**The more Tak learned about Earthlings, the more she questioned the mission…**

"Now, the girls," Baron said, carving out the palate from inside the head of the sheep and passing it to them. "This will make you more diligent and hard working. I have hipbones here for the elder men, as honored guests," he said and served them ceremoniously to the senior men. "Who are the daughters-in-law? They get the breast." He passed the pieces to them. "Who are the married women?" He passed the neck bones to them and one to Tak. "The boys?" They got the kidneys and heart to grow into a man more rapidly. "Who are the sons-in-law?" Once identified, they got the breastbone. "Now, are there any pregnant women?" Baron looked about until one identified herself. "You get this vertebra. Now here are the brains, but not for children. It will make them weak-willed." Baron put servings of brains on plates, with that warning, as some of the women passed them to others beside the children. "Here's an elbow and an ulnar bone. Anyone can have this, except an unmarried woman or young girl, as it will make her left on the shelf with no husband." Baron passed the elbow toward someone who wanted it. When he completed his performance, all done as though he was born Kazakh, he sat down. The rest did not touch their food until Baron, the most honored guest, began to eat.

"Only a true Kazakh would know such things," Dr. Dorogomilov complemented.

"Common knowledge," Baron said in an understatement.

The head of the sheep on the table was facing Tak and it was not just a little distracting. Completely horrified, she tried a bit of a few things to be polite. Then she looked at Baron, who chuckled at her shock, enjoying the effect it was having on her.

When no one was listening, she said to him, "Am I actually asked to consider letting these people go into space?"

Tasked by the Federation of Planets to determine if Earthlings present a threat as they venture into space, Tak, an alien anthropologist, leaves her starship orbiting Earth and takes a shuttle to Kansas. Intending to study humans in the United States—as she has learned no Earth language but English—she is detected while descending through the atmosphere and only evades capture by fleeing to Europe, where she lands in Poland. There, she meets an international arms merchant, Baron Von Limbach, who becomes her guide. She studies "typical" human behavior by accompanying the baron as he fulfills his latest assignment—to get the Dalai Lama back into Tibet. His method of halting the communist takeover of Tibet is to create a race-specific Ebola that will only attack Han Chinese, giving Tak a prime example of how barbaric humans can be. However, the CIA and US military are aware of Tak's presence on Earth and are determined to capture her. And if she is unable to complete her mission and return to her starship—her captain will destroy every living thing on Earth.

# THE VISITOR

BRENT AYSCOUGH

*A Black Opal Books Publication*

GENRE: SCIENCE FICTION/PARANORMAL ROMANCE



THE VISITOR
Copyright © 2015 by Brent Asycough
Cover Design by Chris Buchinsky
All cover art copyright © 2015
All Rights Reserved
Print ISBN: 978-1-626943-22-3

First Publication: FEBRUARY 2015



Published by Black Opal Books **http://www.blackopalbooks.com**

# THE
# VISITOR

# CHAPTER 1

The shuttle doors of the starship opened, and a dark gray, twenty-five-foot-long shuttle exited. Tak looked at the glowing stars and then studied the blue planet ahead as she began her descent. Numbers appeared on the shuttle screen, notifying her of relevant information affecting her intended descent. She choose to descend without power, just gliding, so as not to so as not to draw attention from the planet's defense systems.

In the quiet of space, she pondered whether she'd made the right decision in choosing the language called English. But one language was enough to learn for this mission—or was it? Some of the languages picked up by the starship seemed so difficult to learn. Transmissions were intercepted from major airport towers all over the planet, and they all spoke English. The place called Russia launched more satellites than any other country, but she had been unable to intercept any transmissions from countries where Russian was spoken, except for a few less-developed adjacent countries. A large number of countries spoke Spanish, but there was no detectable space activity from them.

The place called America seemed to be the best choice, given its satellite activity and advanced technology. Its language was also found to be spoken in a number of other countries around the planet, called England, Australia, New Zealand, Singapore, and much of India. And English had been made so much more pleasurable to learn, as she could watch the intercepted movies. The most interesting ones came from America and were in English. So right or wrong, English had been her choice. And she would land in the middle of that country, in a place called Kansas. This was her first assignment alone and she was determined to do her very best.

As she descended through the atmosphere, the outside temperature began to rise. The blackness of space was being replaced below by bluish stratosphere. Descending by gliding so as to create as little heat signature as possible, the shuttle passed through one hundred sixty thousand feet, downward, soon to be pushed in an easterly direction over the surface of the planet by the natural direction of the prevailing winds. All things seemed to be in order.

BONG! A loud warning sounded, and then she heard, "Radar is being received from the surface."

She focused intently on her monitor.

❧❧

On the ground below, Colonel Burkett led a group of four visitors from the Department of Defense and four more from primary contractors whose system was being tested. They were now in a situation room with many monitors and technicians.

"This is our newest and best in terms of detecting a missile attack from above. As you know, in the cold war we were pointing long range missiles at Russia. Now we are anticipating terrorist attacks, such as from a short-range missile, known to NATO as a SCUD missile. They can be launched from relatively nearby against one of our allies. So we have created an advanced system that looks up from the ground and also down from satellites with the latest technology to detect any such missile. We have focused our newest and most sensitive antenna on the areas where a missile launch might be suspected. In this test case, it's over the White Sands testing area. The system will detect a decoy SCUD missile, simulating an attack from a hostile source who could get their hands on such a weapon. In just a short time, the launch will occur."

He looked at his watch and then glanced at the monitors. "There's the launch! The SCUD has been launched from a mobile base, a flatbed truck, much the same as expected in a real situation, except that the truck is remotely controlled, for reasons you will soon understand. This simulation demonstrates what we would do if we suspected such an attack. In this scenario, we put our special 747 airborne laser in the air. In order to take out the mobile base, we bring in a plane. In this case, we will scramble an F-22, which we are now doing from Nellis Air Force Base. The F-22 is equipped with netcentric avionics and will automatically have the location of the launch vehicle displayed for the pilot and locked in from all the sources working together.

"The SCUD you see on the monitors is tracked by the new Space Based Infrared System. The monitor on the left shows what the Geosynchronous Earth Orbit Satellites see. The monitor next to it shows what the Highly Elliptical Orbit Satellites see, and the next one what the Low Earth Orbit satellites see. They are all linked together by the new system. The monitor on the far right is from an older system called the Ground-Based, Electro-Optical, Deep Space Surveillance System.

"Flying over the simulated theater is our special Boeing 747-400F freighter, equipped with our high-energy Chemical Oxygen Iodine Lasers, or COIL, capable of shooting down the SCUD. The huge amount of chemical it takes to fire the big laser several times from the air requires a 747. When we fire one from the ground we have several truckloads of chemical on hand for multiple shots. These impressive lasers actually use the chemical for energy, not like the simple lab ones you may have seen. But the problem in shooting from the ground is in hitting anything. It takes so much chemical that we can't fire it for very long, and we can't rapid fire it like a machine gun. It has to be pumped up with more chemical for the next shot. Firing from the airborne 747, which can be at forty thousand feet or higher, has improved the accuracy many times over, as you will soon hopefully witness.

"Now that the launch has been detected, you can see the 747 changing its course to intersect the SCUD's trajectory as plotted by our new computers."

"Will the laser completely disintegrate the SCUD?" one observer asked.

"No. It'll be badly damaged and largely burnt up, but there will be falling debris. But not to worry—it won't fall on us. The area is some distance away. Some of the area is in use by ranchers, but we have cleared them out from what we've named the 'call-up' area of our test range here at White Sands. The range is three-thousand-two-hundred square miles, and the call-up area adds two-thousand-five-hundred square miles to it when in use. We have an arrangement with the ranchers whereby we can call on them and evacuate them for up to twelve hours a few times a year for tests, for which they are paid a yearly payment and travel expenses."

Burkett continued, "The SCUD will reach one-hundred-twenty-five-thousand feet, traveling from the north to the south end of the range, and then descend. It is nearly at the maximum altitude now. There! You can now see the big image of the 747 on the side of same screen moving in on the SCUD's trajectory. We have the captain of the 747 on the loudspeaker."

"White Sands, Captain Gleason here. The weapon is ready, and we are now within range of the SCUD. Optimal range will be in twenty seconds."

Burkett had put on a headset with an extended cord so he could talk to the pilot and remain standing before the monitors to show the group of important people what was going on.

The computer signaled that the 747 was within range.

"Fire!" Burkett shouted to Gleason, raising his voice to add excitement to the event.

The laser light flashed on the monitors as it hit the SCUD. It lit up brightly on numerous screens.

"It's a success!" Burkett announced loudly and proudly, hoping to raise some enthusiasm and continued funding among the group for the expensive project. "See the glowing SCUD. We just detected and shot a SCUD missile into oblivion in a flawless test, using the new satellites and the airborne laser!"

A sigh of relief could be heard in the situation room from the staff who had been apprehensive that something would go wrong with the test.

"Very impressive," Walters from the Department of Defense complimented, attempting to be polite but trying not to show emotion, so as to remain objective about the test.

"Now," Burkett continued. "The F-22 we scrambled should be close to attacking the mobile launch base from which the SCUD missile was launched, and we can switch some of the monitors to the satellite view of the mobile platform. Then netcentric will set the F-22's computers on target."

The monitors now showed the radio-controlled flatbed truck bouncing along in the desert, simulating terrorists trying to escape. A white missile fuel trail jutted out from the front of the F-22, racing down to the flatbed truck and blowing it to kingdom come.

"Good work, Captain Duncan." Burkett said to the F-22 pilot.

He then took off his headset to address any questions the Department of Defense observers might have and gave them all a great big smile.

Ms. Davis from the Department of Defense looked around at one of the other numerous monitors, off to the side of the one they had all been viewing. "What's that?"

Burkett turned to the screen she was looking at. It was a screen that had been monitoring the high altitude trajectory of the SCUD earlier. Just entering the top of the monitor was a very small object. It had just a hint of a glow, barely visible, but it was the only thing on the dark screen other than the smoldering remains of SCUD missile, well below it.

Burkett put his headset back on, switching frequencies. "Move all available antennas onto that object!"

Adjustments were made to the direction of the moveable antennas of the new system, as well as the older, ground-based optical system. The object enlarged in size from a tiny spot to a larger one as the technicians changed the ratio of the field of view to magnify it. All watched, wondering what the little glow was.

"It's farther up than the SCUD missile that we just melted," Burkett said. "It's at one hundred fifty seven thousand feet. The SCUD did not go above one hundred twenty five thousand feet, and the hit with the laser wouldn't have caused any exploding debris to ascend like that. It might be what's left of an old satellite. Its descent is slow, much like a free-falling object."

"But aren't debris from satellites all monitored by our radar antenna and plotted at NORAD?" one of the group asked.

"They're supposed to be," Burkett said. "And, they're usually going around the globe very fast. So if it was, it would normally fall into the atmosphere at a much higher velocity horizontally."

"Could it be a real missile?" the same person asked. His question turned several heads in momentary reaction to what might be a real threat.

"That seems so unlikely," Burkett answered while shaking his head. "It reflects very little light. Any missile launch would be detected, and NORAD would have picked it up. It must be debris broken off a satellite, probably a Russian. But I'll contact NORAD." He switched the frequency on his radio hooked up to his headset and ordered, "Get me NORAD."

The switchboard operator put him through on a direct military line to the North American Aerospace Defense Command Center, known as NORAD, one thousand seven hundred feet below the surface of the Earth, deep in the formidable natural granite fortress in Cheyenne Mountain, Colorado. "NORAD, Major Hight speaking."

"This is Colonel Burkett at White Sands."

"Good morning, Colonel," Hight said, as he knew the colonel.

The contact was put over the loudspeakers in the situation room, so as not to make it appear to the distinguished guests from the Department of Defense that anything was being hidden, and all in the room had high security clearances.

"We have been monitoring your decoy SCUD launch and the laser shot," Hight said. "Nice work!"

"Thanks, it went well. But we may have something else here. We have detected a small object coming down from space, right over the test area. Do you have it?"

"No, not that I'm aware of. Let me get an update. Can you stand by?"

"Sure."

Hight called to Lieutenant Hawkins by headset across the room, where men and women were watching iridescent monitors. "Lieutenant Hawkins, do you have anything on your infrared in the vicinity of space in the same general area as the White Sands test?"

"Only the F-22," Hawkins reported. Then he said, "Wait! There is something very small and very slow, descending through one hundred fifty five thousand feet."

Hight went back to Burkett. "Yes, now we have it. It gives off only a tiny signature, like a stealth vehicle. It's not burning any visible fuel exhaust."

Hawkins ran the position into his special computer for a statistical analysis. He then said to Hight, "It does not match up to anything orbiting in the database."

"It's not a known piece of debris in our database," Hight told Burkett over the headset. "It is probably a piece of a broken up satellite, probably Russian."

"We have an F-22 out of Nellis already in the air if you want it to take a closer look," Burkett suggested.

"Good idea," Hight replied,

Burkett radioed Captain Duncan in the F-22. "We are sending you the coordinates of a falling object. Proceed to that area, but keep a safe distance until you get a visual of the object. It's still well above you."

"Yes, sir," Duncan responded. "I have the coordinates and will super-cruise to intercept," he said, pushing his F-22 into supersonic speed.

✺✺✺

BONG!

A second warning sounded from Tak's shuttle computer.

"There are two native warships in the area below," the computer reported. "They are both powered by ignited petroleum. One just fired a laser at a rocket with different fuel to destroy it. The other one is smaller and just fired an explosive weapon at a ground based vehicle and destroyed it."

Her screen plotted the current location of the 747 and the F-22 and showed her an image of the SCUD that was destroyed by the laser.

"The smaller one is now traveling toward this shuttle at 1225 miles per hour. The larger one is not approaching, and its configuration makes it unlikely that it can travel significantly faster in the atmosphere than the speed at which it is now travelling, 580 miles per hour."

✺✺✺

Back on the ground, Burkett and Hight, from different

locations, watched the F-22 close in on the object on their screens.

Burkett radioed Duncan in the plane. "What've you got?"

"Standby, sir," Duncan answered. "It'll be in visual range very soon."

✿✿✿

Tak watched her screen closely as the craft behind her and to the left closed the distance between them. How could she possibly have been detected?

Before she had left, the computer carefully set a course so as not to collide with any of nine thousand objects in orbit around the planet.

She touched the manual thruster knob and wondered if she should go back into space to radio an emergency message to the starship, even before she ever got to the planet. What options were there? Maybe she could alter course slightly to another section of America or—where?

"Computer, if we alter our course but still land in the country called America, can we escape the craft in pursuit?"

"Unlikely," the computer answered. "Calculating from the mass it is losing by burning its fuel, it is estimated that the pursuit craft is likely to have sufficient range to be able to follow five hundred miles in any direction if it is to return, or double that if it does not need to return to our present location. But natives on the surface are in communication with the craft, and it can be expected that other craft will follow, if that one expends its fuel. More can be expected if you engage in a chase and attempt to remain within the boundaries of this country. The range of the larger craft with the laser may be much farther, although from its shape, it is much slower."

"How fast can the smaller, faster one travel?"

"There are records taken by the starship showing such smaller aircraft going as fast as 1800 miles per hour. It's currently approaching at 1225 miles per hour."

As Tak considered her options, the F-22 closed the gap, came up within five miles of the shuttle, and continued to close, reducing to subsonic speed.

Duncan radioed Burkett and Hight, who was also now listening to the transmission from NORAD. "I have it in sight now. It appears to be a black vehicle, somewhat resembling a NASA lifting body. It's traveling at two hundred eighty eight knots and descending at one thousand six hundred feet per minute. It appears to be gliding without power. Present altitude is fifty eight thousand feet."

Burkett asked a question that had already been answered. "Did you say gliding?"

"Affirmative."

Duncan expertly adjusted his control stick to move his F-22 in closer to the shuttle.

"The pursuit craft's radio frequency has been located, and the transmissions between it and the surface are now on your screen, translated," Tak's computer said.

"Put future communications in the native language, English," Tak directed the computer. "If the aircraft fires its weapons, take defensive action without my command."

Duncan throttled back, positioned his F-22 right alongside the unidentified vehicle, and then carefully dialed back his speed so he was descending at the exact rate of descent as the other vehicle. He closed the gap, so that his wing tip was only thirty feet away. Duncan took his eyes off his instruments and looked over to see what he could as to how the oddity next to him was flying. To his surprise, through the windshield he saw a very attractive female, with bright red hair, wearing no helmet, and without any oxygen mask, such that her head and face were entirely visible. This was the first actual face-to-face encounter between a human and an alien, but Duncan didn't know it.

"A glider at fifty-eight thousand feet that has descended from at least one hundred fifty-seven thousand feet?" Burkett asked. "How in the hell did a glider get to one hundred fifty-seven thousand feet? And," he added in an unintentional sexist remark, "with a female pilot?"

"Well, if it's a glider, it can't go too awfully far," Hight said. "We'll get working on its speed, the winds, its trajectory, and see where it will likely land if it continues its present course. Hawkins," he ordered. "Get winds aloft data and plot the probable landing of the craft, assuming it is gliding and will continue at its present rate of speed, descent, and direction."

"Yes, sir," Hawkins answered, but he was already working on it as that was the sort of thing he did. "I have your answer," he announced in less than thirty seconds. "Kansas."

"There's no glider that can go up that high," Hight protested.

"See if you can make contact," Burkett said to Captain Duncan. "I want you to force her to land at one of our bases. She is flying in civilian class 'A' airspace with no flight plan. Based on that, you are authorized by me to force her down."

Tak looked over at the fighter pilot while listening to their communications. He was wearing an air force helmet, the dark face shield covering his face, an oxygen tube connected to his mask, and a communications wire to the built-in headset.

He looked like a robot compared to Tak, who had nothing at all on her head, as though taking a boat ride on a lake on a Sunday afternoon.

Duncan switched to a civilian frequency used by aircraft in air-to-air communications, 122.75 Megahertz. "Glider pilot. This is Captain Duncan, United States Air Force. You are being monitored by an air force station at White Sands, New Mexico, as well as NORAD at Cheyenne Mountain, Colorado. You are flying in class-A airspace without clearance. You are ordered to follow me to an airbase."

Tak heard the message. "Computer. What is "NOR-AD"?

"No information," Computer answered.

Nervous, Tak wondered what her options were. She turned to the pilot in the craft next to her and gave him her most attractive smile.

Captain Duncan could hardly believe his eyes. A strikingly attractive woman had just descended from altitudes where only space craft could tread and was now gliding toward Earth, no helmet or even a headset on—*and she smiles*?

"What's going on?" Burkett demanded.

"She's smiling."

"*What*?" he nearly shouted.

"Smiling, sir."

"You order her down!"

"I don't think she has a radio, sir. She isn't wearing a headset."

"Then you motion her to come down!"

"Sir, she's in a gliding craft. She appears to be descending by gravity alone and traveling with the prevailing winds. Since she's already coming down, I don't think she can come down any faster."

"Then you make sure she follows you."

Duncan put up his hand and motioned for her to follow him.

"What is she doing now?" Burkett asked.

"Still smiling."

Tak heard that on her radio, which was monitoring their frequency. She had to make a decision and quickly. Abort the mission or go on? She could thrust out into space and call for the starship or stay and try to complete her mission. At any rate, Kansas appeared to be out. Perhaps the next the next large land mass known as Europe would do.

"Computer, find a sparsely populated area well within the land mass called Europe and plot a course. Engage the thruster."

The roar of the powerful thruster overshadowed everything else. The shuttle was soon traveling at seventeen thousand miles per hour while still in the atmosphere, and then it went up and east, leaving the Earth.

"My God!" Duncan gasped. "Did you see that?"

At NORAD, Hight could see the shuttle image on his screen. It was traveling at a tremendous speed, climbing, and leaving the continental United States. "That couldn't be the glider you were pacing, could it?" he asked Duncan sarcastically. "A glider at seventeen thousand miles an hour?"

"It's some kind of rocket," Duncan said.

"No shit. I have it on our satellite heading over the Atlantic toward Europe. We can switch to another satellite and see if we can pick it up in Europe. We should be able to trace it there, if all goes well. This used to be written up as a UFO, but we should report this to Homeland Security. This is some sort of new vehicle we have never seen before that can travel at hypersonic speeds. Not even our experimental hypersonic rockets can fly anywhere close to that speed. This could be a real threat. But from who?"

The government people, who were there for the test, looked to Colonel Burkett for an explanation of what had just happened.

❧❧❧

In space, the computer shut down the thruster.

"Have you set up the new landing spot?" Tak asked it.

"Yes," it answered.

Her screen showed the landing spot on the section of the map called Europe. The area was on the dark side of the planet but the computer showed the land mass clearly.

"Select a spot in a remote area, as far as possible away from any large cities."

She figured that seemed like a good possiblity to land without being noticed.

"Acknowledged."

The computer selected a spot from its mapped topography, showing it on the shuttle screen. It displayed the topography of the landing spot, the weather there, and other factors needed to make a perfect glide slope. It also displayed calculations of the weight of the shuttle as decreased by use of fuel to land in Europe, gravity of the earth, speed at all times, drag of the atmosphere at all relevant altitudes, effects of the known and measurable winds, and the incidental gravitational pull of the sun and the moon. It had the ability to determine if it was not on the calculated course of glide slope and to make corrections.

The selection was on the pasture of a farm. A lush, green field presented itself within eyesight range ahead. It was night, but there was illumination from a bright moon, and Tak could see the landing field visually through the canopy. It was filled with new grass coming up, following the winter.

The craft was designed to land slowly on its belly skids, as it was not intended for repeated use. With trepidation, Tak held her breath as the shuttle touched down at a very slow speed and slid to a stop.

A rush of excitement overcame her as she landed. This was her first mission alone. She looked through the windshield at the lush, green pasture. *It's a farm!* There were no warships to intercept her. The computer had successfully selected a remote spot, not close to natives. *People, the word is. From now on, it is English. Or, do they speak English here?*

She raised the canopy and took her first breath of Earth's air. It was cool and refreshing air, full of the delightful odor of farm vegetation and moist, tilled soil. The exhilaration of the mission, along with the fresh air, filled her lungs and fueled her ambition. She set the computer to warn of native vessels, got out, and reached in for her satchel. It was too dark to venture out now. Had she been detected? Were more warships on their way?

The best move, she concluded, would be to wait, without destroying the shuttle in case warships came, in which case she could climb in, head back out of the atmosphere, and call for her starship.

She leaned against her shuttle, waiting for night to pass, absorbed in the mesmerizing odor of the farm with the beauty of moonlight.

Off in one direction, she noticed the outline of a farmhouse. She could walk there at first light. But she would have to destroy the shuttle, so as not to leave evidence of her visit. That was an apprehensive notion after the encounter earlier. But here she was on a mission.

After a while, light could be seen in the sky to the east. High cirrus clouds began to refract shades of pink, presenting a delightful greeting to her entrance on the planet. Rain was on its way, perhaps later in the day.

There being no apparent threat, she decided to carry on with the mission. She checked her computer bracelet on her wrist to see if it was functioning, just to be sure. It was. Resembling a large wrist watch, it had a screen and a removable blue object that looked like a lapis jewel.

She took from the satchel one of several small balls, each just a bit bigger than a large grape. Touching one to her wrist computer, she commanded it to determine the mass of the shuttle and to activate the self-destruct in three minutes.

"Acknowledged. Disintegration will be in three minutes. Move away from the shuttle."

She put the ball into the shuttle and began to walk toward the farmhouse to the east. She then turned and looked back. The shuttle began to glow and then disappeared. *It's gone!* Loneliness and an empty feeling set in with the absence of the security the shuttle brought. Her escape had vaporized with the shuttle.

*On with the mission,* she ordered herself, trying to fortify her resolve. She bounced a bit due to lighter gravity than what she was used to. As she walked east, the sunlight crept out, reflecting against the high cirrus clouds, creating a beautiful pink color—her first such early daylight sight on the planet, and one she would always remember. The morning dew soaked the growing vegetation and her boots.

After a time, she could make out not one, but two structures ahead. She could see that one was a dwelling, and the other a storage place. *Barn* was the word.

Two men had just driven up on a tractor, gotten off, and gone to sit on the porch. Both were middle-aged men. Early rising farmers. It had become their practice to meet once a week to talk.

As she approached, they noticed her, stopped talking, and stared. There had been no hikers or pedestrians at that farm before.

Tak had chosen, in an attempt to blend in with the native dress, an outfit of black boots, black pants, a gray sweater, and a black jacket made of a substance that resembled leather. But her clothes were certainly not those of a farm girl, or a nature-loving hiker. She was quite out of place as far as the two men were concerned. They continued to stare and said nothing.

She got ready to speak the first words to the human race. "Hello. I wish to go to the nearest town."

The men began to talk among themselves in a language Tak did not understand.

"English," one of them said, a relief to her as it was the first word she understood.

Her wrist computer was on all the time and recording this language so as to learn it. The computer would remain on during the entire Earth excursion.

"I speak little English," said the younger man, holding up his hand with his thumb and forefinger an inch apart to indicate a measure of a small amount.

"Would either of you be willing to take me to the closest town?" she asked.

The one who spoke translated her request to his friend. They looked at her, then at each other, and then back at her, evaluating her request. Both of them then began a very intense discussion in their native tongue over the topic. Their voices rose at times, and the conversation elevated to a debate. Strong views were expressed

The English-speaking man turned to Tak. "He does not think it proper to take a young woman to town. But I do not agree. I would take you to town. But neither of us have a car and I do not drive."

*How strange that they debated whether or not to do what they cannot even do.* It was time to move on. "Thank you. What's the name of the next town?"

"Wieliczka." He pointed down the only road.

"Thank you."

Off she went on foot, along the rough dirt road, on her mission to learn the ways of the natives of the planet.

# CHAPTER 2

Raymond Houser, Homeland Security Director, came in early. He worked long hours and wanted to be advised of any new developments, if at all suspect, immediately. He required his staff to condense situations into brief summaries to save time. Sixty, gray hair, medium build, and very well dressed, he was often called on with short notice to see the joint chiefs, the president, the head of the FBI, the CIA, or some other very important person.

Richard Ralls, formerly with the CIA and now one of the top operatives under Hauser, waited for his turn to see the director about a new development that was indeed curious. Richard was thirty-nine, in excellent shape, just under six feet tall, dark hair, and had a ruddy complexion.

It was 8 a.m. when he was ushered in. The director, already sitting at his desk, motioned for Ralls to take a seat. A secretary brought over a tray with an insulated coffee flask, sweeteners, and cream so he could fix his coffee as and when he preferred. Ralls fixed himself a cup and began his presentation without further delay. He needed to utilize the time he had, as they had to deal with all the world-wide threats that came in every hour of the day.

"Director, we have something quite unusual. The military was conducting a test yesterday with our 747 mounted laser to knock out a mobile-based SCUD missile over White Sands. During the test, an intruder aircraft, somewhat resembling a NASA gliding craft with almost no radar signature, glided down over the test area from very high. It was first recorded at one-hundred-fifty-seven-thousand feet—which means it presumably started higher—and then, at over fifty-thousand feet, when approached by our F-22, which was airborne as part of the SCUD missile test and armed. The jet was sent to intercept and order it down. Instead of complying, it sped from its slow glide to seventeen-thousand miles per hour while still in the atmosphere, then it headed up and east, out of the atmosphere. We then tracked to a spot in rural Poland where it landed."

"What have you been smoking, Richard?" the director joked. "Nothing can go seventeen-thousand miles an hour in the atmosphere."

"I know it seems like a mistake, but we have it recorded by NORAD and then by all of our systems and two satellites. The speed is confirmed. It had a radar signature when accelerating. But then, when its engine shut off, as it had no radar signature. We were only able to follow it visually via our satellite, which was very compromised. It landed at night, and then clouds came in and covered the area, preventing visual tracking. By the time the sun rose, and the cloud cover thinned, the craft was nowhere to be seen."

The director was still just getting started for the day. He frowned. "This occurred yesterday and I'm only now being informed?"

"Well, you see, the notification came from NORAD, and it seems that this is the first time since Homeland Security was established that NORAD has had cause to notify Homeland Security. And, when the report was made, our own staff did not at once consider it important enough to notify you on the golf course on a Sunday that a UFO was identified leaving the United States, as opposed to entering it. Frankly, it seems that some of the staff doubted the validity of the report. We just don't get UFO's like that. So it was passed on to me last night, and I thought this morning was soon enough."

The director pursed his lips, leaned forward, and rested his forearms on his desk. "Go on. More details."

"It was first detected on radar entering the atmosphere, apparently gliding down, from one-hundred-fifty-seven-thousand feet above White Sands. As it was gliding, it gave off a reduced heat signature. We don't know how high it started from. It was first seen visually seen at fifty-eight-thousand feet by our F-22 Air Force pilot. He did not have cameras on his plane, only radar. He described it as a black, stealth-shaped aircraft, twenty-five feet in length, gliding down into the atmosphere in the direction of the jet stream winds. It had a shape similar to one of those NASA lifting bodies, which glide well without long wings, and are not super-streamlined like a hypersonic rocket. Our pilot said he could see the pilot, who was, surprisingly, a red-haired female without any helmet or oxygen mask."

"Russian?" Houser asked.

"I contacted Russia to see if it was a Russian test vehicle, or if they knew anything about it, or would admit to it. I was told no, and they confided that Russia had also tracked the craft at their Armavir Radar Station which tracks incoming missiles to their west. Anyway, why would Russia test something over the US, rather than off in northeast Siberia, where it would be hard for us to detect? To do it over the US would be a very serious provocation. I rule out Russia."

"You say it sped to seventeen-thousand miles per hour while still in the atmosphere?" Houser asked, unable to believe what he'd been told. "Are you sure about that?"

"That's the bombshell. It achieved that speed while still in the atmosphere. Anything we have, or know of, would have been incinerated at those low altitudes and that speed. Also, it did not accelerate faster than seventeen-thousand miles per hour once it left the atmosphere, as you would expect it to. It just went to seventeen-thousand miles an hour as though the atmosphere had no effect on it."

"Any clues?"

"Nope. It's a mystery. I have spoken to our F-22 pilot,

and he has no additional information to offer. I'm having an FBI criminal sketch artist make up a drawing of the pilot's face, but our pilot was looking through his face shield, through his canopy, and through the canopy of the mystery craft. So his view was compromised as to minor details.

"One theory is that it is a privately made craft sent over to us to us as a warning that whoever made it can reach such speeds with a bomb—even a small, dirty bomb. And since it can go so fast, it could be launched from a ship or even the ground in nearly any country and reach us at low altitudes, for which we are not prepared. We have nothing that could intercept it and knock it out. It could be a warning from someone with a future extortion threat, possibly to release some Muslim prisoners or something like that. Maybe some lunatic with Arab oil financial resources sufficient to have such a craft built."

"Do you think that whoever sent it will want to request ransom?"

"That seems hard to believe," Ralls said. "Catching the group that would collect a monetary ransom would be all too easy, and they could most likely never get away with it. More likely, it's something else, but I'm not sure what. Maybe a release of prisoners, or maybe pulling out of some country or military base we have somewhere."

Director Houser shook his head and sighed. "Putting in a young woman with no headgear, instead of, say, a regular pilot or a robotic pilot must have been to make some kind of statement. I can't imagine a Muslim nation doing that, since they won't even let women drive cars. It would be an insult to the Koran, or so many of them would think."

Ralls nodded. "Good point."

"Do you have any idea at all where the craft might have come from?"

"None whatsoever. One remote possibility is that it might have come from one of those crazies with their homebuilt rockets, trying to show off. But the person did not claim any glory, and she could have made it a media event if she wanted to. Or it could possibly even be some disgruntled engineer who wants to get even with the US, or someone in it, and wanted to show what he knows and we don't. But we have no knowledge of anyone who can build anything like that."

"We can't let anything with that much intercontinental travel capability and tremendous speed go unhampered," Houser argued. "This is especially true since we don't know who built it. Someone could send over a nuclear bomb, even a small dirty bomb, and hit a target city here before we could knock it down. The very purpose of the SCUD missile test over White Sands is to stop such a missile if one was tracked coming in to our territory from a relatively nearby launching station, such as a ship near us or a territory nearby or one of our protectorates. Where do the satellites show where it landed?"

"The exact coordinates have been plotted by satellites," Ralls said. "So we can determine where it landed by GPS satellites."

"I want you to go over to where it landed and check it out. Maybe there's a hanger around somewhere or some evidence as to what happened to it." Houser turned to the monitor on his desk and typed in an inquiry. "We have a military base in Lodz, Poland. I'll see if I can get you a special military aircraft today to get there so you won't have to go through commercial flights with several plane changes to get to Poland. You can pack a weapon that way, in case you need it. I'll arrange a military chopper there and a few soldiers to help look for that craft, whatever or wherever it is. I'll get my contact at the National Security Council to make the calls to arrange things and put you in touch with the CIA. I want you to leave today if you can, so no more time lapses to let whoever flew that craft hide it."

# CHAPTER 3

The Dalai Lama concluded His speech at the University of California at Long Beach with:

"For as long as space endures,
And for as long as living beings remain,
Until then, may I too abide,
To dispel the misery of the world."

"How perfect!" a beautiful East Indian woman in the audience blurted out, although not very loud.

She produced a handkerchief from her purse and touched the underside of her eyes, which were moistened by the experience.

The young man sitting next to her glanced her way. "Yes, He's fantastic. This is my first experience."

Feeling comfortable with this man who shared a common interest, she asked, "Would you be like to come to our conference group meeting in an hour, the Followers of His Holiness? It's being held in conjunction with a chapter of the Students for a Free Tibet."

"Could I?" the young man asked, uncomfortable at intruding.

"Anyone interested may come. You may come with me as my guest, if you feel uncomfortable going alone. There will be several speakers who are very knowledgeable about His teachings."

"Great! Is it nearby?"

"Yes, it is right here on this campus. You may follow me if you like. It's only a ten minute walk."

The two of them worked their way through the crowd of seven hundred leaving the meeting hall. Just outside, the noise of the jabbering throng subsided, so she looked at him and introduced herself. "I'm Shanta Laxshimi."

He was able to better see her attire outside. It was foreign to him and so exotic. She looked East Indian, early thirties, and extraordinarily attractive. Her beauty was enhanced by a magnificent sari which she wore so very well. It was of maroon and gold material. Her mid-section was left bare in the traditional sari fashion, and she was without stomach fat. She wore a thin gold chain around her bare waist and another on her ankle.

She looked at him, waiting for his name and, finally, he realized that he was staring at her without talking. "Oh, sorry—I'm Andrew Saunders." He paused, clumsily, and then added, "Ah—actually, if you would rather ride than walk, my car is here."

"Why, yes. But there's no parking here or near the next place. We have to walk."

He looked up toward the street, a signal to his driver. In the dark, people were walking to their cars, some a considerable distance away. Double parked, with an attendant driver, was a shiny black Mercedes sedan. And, seeing Andrew, the driver turned on the lights and drove forward. A chauffeur in black exited smartly and opened a door.

"Wow!" Shanta was awestruck. "Is this yours?"

"It's either a company car or Roger rented it," Andrew said, gesturing at the driver. "Just tell Roger where."

The meeting of the Followers was held at a smaller conference room on the university campus. The group's volunteer organizer was Warren McLaughlin, who had been instrumental in inviting His Holiness to UCLA Long Beach and had sent a newsletter to the Followers as well as the Students for a Free Tibet, who now congregated at the meeting, following His Holiness's speech. Andrew was handed a newsletter at the door, which contained words of wisdom imparted by His Holiness, along with news of current events in Tibet. Within a short while, over two hundred people had come in, chatting and discussing what they had heard.

McLaughlin took the podium, which brought about a respectful silence as people stopped talking. "For those of you who are newcomers, I usually give a short update on what is happening in the land where His Holiness belongs and from which he has been exiled. In Tibet, atrocities continue. World news ignores this. More than six thousand monasteries and their contents, irreplaceable jewels of Tibetan culture, have been destroyed by the demonic communist Chinese government. Tibetans are routinely imprisoned and tortured for non-violently expressing their views, which includes support of His Holiness. They are detained indefinitely without public trial, tortured, and often killed. One million two hundred thousand Tibetans have died from torture, starvation, and execution. Nuns are brutally raped in Chinese prisons.

"Why is it that Tibet is the only area of The People's Republic of China where foreign journalists are not allowed? The tortures that we have documented include severe beatings, whippings, use of electric batons on mouth, body, and genitals, being kept in irons continuously, suspended by their arms, deprived of sleep or food, and exposed to intense cold.

"Tibetan women are forced to have abortions. They are given the option of paying a fine of seven thousand Yuan, usually the equivalent of five years annual income, unless they terminate their pregnancies by abortion. Mandarin had replaced Tibetan as the official language."

McLaughlin began to work himself up. "The Chinese government offers tax breaks and military promotions to those Chinese who will move to Tibet as part of a population transfer to destroy Tibet's culture. Huge numbers of Chinese, an estimated seven and a half million, have been sent there to dilute the Tibetan population, which is estimated at six million. The Chinese exploit the natural resources; ease over-population of China by expanding their territory; obtain strategic military locations over Asia, especially to station missiles directed toward India; and promote their racist, imperialist policies. The Chinese are destroying the environment by constructing pipelines; wholesale clear cutting of forests on an unbelievable scale; and dumping toxic waste, including spent nuclear fuel, on Tibetan soil."

He paused to calm down and then continued. "His Holiness proposed a five-point plan for the restoration of peace and human rights in Tibet. First, the transformation of Tibet into a zone of Ahimsa, a demilitarized zone of peace and non-violence. Second, abandonment of China's population transfer policy. Third, respect for the Tibetan people's fundamental human rights and democratic freedoms. Fourth, restoration and protection of Tibet's natural environment and abandonment of China's use of Tibet for the production of nuclear weapons and dumping of nuclear waste. And fifth, commencement of earnest negotiations on the future status of Tibet and relations between the Tibetan and Chinese people."

McLaughlin opened his arms as though in despair. "And what does the mighty American government, the policeman of the world, do? It normalizes relations with China, completely ignoring the atrocities and the ruination of Tibet. When the oil of America was threatened by Iraq entering Kuwait, America and her allies went to war. This was not to save the anti-American Emir or the Kuwaiti people who believe Americans are Satanic infidels, but for oil. Yet for Tibetans, they remain crushed by no less villainous behavior. Now Americans and their allies have attempted to police Iraq and Afghanistan, all because of oil, but in the name of addressing terrorism. But what of the terror in Tibet?"

The speech continued for an hour and a half, after which Roger took Andrew and Shanti to a place he had located while they were at the meeting, an after-hours pizza/Italian café, just off campus. The tables were candle lit and the best little round table next to a window had just become available. The young maître'd put Andrew and Shanta at that table ahead of two other parties, deciding they had a reserved seat there, his decision motivated by Roger passing him a hundred dollar bill.

At the table, the candle light gave radiance to Shanta's brown skin, glowing with the rich oils she rubbed on her skin, memorizing her onlooker.

"Do you like my sari?" she asked to give him license to continue staring at her body.

"I've never known an East Indian girl before. I'm from the south and there were no East Indians there when I grew up. I think your outfit is beautiful. What do you call it?"

"It's just a sari. I got this one in Jaipur. Have you been in India?"

"No."

"This is my first trip to the United States. I'll not be able to go to the south, but I have heard it is very nice."

"Please tell me about yourself," Andrew asked.

"I must tell you that I'm married."

Andrew went into shock. "Married?"

"Well, it is not exactly what you might think, but still I'm married."

"What do you mean?"

"My family moved from India to Singapore, where I grew up. My parents made an arranged marriage for me with a Singaporean, an Indian doctor, who had by then moved to New York to practice. I had no say in the matter. The doctor did not want an arranged marriage and refused for a long time. Finally, his mother told him that if he did not come back to Singapore to marry me that she would commit suicide—and she convinced him that she meant it. And she probably did. So he agreed and came back for a traditional Indian wedding. But he never consummated our marriage and left the next day to return to New York. I was left no longer eligible to marry another, even though the marriage was not considered valid since it was not consummated. But I had nowhere to go, and I was no longer eligible under Indian tradition, like used goods. I was very hurt and left to go to an ashram in India."

Andrew could hardly believe the story. "Seriously?"

"Oh yes, quite seriously. I had been following Hindu religious teachings all my life until I discovered the truths of the Dalai Lama. I'm fascinated with Him. I find no conflict in His words and my Hindu upbringing. It is very harmonious."

Andrew was fixated on the sexual aspect of her story. "You never consummated your marriage?"

"I'm still a virgin."

# CHAPTER 4

Tak approached a small sign alongside the road that had the number "4" on it. A passing car slowed to a stop just ahead of her. It was a small blue car, with only the driver, who reached over and cranked down the window on the passenger side. He said something that made no sense to her. She let the sound reverberate in her mind to detect what it was. He repeated it.

Was he asking her name, she wondered? "Tak," she told him.

He leaned over and opened the car door, obviously offering a ride. She climbed into the car and off they went. He began to speak to her, but she could not understand him.

"I only speak English."

"Ah," the driver said, shrugging his shoulders and smiling. "No speak."

They rode along, not speaking, the spring green color of the countryside a delight. Before long, a sign appeared: WIELICZKA. The driver turned and looked at her as though to ask if that was where she was going.

She assumed this town or place, whatever it was, would be as good as any, since she had missed Kansas. "Yes, this will do nicely."

The driver slowed his car and turned into a parking area. A number of vehicles were parked there, including several small busses. The car stopped and Tak pulled on the silver crank to open the door. When the door did not open, she pulled harder. Hadn't he pulled on this when he initially opened the door for her? She'd thought for sure that he had. The chrome handle came off in her hand. She looked over sheepishly at the driver, who took it from her and set it down between the seats. He then leaned over her and opened the door for her. She got out of the car, closed the door, then leaned through the window, and said with a smile, "Thank you."

The young man nodded and drove away. Tak saw some kind of travel office. In front of the congregation of people, a young lady stood behind a ticket counter. Off to the left was a metal-framed glass door to a shop.

Tak headed for the shop. Inside several clerks were standing about, assisting customers. Tak went up to a table with picture books on it and noticed that the books came in a number of languages. She picked up one in English, and read the cover: *WIELICZKA SALT MINE.*

It showed a map of where the town was and gave the name of the country, *Poland.*

A salt mine! A place where salt came from on this planet! Best to go inside to learn how that was done. But how could she do that?

Outside the shop, people were lining up line next to a structure containing an elevator down to the salt mine. A group of tourists, speaking English, exited a tour bus in the parking lot. Some went inside the gift shop to use the water closet, and the tour leader went up to the ticket window to get them admission. They then gathered at the request of their tour leader near the elevator. Tak sheepishly melted into this group.

An official guide approached the tour leader and took over. His uniform was all black, the top a tunic with gold and red epaulets with polished brass buttons and his head was adorned with a distinctive cap. He went to the ticket office, where he was handed a slip with the tally of visitors, and then beckoned for them to come to the elevator door.

There were twenty-four of them, twice as many as could fit into the elevator at one time. The guide then motioned to the group to collect in a queue at the elevator. The tour leader repeated his request to be sure that his group knew who their guide was.

"Come with me to the elevator," the guide said. "There will have to be two groups, as the elevator only holds twelve."

Tak walked with them toward the elevator as though she was one of them, mixing in toward the middle of what would be the first group going down. The elevator consisted of a metal cage with unpainted, metal sides with quarter-inch holes close together. The guide motioned the group to get in and crowd together, while he would follow, taking the second half of the group down. The door closed. The elevator descended so fast and it was so dark that many in the group were scared to the point of shrieking.

The landing area was dimly lit, but the frightened crowd welcomed it. The light came only from a few exposed bubs on the low ceiling. The temperature was considerably cooler than above, and the high moisture content in the air was very noticeable. The dampness of the mine produced a salt-water brine that gave off an unusual odor, although it was not unpleasant. The walls and floor were slightly damp, but not enough that they were muddy.

The second half of the group soon arrived, accompanied by the guide, who then started to count the number in his group.

Tak moved out of that group and over near another one speaking a different language until the other guide had counted the number of heads to see if all were there. Then she returned.

"Well, here we are," the guide began. "I bet a number of you have used the expression, 'I'll be at the salt mines'. Now you can say you have actually been to a real salt mine!" His joke was followed by a big smile, showing crooked teeth.

"This mine has been in continuous operation for over seven hundred years. The mine ranges from sixty-four to three-hundred-twenty-five meters below ground. It's a labyrinth of over two-hundred kilometers of corridors and two-thousand-forty chambers, which are the excavated areas where salt was taken from. But don't worry. I'm only going to take you on a short bit of it."

Tak was led along square mine shaft tunnels six feet wide, and not much taller in spots, then into a chamber filled with life-sized carvings of people in the gray-green color of the natural salt, where the guide amassed the group again.

"The Wieliczka rock-salt deposit formed fifteen million years ago, in the Miocene epoch, Cainozoic era. In later times, the deposit underwent being folded in the uplifting process of the Carpathian Mountains. Before people reached the deposit in this mine, salt was obtained by evaporation from the water of brine springs on the surface, going back as early as 3500 BC. As surface supplies ran out, people started looking for the salt in the depths of the Earth. At one time, over a third of the world's salt came from this very mine. Now, it is only mined to keep the water from overtaking it, as it is no longer economically profitable to mine salt here." He beckoned to the group. "Please follow me."

In the next chamber, he continued. "This is the Nicholas Copernicus Chamber. This mine is noted for its many carvings of salt. In a number of the salt chambers, the miners left about two meters of salt around the walls for artists to make carvings, and you will see a number of those chambers on the tour. This is—" He gestured at the life-sized statue of the dark gray-green salt next to him. "—a statue of Nicolaus Copernicus. It was created here on the five-hundredth anniversary of the birth of the great Polish astronomer, who once visited the mine. Many heads of state have visited the mine when they come to Poland." He beckoned again. "This way please."

Fascinating, Tak thought. What a stroke of luck! She

had not heard of this place in her studies of the planet. She was led into an enormous hall that resembled an elaborate palace ballroom. The entrance was from a balcony in the rear of the magnificent chamber, with steps leading down to the floor. The gray-green salt walls were carved in elaborate, life-sized scenes of people and places, and chandeliers hung from the ceiling.

The guide led the group down the long stairs to the floor of the huge room, which floor had been carved into hexagonal tiles of salt, to resemble a stone-tiled floor. He stopped to wait for the group to gather around him and then began again. "This is the Chapel of Saint Kinga. You will see various religious carvings on all of the walls, including one of The Last Supper to your left. Everything in the room is carved out of salt—the railings, the alter, even the chandeliers, which were carved from salt crystals and, of course, lighted with electricity that we have brought in. Excavation of the room was started in 1896, and the carvings were done in stages in the following years. The chamber is fifty-four meters long, eighteen meters wide, and fifteen meters high. The floor is one-hundred-and-one meters below the surface. This chapel is still used on special occasions and can be reserved for weddings. It is the only place where underground worship exists."

Tak was amazed. Underground worship of the Earthlings' concept of a creator in a big chamber, 330 feet below surface, in a cathedral carved out of salt!

Another group of adults entered the chamber and milled about, looking at the carvings as her group did. The guide for Tak's group stood over by the steps leading out, waiting for her group to complete their examination of the carvings and press on with the tour. Once the group had gathered around the guide, he began to count heads to see if all were there.

*Oh, oh! Another head count!* Tak moved toward the other group so as not to be counted. The guide then collected the group and escorted them back up the steps to the exit, taking care that the number in his group was complete, making it impossible for Tak to remain in that group without being detected.

She realized that she was left where she was and wandered over to the other group that was forming about their guide. He began to speak, but the language was not English.

*Not English*! Tak was on her own. She went up the steps alone to the tunnel to follow the tour group. She caught up and joined in the back. Another chamber appeared and the group went in, Tak in the rear. It was a very tall room, without carvings, and had a walk-bridge over an inland pond. The upper part was unlit. Off to the left were wooden steps leading behind a rock in one direction, and another set led up a steep incline toward an opening somewhere near the top. Tak decided it was obviously not part of tour, due to the narrowness of the steps.

The guide gathered the group on the bridge over the middle of the pond and began. "There is much water in the Earth here. It has always been, and remains, a threat to the mine shafts' integrity. As you can imagine, the water is so extremely concentrated with salt that it's a brine. It's concentrated to the maximum amount of salt that water will hold. The climates of these salt mines are especially favorable to humans as they do not contain most allergens and micro-organisms, such as bacteria, viruses, and fungi that exist on the surface. On level five, which is not part of the tour, there is an allergologic sanatorium where patients come to stay for their health. Patients inhale the air, rich in sodium, calcium, and magnesium chlorides, which cures diseases of the upper respiratory tract. That level is one-hundred-thirty-five meters below ground, in the Wessel Lake Chamber, and there is excellent medical care there. Appointments can be made for treatment there, and if you have asthma, allergies, and respiratory ailments, you might find it beneficial."

The tour guide motioned for his group to continue and let them pass along beside him, again counting to be sure he had everyone.

*Oh, oh*! *Not another counting*! To the left was the narrow wooden bridge, leading somewhere, its direction obscured from the main path by a large rock six feet high and three times as long. *Behind this rock will do.*

When the guide turned his head, she quickly went over the wooden bridge and hid behind the huge rock.

*Well*, she thought, *I'm on my own now*! She could wait for another English speaking group. That was probably the best plan—to hide out here for a while. *Time for a rest.*

Tak sat down behind the huge rock, contemplating the day. She had, after all, left the starship, entered this planet's atmosphere, gotten detected by a warship, gone back into space, and managed to land safely in a place called Poland. A short rest seemed well deserved.

The group that was in the big chamber behind her original group, the one with another language, came along. Tak remained behind the rock. The group leader stopped on the bridge over the brine lake, and the guide explained something to them. That group moved on, and no other groups followed for nearly half an hour. Then she heard voices in the brine lake chamber. Tak stood up and carefully peaked around the rock. It was not a group, but instead only two people. One was a guide in a black uniform, the other a tall, good-looking man, who appeared to be nearing forty years of age, with blond hair and very well dressed as compared to all of the other tourists. Why was there only one in this tour? Maybe he was an important person.

Tak quickly crouched back down so as not to be seen. The two men walked to the bridge, to the widened part over the lake, where her guide had stopped the group to speak. The guide began speaking to him in English. 'This is the Weimar Chamber."

"Didn't the Nazis build airplane parts in these mines in the war?" the man asked.

"Yes," the guide said. "In 1944, the Nazis set up a plant here. They thought that building the parts here would save them from being bombed as was the case at so many of their factories. The factory here was manned by Poles of Jewish origin, detained in a temporary camp located in the Kinga Park. The plant was disassembled at the time of the Soviet offensive, and the prisoners were taken to Belzec and other camps by the Nazis, where they were killed." Hearing no more questions, the guide asked the man, "Are you ready to move on now?"

"Tak," the tourist said.

She heard it clearly from behind the rock in the salt chamber. How did this man know her name? She came out and walked around the wooden bridge to the two men. Tak felt sheepish, caught, or so she thought, and approached him. "You know who I am?"

He stared at her, looking dumbfounded at her question. "I'm afraid not, madam. But allow me to present myself. I'm Baron Von Limbach."

"Tak."

Clearly surprised, he said, "Oh? Do you know of me?"

"Oh, no. I do not know of you. Why do you ask?"

"Because you said *Tak* when I told you my name and title."

"My name is Tak."

"Seriously?" Baron said, leaning toward her slightly as if to make very sure he heard her answer. "In spite of the many languages I speak, I have never heard of a person with the name of *Tak*."

"Yes. Tak."

Baron laughed a hearty laugh which resonated in the quiet air of the big, salt chamber. Then he asked, "Where's your guide?

"I seemed to have lost him."

"I see why you got lost. Whenever one of the guides said 'tak,' you thought you were supposed to follow. *Tak* means *yes* in Polish, which is one of the many languages I speak. So when I said tak earlier, you thought I was calling you!" He began to laugh again.

The contagious laughter of the man called Baron

moved to his guide, who also began to laugh, and then it took hold of Tak, who laughed for the first time on Earth.

"Tak, since you are without a guide," Baron then told her, "perhaps you will permit me to allow you to use mine and let him accompany us both to the surface?"

"Thank you, yes."

After visiting two more chambers, Tak followed them back up to the surface, where Baron gave his private guide a handsome tip.

Up on the surface, with better lighting, Baron looked at her curiously, attempting to evaluate just who she could be. She was an extraordinarily attractive woman, perhaps in her twenties, with thick, red hair; a super build; strong bone structure; and had been wandering around over three hundred feet below ground in a salt mine. A runaway? But she looked clean and fresh. Perhaps escaping from a volatile husband or lover? One of those women who claimed abuse by a husband or lover? A fugitive? But she was so attractive that he wanted to believe the best about her.

An enormous, white car approached. "There's my driver," Baron said.

A sprinkle of rain drops began, and it looked very much like it would soon rain. Tak was all that much more vulnerable, as she found herself outside with no shelter she could go to. She noticed that Baron's approaching car was significantly different from the others she had seen so far. The car was six feet tall, white, and had a very long, high hood. Two enormous chrome headlights, each a foot in diameter, proudly stood attached to the sides of a huge radiator. Two long claxons protruded, one under each light. The front fenders tapered back into running boards under the doors as a step into the car for passengers. Atop the huge radiator was a silver figurine, a lady with wings.

Wondering whether or not he might be inviting trouble, Baron decided that at least he could offer the attractive woman a lift. "It is going to rain. Have you transportation?"

"No, I don't"

"Where are you staying? Perhaps I might offer you a lift."

"I just arrived and do not yet have a place to stay."

This was indeed curious, he thought. But given her beauty, and he being one who was always interested in women, he decided to dive into whatever trouble might be following her. "I recommend my hotel. It is the Forum, situated above the bank of the Vistula River in Krakow, and it is certainly the best. Would you like to follow me there?"

She wondered if this was an offer in exchange for something she was to provide, which it most likely must be. But here she was, in a very strange land, where English was not the native language.

She acquiesced. "Okay."

The driver stopped the car and opened a rear door. "Lachhiman, to the Forum," Baron said.

Tak stepped into the back and sat on the plush leather seat, upholstered much like a posh leather couch, where the rich odor of leather consumed her. Other tourists took pictures of them in the car with little cameras. She concluded that they were interested in the fancy car.

A lovely spring rain began to pour down as the car went toward Krakow. Music, as well as fresh air, came from the deck behind the rear seat, and Tak felt comfortable with her host.

Baron leaned forward to the center-dividing window, which was open, and asked of his olive-skinned driver, "Lachhiman, were you able to find out if the mushrooms are in season?"

Lachhiman turned. "Yes, sir, they are indeed."

Baron looked at Tak. "They have a very special mushroom that grows here. It makes a delicious soup. You haven't tried it?"

"I only arrived today. What's a mushroom?"

He looked puzzled and answered her question with one of his own. "Would you like to join me this evening to try it?"

"Oh yes, thank you."

"Will you be in Poland long?"

She realized that there was much more to the question than just a simple answer, and that he, obviously seasoned at language, could detect much from the nuances of how she answered. She must be careful. But, on the other hand, this very kind person was helping her, and she had known that she would have to take chances on her mission. He was the best choice—in fact, the only choice, at the moment. She decided on an answer. "I'm traveling and am flexible."

Baron chuckled. "Ah yes, *flexible.*"

Tak looked around inside the beautifully appointed car interior. "This is a very nice car. Is it a popular model?"

He looked at her, again puzzled. "No, it is not what you would call a *popular* model. It is a 1936 Rolls Royce Phantom III with a Parkward Razor Edge body. Only six were ever made. I had it modernized mechanically, so it would be reliable, and added comforts like air conditioning and things not available when it was made. I keep it here in Europe."

The majestic car continued through the green fields of the countryside, the lovely spring rain pounding down against the music, an ambiance she would always remember.

Baron pointed ahead. "There's the Vistula River and the hotel."

The picturesque hotel was situated on the river bank. Two uniformed hotel doormen came to the car, one on either side.

Lachhiman came around to stand near Baron. "Sir, will you be going out for the mushroom soup this evening?"

"Why, yes."

"What time, sir?"

Baron looked at Tak, who did not respond. "Let's make it eight," he said. "Check with the concierge on where the best place is just now and how to get there. We'll go relax and freshen up."

"Very good, sir."

Baron led Tak into the lobby. The concierge, recognizing the wealthy guest from previous stays, came out at once to greet him with old world manners. He bowed to Baron. "Good afternoon, Baron. It's so delightful to have you back and to have nobility in residence once again. It distinguishes our hotel. Have you any immediate requests?"

"I'd like to arrange an additional room for my guest, adjoining. Then we would like you to make reservations for two at eight at the absolutely best place for the mushroom soup. Please tell my driver how to get there."

"It would be my honor, Baron."

Baron and Tak followed the concierge to the greeting counter. The concierge summoned a female clerk with a wave of his hand, but he stayed on the outside of the counter to better serve his royal guest.

After a few words with the clerk, he turned back to Baron. "Baron, the rooms on either side of your suite are taken, but one of the guests has not yet arrived. We are putting that guest elsewhere so you can have the adjoining suite. Could we have the name of the guest?"

"Just put the room in my name," Baron said.

"Yes, of course." The concierge filled out the card as just "Baron von Limbach," and then filled out a second card for his guest as "Baron Von Limbach, Second Room." But he was obligated to put down the responsible person for the second room, just in case Baron was not going to pay for it. The concierge turned to the woman. "Madam, how would you be paying for the room?"

Tak looked at Baron. "If you would be kind enough to lend me some money, I have something in exchange that you might take."

His eyebrows rose. He turned to the concierge and said magnanimously, "Put her room, and whatever she wants, on my bill."

"Very good, sir." The clerk made magnetic entry cards for them, which the concierge handed to Baron and the woman.

Tak looked at it curiously.

Baron's bags had been collected outside from the back of the car, brought inside, and on put on a brass trolley.

The concierge then looked at Tak. "Is your luggage here, madam?"

She raised the shoulder strap on the satchel she had slung over her shoulder. "I only have this one."

Discrete as the best concierges must be, he simply wrote on the registration card, gave the bellman the number of Baron's room, and said, "Second room, no bags." He turned back to Baron. "Very good, sir, I'll see to it that your chauffeur has the usual accommodations and whatever he needs. He can place your car in the special, secured, and monitored spot in our garage as usual. Will there be any-thing else at this moment?"

"Only the reservations for us at eight at the place that has the absolute best mushroom soup."

"Of course, sir. It's in season. I know just where to send you. I'll make reservations for two and tell your driver how to get there."

"Excellent."

The concierge snapped his fingers at the bellman and off they went to the rooms. The bellman took the cargo ele-vator, and Baron and Tak the regular one, intended for guests.

In the room, Tak went right to the balcony overlooking the fabulous view of Vistula River with a castle just across in a beautiful sunset.

Baron followed her in. "Will this do?"

"Oh, yes, thank you, Baron. This is wonderful!"

"'I'm glad you like it. It's the best in Krakow." He tipped the bellman, who then left in the tradition of old world Poland, by backing out of the room.

"I'll be just next door if you want anything," Baron then said to Tak. "If I don't hear from you sooner, let's meet at eight in the lobby. Is there anything you need?"

"Yes. I do not have any of the local currency."

"That's all right. Just charge anything you want to the room."

"Thank you, but I can pay for myself. I understand the need for money and brought something to trade."

"Now, what on earth might that be?"

Tak opened her bag, reached inside a pocket, and took out ten bars of pure gold, each five inches long and an inch wide. "I understand that these are valuable here? Can you trade me your currency for these?"

Baron frowned. "Tak, you continue to surprise me. Those are worth a fortune! You hardly appear to be the damsel in distress." He took one of the pieces in his hand to judge its weight. No stranger to wealth, he knew what to do. "I think I know what's best for you. I'll take them to an exchange for you tomorrow and make sure you get a good rate. There will probably be a commission loss of a few percent. Will that do?"

"That would be good."

"Keep them until then, but you'd better carry them with you all the time and do not leave them in the room—although, there is a safe if you wish to use it. In the meantime, let me treat you. Let's freshen up and dress for dinner which is at eight. Oh, sorry, I forgot you have no luggage. Well, just wear your outfit, as it will have to do."

He went into the adjoining room through the passage door and closed it. In spite of his vast experience, he was bewildered. He had learned that truth was often stranger than fiction, but this was definitely a first.

In the privacy of her room, Tak realized that it was time to send a message to the starship. It had placed a geosynchronous satellite, high above Earth's satellites, which would relay any messages. It was designed to follow her wrist computer wherever she went on the planet, so it should be directly overhead.

Tak spoke to her wrist computer in her own language. "Computer, send the following message to the starship: 'Entry into planet's atmosphere over initial landing site detected. Alternate spot chosen in a country called Poland on the other side of the planet, but in the same northern hemisphere. Landing safe and mission underway.'"

"Message sent," the computer told her.

Tak then decided to try out the bathing facilities to prepare for something called "mushroom."

❧❧

The waiter pushed the serving cart over to the table with two huge, freshly baked, hollowed out bread loaves, that looked like large round buns, each on a serving plate.

"The mushroom soup is served in this fresh bread," Baron explained. "The top, you will find, has been sliced and can be lifted off."

He demonstrated by lifting the top off his, and she followed suit, allowing an enormous, steamy cloud of highly aromatic fresh mushroom soup and freshly baked bread to intensely satiate the senses.

The aroma consumed her. "This smells wonderful!"

As she inhaled its magnificence again and again, the waiter poured two glasses of wine that Baron had chosen.

She inhaled again, consumed in olfactory extravagance, and let out a "Hmmmmmm!"

Tak waited to see how Baron handled this strange object. He broke off a piece of the bun top with his fingers and took a spoon in his other hand. Sipping the steaming soup with the spoon, he ate the piece of hot bread. She copied him, sampling the sumptuous concoction.

"Delicious!" she found herself saying, involuntarily. She sipped the wine, savoring it, and looked at Baron, smiling. "I had no idea there were such wonders here."

"Do you have mushroom soup where you come from?" he asked.

"Nothing like this, to be sure."

"Tak, I speak quite a few languages and pride myself that I can tell where many, if not most, people come from.

But I confess, I cannot place your origin from your accent. Perhaps, you have not obtained a particular accent because you travel so much. Have you traveled a great deal?"

"That much is certain." She wondered if he would continue to press. She could tell him she was from Kansas as that was where she had planned to land. But she did not know what a Kansas accent sounded like or much about Kansas itself. And most likely, a linguist like Baron would know right away that she was lying. Better not mention it, she decided, as he might turn her in to the authorities.

Baron took the cue that she did not wish to reveal her origins and left the subject alone to concentrate on the fabulous soup. His evening was, after all, adorned with a very beautiful young woman and so, he concluded, why not enjoy it to the fullest?

"What have you in store for the rest of your visit to Poland?"

"I want to learn as much as I can."

"Have you had a chance to visit Auschwitz and Birkenau?"

"No. Are those people interesting?"

Baron blinked and sat back in his seat, as he could hardly believe her naiveté. He wondered if it was possible that someone had not heard of Auschwitz? She did not seem stupid. She seemed foreign, very foreign—and as charming as she was beautiful. He wanted her.

"Those are not people, but places. I'll tell you what. I have business tomorrow, and now that includes exchanging gold for you. And, of course, I've already seen Auschwitz and Birkenau. Why don't I have the concierge hire an English-speaking, private driver and a tour guide for you with a car and send you off to see them tomorrow? We could then meet for cocktails and dinner later. I'll have your currency for you then. What say you to that?"

"That would be excellent."

# CHAPTER 5

Hot breath exhaled from the man and woman like low flying clouds as they plodded up the steep, snow-packed road, leading up to a plateau in the mountains nine miles from remote Stepnogorsk, Kazakhstan. Spring, that had come elsewhere, was still absent there.

The man carried a plastic bag with something in it that was fairly heavy.

The bus had dropped them off at the spot where there used to be a half dozen armed Soviet soldiers at a guard station, an electrified fence, a radio to call to verify any questionable identities, and a weapons carrier, all now vanished.

Dr. Borislav Dorogomilov was tall, gaunt, and pale-skinned. His hair receded on either side of his head and gray filled his sideburns. His mouth and lips had an unfriendly thinness, and his nose was long and slender. His expression gave no hint of welcome.

Dr. Anastasiya Volkova, his assistant of many years, was almost as old. She was tall, slender, with long, thin legs; thin, broad shoulders; and a tall, thin head with blondish hair. She was attractive, but she took no time to apply makeup nor fuss with her looks. Her manner was very domineering.

"It's so good to have you back," she said to him. "The funeral for Karina was very touching, and I cried for her loss. But yet, she was suffering, so it was a Godsend that she finally passed."

"Thank you for everything and for the food you sent over to the house, Anastasiya."

"I'll do my best to take care of you now and please you, as I always have. But there's something happening soon that you probably don't know about since you've been gone. Some American diplomat, a woman from the US State Department, is coming to inspect the lab in a few days, as most of our financing for the fungi is now coming from the United States. As usual, there will be a few people from our government accompanying her, trying to talk the United States into providing more money. They, of course, will want the money to come to them to administer it. The woman will be here on a tour of several countries to give talks on why they need to stop allowing the production of drugs. She will report back to the United States on the need for additional money to continue the funding of our fungi research, and also for money for the dismantling of this building. She is on a tour of the Ukraine, Uzbekistan, Tajik-istan, and her last stop will be here."

"What kind of nonsense is this?" he spat out angrily and thought of the stupidity and the hard times he was suf-fering. "This childish nonsense to make friendly fungi that kills opium, and is harmless to animals and humans, is set up to make it appear that the government is not allowing drug production. Ridiculous! Government officials them-selves are in the drug trade. They get payoffs for allowing drug production, although no drugs come from this lab. What'll I tell her? That I'm close to eradicating all drug production with my fabulous new fungi? The American government lives a lie to itself and its people. And I'm sup-posed to babysit some fucking cunt-for-brains idiot! Those assholes in the US send women to Muslim countries, and you know what they think of that and what they say about them when they leave."

"Well, it is the funding of fungi growth to kill opium

that keeps the lab open," Anastasiya replied, trying to calm him. "Without that, we would have nothing, and you would not be able to keep your special room." She referred to the special room where he kept live viruses that the Soviets had brought from Africa years before. "And it is not as though the Soviet government was ever truthful with anyone."

"Better nothing than this," Dr. Dorogomilov decreed in angry protest, but he really did not mean it.

They entered the doors of the huge Building 221. Moss blanketed the outside of the building, with its broken windows covered with plywood in place of more expensive glass.

Building 221 was dark, run down, the length of two football fields, and six stories tall, with four stories above ground and two underground. The underground stories were put there to assist containment of volatile bio-warfare agents should there be an accident—and there had been. He opened the door. Its unoiled hinges squeaked. The inside was dark, drafty, damp, and eerie. Airtight locks, put there to contain the horrific products made there, now hung open. No lights were on, and the inside was not heated, save for one section where his lab remained. It was still the most sophisticated lab of its kind on Earth, used for the experimentation of killing people with chemical and biological means. It was now used only for the façade of fungi experiments, modestly funded to create an environmentally safe formula to kill opium poppies. Although now dated, most all of the exotic equipment remained, however, for the making of bio-warfare agents, which was why there was partial funding for the fungi—to lower any interest in it being fired up again to make anthrax, staphylococcus, and experimentation in bio-warfare agents. Run down as it was, it was still a level four bio-warfare lab, like no other in the world, where biological warfare agents could not just be made, but mass produced.

To keep one from falling, illumination was provided by a few lights. The lack of heat and the drafts made the inside seem colder than outside. No one spoke as they passed through the cold, echoing, abandoned, anthrax-fermenting room. Instead, they waited until they got to their less hostile lab downstairs. The elevator no longer worked, and there was no money to fix it. Their lab was kept in the best part of the building. Building 221, like 241-244, and 231, were equipped with bio-containment systems with high efficiency air filters and fans for maintaining negative air pressure, individual air supplies, sterilization autoclaves, and submarine doors. The system in 221 still worked, due to continued maintenance. The modest amount money coming in was enough for utilities to heat and power his private lab in a small portion of the huge building.

They walked through the unheated, huge, fermenting rooms, now inoperative, where the Soviets had built ten, five thousand gallon fermentation vats for brewing anthrax microbes.

He put down the plastic bag which contained animal remains for his special Ebola. He would later suit up in one of the special pressure suits, clean the special area of Ebola, and add the new food.

Dr. Volkova made Russian tea for them in glass cups with metal bases.

He continued complaining. "I'll probably have to destroy my beautiful samples one day! Using part of my paltry salary and favors, I have continually brought in animal tissue to keep alive samples of Marburg virus from Uganda, Zimbabwe, South Africa, and Kenya. I kept alive the magnificent Ebola from Zaire—now called the Democratic Republic of the Congo by those savages—and from Sudan, Central African Republic, Gabon, Nigeria, Ivory Coast, Liberia, Cameroon, Kenya, and also Uganda. And, of course—" He smiled. "—my special variant with altered RNA. I can make it work on a given race and keep it reproducing that way. But who will pay me for what I can do? Probably no one, except those lunatics in the Middle-East and who would lead to our being caught for sure.

"If I do have to destroy my samples, the variants that I

have created will be lost. My genius will go down the drain! I'll probably end up continuing to work on producing the ridiculous fungi that the government claims will be used to eradicate the growing of poppies, as though the dope trade of this region is going to be eradicated. Ridiculous! My life's work has become an unwanted commodity. I'm an unwanted commodity."

She came up behind him and gave him a strong hug. "Darling, you're a wanted commodity to me."

He calmed down, accepting her embrace. He then directed his attention to the moment. "What about this American female who's coming? Do you think that her arrival will speed up the money from America to tear down the interior of this building so that I'll have nowhere to keep my specimens?"

"I don't know," she said. "Why don't we ask her?"

# CHAPTER 6

By coincidence, and because of the difference in time zones, just hours before Doctors Dorogomilov and Volkova had their conference, an expert from the CIA, Dan Horn, was briefing Christine Rhyes-Walters of the State Department for her mission to that very facility. He had numerous pictures of the inside of the buildings, all of which had an address of only Postal Mailbox 2076. Additionally, he had a stack of documents and satellite photos, all of which were labeled top secret.

Rhyes-Walters had been with the State Department for two years, her appointment arranged by her father with his political contributions to the president. She kept her family name when she married and used it with the hyphen. Although never slender, she had gained weight since she'd taken the job, and her blue business suit, one of which she bought when appointed, was now too tight. She was headstrong, opinionated, and not too bright.

As Rhyes-Walters looked at pictures of huge vats used for making anthrax, Horn said, "As you can see, this Stepnogorsk facility is set up for big-time production of weapons-grade anthrax. Other chemicals can be made there as well. Here are pictures taken inside Building 221."

The picture depicted row of enormous tanks that were so big they looked like something found at a shipyard.

Rhyes-Walters' eyes opened wide in amazement.

"These were used just to make anthrax? My God, they could kill the whole world with these!"

"Well, they could have killed a significant part of it. Check out these five thousand gallon vats. The solution of bacteria grown in the fermenters was transferred to seven centrifugal separators on the floor below, which spun at five-thousand revolutions per minute to separate the bacterial cells from the nutrient media and other waste products. When in operation, in a single three-day production cycle, one-and-a-half metric tons of concentrated bacterial slurry was produced. When in operation, it would have made Anheuser Busch jealous at the capacity.

"As you know, the Kazakhstan government is upside down due to lack of money, inflation, joblessness, and corruption," he continued. "We don't want this place turned into an anthrax producing facility again, and that is what we are hoping to continue to prevent.

"In case you are having thoughts that the place might be converted to some other use, you should know that you're not the first. This was the only major Soviet germ installation that had been built outside the Soviet heartland. It was built in 1982, ten years *after* 1972 when the US and the Soviets signed a treaty banning such bio-weapons, called the Biological and Toxin Weapons Convention. It was only in 1979, when there was an accidental release of anthrax at a place called Sverdlovsk, Russia, that killed sixty-four people as well as livestock thirty miles away, that it was confirmed the commies were making anthrax. They then moved the production to Stepnogorsk and funded this huge facility. It was built there, as opposed to inside the heartland of the Soviet Union, mostly because it was so remote and isolated, but also because the Soviets used those Muslim nations as dumping grounds. Russians did not care if there was an anthrax leak in a Muslim country.

"Soviets used other areas of Kazakhstan for military programs. As an example, only ninety-three miles from a town called Semey, there is a spot that was used for testing nuclear bombs. Get this—over four-hundred-seventy nuclear bombs were exploded there above ground from 1949 to 1989, causing inhabitants of Semey to suffer radiation poisoning that continues even today. And as for testing biological weapons, Soviets used Vozrozhdeniye Island, located in the middle of the Aral Sea, the northern third of which is in Kazakhstan, for open-air testing of such weapons.

"In its heyday, the very best bio-technologists and talented young scientists from the best universities in the Soviet Union worked at PO Box 2076. Specialized courses at leading Soviet research institutions were developed to train new personnel to come to this facility. In 1984, the facility had three hundred-fifty people. By 1991, it was eight hundred, with seventeen scientists who had doctoral degrees and one-hundred researchers. Building 221 had fermentation equipment and a genetics and microbiology research laboratory with a high containment system.

He handed her a picture. "This is a building, known as 600, which also has a high containment system and a specialized chamber for testing biological warfare munitions. Made of stainless steel, the chamber is two-hundred cubic meters in volume, with walls one-and-six-tenths centimeters thick—imagine the expense of that!

"Buildings 241 to 244 and 251 to 271 are underground bunkers with reinforced concrete walls two meters thick, designed to survive a nuclear attack. Buildings 241 to 244 contain weaponization lines where special machines filled bomblets with concentrated slurry or pathogenic microorganisms and then sealed them. Explosive bursters were attached, after which the bomblets were installed on aerial bombs or missile warheads. Buildings 251 to 271 contain refrigeration rooms for storage of the biological agents, capable of sustaining temperatures down to minus forty degrees Celsius with a volume of eight hundred cubic meters. Buildings 251 to 271 are connected by a railway spur with loading equipment and have a small helicopter landing site nearby. When operational, three hundred metric tons of anthrax could be made in weapons-ready form every ten months.

"Are you an animal lover?" He shot her a sinister smile and continued. "Monkeys, rabbits, and other animals had been kept in cages in the vivarium, used for tests in the aerosol chamber. But after a few years of operation, a better method of experimentation was found. Humans were actually brought in for testing! When someone was sentenced to death in the Soviet Union with little or no family for a funeral, the person might be sent to Stepnogorsk. They found that bringing in humans was actually cheaper and less trouble than bringing in monkeys from far away countries. As the prisoners were to die anyway, the testing of lethal agents on them worked out well for all concerned."

Rhyes-Walters leaned forward, obviously upset at what she was hearing. "And we're supporting this monster Dorogomilov who was in charge of such evil?"

"Well, you know how things work," Horn said. "If we don't continue to put money in there for research on the fungi to kill opium, the corrupt Kazakhstani government officials might very well let someone use the facility to produce anthrax or another bio-warfare agent for fanatic Muslims who will pay anything for them. So it is the lesser of two evils, or at least until money is raised to tear the facility down.

"Let me give you just a little more history. After the collapse of the Soviet Union, Kazakhstan inherited this facility, and it remains the world's most impressive biochemical production facility. Funding was cut off. It was abandoned and left to Kazakhstan. Since the facility had been controlled by central Moscow agencies, local Kazakhstan authorities had little or no idea about the activities there.

"Kazakhstan, with the inducement of our money and a few others', set a goal to convert the Soviet's horrendously expensive investment to civilian use rather than let it go back to making bio-warfare or chemicals for oil rich Muslim nations. The Kazakhstan government, in 1993, formed an enterprise for civilian industrial development, called Bi-omedpreparat. Genetically engineered insulin, the antibiotic called roseofungin, and other pharmaceuticals were tried. But that all failed due to high costs. Next, with US money, a joint venture called Kamed Resources was founded with our support and the US firm of Allen & Associates who make pharmaceuticals. However, that closed down after Bio-medpreparat failed to pay the utilities, initially funded by Kazakhstan. From 1993 to 1995, Kazakhstan maintained a life support regime for the buildings, but that was as far as it went.

"In 1995, Kazakhstan stopped providing funds, and measures were taken to mothball the place. The conversion to civilian use, therefore, never really happened, and that is the danger. By 1998, only a handful of activities were still carried on, making miscellaneous medical items, such as syringes, but that is all gone.

"The bottom line, from an economic sense, is simply that this facility, which cost millions just to keep going when making bio-warfare chemicals, cannot support itself when converted to civilian use. Too remote, too costly to heat, maintain, and power, it is a modern dinosaur. So we want to keep it minimally funded until it is torn down or converted so that it will not be used for chemical warfare production."

"Why did this Dr. Dorogomilov not go with the Russians when the USSR broke up?" Rhyes-Walters asked.

"As far as we know, there are two reasons. One is that he married a Kazakh woman. Her family is from a nearby town in the steppes below Stepnogorsk. But soon thereafter, just before the collapse of the Soviet Union, she came down with cancer. It took her years to overcome it, as it went in and out of remission. With the cancer, she needed the help of her local family, and Dr. Dorogomilov refused to leave her. He refused to accept a low-level research position back in Russia, staying on until her passing recently, so she could be with her family and in her homeland. He lost his privileges with the collapse of the Soviet Union and lives on whatever we provide, plus a pittance from the Kazakhstan government. Our profile on him is that he is bitter with life."

"Can't he just leave now that his wife is dead?"

"I suppose so, but then there is the second reason. Russians have cut back enormously on military spending, and his specialty is chemical and bio-warfare agents. There is no longer a demand for a scientist with the specialty of killing millions with bio-warfare.

"He could have, and probably still can, get a low-paying and lackluster job teaching biology or chemistry in a Russian university, but nothing with any of the importance that he used to have. What we are concerned about is that he has the complete ability to make anthrax and other deadly chemicals in quantity, and if a rogue nation or one of the lunatic Muslim leaders wants to make an order, it could be done there.

"The Kazakh government officials could easily be bribed not to notice. If such an order were allowed to be filled, even a small order of enough for a terrorist attack, he could make a relative fortune—imagine what a million would look like to someone who can no longer afford a car! So we want to spend money there for anything we can that will help prevent that from happening.

"The fungi research to kill the opium poppy, of course, does little good as it has not come to anything yet, but it makes good press and also gives us the right to go in and inspect the facility to make sure it is not being converted to anthrax or bio-warfare production."

"So I'm supposed to go check up on him and report back with recommendations on whether or not to continue funding for the fungi experiments and conclude that we should after this inspection?" she said.

"Yes."

෴

Ralls peered out of the helicopter window as it repeatedly circled the exact landing spot of the menacing craft as shown by the recorded GPS.

He communicated with the pilot over the headsets. "Anything at all?"

"Zip. Whatever grass that is growing there does not look to be flattened by something landing. But there was just a rain here, so that might have brought back up any grass that might have been pushed down. I think this is a dead end. We had better go back now. We've been here an hour, and we have to get started back or we'll run out of fuel."

"Okay. I'll arrange a car and take it from here on by ground," Ralls said.

He called Hauser, later on from his room in Lodz, on the secure satellite phone. "Nothing found. It's as though someone picked up the craft and took it away. There was no runway, no hanger, no nothing. Perhaps the pilot had some accomplices ready to cart the craft off? But there were no vehicle tracks in the vegetation in that area."

"With no explanation, the more that I think about this, the more concerned I'm becoming," Houser said. "Someone could propel a nuclear bomb, even a small, dirty bomb, at us in the US at seventeen-thousand miles per hour from almost anywhere on Earth and we would not be able to stop it. We have to find out who is behind this. Chase any leads you can find, and find something. Contact the CIA. This is too large of a potential threat to ignore."

# CHAPTER 7

Good morning, Andrew!" Shanta said exuberantly, announcing it practically to the entire hotel lobby. Exciting the elevator like a fashion model on a ramp, she wore faded blue jeans, a matching faded denim shirt with the bottom shortened by tying the shirt tails together in a knot in the front, matching high-heeled shoes of light blue leather with several crisscrossing straps across the front of the foot. Her jewelry was a three-inch wide bracelet of real elephant tusk with semi-precious stones and gold, circular earrings. Her olive skin made her look like a movie star. Dark, as if from tanning, it was accentuated by the faded denim. Others stared at her beauty, as well.

Unsure of himself, and taken aback by her new look, he did not respond immediately. Instead, he just stared at her as he had done when he met her the evening before.

To ease his tension, and to give him reason to continue to stare, she stopped and posed, turning around to make it more comfortable for him to be gawking at her. "You said to dress casually. Will this do?"

"You're beautiful!" Andrew blurted out clumsily.

"I'm glad you like it. I haven't too many things, as I like to travel light. And now too, the airlines charge you extra for bags." Shanta held out her hand to take his. "Shall we?"

"Yes."

He let her lead him the first few steps toward the glass
door entrance to the hotel.

Outside, the black Mercedes was waiting patiently with
Roger standing by at attention, not altogether unlike a Swiss
Guard at the Vatican.

Inside the car, Andrew looked at her. "What sort of
food would you like?"

"It's such a nice day. Why don't we go to someplace
where we can sit outside?"

Since Andrew seemed to have trouble selecting a spot,
Roger volunteered, "It is a little brisk for the ocean, ma'am,
but I know of several places that have outdoor seating,
where it would not be uncomfortably cold."

Shanta looked at Andrew, who was silent, and then
said, "Roger, why don't you pick one?"

"Any particular choice of cuisine, ma'am?" Roger
asked, as she was Indian, and he knew enough to know
some Indians didn't partake of pork, such as Pakistani Muslims. Some were vegetarian and didn't partake of eggs. The
majority did not partake of beef. And others might have
strange diets he did not know about.

"I eat nearly everything," she answered. Then she corrected, "Well, not like the Chinese, who eat everything that
walks, flies, swims, or crawls underground." She turned to
Andrew and smiled. "I'd like to try something local, as this
will probably be my one and only trip to America. Is there a
local sort of food?"

"We are close to the Mexican border, and there is much
Mexican influence," Roger answered. "I've been told of a
place that serves an Americanized version of Machaca,
fixed as an omelet with Spanish tomato sauce, marinated
beef, onions, and lots of peppers. How does that sound?"

Shanta looked at Andrew but he left the decision up to
her. It being apparent that she was to decide, she said to
them, "Let's do Machaca. I love peppers."

❧❧❧

"Oh Andrew, this is wonderful!" Shanta said, savoring the Machaca as they sat outdoors.

"Nice," Andrew agreed, being inexperienced with foreign foods. He then addressed what was foremost on his mind. "Do you believe that the Dalai Lama is the reincarnate of Buddha?"

"Yes. Don't you?"

"It's all new to me. Last night was the first time that I saw Him in person. I had a very strange feeling come over me at the session. Have you seen Him in person before?"

"Oh yes. Last night was the fifth time. Except for once in London, all the others were in Asia. I went to Tibet but, of course, He was not there, as He is not allowed. I saw Him in Dharamsala, India, where I stayed for several weeks. That is the seat of the semi-official Tibetan Government In Exile and is known as 'Little Lhasa.' The original Lhasa is a city in Tibet."

"Tell me some of the things you have learned."

"Sure. Well, let's see…where to start. Mental poisons. He teaches of mental poisons. There are negative states of mind, which He calls Kleshas, afflicting emotions. These are attachment, aversion, and ignorance. One can be cured of these once one achieves liberation. Without achieving liberation, there is illness, which includes mental illness.

"There are the positive emotions. These are such things as kindness, love, and compassion. The Buddhists have these qualities present in their minds but, while having these present, they have also a direct comprehension of emptiness."

"I'm not sure I comprehend emptiness, but the rest I think I understand," Andrew said.

"It takes some time, Andrew. At the heart of Buddhist philosophy is the notion of compassion for others. This is not the usual love for family. It's love one can have even for another who has done one harm. He believes in universal compassion, based on spiritual democracy. Selfishness is destructive to the individual, and to society.

"There are ten virtuous acts spoken of in Buddhism. Three concern the body: one must not kill, steal, or engage in sexual misconduct. Four others are verbal: lying, defaming others, offensive words, and engaging in frivolous conversation. The last three virtuous acts are mental in nature: do not develop covetousness, do not practice malice, and do not hold false or perverted views, which denies spiritual perfection."

"Do you practice these?"

"I try. I believe that you Christians have similar goals, do you not? The ten commandments?"

"Yes. I know of those." His answer was hardly that of an Oxford scholar on religion.

"He speaks of clear light as the Primordial Buddha," she went on.

"Have you seen the light?" Andrew asked,

"No, not yet," Shanta admitted.

"What does the Dalai Lama intend to do about His exile from Tibet?"

"He wants, most of all, to have Tibet returned to Tibetans. You heard the speakers last night. In a sentence, you might say that He says that the freedom struggle of the Tibetan people is at a crucial stage, and that the sinicization of Tibet is cultural genocide."

"You've been to Tibet," Andrew said. "Do you think there is any chance of the Chinese reversing what they have done to Tibet?"

"Not even a faint chance."

"Something must be done! What?"

"The only thing that can save the Tibetan culture and the home of the Dalai Lama is for the Chinese to leave."

"How on earth would you rid Tibet of seven and a half million Chinese?"

"Well, the government of China has no intention of requiring them to move—just the opposite," she said. "China continues to place Chinese there, deliberately, to dilute the Tibetans and their culture"

"You've traveled so much and know so much."

"Well, thank you, Andrew, but I've traveled mostly in Asia. This is my first time to America. Travel is very expensive. And my parents are supporting me still. I'll probably take a job sometime soon, most likely in Singapore. I could never get a work permit to come here."

He looked at a schedule he'd picked up at the door of the meeting hall. "I saw in the schedule that He is going to speak in London next. Will you be following to hear Him there?"

"Oh my, no! I can't afford that!"

"Would you go to London if you could?"

"Of course."

"I've decided to go. Would you like to come with me? My treat."

Utterly surprised, Shanta blinked. "Oh, I couldn't accept such a generous invitation, but thank you."

"It really won't cost anything. I'll be taking the company jet if I go, so you would just be riding along. And, on the trip, you could tell me more—there is so much that I don't understand."

"Company jet?"

"Yes. I'm the sole beneficiary of a trust that my father left me. The company has its own jet. As one of my benefits, I can call for it whenever I want."

"Is your father dead?"

"Yes. Actually both of my parents are gone. Mom died of cancer seven years ago, and Dad died a year ago. I'm an only child."

"I'm sorry for you that you are left alone with no family."

Andrew did not respond, but just stared blankly out into space. It was apparent that he was genuinely lonely without family, and perhaps without direction in life. Now he seemed to have found it.

To change the subject she said, "I've never ridden in a private plane before. If I could ride along, I guess it wouldn't cost any more. But then there would be the hotel which would be very expensive in a place like London. I must decline."

"Not to worry," he said, nonchalantly. "I'll get you a room in my hotel of your own as my treat."

She was without words, as nothing like this had ever been offered her. From her jilted marriage, after which she fled to an Ashram in India, all operating on a budget like that of a student, here she was offered more than she could imagine.

But she must not accept such an offer. If accepted, would she have to offer bedding with this man, not her husband, to pay in kind for the favor? Would she be impetuously sacrificing her virtue preserved for her one and true husband, yet to come? As the first husband never consummated the marriage, at least before God, she hoped, she was still available.

It was the most difficult decision she'd had ever to make. But also one that had to be made in an instant. It would dramatically alter her life, either sending her back to Singapore, or in a direction she knew not where.

Shanta's resistance faded to temptation. "Okay," was all she could muster in the face of such power from wealth. She felt as though she had just been raped, or maybe that she would be. Maybe it was time?

✁✁

Roger drove through the gate of the private jet parking ramp at the Long Beach Airport. The steps to the Gulfstream were down and ready. The steward inside, Sheldon, stuck his head out, keeping a constant vigil for them while trying at the same time to put things in better order for the wealthy young master. He saw them coming and hurried down the steps, well ahead of the arriving car. He wore black pants and vest, white shirt, and a black tie tucked neatly into the vest.

"It is very good to see you, sir," Sheldon said as the door opened.

"Hello, Sheldon. How've you been?"

"Very good, sir. It is so kind of you to ask. And good morning to you, Ms. Laxshimi."

Sheldon, advised as to who was coming, tried to find out how to pronounce her name by calling the Indian consulate. When he was put on hold indefinitely, he then phoned an Indian spice store and found out how to say it. He found out the pronunciation and that her name is that of an Indian Goddess, and pronounced *lek-shmee.*

Roger got their bags from the rear of the vehicle as the two pilots in the cockpit made the jet ready, one calling in to confirm the flight plan to New York and the other obtaining the latest weather briefing.

Shanta walked slowly into the Gulfstream, amazed by the luxury. There were only eight seats, four on each side in a club arrangement, with two seats each facing one another with fold down tables in between.

"Show her around, Sheldon," Andrew said, then he went forward to talk to the pilots.

"In the back, there is a bathroom, dressing area, and bedroom," Sheldon said. "There is a forward bathroom, and my station. We'll be about five hours to New York and a little longer to London. There is a stock of classic and current DVD movies and a large screen. There is also an active Internet connection. You will not hear the jet noise as the interior has ambient noise cancellation."

Andrew returned, held his arms out, and looked around. "So do you like the plane? The company just bought this one. It's a Gulfstream. The interior is custom."

Shanta looked around in amazement. "This is fantastic!"

"Say," Andrew then said. "I notice you have never asked me the what my company does."

"I felt it was not my place to inquire. I thought that if you wanted to tell me, you would do so."

"My father built the largest chicken franchise business in the world. Now the majority of it is held in trust for me."

"Wow! It must sell a lot of chickens."

ოჯოჯ

"There's Roger."

Upon their return from London, Andrew waived excitedly at the comforting sight of his driver. Shanta came to the doorway of the Gulfstream. Andrew pointed to a white, stretch Lincoln limousine that had just stopped on the tarmac. Andrew led Shanta down the steps of the plane at the New Orleans airport.

"So nice to see you, sir, and you, Madam Laxshimi," Roger said. "I only received your change of destination to New Orleans yesterday, and I had to rush here to put things in order."

The limousine pulled up to the circular drive of the New Orleans Windsor Court Hotel. Andrew, familiar with the hotel, went right to the reception area, which consisted of several large, luxurious, private desks with comfortable chairs across from an individual host. A man behind one desk recognized him and stood.

"It's always a pleasure to see you again, Master Saunders."

"Thank you. It's nice to be here again. This is my guest, Shanta Laxshimi."

"It is indeed a great pleasure to be introduced to such a charming lady,"

With an enormous smile at being treated so royally, Shanta said, "Why, thank you." She sat next to Andrew in the overstuffed, green leather seat beside his.

"I heard that Mr. Eschmann is staying here full time now," Andrew said. "I hope he's in."

"He may be in his room. Shall I call on him to announce your arrival?"

"No, not like that. That would be rude. Why don't you

give us rooms, and send him a written note that we're here, and to call on me at his convenience if he would be so kind?"

"Would you like a high room facing on the river side, as usual?" The receptionist remembered and kept on record what his wealthy guest preferred.

"Yes, river view. But make that two adjoining suites please."

⌘

"Sautéed French Foie Gras with Aromatic Pearl Couscous Fig Demi-Glace and Cumin Crackers for my appetizer." That was Mr. Eschmann's choice. He turned to the lovely Shanta. "What would you like?"

Mr. Eschmann was treating the couple to the Grill Dining Room in the hotel, a grand place to dine. He was in his own, in a world of the best foods anywhere.

She was ready to read out from the menu. "Crisp Potato Galette with Smoked Salmon, Vodka and Caviar Crème Fraiche. That sounds soooo good."

"Andrew?" Mr. Eschmann turned to him.

Looking to the waiter for help, as many of the menu selections were foreign to him, Andrew asked, "Is there a special tonight that you recommend?"

"Sir, you might enjoy the Char," the waiter said.

No one explaining what Char is, Andrew felt dumb. "Isn't *Char* what we do to new oak barrels before we put in bourbon for aging?" One thing he knew well was the making of Kentucky bourbon, common knowledge of those who grew up where he did, not to mention the fact that his trust owned one of the major distilleries and he had visited it often in the years prior. No one came to his aid. "In fact, our barrels are so much in demand that after we use them once, the discards are sold to Scotland for aging Scotch, which they use for aging for 12 or more years and then call it single malt, as though that was something special," he said.

"The used barrels are also sent to Jamaica for aging rum and also to Louisiana for aging Tabasco."

Eschmann finally came to his rescue. "*Char* is fish but I'm not sure where it is caught." He looked to the waiter for an answer.

The waiter promptly complied. "That's a fish similar to trout, normally found in the mountainous districts of Wales but, in this case, Alaska. It's called Arctic Char, and I recommend it, as it's splendid."

Andrew relaxed. "Okay, I will take that at the appetizer. It is here on the menu. It is called the Arctic Char Sautéed with Fresh Chanterelles and Peanut Potatoes Tarragon Oil and Smoked Butter."

Mr. Eschmann then picked his main course. "I'm going with the Prime New York Strip with Braised Endives and Leeks, Truffle Parisienne Potato, Cuban Oregon Sauce. And please bring me some truffle salt for my beef. I can only take a little salt at my age, and I like it to flavor the beef well. How about you, Shanta?"

She had a look at the goodies on the menu and picked one. "Seared Maine Lobster with Miso Glaze and Taro Root Parsnip Puree, Ginger Soy Sauce. I don't know what all that is on the lobster, except for the ginger soy sauce, but it sounds delicious."

"Andrew?"

"Rack of Lamb with Chick Pea Puree and Artichoke Ragout, Lemon Oregano Jus."

The waiter left to set in motion the gastronomic extravaganza. Eschmann then felt it would be the time and place to ask what Andrew had come to see him about.

Andrew spoke first, politely, with southern manners, not jumping into the subject. "So how've you been, Mr. Eschmann?"

Eschmann sipped his Johnny Walker Blue Label. Notwithstanding the fact that the trust he was in charge of administering, which owned a Bourbon distillery, he preferred Blue Label when the best was served. But he always took bourbon over cheap scotch, unless Blue Label was available. "Andrew, now that I'm retired, I conduct such minor matters as seeing an old acquaintance over a wonderful meal. I've moved here from Kentucky for that very purpose. You know, I don't play golf or engage in any pursuits other than epicurean."

The three of them sat in a circular booth where they could all face one another equally, that arrangement having been selected by Eschmann, a master at conducting meetings.

Eschmann took a sip of his pre-dinner scotch. "I haven't seen you since the funeral last year. What have you been up to?"

"Nothing much. Since Dad died, I've just been traveling about. I just came back from London yesterday with Shanta. Did you sell your home when you moved in here? I used to love it when Mom and Dad brought me over there when I was little."

"Yep. When Charlotte died, I felt very lonely there. And there was always so much upkeep. Charlotte took care of the gardens, you know, and that was quite a lot of work, even with help. I decided to sell and pass out all the antiques and things to our three kids. What they didn't take was given away. Thanks to the retainer your father provided me, which still continues, I'm able to afford to live here in this hotel. It is funny—when you are young, you think one day you will own a castle, and you strive to build up a big estate. We ended up with a big place, as you recall. Forty acres. But then there comes a time, or at least it did with me, when you realize that collecting things is more of a burden than it is rewarding. Things require polishing and maintenance. Many bathrooms mean more leaks to fix. Carpet care. Drapery cleaning. Wood floor refinishing. Fireplace maintenance. Appliances breaking down. Endless. Keeping up the big place was nearly a full time job for one person, even with a full time-servant."

"How is Sherman?" Andrew asked, referring to the

wonderful, huge, black man that used to work for Eschmann.

"Sherman's fine. He now lives with one of his kids. He'll be eighty-three this year. He was with me for forty-five years."

"I sure like him," Andrew said, reminiscing. After a pause for remembering good times, he asked, "How do you like living in this hotel? Don't you have to have almost no possessions to live in just a hotel?"

"It's wonderful! I have only a few clothing items and personal effects. I collect nothing! I get cable on the big screen in the room and can order anything around the clock. The room is made up daily when I step out, and all I have to do is put my clothes to be cleaned in a pile. They return the next day, placed properly in the closet, all ready to wear. And all of this is just two blocks from the French Quarter. I'm close to some of the finer restaurants in the US. And you know I love food!"

He chuckled. "So, what might I be able to do for you? This old, retired attorney isn't what he used to be, you know. I have aches, pains, and arthritis. I have to take medicine for high blood pressure."

Andrew came to the point of the visit. "Shanta and I need your help. I've taken up following the Dalai Lama. Do you know of Him?"

Playing dumb, Eschmann said, "A little. He wears those orange robes and has the round glasses. He seems to get invited to dine with heads of state quite a lot. Seems to me they gave him a Nobel Peace Prize—that is what they do when you are an exiled leader."

"Yep! That's Him."

"So what might I possibly do that could help out with the Dalai Lama, who, I believe, is supposed to be a holy man? I'm just a small town lawyer who moved to New Orleans to retire."

"You always had some fantastic connections and resources for Dad. I remember him telling me how he could not get those in authority to open our chicken franchises in parts of Asia, and you found the way. I'm interested to see if there's something that can be done privately to somehow get the Dalai Lama back into Tibet. If anyone could, it would be you."

"Andrew, you know I was practically a sole practitioner, with only one assistant lawyer and a staff of only two secretaries, and I do not have all those connections like those lawyers with friends in the White House. I think you have too big of an image of what I can do."

"As I recall," Andrew said, "it wasn't political influence that got the chicken franchises opened in several countries in Asia which were not allowing it, but very private influence—yours, to be exact."

Eschmann looked at Shanta so that Andrew could see him looking, his way of communicating the question of how much he should say in front of her, a stranger to family business. Andrew saw the gesture. "Don't worry about Shanta. She and I are together."

Eschmann paused for a moment, wondering how much to say. It had been years since the bribes were arranged, too long ago to still be sensitive to discuss. And, after all, the beneficiary of the trust that he himself had set up was Andrew, who was sitting across from him asking him for help. Financially, Andrew was in league with the richest. Also, Eschmann owed a duty of loyalty and respect to Andrew's father, who had told him to look after his only son. Andrew had gotten himself in miscellaneous trouble over the years that Eschmann had been able to fix. Nothing too serious— he had been expelled from a university for various antics, and Eschmann was able to get him back in by arranging a large endowment. But Andrew dropped out later, anyway, and never got a degree. Andrew was not the most stable of persons, and he had seen various counselors and a psychiatrist for a time in order to stay out of jail. He did not show any signs of having the wherewithal to take over the business. Consequently, the trust was set up so that the business was run by professionals, and the profits, which were huge, went to Andrew. Eschmann could hardly refuse, although he doubted the wisdom of private intervention into political matters.

He decided to risk discussing it in front of this new woman with Andrew, although he doubted the longevity of this new relationship. "The main method used was what the Chinese call *fragrant oil.*

"*Bribes!*" Andrew guessed at the interpretation and blurted it out loudly.

Eschmann, the seasoned trial lawyer and trained like an actor in use of body language, staged a flinch as though someone fired a shot over his shoulder and he had to duck to miss being hit. He looked around, as though to see if anyone was listening, a physical signal to Andrew to lower his voice and select his choice of words more discretely. Andrew clearly did not have the subtlety of a seasoned pleader.

"The skill was in finding out who would have the power to let the company come in," Eschmann said, "and who would be amenable to it—and to our fragrant oil. What is it that you seek to do?"

"To bring about the return of the Dalai Lama to Tibet."

Eschmann sat back. "Well, that should be easy. Hardly a phone call should be enough," he said sarcastically. "So you think that I've the kind of contacts who can make happen what our government and the rest of the free world has not been able to accomplish?"

"You are the only person that I know to ask. It's something I really need."

"Well now…let me think." Eschmann looked up, realizing that he would have to go along with his sole, impetuous client, the heir of his father's huge estate. *After all*, he thought, *it's now this young man's money.*

"I may know someone that might help. He's a hard person to forget. His name is Baron Von Limbach."

∽∾∽

The phone rang in Andrew's room. Andrew was awake, but not yet out of bed. He rolled over, picked up the receiver, and drawled out a "Hello."

"Eschmann here. Good morning."

"Good morning, Mr. Eschmann. So nice to hear from you."

"You don't sound like you are awake just yet. Shall I call back?"

"No, I'm awake. Go ahead."

"I've made the contact for you. What do you say we have brunch at the Commander's Palace? This is Sunday, and they have nice jazz there. In two hours?"

"Sure."

Andrew called the suite next door. "Shanta?"

"Yes, dear?" The bond between them had grown.

"Mr. Eschmann wants to take us to brunch. He has something for us. Can you make it in two hours?"

"Yes, dear. I have been up for a long time. What should I wear to that place? I don't have much as you know. "

"It's a little fancy. One of your saris will do just fine."

∾∾∾

Inside the restaurant, the three of them sat at a table near a window, but it was much too hot outside for any window to be open. Jazz music saturated the atmosphere with a wonderful ambiance unique to New Orleans.

"I've managed to reach the baron. No small task—you might be surprised what that took. It seems he has insulated himself from people who are trying to find him for whatever reason. He has numbers in Berlin and Taipei. When I explained who I was to one of his secretaries, he finally called me back from God knows where. I did not mention anything about what you want him for, as such topics really must not be discussed over any phone line. It was only because of our past relationship, whereby I had hired him for your father's business, that he returned my call. I told him about you, and that you wish to see him at any place he chooses. He says he will phone me today and tell me where he will be in several days. Will that be satisfactory?"

Andrew smiled widely at the news. "You're the best, Mr. Eschmann. What do you think?"

"I really can't say. But given the nature of, and the magnitude of, your plight, this is the very best that I can do. If he can't help, I can't help. I don't have unlimited resources, you know."

"I think you do," Shanta said and then leaned over and kissed him on the cheek.

"Well now, I had no idea I was so good!" He laughed and motioned to a waiter for what would be, especially with Eschmann's local knowledge of just what to order at the restaurants he frequented, a breakfast to remember.

# CHAPTER 8

"Work Brings Freedom," the female tour guide said, translating the sign—*Arbeit Macht Frei*—above the entrance gates to Auschwitz, as she took Tak on a private tour arranged by Baron. She was fifty, blonde, and somewhat attractive. "My family for several generations has lived very close by, and we have first-hand knowledge about this place."

Tak looked about as the guide walked her through what many consider the bowels of evil.

"The sign you see above was placed here by Rudolf Hoss, the Commandant. It was intended to be a kind of mystical declaration that self-sacrifice in the form of endless labor does, in itself, bring about spiritual freedom.

"The estimates are that there were, in total, between one million one hundred thousand and one million six hundred thousand prisoners here. The vast majority were Jews. Many Jews of the world contend there were more here, but this is what my family and the local historians believe. There were gypsies and others cremated here as well."

"What's a Jew?" Tak asked.

The guide assumed Tak asked the question in a philosophical sense as of the time of the camp's operation, as no one asked such a question in present tense. The guide was an expert on the subject with the benefit of generations of her neighbors' proximity to the death camp. She gave what she considered to be the best answer. "Well, to quote Hitler, 'A Jew is a parasite living in someone else's country.'"

The guide led Tak into an underground chamber to a room with two ovens that had rails leading to them. "Here, at Auschwitz, this first crematorium was built. It was later considered too small and was torn down to build a bomb shelter. They saved the iron doors and parts, so the Polish government reconstructed the ovens you see here."

"Was this brought about from hatred of Jews?"

"Actually, many think it was Hitler's subordinate Goebbels that truly hated Jews, but clearly Hitler, as ruler, deserves the majority of the credit for the mass murders. The intent of the *Reich* was to purify the races of Europe and to do so by the elimination of inferior races.

"The people were gassed in the room we just came through with Zyklon B, a hydrogen-cyanide poison gas. Then other prisoners, used as workers, loaded them into the ovens.

"Himmler inspected Auschwitz on March 1, 1941, which led to an order for five three-retort ovens. The new ovens were constructed at Birkenau instead of Auschwitz. Those together burned five thousand people a day."

"Amazing," Tak said. "Killing and cremating five-thousand members of a race of a people in a day. And in such small ovens. How could they do that with so small and so few ovens?"

"Initially, they loaded two corpses in each oven. As time went on, to reduce loading time and increase efficiency, four or five corpses were loaded in an oven each time. It took twenty minutes to cremate three corpses, and it was learned that it was more efficient to spend twenty five to thirty minutes to cremate four to five at a time and to reduce loading time. There were a few times when the Nazis wanted to cremate more than the ovens could handle, and so they burned them in a pile outdoors nearby. My parents, now dead, recalled the stench of the burning bodies on those occasions."

❧

At nearby Birkenau, the guide continued. "As you can see, although much larger, there is less of Birkenau left. The brick entrance arch remains, with the train rails in place. Inside you can see the field with the foundations of where there used to be wooden barracks, which were burned by the fleeing Nazis. In the rear, you will see the remains of the gas chambers and krematoria that the Nazis exploded when they left.

"Auschwitz had twenty-thousand prisoners, whereas at Birkenau had over one hundred thousand. There were three-thousand-five-hundred German soldiers here to run the camps and guard the prisoners.

"Many think that the most evil man here, and also in the world, was Doctor Josef Mengele. He was known for carrying a riding crop, and there is a picture here of him inside with it.

"To study what was hereditary and what was learned from the environment, he thought answers existed in studies of twins, and so he haunted every arriving convoy he could, in search of twins. He was obsessed with the controversy of environment verses nature—he wished to demonstrate that heredity counted for the important things, as opposed to the environment. Since, sometimes, ten thousand new people arrived daily, he had a large censes to find twins for experiments."

"Mengele performed experiments on one-thousand-five-hundred pairs of twins," the guide continued as they walked through the camp. "He believed that which was identical must be hereditary, and any difference was from environment. His experiments involved injections into eyes, spines, and inner organs, incestuous impregnations, removal of organs and limbs, injections with lethal germs, transfusions of blood from one twin to the other, and exposure to various stimuli. The tests usually ended in dissection of the body for examination.

"On January 18, 1945, as the Soviet Army was near, Mengele fled and lived in Paraguay and in Brazil, receiving money from his German family, until January 24, 1979, when he drowned while swimming in the ocean in Bertioga, Brazil."

Walking to the back, they came upon the gas chambers and krematoria. "These have been maintained as they were left by the Nazis," the guide said. "Although blown up with explosives, you can clearly see the gas chambers and the rails to the ovens."

They walked back along the railroad tracks to where the car and driver were waiting. About half way to the gate, Tak stopped.

"What is it?' the guide asked.

"I feel something here in time. Something happened here, involving many souls."

"This is where the train stopped and let out the thousands of prisoners nearly every day," the guide said. "It is from this spot that they were told to go to the back, which is the gas chambers, or the other direction, which was for forced labor. Do you have a special sense for such things?"

"I do have a special connection with time," Tak said.

On the return trip in Tak's private car, a hired, black Mercedes sedan, Tak asked the guide, "How, in just the span of a human life, could there have been such brutal extermination of so many of one people by another?"

"There was much suffering then," the guide answered. "Even those that were not prisoners had hard times. And the death camps were only a small number of the total people killed in the war. The Russians lost over twenty-six million in battles and, in some cases, starvation."

"Do you think that humans have changed very much since the time of the death camps?" Tak asked her.

"I belong to an informal association of local guides," the guide said, "and they encourage us to be cautious when rendering personal views and opinions that are outside the objective, historical facts of the historical monuments that we guide tourists through."

Tak looked her in the eyes, trying to determine what she was concealing.

The guide realized that Tak could detect her deceit. But then, as she made more from tips than from her modest salary, she decided to please her client and answer. "There are many Jews that come here from all over the world on prayer missions for lost ancestors and they treat the entire camp as a highly solemn event. However, there are others, not Jews, who come just to witness what Hitler did with the Jews. It would be fair to say that some of the clients actually find the experience stimulating."

᠑᠑᠑

The phone rang in Tak's suite. "How was the tour?" the now-familiar voice asked.

"Stimulating."

"Stimulating? Well, I hope you enjoyed it. Would you like to meet in the lobby bar for a drink in about half an hour? I have your currency."

Tak went down early to see if there were any interesting people in the lobby that she might observe. A group of Hasidic Jews were occupying most of the lobby area, having just arrived to go to Auschwitz for special prayers for lost family members. They wore their characteristic black outfits, hats, beards, and long hair. Even the sideburns were very long, hanging down below their chins. To her, they appeared alien, compared to the other humans she had encountered.

She concluded the all-black outfits were uniforms, having seen the black uniform outfits of the guides at the salt mine. She decided to ask and sat at a table with one of the Hasidic Jews who was sitting alone.

"May I ask what that uniform signifies that you do?" she asked.

"I'm a Jew, here on a special prayer mission."

"Oh yes, I learned about Jews today. You are a parasite living in someone else's country."

The Jew's eyes opened wide, and just as he was about to say or do something, Baron fortunately approached. "Tak!"

She looked at the angry Jew. "Excuse me, I must go now."

She got up and went to greet Baron, who had unknowingly rescued her, and who was already generating looks by his elegant presence in the lobby.

Baron led her to a quiet table at a widow overlooking the river, away from others, where they could talk. He handed her a large, stuffed, manila envelope.

Inside was a huge stack of Euros. "Oh, thank you, Baron. How much do I owe you for what you have spent for me?"

"Nothing. The room is on me. But I see you are hardly impoverished."

"I did promise to repay you," she said.

"Oh, no, I insist. Now, let's have a drink. What would you like?"

Tak had not the slightest clue what to ask for. "Whatever you are having."

Baron ordered for them. "So tell me about your day."

"Auschwitz and Birkenau were fascinating and the history of just such a relatively short time ago was very informative. Has anything like World War II occurred since 1945?"

"Did they not teach you history in school?"

"My studies were not of Earth's history, but rather of human behavior in the present to determine the predictable future. But it occurs to me that, after the tour of the activities of Auschwitz and Birkenau, I should acquire knowledge of any similar events since that time, as it might affect my predictions as to probable future conduct. Are you knowledgeable on the subject?"

"I am no historian. But I have some knowledge of the history of wars since World War II."

"I would appreciate hearing from you on that subject."

"Well, the history of war over even such a relatively short period of is no small question. How to put together such an answer without taking all night? There are libraries of books on the subject. But, yes, there have been many wars since World War II."

"Would you mind imparting some of your knowledge to me on the subject of wars since World War II?" Tak positioned her wrist computer more prominently in front of her so as to be able to record the lesson she hoped to learn—a lesson in human behavior.

"Well, let's see…as just a short history, to be sure, there has been much of the same sort of activities since 1945, but not on such a large scale. Although not a war, the Soviets and the United States have had thousands of nuclear missiles pointed at each other since just after World War II but which were never used. But there have been numerous actual wars or conflicts. Just to name a few, the Chinese killed many in the communist takeover and the later so-called 'Cultural Revolution' starting just after World War II. The Muslims from Pakistan fought with the Hindus in India just after their independence from England in 1947, and there have been numerous clashes since, including presently in Kashmir. There was the Korean War in the early fifties with people of the same race killing each other over differing forms of government, involving a war of allies of democracy fighting North Koreans, Chinese soldiers, and Russians pilots. There was the Vietnam War from the mid-fifties to about 1975, followed by political violence and many executions, with several hundred thousand 'boat people' dying at sea, trying to escape, with an estimated total of 3.8 million Vietnamese killed.

"There was wholesale murder in Cambodia by the Khmer Rouge from 1975 to 1979, by execution, starvation, and forced labor, killing 1.7 million people, about a quarter of the population. The Arabs fought Israel in wars off and on that were nearly thirty years long, and fighting continues regularly between Israel and some Arab states. There has been fighting in the north of India in the Punjab on several occasions. Groups of Catholic Irishmen were blowing up English Protestants with terrorist bombs to keep alive a vendetta for decades in retaliation for past horrific acts of the British against them. There were race riots between the Chinese and Malay in Singapore in 1965, followed by the riots in Malaysia a year later. There was the Falklands Island war of 1982, between Argentina and the British, which was actually decided by Gurkhas, like my driver Lachhiman, who, working for the British, landed on one side of the island and chased the Argentine Army across the island to defeat. Clashes in Africa occur regularly, with hardly any country there able to run itself. There has been massive slaughtering in some African nations, like the racial slaughtering there between the tribes of Hutu and the minority Tutsi, both blacks but of different tribal origins.

He paused to take a quick breath. "There was fighting and extermination of races not far from where we are now, in Bosnia-Herzegovina with the Croats, Muslims, and Serbs fighting among each other, resulting in an accord in 1995, dividing up Yugoslavia into new territories and creating the Serb-controlled Republika Srpska. There is much hatred there among those groups, and it is only the presence of the NATO-led foreign troops that keeps fighting from breaking out again. Then there is the routing out of the Chinese by the Muslims in Indonesia not long ago. The US president Carter turning over Iran to Muslim radicals was the precursor to Muslim terrorism. There was Iraq with its leader Hussein killing Kurds in the north of the country, using anthrax on his own countrymen, funding terrorists in other countries, and then sending his army into Kuwait. US presidents made war to rid Kuwait of occupation, then to rid Iraq of Hussein, and they to continue to war in Afghanistan. There is much warring presently in many parts of the world by

Muslims intent on killing innocents that are not Muslims, or that are not of the same Muslim sects, fueled by religious fanatics. In Russia, and other places, Muslims attack non-Muslim Russians often over who is the true God, the Muslim Allah or the Orthodox Christ, although that is just an excuse for killing. There are about eleven million illegal Muslim immigrants in Russia. Muslims now bring their terror in the form of suicide bombers to civilized places and blow themselves up along with innocent victims in many countries. There are also wars over who is to control the country, such as in Syria."

"Have Muslims always done these things?"

"Well, if you go back much farther than World War II, there is a huge history of religious wars, and not only Muslims. But your question was concerning matters since World War II. Much of the cause of current terrorism stemmed, or at least began, from US President Carter, arguably the worst US president ever, giving up Iran to medieval religious Muslims by withdrawing support of the Shah of Iran years ago, for what he called a poor civil rights record. Muslim fanatics learned they could then control countries, especially those with oil reserves."

With that, he leaned back and sighed. "I'm sure I have left out many."

"Are the wars and killing finally over, or continuing?" Tak asked,

"Oh, continuing, to be sure. The US and its allies are at war in Afghanistan. There are outbreaks of minor fighting in many parts of the world. There is war in Syria, Muslim against Muslim. There is killing by Muslims of other Muslims in Iraq. There is fighting in parts of Africa.

"Humans are a primitive lot, as evidenced by their adherence to numerous religions and blindly following religious leaders. Today is not much different from medieval times and the Inquisition. Religious leaders, and there are so many, seek power by wanting to be exclusive. Most people, excepting the Hindus, believe in a single God, but of course they have different notions of what the true God is. Most all believe that their notion of God is the one and only true God, and all other Gods are false. It is sort of like saying, 'I believe in the one and only true God, and He is merciful and wonderful. And if you don't believe in Him, I'll kill you.'"

Baron smiled at his little joke, but Tak did not take it as humor and listened intently. "But, I must say, it's good for business," he added.

"Good for business?"

He backed away from the admission. "Oh, it's just an expression."

*Then*, she wondered, *why did the Federation send me to this barbaric place? Was it just to confirm the obvious? Was it just a training mission for me as my first mission alone and, in actuality, unnecessary?*

Baron looked at his watch to avoid further interrogation. "Will you join me for dinner? There is a delightful, elegant restaurant downtown, overlooking the square that has the most wonderful Polish food. I've reserved a table in two hours."

"Oh, yes." Then she looked down at her clothes. "I believe that the custom is to dress differently at elegant restaurants, and I would not look appropriate at your table, so maybe I should decline."

"Nonsense!"

Baron looked about for the concierge and saw him at the end of the lobby. Baron signaled for him to come over by raising his hand.

The concierge hurried over to the distinguished guest. "How may I serve you, Baron?"

"My guest will be joining me for dinner in two hours. Will you please tell Lachhiman where to take Mademoiselle for the best dress shop in Krakow? And call ahead and have the shop charge whatever she wants to me here on my hotel bill."

"Of course, Baron," the concierge said.

"I'll stay here and have another drink or two," Baron

said to Tak. "Why don't you go now before the shops close? Have fun."

❧❦❧

Tak sat across from Baron at a little table for two in a bay window at the quaint restaurant on the second floor, overlooking the square in downtown Krakow. The guests were more formally dressed as Baron knew they would be, and Tak looked beautiful in her new outfit and shoes.

"Is this outfit good?" She had bought a simple, one piece, black evening outfit and black, high-heeled shoes, all of which the shop keeper recommended.

"You look like a supermodel."

The waiter came, and Baron was prepared. "Definitely the duck." He then selected a wine.

The waiter looked at Tak. She smiled. "Definitely the duck."

Baron laughed and then announced his plans. "Tak, tomorrow I'm scheduled to go to Germany. I assume you'll be staying on?"

"Is that far?"

"No. I'll be going by car. The drive is through the countryside and, with a stop or two to stretch and eat, it should take one day. Do you know Germany?"

"No."

"It is quite different than Poland. Would you like to join me? You have seen the main highlights here in Krakow." Then he said something satirical but it was not understood as such by Tak. "Or perhaps tomorrow you were going to stay on and do some shopping for Polish crystal?"

"Oh no, it would be inconvenient to collect native artifacts." After she said that, she realized somehow *collecting native artifacts* did not seem like the best choice of words.

But if Baron noticed her faux pas, he did not mention it. "Then why don't you join me?"

"That is across another governmental border, correct?"

Baron again raised his eyebrows at the curious question. "Yes, we cross the German border."

"What would I need to cross the border?"

"Well, since the two countries are both part of the European Union, you do not need a passport. But if you want later to go elsewhere, you'll need your passport."

"Thank you, I'll join you. Where do I get a passport?"

෧෩෧෩

The morning view of the Vistula River from her balcony at the Forum Hotel was a sight to remember.

Both Tak and Baron went down to the restaurant for polish sausage and coffee.

"We'll be leaving in an hour," he told her after they enjoyed coffee and sausage together.

He left for his room to make ready for the journey to Germany. Tak had nothing to pack other than her satchel and her new black dress and shoes, which fit neatly into her bag, and which she had already packed. So she stayed on to observe more human behavior.

After Baron had gone to his room, four men came in from the outside, apparently not staying at the hotel, and sat near to Tak. They ordered coffee. Their appearance was rough and disheveled. They were wearing inexpensive suits that had not been pressed recently and had on wrinkled shirts with soiled collars and without ties. The pockets in their suits sagged, as if from carrying things. They were not clean shaven. Tak detected a slightly foul body odor from the one sitting nearest to her. They were speaking what she recognized as Russian, although she didn't understand the words, and did not seem to belong in the hotel compared to the other guests.

She could see outside the hotel glass doors to the area where the cars arrived. A small crowd of on-lookers was gathering around as Baron's grand, white car pulled up. Out of the car came Lachhiman, muscular and fit, in command of the car and his surroundings. The four men in the lobby all looked toward the Rolls Royce and spoke to each other about it, but so did everyone else who saw it. They then got up and went outside to the parking area.

"Good morning, Tak!" Baron's louder than normal voice vibrated the air from behind her as she was watching outside. Tak turned to see Baron, eloquently dressed, adorned with a fedora hat.

"Baron! Good morning!" she said, trying to return his exuberance.

A baggage man came along with Baron's luggage on a brass hotel luggage cart. His bags were four in number, of cloth and natural saddle leather from the best of London's shops, and in slightly descending sizes. Lachhiman placed the bags on the luggage rack that folded down horizontally off the rear of the car, making it into a shelf. He strapped them down with matching leather straps, the largest on the bottom. The bags actually added to the unique effect of the car.

When Lachhiman finished strapping the bags on, he came around to stand at attention for Baron. Then, at just that moment, as though on cue in a movie, out he came from the hotel doors, with all four of the doormen standing at attention in a row to bid him goodbye, the concierge having orchestrated his leaving. Hotel guests outside stopped to gaze at the sight of this most interesting man entering his car, as if it was a major event. Lavish tips were passed out by Baron, with the most to the concierge. Tourists took photos of the car with their small-point-and-shoot cameras or cell phones, while Baron fed off of the attention. Tak then followed Baron into the car.

The spring scenery through the countryside was gorgeous, initiated by a light shower, followed by sunlight, with the delightful odor of spring in the air. After a while, Tak, curious about the driver, asked, "Baron, Lachhiman has brown skin. Where is he from?"

"His name is Lachhiman Thapa, PVC. He's a Gurkha."

Ignoring the fact that Baron might wonder about her wrist computer, Tak commanded her wrist computer for an instant translation of what was being continuously recorded for PVC in English. It showed an answer, polyvinyl chloride.

She turned to Baron. "He's named after plastic?"

Baron laughed aloud and announced his driver's new name: "Lachhiman Thapa, polyvinyl chloride!" He laughed again. "PVC stands for *Param Vir Chakra*. It's the post-independence equivalent of the Victoria Cross."

"Is that like *Baron*?"

"The difference is that baron is usually a title from birth for a nobleman, although there are exceptions. PVC is earned after birth through achievements. In the case of Gurkhas, most of the awards of the Victoria Cross or the Param Vir Chakra have been given posthumously—that is, after death."

"I see. He comes from Gurkha. Please tell me about them."

"Gurkha is not a place, but a soldier. The Gurkhas come from Nepal. They are not just soldiers, but soldiers for hire. They have been hired by the British since 1815. They are also hired by the Indians, as was Lachhiman. They have been hired by a number of other countries as well. Until India gained its independence from England in 1947, the award given for bravery was the English award of the Victoria Cross. More Victoria Cross medals were given to the Gurkhas than any other group of people. They can still get a Victoria Cross if they were actually serving in the British Army, but if hired by India, the medal is the Param Vir Chakra, or PVC, and if from Pakistan, the Nishan-i-Haider. Now, Lachhiman enjoys the title of PVC. It's quite an honor."

He paused to see if Tak was absorbing this. Hearing no questions, he continued. "His efforts inspired his platoon to capture a vital strategic hilltop. Nearly dead from injuries, in the freezing snow and thin air, he refused to die. When his platoon finally took the hill, he was taken 'to hospital.' He spent over three months 'in hospital' and was awarded the medal Param Vir Chakra. His commander thought his injuries too severe to have him return to active combat, and I was lucky enough to hire him. He is fierce and will not back down."

"Why do you use such a formidable warrior just to drive your car?"

"He is not just my driver, but also my bodyguard."

"Oh, I see. You need a soldier to protect you. What sort of weapons does he have?"

"He carries only his kukri, a long, curved knife, and a smaller blade. He is very good with them, and there is no prohibition against taking knives across borders, contrasted with guns. So it works out very conveniently for him to drive for me in countries where I do not have a local body-guard with a weapons permit."

"Convenient," she responded.

The grand Roll Royce came over a hill. There were fields of rye, oats, and potatoes on either side of the road in the beautiful Polish countryside. No other cars were in sight. As they came around a curve, two stopped cars were ahead, apparently in an accident, blocking the road. The occupants, a total of eight men, were outside the vehicles, looking, pointing, and talking as though they were in disagreement as to who or what was the cause.

"Problem ahead," Lachhiman warned.

Baron leaned forward to evaluate. One of the cars was cross-ways in the road, pointing to the left, the other apparently having hit it in the rear, resting with its front bumper touching the left rear of the other car, blocking any car from passing. The shoulder of the road on either side was narrow and then dropped off six feet at that spot, such that no car could go around.

"What do you make of it?" Baron asked.

Lachhiman slowed the Rolls Royce down to a crawl. "We can't go around."

Tak looked at the men and recognized some of them as the men who sat at the table next to her at breakfast. "Baron, four of those eight men sat next to me during breakfast at the hotel."

Baron sized them up with their disheveled clothes and concluded they could not afford to stay at the Forum Hotel. This meant that they were Russian gangsters, involved in a carjacking. They would take the car back to Russia where a stolen, expensive car could be sold in an instant. There were no reciprocal agreements between countries to recover a stolen car from the corrupt Russian government. But there was danger to him and his passengers, as they would all be witnesses.

"Lachhiman, get ready. They want the car and may kill us!"

Lachhiman stopped the car and tried to put it into reverse but, before he could, most of the men stormed the Rolls Royce, pointing Russian pistols at the three of them through the car's windows.

"*Get out car now!*" one of them yelled, pointing his Russian pistol, correctly assuming that they spoke English as the men had heard English spoken earlier by the driver and the baron at the hotel.

Baron spoke softly and quickly to Tak. "They're Russian bandits. They intend to steal the car, take it to Russia, and rob us of our valuables. Be very careful. They may decide to kill us to leave no witnesses."

Without moving his head or looking down, Baron lifted one of the armrests of the luxury rear seats in the Rolls Royce, which had a hidden compartment with a hinged top covered in leather that pivoted to one side. When closed, it was completely unnoticeable. Open, it exposed a 9 millimeter semi-automatic pistol. He slipped the equalizer into his suit jacket's outside pocket.

They were ushered out of the car at gunpoint. Tak put her satchel strap over her shoulder as she exited. The three captives were then held at bay outside the car with guns trained on them. The Russians became excited at their spoils, as their usual bounty was a late-model Mercedes. This super car could sell for several hundred thousand euros to one of the Russian billionaires or a Russian drug dealer, as it was very rare, eye-catching, and handsome.

The bandits gazed in delight at their bounty, with one getting in the front and another in the back, behaving like children with a new Christmas toy. Filled with exuberance, all but two went to look at the prize, leaving just the two to guard their victims at gunpoint.

Jokes were made about having such a car themselves and how it would bring girls and recognition if they had such a trophy back home. To the Russians, the three victims posed no apparent threat. Lachhiman looked like a harmless, third-world chauffeur; the baron like a wealthy industrialist, with his flashy clothes and car; and the young girl possibly his niece, since she carrying her satchel over her shoulder like a school bag, as opposed to a designer handbag. Finally the Russians decided that everything was under control, and they walked away from the Rolls Royce, except for one, who remained behind the wheel. He was the one who was to be the driver back to Russia and was familiarizing himself with the controls. The others came over to where their three captives were standing and began to talk.

One of them said to his comrades, in Russian, "This beauty will be extremely easy to spot once it is reported stolen, unlike an ordinary black Mercedes sedan that we normally score. If we turn these people loose, they will report what happened, and the Polish police will be alerted to stop this easily seen car before we get it across the border out of Poland. We should kill them and then we can get across the border."

"I agree," one of the others said. "Let's shoot them here and leave them in the ditch."

The most senior, Pyotr, disagreed. "Murder is a completely different crime than auto theft. I don't like the idea of killing them."

"Pyotr, this will not be the first time we have killed," another said. "Think how much this car will bring us back home. We can sell it for a fortune. If we don't kill them, they will report the theft and the border guards will be looking for the car. I say we kill them."

Another, one holding his Russian Stechkin pistol on the victims, came to Tak and took her satchel off her shoulder. He sat the bag on the ground and began looking through it. "What have we here?" He pulled out the black outfit and high heeled shoes she had bought. "Evening wear," he said, laughing and holding up the dress and the black high-heeled shoes. "She must be the fat one's girlfriend, not his niece."

The rest of them laughed after they saw the evening outfit. Then the man found Tak's stack of Euros Baron got her for her gold in the bottom and held it up.

"Look! She has a fortune! She must be the fat one's wife or whore!" Holding it up, he turned and flashed it, to let all of them see the bounty. His big smile showed his bad teeth. "We're already rich!"

The laughing subsided, and then the first one that had said the captives should die, said, "Let's shoot them." He looked around at the group. It was clear that they had no particular leader and a consensus was needed.

"I agree," the one with Tak's money said. "Let's do it before someone comes along."

This time no one else objected, not even Pyotr.

By now, as there was no apparent threat to the Russians, all but two of the six who had pistols had put them away. Two of them went to the money to see how much there was. It was a moment when only two guns were trained on them, and the last chance to react. Unbeknownst to them, Baron understood Russian and was alerted to their evil intent.

He nodded to Lachhiman, who leaped like a jungle cat. In his practiced move, he pulled his razor sharp, long kukri down from its blade-up position where it was held in a special knife holster under his tunic. He brought it down in a blindingly fast swinging motion then added his other hand to the handle while still swinging it, to maximize the force. He swung it up and around then brought it down with tremendous force right over the arm just below the elbow of the man holding his gun on Baron and Tak. In his bravery, he chose to save his employer before himself. In the move, he stepped forward to strike and to one side of the gunman who was pointing his gun at him.

The arm, just below the elbow of the Russian holding his gun on Baron and Tak, came off quickly and neatly. The hand, still holding the gun, fell to the ground. His swing was not slowed by the contact with the Russian arm, and he brought it up once again, adding a twist to it by turning his body, holding the kukri out to add velocity. He swung it around at a blinding speed until it found its next target, the neck of the Russian holding his gun on the spot where Lachhiman had been standing an instant before. The force of the swing, with his arms extended, was so much that the kukri went right through the neck of the Russian, and his head literally rolled off his shoulders and fell to the ground ten feet away. The headless Russian got a round off with his pistol before his head left him, but it went harmlessly through the spot where Lachhiman had been standing a second earlier. An eerie sight, the body of the headless man did not fall to the ground immediately, but instead remained erect as blood squirted out of his neck.

Baron pulled out his weapon, shot one of the Russians twice in the face, then shot another twice in the chest, dispatching them both. As Baron fired, another Russian was taking his pistol out of his pants pocket. Lachhiman moved to him, bringing his kukri up and then down. Landing on the man mid-shoulder, it buried itself several inches deep into his body, severing the clavicle of his gun arm. The Russian's useless arm dropped the pistol, and he fell to his knees.

Another, who had put his pistol in his suit-jacket's side pocket reached for it, but hesitated when he saw the carnage. So he let it stay inside the pocket and surrendered, hoping to live. He, unfortunately, had never met up with a Gurkha like Lachhiman, who did not take prisoners. Lachhiman slit his throat deeply, dispatching him.

A Russian, who had no weapon showing, leaped to pick up a fallen pistol off the ground and quickly moved behind Baron. He stuck the pistol to the side of Baron's head. "Drop gun!"

Lachhiman froze to prevent his employer from being shot. Baron did not drop his pistol, knowing the Russian meant to murder him, so there was no point in dropping his weapon. There was one other Russian left, the apparently unarmed man that was in the car behind the wheel and who was now getting out.

Tak decided that she needed to act or die. She lifted the lapis colored device off her wrist computer and pointed it at carjacker behind Baron, who was holding his gun at the back of Baron's head, and commanded it in her own language. A section on it lit up, and a thin, blue, laser targeting beam targeted the Russian, reflecting off his midsection. She rotated it up until the beam shown on the side of the carjacker's head. As she pushed on it, the beam widened to cover his head. Another push caused it to make a "snap" sound, and an extremely bright, powerful blue laser emitted from it and engulfed the carjacker's head, toasting it instantly. Ashes fell on Baron's shoulder, depositing themselves rudely on his suit.

Lachhiman watched this, as though he saw ray guns every day, and nonchalantly walked toward the Rolls Royce where the remaining Russian was getting out. On the way, he walked by the Russian with a deep cut through his shoulder and who was on his knees groaning loudly in pain. As Lachhiman passed, he swung his kukri, using only one hand, so that it cut right through that groaning Russian's throat, finishing him as though cutting an undesirable weed.

Lachhiman was then at the Russian coming out of the Rolls Royce. The Russian appeared as if he wanted to surrender and raised both arms and hands, yielding. But Lachhiman was in no mood for that and, with both hands on the kukri handle, he ran it into the man's stomach, then twisted it once, and removed it. When the man fell and kneeled over in pain, Lachhiman brought the kukri down over the back of his neck, cutting the spinal cord as neatly as though by guillotine.

The one still alive, who had an arm missing, was Lachhiman's next target, and he dispatched him very quickly by cutting his neck wide open, blood spurting out like a faucet.

Eight dead Russians lay about, covered in blood. Lachhiman had blood splattered all over him as well, as if he was a doctor who had just performed open heart surgery on several patients in a war theater.

"Lachhiman, recover Tak's property," Baron said. He then turned to Tak. "We must hurry out of here. If there is any detection of our involvement, we will be detained."

Lachhiman collected Tak's money and evening wear, put them into her satchel, and gave it to her.

"How long would they detain us?" Tak asked.

Baron thought a moment. "Well, they would try to sort everything out, and they would want to hold us for an inquest, with the possibility of bringing charges against us. I'd have to call on my connections to get us out but that could take days if we are unlucky." And then he looked right into Tak's eyes, as though he knew more than he was letting on. "If you can't prove your identity, you'll never be released."

She worried that she could be put into a jail and waste the rest of her stay, learning nothing more of humans. The starship would have to be summoned to come for her, and that might make quite a scene. To avoid that, she concluded it was time to take charge.

She faced Lachhiman. "Let's put the bodies in a pile."

Lachhiman looked at Baron, who nodded his approval. Lachhiman and Tak dragged the bodies and parts to the side of the road parts, Lachhiman taking either the arms or the legs and Tak the other half, and piled all eight of them up.

"Unless you want their weapons, put them in the pile as well," Tak said.

Lachhiman collected their weapons from the ground, as well as the spent brass from the automatics that had been fired, including Baron's, and put them in the pile of Russians.

From her satchel, she pulled out a disintegrator, one of which she'd used to destroy her shuttle. She put it on top of her wrist computer and gave the computer several commands in her own language. The computer then imparted information to the disintegrator. She then took it off the computer, carried it over to the pile of Russians, and stuffed it in between the bodies and their weapons.

"Stand back," she said, moving back herself.

She gave another command in her language, and there was a loud sound like an explosion. The bodies became covered in a ball of blue colored energy, disintegrating the pile, leaving smoldering fumes and strange odors. However, in her haste, she had miscalculated the charge. The overkill disintegration not only toasted the carjackers into infinity, it also evaporated a hole in the ground ten feet deep.

Tak walked over to the hole and looked in. Smoke was coming out of the ground. "I guess I miscalculated a bit." She then turned to Baron. "What about their cars?"

"Those too," he said.

"Put them together on the side of the road," Tak said to Lachhiman.

He complied and put the cars, one in front of the other with their bumpers touching, on the roadside.

This time, Tak took off the blue device resembling lapis and pointed it at the two cars. She pushed it and a laser light with a narrow beam came out. She pushed it again, and the blue laser widened until it covered both cars, determining their mass. She put another one of the disintegrators on the wrist computer, and it took in the information gathered from the beam.

"Stand back," she said, but it was unnecessary after the

first explosion of energy, as and Baron and Lachhiman were already quickstepping backward, filled with apprehension.

Tak spoke a command and there was another snap, and blue light glowed about the cars. They neatly evaporated, leaving only smoke and fumes.

Tak went back over to where the cars had been and, seeing no hole in the ground, said, "That's better."

"Lachhiman, get the European road hazard triangle out of the trunk and put it in front of the hole so no one crashes into it," Baron said. "We'll stop ahead somewhere for you to change. It looks like I have to also." He looked at the gray ashes from what used to be a head that had landed on his shoulder, an imperfection of his near-perfect presence.

# CHAPTER 9

On the road, after a stop to allow Lachhiman to change his clothes and Baron his suit top, a new conversation was begun.

"Tak, I think it's time we had a little chat."

Tak looked sheepishly at Baron, as now it had to be clear to him that she was empowered with a weapon not available on Earth.

"Tak, it is obvious that you are not of this Earth."

"Was it the weapon?"

"That only confirmed it. I've known for some time."

"How?"

"Your speech. You have no discernible accent. I speak many languages. I'm able to place most people's origin very closely because of accents, vowel drawls, choice of words, or idioms. I can do this in a number of languages, and certainly in English.

"You have no accent whatsoever in English. There being no trace of British accent, that eliminates England, and certainly Scotland and Ireland. It eliminates English former colonies or territories such as India, Malaysia, and several islands where English is spoken. Obviously, Australia and New Zealand are out, with their extreme accents. Canada is out with their *uut and abuut* for *out and about*. There are a few places like Nigeria where English is spoken, but I have ruled these out as they have a distinct accent.

"That leaves America. Focusing there, you have no vowel drawl of the South, the Midwest, the Texas *yee* or the *y'all,* none of the long Os of the border to the northeast, no country or small town drawl, nor any trace of that easily discernible accent from New York, Boston, or whatever those other US states are called around there. The lack of any accent indicates higher education and in diverse locations, such as having gone to several schools in different parts of America and more likely Europe as well, and with much travel so as not to pick up an accent or vowel drawl. For example, you might have been a diplomat's daughter and traveled all over the world, with the best schools or tutors. But the possibility that you had an extensive education with wide travel experience cannot be, due to the simple fact that you have not even the slightest bit of knowledge of places or history—not even the last Great War. So, as the saying goes, where on Earth did you learn your English? The answer has to be, you did not learn it on Earth."

He paused, looked at her silently for a moment, and, hearing no comment, continued. "Then we have the fact that you travel with gold bars and no currency. You have no luggage, only one outfit. No passport. No surname. No opinions of Earth things, which is impossible for anyone who has grown up here. How could anyone be traveling in Poland and not know that *tak* means *yes*? And, of course, there is that wrist device of yours that has not been invented yet. Then I just witnessed those little balls that generate an energy pattern, disintegrating things. And, not to forget," he said, smiling. As he spoke, he reached for her wrist and held up her hand. "You have seven fingers."

"Seven toes too!" Tak said. "And, they are like fingers, instead of toes. I can use them like your fingers. I think the term is opposable with the big toe. But are you not shocked! No contact has ever been made with Earthlings by the Federation."

"But you must tell me, where did you learn your English?"

"On the starship, I intercepted and studied Earth transmissions."

Then Baron turned toward the front of the car, straightened his tie, sat up very straight, and leaned toward her formerly. "Tak, it my distinct honor to be the first human to be introduced to a member of an alien race. On behalf of the inhabitants, I welcome you to Planet Earth. Would you allow me to be the emissary for humans with the Federation of Planets?"

"Yes, that is acceptable."

By the most unlikely of selection process, the emissary for Earth had been picked to meet the first alien from outer space.

Tak appeared anxious that her cover was blown. As she wondered if he would turn her in, the answer came.

"Mademoiselle Tak, I extend an invitation to our planet. I suspect that you are desirous of not being introduced as an alien to anyone other than me, and I, therefore, give you my word that your visit here shall be kept confidential. Should you decide to make your presence public, however, you might mention that I was the first to introduce you to the planet."

She responded in kind. "It's indeed a distinction to have the first contact with such a gracious and talented host. But please leave my presence here unknown. My mission does not allow me to make an introduction on behalf of the Federation."

"You have my word that knowledge of your introduction to the planet stops here. And you need not worry about Lachhiman. To say that you can trust him with your life is an understatement."

"Thank you. This is my first mission alone. I only arrived the night before I met you."

"May I ask—just what is your mission?"

"I'm here to examine and evaluate the inhabitants of this planet, that is, humans. Our Federation wants a first hand, accurate report. As my race is, in many ways, close to humans in size, comes from a planet with similar gravity, breathes oxygen, and has a similar diet of eating animals and vegetables, I was chosen to come and mingle with humans to examine your typical life, what you do, if you have wars—and, if so, would you bring them to space if allowed off world, and other facts about your existence. As your race is reaching out into space, although just barely, I must compile a report on human activities and the likelihood of you being a threat to others."

When she paused, Baron seized on the chance to learn more. "Have you traveled to other galaxies?"

"Yes."

"Can you tell me how you travel?"

"No, Baron, I was not sent here to educate humans on how to travel in space in order that your warring race can bring wars to others."

He had to press for whatever he could get about the universe. "Would you mind telling me how many planets are there just in the Milky Way that are like Earth?"

She decided to continue revealing what she could, as payment for his care of her and upon his assurance that he would not expose her. "Baron, assuming you are asking about planets that are covered with water, like Earth, with stable atmosphere, capable of supporting life, there are over nine hundred thousand in the Milky Way alone."

Fascinated beyond his wildest imagination with the information, he pushed further. "How many planets in the Milky Way have intelligent life such as our Earth?"

"Baron, Earth is not considered to be a planet with intelligent life. Your constant wars prevent that."

♥♥

Not about to miss the biggest opportunity for any human, Baron proposed, "What if I invite you to join me as your guide for your tour on Earth? I'll take you about for your entire visit. As you can see, there are perils for you here and I'll be able to make your stay safe, as well as to provide you with the representative sample of humans and their conduct that you seek. And, since you do not have travel papers or knowledge of how to get about, you might very well end up detained, that is, in jail somewhere unless you have someone like me to prevent that."

"Do you think that if I travel with you, I will experience a true representative sample of humans on the planet?"

"Without a doubt," he lied.

Baron considered the magnitude of this moment in his life, one that was of the most unimaginable royal status for himself and as that of the as yet unrecognized emissary for the human race for the first alien contact. In furtherance of his promise to be certain that her presence here would remain unnoticed, they motored the majestic 1936 Rolls Royce toward Germany with all of the stealth of Attila the Hun coming over a hill, in 450 AD, toward a city to conquer.

∽∾∽

Baron instructed Lachhiman to make their destination *Rothenburg ob der Tober*, a picturesque town on the Romantic Highway in nearby Germany, a site he felt sure Tak would like.

Upon arrival, Baron saw that he was right about its effect on her. Inside the protective city walls, Tak was delighted and amazed. She turned about, soaking in the picturesque town. "This is absolutely beautiful!"

They strolled along to the hotel. The reception area was made of handsomely carved and detailed wood. The floors, desks, stairs, bannisters, and walls were all in the same wood. Out from the back, bounced a pretty German girl in her teens.

Baron announced himself in German. "I'm Baron Von Limbach. I have reserved your two best rooms."

The hotel restaurant provided the ambiance that Baron

had intended, much like that out of a story book.

"Tak, I remember that this place is known for excellent goose. How does that sound? It's something like the duck you had in Poland, but perhaps more exotic."

"If that's what you recommend."

The two of them satiated themselves with fabulous goose and wine and began to focus more intently on each other. It had, in fact, been quite a day with the two of them nearly killed on the road by Russian carjackers, clearly a trying event.

Finally, Tak looked at Baron, wine in hand. "Baron, I'm very much interested in trying out sex with a human. Would you mind if I did that with you?"

Baron nearly choked on his wine. "Although it will be a great sacrifice for me, I reluctantly agree to do this for you."

"I think you may find it something different and very interesting, which I'll call *Alien Style*," Tak said with a grin.

Baron asked the girl at the desk to send up another chilled bottle of delicious Rhine wine and asked if she had candles for power outages to avoid giving the real reason.

"I'll send up another bottle right away," she said. "However, there are already candles in the desk beside the bed."

"Do you have power outages so often?" he asked.

"No," she said. "This is the Romantic Road, and many people ask for candles."

In the room, there was a radio on the desk, and music was found. Candles illuminated the room and flickered off its vaulted ceiling. The four poster bed made an alluring nest.

Tak disrobed in front of him as he watched and, to his surprise and delight, she was indeed different from humans. Her feet with seven toes were agile, like her hands, with the big toe opposable, and extraordinarily useful.

Her sex was large and defined, with its own muscular system.

The two of them engaged in what was the first such encounter of humans and aliens, a novel and exciting adventure for both.

# CHAPTER 10

Ralls returned to the farm by car, but it cost another day. He and his Polish interpreter, Klara, a blonde woman of forty-five, headed for the farmhouse on the property where the GPS showed the landing spot.

They drove into the farm and up to the farmhouse that they had seen from the helicopter. An elderly man came out, and greetings were exchanged in Polish.

"Did you see any strange aircraft landing in your farm several days ago?" Klara asked.

The retired farmer looked at them like they were crazy. "Strange aircraft? What are you talking about? This is a farm, not an airport."

Ralls showed him the drawing of the pilot. He had brought a colored drawing of the pilot, as made by a sketch artist from the description of Captain Duncan, the F-22 pilot, since the person of interest had red hair, which was perhaps her most distinguishing feature from what little the F-22 pilot had been able to observe.

The farmer looked intently at the drawing for a while, holding it at a distance. It was obvious that his vision was not very good and he needed glasses.

Then he hesitated, as though to avoid making a mistake. "I'm retired, and others now work this farm. I meet with my retired friend early one day a week for coffee to discuss things. We were meeting here when a young woman walked up, asking for a ride to town. She had red hair, but I cannot say if that was her or not."

"What direction did she come from?"

He pointed out to the farm. "That way. She was on foot coming across the field. I think she was one of those nature lovers on a spring hike somewhere."

"Did she say where she had come from?" Ralls asked.

He thought a while. "No. She wanted a ride to town but we told her that we could not give her one. She left down the road toward the highway."

"Was there anything unusual about her?"

"No. But, she did not have one of those huge back packs like the hikers usually have. She only had a small shoulder bag. She was very pretty and had red hair."

Ralls and Klara thanked the old man and headed down the road.

"The first congregation of people on the road will be the salt mine, a tourist attraction," Klara said. "I think we should try there."

There were tourist buses with groups getting on and off. People milled about, going down the mine, in and out of the gift shop, and to the bathrooms.

Klara and Ralls went into the gift shop to see if anyone knew anything.

A Polish sales lady of fifty years approached them. Ralls thought she might speak English since she was there for the tourist trade. She did.

"Hello. I'm looking for a young lady with red hair." He showed her the drawing. "Have you seen anyone recently resembling her?"

She looked carefully at the drawing. "There are many tourists that come here. But I do recall a few days ago a young lady with red hair accompanying a man into a very fancy car, a big white one. The car was one of those older, classics. It drew quite a bit of attention."

"Do you know which way they went?"

"No, but Krakow is near. They most likely went there,

as that is where most tourists come from to visit the salt mine here."

Ralls and Klara headed for Krakow. As there was no one else to discuss the search with, Ralls discussed the possibilities with the interpreter en route. "What do you think?"

"There are a lot of pretty girls here that will escort for cheap," she said. "If she came in some rocket, where is it? We should look further into just who is this person with the fancy car."

"It's the only lead we have, so let's check it out," Ralls said. "If the man she caught a ride with is rich, where in Krakow would he likely take her?"

"Oh, that's easy. The best hotel is the Forum on the Vistula River."

At the reception of the Forum, Ralls, with Klara next to him in case translation was needed, asked the lady clerk, who spoke limited English, "We are looking for a man in a classic car, a big white one, and he may have been accompanied by a red-haired young lady."

As she was well trained, she did not respond, but instead went for the manager. A man dressed in formal black clothes approached and asked, "How may I help you, sir?"

"I'm from the United States Government. This is my official interpreter and assistant." He had just elevated her to assistant. He produced an identification card with his picture on it with a US seal, along with a badge. "We're looking for a man with a young lady with red hair who may have checked in here recently. They would have been in a huge, white, classic car."

The manager could care less what governmental agency wanted to probe into hotel business and interfere with his high-stepping guests who took the expensive suites and depended on anonymity. "I'm so sorry, sir. We are known for discretion with our guests, and even if I did remember them, I would not be able to say if such a person was or was not a guest here."

Ralls realized that he would get nowhere by the front

door approach. He decided to get rooms and see what could be learned from hotel staff or other guests. "Very well, thank you. How much are two regular rooms?"

"We have two regular rooms," the manager said. "River facing, or city facing? Those facing the river are at a higher rate than those on the other side." He gave them the rates.

Ralls, shocked at the prices, and remembering his limitations on expenditures for travel and hotels away from home, asked, "The US Government requires travel away from home to meet a per diem limit set by the Internal Revenue Service for federal employees, which is the same that is allowed for deductions for taxpayers. Do you give a discount for government employees?"

❧❧❧

Once settled in what Ralls considered as outrageously expensive rooms, he sent Klara out into the hotel to find out who might talk.

She returned an hour and a half later. "No luck with the maids or the porters. There are a number of rich or important people that stay here, and I either could not get anyone that remembered or perhaps they were too well trained to speak, for fear of losing their jobs. However, the bartender, when I told him I was a classic car buff and asked if he had seen any classic cars recently, he said that there was a beautiful, classic, white Rolls Royce belonging to a rich guest at the hotel recently. He recalled that he was an aristocrat. That's all I could get from him."

"That could be our man," Ralls said. "I have an idea. Maybe he went into town to eat, and the staff there would not be under instructions not to speak about customers. Why don't you go back to the concierge and find out where the best restaurants in town are? We can then go to into town this evening and ask."

The hotel recommended a short list of the best places in

town for dinner. That evening, Ralls and Klara began to hit them, one after the other, until they found one that announced that they had a special guest called Baron Von Limbach who had arrived in a classic Rolls Royce car with a beautiful young lady.

"We have his name," Ralls said to Klara. "Now I can check on him."

Back at the hotel, Ralls phoned in to Washington, where it was morning, on his military, secure satellite phone. "Good morning, Director. Ralls here from Krakow, Poland."

"Any news?"

"I circled the exact landing spot and surrounding area many times in a chopper, but there were no clues. The exact landing spot was in the middle of a pasture—there has been rain since, which might have made the grass rise up from landing gear impressions. There was no landing strip, no hanger, and no tracks from trucks to collect any such craft."

"What? That seems impossible! She must've had a way to get the craft out of the area."

"The only clue at all is that, on the morning following the landing, a red-haired female appeared at a farmhouse not far away. At the farmhouse we met a farmer who said that a young lady with red hair came to his house early in the morning after the landing, on foot, and wanted a lift into town. He thought she was one of those back-packers, but she did not have a back pack, only a satchel, which means she was most likely not camping out. When she could not get a ride, she left on foot, walking toward the highway. I assumed there was no one waiting for her at the landing site so I went to the nearest congregation of people, which is an old salt mine turned into a tourist attraction. A young lady with red hair was seen leaving with an older man in a classic, white, expensive-looking limousine. It's a long shot, but it's the only lead I have so far. I came to Krakow here, following those two, and was successful in finding out where a red-haired woman and a rich man stayed at this very hotel, the Forum. His name is Baron Von Limbach. I could not get a name for her. They left together in his car. Run his name for me please."

"I'll check on him," Houser said. "What do you think the chances are that the redhead is out pilot?"

"The entire situation is an enigma," Ralls said. "She could just be the wife or girlfriend of this baron, a hiker, or even an escort girl. On the other hand, maybe he is the sponsor of that radical craft as he might be able to afford to fund such a project. What do you think?"

"It seems so hard to believe that a young lady with a craft that can descend from space into the atmosphere on some sort of rocket, in which she then travels seventeen-thousand miles an hour from one continent to another, would be hitchhiking for a ride," Hauser said. "What do you intend to do now?"

"The only lead is this Baron Von Limbach, and that's a long shot. The redhead might be some girlfriend or even a local hooker. But I think they headed for Germany, so I'll head that way now. How soon will you be able to get me details available on this baron fellow?"

"I'll get to work on it now. I should have some for you in a few hours, and more later. Shall I send them to your laptop?"

"Do that. I'll sleep here in the hotel in Krakow and head out in the morning, depending on what you find."

❧❧❧

In the morning, Ralls awoke early to see what Hauser had dug up on this Baron Von Limbach. Hauser's email was as follows:

*Baron Von Limbach has German and Taiwan passports, and he has offices in Taipei and Berlin. He is described by some as an arms merchant but, in actuality in these times, the actual sale of weap-*

*ons, unless it is on a small scale, is done directly between the weapons manufacturer and the end-user country. Taiwan, for example, has a law that forbids Taiwan and its army from purchasing weapons unless directly from the manufacturer. These laws are designed to prevent weapons from falling into the wrong hands and to prevent the governments from paying excessively for the weapons because of bribes and graft. However, there is much graft in Taiwan, and the baron brokers a number of these transactions and is paid outside of the actual purchase. But that is just for the actual weapons themselves. There is a much larger business in military support for all sorts of military and related equipment, such as special sighting systems for tanks and mobile guns like Howitzers. These are very expensive.*

*One of the programs that he initiated was to fix the problem in dealing with rocket-propelled bombs that have rocket fuel and explosives that have a shelf life of several years and can become unstable or not function. There is also another problem with old weapons, which is the expense of getting rid of them when they are beyond their shelf life. Most countries are part of a treaty which bans dumping these into the ocean. His solution was to simply load up the rockets that are older first and the newest ones last. Imagine enemies dying from weapons just to get rid of the weapons!*

*He was behind a sale of a number of American-made Robinson helicopters to the Taiwan Government to use as observation platforms in their constant vigil against Mainland China. In Taiwan, the baron had a French-made FLIR (Forward Looking Infrared) camera mounted on the helicopters to patrol the Taiwan Strait. That FLIR will pick up a person on a boat in relatively high seas at night. Those FLIRs sell for over a half million each. As the Taiwanese, like other Chinese, are not known for flying skills, he also set up a program to train the Taiwan helicopter pilots, from which he profited handsomely.*

*He is behind, or a part of, a company that is presently retrofitting older and desert-worn Saudi Humvees with armor and a French 20 mm gun on a turret with a very expensive targeting system that shoots on the fly at full speed. The retrofit involves an interesting program of having the Humvees come to a Saudi hanger. There, a company that he is behind, completely strips the Humvee, and then all parts that wear out are replaced, such as the motors, drive train, half shafts, etc. A new US diesel from Cummins in Columbus, Indiana, or one from Volvo in Europe is installed along with all new parts that wear out. All the electrics are replaced. The result is sending out a sort of zero-time Humvee, guaranteed to give as much life as a new one, but for half the price, and it is supposed to be better than new. However, when in the hanger, they added the armor on the floor, the sides, and weak point, along with special windows, to reduce the killing effects of bullets and Improvised Explosive Device (IED) bombs of the Taliban. He also adds a 20 mm turret on a number of them. All of this is very expensive.*

*He is known to be very rich and travels and lives in very high style. Could he be behind the flight over the US? If any individual would be capable of creating such a craft, it might be him. But why? What motive? What could he possibly gain from making such a daring, public statement, especially when his business and wealth come from keeping a low profile?*

*As far as we know, all of his business is on the*

*side of the West and Western allies. Has he gone crazy? There has been no ransom or other signs of him, or anyone for that matter, wanting something. And the ability to create a craft capable of going seventeen-thousand miles an hour in the atmosphere is beyond the capability of any country or, as far as we know, anyone. There now are some private flights into the edge of space, planned by an outfit called Virgin Air, but there is no reason for those people to take off without a flight plan, and they cannot go that fast in the atmosphere.*

*We have not got much to go on. I am in touch with the CIA and will try to see if this baron is up to something. I am asking the CIA to assist. I am sending a contact number. I want you to tell the CIA that I want to see if their people can get us a DNA sample of that woman.*

*(End message from Director Hauser)*

# CHAPTER 11

The following morning, Baron and his alien lover sat in the picturesque hotel restaurant to have breakfast. As they sat, sipping strong coffee, they smiled at each other, with little talk at first.

He prepared her a freshly baked roll, spread with butter and locally made blueberry preserves, a delicious way to start any day with a new lover, even if she was from outer space.

"The different foods have certainly been one of my greatest experiences here," Tak said. "Is the German food different from Polish?"

"Well, there are subtle differences, even if you are from a different planet. In Poland you had Polish sausage, and here you can try something similar, but it's still a sausage. The countries are close together, at least on a map of Earth, so I suppose the foods will seem much the same."

He made his order to the pretty young waitress, who was the same girl working at the desk the day before. "*Bitte…*" Then he realized he must speak in English so that Tak could experience the moment. "Make us each two Bavarian Weisswursts, boiled in water, with a sprig of Italian parsley, or your equivalent, to remove any odor. Serve with Bavarian mustard." As she left, he decided to broach a subject with Tak. "Last night was the most amazing sex I've ever had. You have something extraordinary in your *Alien Style.*"

She turned to him with a sobering observation. "Human evolution has unfortunately left you with sexual components whose operations do not fully satisfy human desires, which seem to occupy a great deal of your thoughts, during waking hours. This is why, I now believe that I may have confirmed the reason that humans engage in what you call oral sex. It seems to me, as an anthropologist, that oral sex is a perversion of what parts of your bodies were intended to be utilized for reproduction. You will have noticed that last night, with my race, that it should not be necessary to pervert the use of our bodies to use oral stimulation for gratification and the organs that we have are sufficient."

All Baron could muster was, "But then why did you try it?"

"Well, I am a field anthropologist," she said sheepishly.

"Will it further your study if we have alien sex again?" he asked.

She smiled. "It may take additional practice. What have you in mind for today, or would you like to spend the day in the room practicing intergalactic sex?"

"The answer is simple. We will go back to the room for more practice and then out to the village where we can look about, window shop, and enjoy the scenery. Oh, I want to tell you something. In order to show you places other than these European nations that are part of what is called the European Union, it is necessary for me to get you a passport. I can take you to Berlin if you wish, where I have an office and influence, and I can get you one there. However, I must have your solemn promise that you will not report to any Earth authorities how I got you the papers."

"As I trust you not to reveal my existence, I'll reciprocate and do whatever you ask. Are there any other perversions of sexual reproduction that you wish me to experience?"

He grinned then nodded.

"Is there a name for my anatomical differences," she asked.

"Yes," he said. "Area 51."

❧❧❧

Later, window shopping and absorbing the ambiance of the quaint village, they came upon a small watch shop. They turned in as Tak was infatuated with the mechanical devices.

She asked to see a skeleton pocket watch with both sides of the watch in glass, showing the many gears turning about.

"This is amazing! This sort of thing has not made for many ages. Where I come from, time is not measured by gears and springs. This is an art of the far distant past. Imagine how much time it must take to make such a device!"

"You could fix this to your waistband with a chain and put the watch in your pocket," Baron said.

Tak, mesmerized by the device, continued to look at the gears going round and round.

"Is the case on this piece solid gold?" Baron asked the shopkeeper.

"Oh yes," he said. "Solid twenty-two karat. It's from Switzerland."

"Have you a gold watch chain?" Baron asked.

"Of course." The clerk produced a thin, black-velvet-lined drawer with many chains, in silver and gold, and laid the drawer on the glass.

Baron looked at his alien. "Which of these do you like?"

"This one." She held it up as though it was a treasure.

The shopkeeper attached it to the timepiece.

"How much for both?" Baron asked.

"Well, you know, the price of gold has skyrocketed."

Engaging in the fun of bargaining, although it mattered not, other than the fun of it, Baron said, "You bandit! You did not pay those prior prices for these pieces. We can always come back next year if we decide to come back again, when the price goes down, when you still have this unsellable relic."

There being no other business that day, or almost all week and, with a poor European economy and few customers, the shopkeeper quickly came to a reasonable price for the two pieces.

Baron was content with the bargain. Tak, mesmerized with what she considered a priceless antique, accepted his magnanimous present.

"A small present for my favorite alien," he said when they were out of the shop.

Tak flushed at the wonderful present from her new lover. She gave him a hug "Thank you, Baron! This will always be very special to me." She attached the watch chain to her waist band and let the watch drop into her pocket. She took it out a few times to admire it.

෴

In Berlin, Baron showed her into his office, a two-room suite, with only a single secretary. She was attractive, tall, blonde, and forty, with amazing efficiency. Her name was Ingrid.

Tak was sitting in front of Baron's desk, behind which was a large window of the city, when Ingrid came in with papers in hand. She handed them to Baron for approval. He looked at them and seemed pleased.

Baron looked at Tak. "I have something for you."

He handed her the documents, a certificate of birth, marriage certificate, and a passport. All were obtained by Baron's influence, and all were recorded in official records in case anyone checked. All were fraudulent, but very official. Tak looked at them strangely, not having any idea what to expect. She read the passport with her picture. It read, *Baroness Von Limbach.* "It's me! I'm a baroness!"

At a sidewalk café near the Berlin office, they sat outside for a light lunch and to watch the people go by.

"Tak, I have a decision to make, or perhaps I should say you have one to make. I absolutely insist on being your guide on Earth for the duration of your stay. I will take you wherever you want to go, or if you do not know, I will take you where I think you would like to go. But I know you are not here to see the tourist spots of mountains and canyons, but people.

"Now, if you like, I can allow you to join me in my business, which I think you will find informative and interesting. However, I must have your absolute assurance that you will keep all details of what you learn a secret from everyone on the planet.

"The choice is yours. Would you like to accompany me on some business and learn a bit about how the Earth business works, or would you prefer to simply learn more about humans that are not engaged in any such activities? Either is fine with me."

"I'm quite sure I should go should with you on your business," she answered. "And I will keep what I learn a secret."

"Very well, that is settled."

As they sat at the café, they saw many high-fashion women out shopping, walking right by the table.

"I don't understand something. Earth females want to be treated as equals to males, right?" Tak asked.

"That is so."

"Then why is it that the females paint their faces and nails but men do not?"

"Good question."

"Is it that the females would be less attractive to the males if they did not use paint?" she continued.

"That is so."

"Would I be more attractive to you and others if I painted my face?"

He looked around at a huge department store just nearby. "Why don't we go into that store to a makeup counter and find out?'

"I would like to try that."

"You alien females are all the same, always worried about your looks."

☙☙

Ralls and Klara headed in the direction of Germany, where a few witnesses had seen the Rolls Royce going. After a time, they saw a group of men wearing reflective green vests, the road hazard kind. The nearest had a stop sign in hand. The traffic was reduced to one lane traffic. By a hand signal to another man fifty yards down the road, the traffic was be allowed to pass from one direction, then the other direction was allowed to pass. There was enough room on one side of the road for a lane of cars to pass, but not enough for two lanes, especially with all the pieces of equipment involved, occasionally coming into both lanes. There were no cars in front of them when he arrived, but a few were building up in a queue behind his car as he sat there.

Frustrated by the delay, Ralls sighed and tried to relax, looking about. He tried to see what the cause of delay was. There were two, huge dump trucks filled with dirt, with one dumping its load into a huge hole in the ground. The other truck was waiting its turn to dump its load.

Ralls realized that this was most unusual. He pulled over his car to the shoulder of the road and got out with Klara. The man with the stop sign did not seem to mind, as Ralls was not holding up traffic.

Ralls walked up to the hole in the ground. It was ten feet deep and being filled with dirt as they watched.

Klara asked the crew superintendent what had happened. She then turned to Ralls. "He does not know what happened. Some driver reported this huge hole in the road, and this crew is filling it up. He said that the dirt from the hole is missing. It is not stacked up anywhere, nor is there any debris. So they are having to truck in loads of dirt for the fill."

"What on earth could have caused it?" Ralls asked, as though she might know.

"I've no idea," Klara said. "If these highway repairmen do not know, I certainly do not. But where the dirt might have gone is the real mystery."

"I wonder if this huge hole is related to our mystery woman and her fast vehicle," Ralls said to Klara. "A large hole in the road and many yards of missing dirt. A seventeen-thousand-mile-per-hour female. Are they connected?"

Klara answered with a question. "Why would a female pilot that can go seventeen thousand miles an hour want to make a huge hole in the highway?"

"Where's the dirt from the hole?" Ralls said. "Both events are very strange. I am going to find that woman. I think she may have some answers."

# CHAPTER 12

The next stop for Tak and Baron was Paris. He flew her there, now that she had identification to show at the airport. At their hotel, during a petit dejeuner, Baron suggested one of two ideas for the next leg of her Earth adventure.

"We could go by car south to the Loire Valley to stay at one or two converted castles and sample the fabulous cuisine, or to try the rapid train down to the south of France and then on to Spain."

"How rapid?"

"It's called *Train à Grand Vitesse*. The speed may be nothing like you are accustomed to, but it averages 300 kilometers per hour, which is 186 miles per hour, in case you haven't converted to metric yet."

She chose. "Let's do the train."

"Very well, we'll leave tomorrow morning. I suggest Paris to Bordeaux where we can have a wine tasting."

☙❧

In the wee hours of the next morning, five Muslim men, dressed in dark clothes and hunched over so as not to attract attention, cut through the bottom of a security chain-link fence and snuck up to the rails of the Train à Grand Vitesse railroad in an unpopulated area south of Paris.

Through the fence they dragged a four-foot-long oxygen cylinder, a special torch, two hydraulic cylinders, a small car battery, a small bundle of rods that were three feet long, and a sledge hammer.

At the train rails, one hooked up the oxygen cylinder to a hose from a device resembling a pistol that held a special, three-foot rod so that oxygen would flow through the gun and out through the special rod. The rod held eight different thin strips of metals, including thermite, which only partially filled the diameter of the three eighths inch copper rod, so that the opening would allow the oxygen to flow alongside the metals. The metals, with ignited oxygen, created an exo-thermite reaction of 10,000 degrees Fahrenheit out of the end of the rod, which would melt anything. The rods would expend rather quickly, in about a minute. It was not a very efficient device, but devastatingly effective as it could cut through metal, concrete, or anything else.

The battery was set nearby and the operator of the gun made ready with leather welding gloves and goggles.

One turned on the regulator on the oxygen cylinder, and the gun was ready. He opened up the regulator to 100 pounds per square inch, which would maximize the reaction and temperature over and above the normal 65 pounds. The operator pulled the trigger. The flow of oxygen could be heard hissing from the end of the small rod that was fitted into the gun. He took the electric striker, which was wired to the battery, and held it to the end of the rod, creating sparks.

*Whack*! was the sound of ignition, and several feet of sparks began to blast out of the end of the rod, a scary thing to work with. The man with the rod holder held it up to one of the rails and pulled the trigger all the way.

Whoosh! The flames came out of the end of the rod loudly and menacingly. The operator held the rod up to the top of the rail again and began a cut. In less than a minute, the rail was severed. He repeated the operation on the other rail. He then walked down the line with his assistant carrying the oxygen cylinder and battery. He cut off the spikes of the rails on both sides until he was one hundred paces down from the starting place, adding new rods as they were used up. He then cut both the rails at that spot. One of them whacked the train rails with a sledge hammer to loosen them.

The group then placed the two hydraulic cylinders, one near each cut in the rails, set to push outward, fitted just below the top of the rails. He adjusted the cylinders until they were tight against the section of steel just below the top of the rails. The hydraulic cylinders were connected to each other with a hydraulic line and then to a reservoir and pump, already connected to each other and the pump in advance, so as not to have to bleed the system in the field. The same battery used for ignition of the torch was then hooked up to the hydraulic pump and then to a receiver with a switch. A cell phone was hooked up to activate the receiver. All was in place. When the remote receiver was activated by cell phone, the pump would start pumping hydraulic pressure into the cylinders, pushing the rails apart, as they were now no longer fastened down.

All that was needed was the phone call.

The terrorists scurried away, taking the equipment that did not need to remain.

⚜

They intended to take the first train, but Baron was a bit slow that morning, after another marathon session of alien sex with Tak. And, with a traffic jam on the way there, they arrived a few minutes too late for their scheduled train. He bought tickets for the second train and decided to burn up the time by taking a coffee and relaxing in a café in the station.

On the walls in the café were two big screens TVs, for the waiting train riders, showing a soccer game.

There was a commotion in the terminal. The TV monitor screens switched from soccer to an overhead view from a news helicopter of a spectacular train crash on the TGV track. None of the train cars were in their normal position. One was standing up, another upside down. One was across the tracks and upside down, and some were crushed. None of the passengers could be seen moving, and they could bloody bodies all about, looking very dead.

The news channel reported as the helicopter flew above the carnage. "…a short while ago, the TGV train from Paris to Marseille was derailed. It was traveling at 300 kilometers per hour. As you can see, cars flipped, spun, and tumbled. The number of dead is not known, but it is believed that there were 285 passengers plus crew aboard the train. A local hospital is said to have received the first few passengers, all of whom were dead on arrival or died shortly thereafter. The death toll is feared to be very high, and it is feared that all may, in fact, be dead. Just minutes after the incident, an anonymous call was received by a Paris news stations, claiming it was done by al-Qaeda in retaliation to the French law prohibiting Muslim females from covering their faces in public…"

"We were scheduled to take that train and we would be dead if we had," Tak said.

There was little to say as they watched, in horror, the carnage and suffering as shown on the news.

Train travel was suspended, although no one wanted to take another train at that time. As they needed to change their plans, the two headed back to the hotel to see if rooms were available. They could then decide what to do, having just missed death by a lucky few minutes' delay.

☙❧☙

Baron took her to Le Jules Verne Restaurant in the Eiffel Tower for dinner that evening. As they sat, Tak wanted to discuss the terror attacks.

"Tell me more details about these terror attacks, Baron.

Is this something that's going all over the planet?"

"Yes. In the recent past, there have been tens of thousands of bombings, many of them suicide bombings, killing hundreds of thousands. This particular attack appears to be a way of making a statement that those who are not Muslims, who they consider infidels, cannot prevent Muslim women from covering their faces in public. The Muslims have a tradition of making the women cover their faces in public. Some require the women to cover their entire body and head in a black or blue robe called a burqa. Some require a scarf called a hijab. France passed a law forbidding the covering of faces with the burqa in public in 2011. This act of terror is a protest, or so they claim."

"To get attention, these people kill innocents?" Tak said in amazement.

"It seems to be the only way they can get any attention."

"All of that killing just because the government passed a law that forbids women from covering their faces because of a religion?" she asked.

"Exactly. Or at least that's their excuse. Killing is what they have in mind, and any number of excuses will do. The vast majority of the killings are done by Muslims. Many make whatever war they can with their primitive tools against non-Muslims, whom they call infidels, or non-believers, whom they also accuse of being without faith."

"Are any of the Muslim countries advanced with space probes and electronic inventions?"

"Yes, but religious fanaticism is fueled by ignorance. However, religious fanaticism and ignorance are not confined to Muslims. There are Christians who murder medical doctors for performing abortions. Many Christians pray daily for minor favors from their God."

"How many Muslims are there?"

"About 1.6 billion, or about a quarter of the world population."

"That is a huge number of humans, considering that

this warring pits so many humans against others. Are they all bad people?"

"Not at all. Many are wonderful."

Still in shock at having come so close to death, she said, "Baron, it's a good thing that I wasn't killed in that terrorist attack. The captain of the starship might have done something about it."

Baron was all ears. "What would that be?"

Tak thought a moment. "Well, there are two schools of thought. The first is that since my murder would not have been targeted at me specifically, the captain might decide not to intervene and just write my death off as an unfortunate casualty of an anthropologist sent on a dangerous assignment to a primitive and barbaric planet."

"What is the second school of thought?"

"Eradication of humans."

Baron could not let this go and thought he might get more out of her on this. "Could you be a bit more specific on how the captain might eradicate humans?"

"Well, there are quite a few options available to a starship captain. An angry response would be to steer a couple of large asteroids into your planet, one for the each hemisphere. That would do huge damage and cloud the planet with dust for years.

"One would be to blast your sun to create a solar flare so huge it would burn your planet's surface and destroy all human, animal, and plant life.

"Or he might blast your planet's core by firing down a volcano with a strong laser that would reach the core and heat it up to the point of neutralizing your planet's magnetic field which is necessary to protect your planet from radiation and gamma rays from the sun. This re-alignment of the magnetic field would create volcanic activity on a major scale, spreading volcanic dust in the atmosphere, which would include sulfur dioxide. The sulfur dioxide would mix with rain, become sulfuric acid rain, and destroy most all life remaining. In that case, there would be a cloud of the gas around the planet for several years, blocking the sun and chilling down the surface. That would be my favorite. The best English that I can come up with is that these options would create a *fresh start*, or a *do over*."

"Your *favorite*? A *fresh start*? A *do over*?" Baron repeated what she said like a Brazilian parrot, shaking his head.

The waiter appeared and asked for their order.

"What is the specialty tonight?" Baron asked in French.

"Canard au sang," the waiter answered.

Baron looked at Tak and translated into English. "The specialty is Canard au Sang."

"What is that?" Tak asked.

"*Canard* is duck," Baron said.

"Oh, you gave me duck in Poland," she responded. "It was wonderful. What is the other part?"

"It means served in its own warm blood."

"*Baron!*"

☙❧☙

The next morning, the couple was up in their room. Baron phoned the front desk for petite dejeuner with coffee and juice. In only a few minutes, a young lady appeared at the door with a tray of the usual breads, butter, jam, coffee, milk, and orange juice.

As they ate, Baron opened his laptop and read messages. "I'm requested at my office in Taipei. Would you like to see Taiwan and parts of Asia? With this terror attack on the train, you might not want to continue here in France."

"I would now prefer to leave here," Tak said. "Let's go to Taiwan."

"I'll get busy making reservations," he said.

Her clothes were still in the bathroom on the towel rack drying. Baron brought them out before he started his shower. They were almost dry.

"Tell me about your clothes. You have only this one

outfit, not counting the one you bought in Poland. How do you manage with one outfit?"

"My clothes are unlike yours. I can wash them and hang them up to dry. They are made of a material that holds a constant temperature, and if wet, they dry right away. It keeps me at the temperature that is just right for me at all times."

Baron blinked, stunned, then started at her. "A constant temperature? Air-conditioned and heated clothes? I could make a fortune with this!"

She followed him into the shower. While they were both occupied in the shower, a different person came into the room who was not the same one who brought the tray. She was a woman in her late twenties with short, dark hair, black slacks, dark red shirt, and black jacket. She also wore latex gloves. She put the used cups and glasses on the tray and took the breakfast tray away. Outside, down the hall on the staircase, when no one was looking, she put the cups, glasses, and utensils into plastic bags and put them into her oversized purse. She carried the tray down the steps to the reception, and set it on a desk when no one was looking. Then she left. She was a CIA operative.

☙☙

The secure, satellite phone rang for Ralls in his Frankfort hotel.

"Mike Winger, CIA, here. We found the girl you wanted and the baron at a hotel in Paris. They are married, and she is a baroness. We don't have the marriage records yet, but believe it was a recent marriage by an administrative official in Berlin. We were able to get their cups, glasses, and eating utensils in Paris and have sent them for analysis of fingerprints and DNA."

"How did you find them so quickly?" Ralls asked in amazement.

"We've been looking all over for them," Winger answered. "Then there was the terrorist train attack the day before yesterday. The French Government collected video recordings on solid state recorders of the train terminal in Paris looking for suspects. They got a clear shot of the couple you described, sitting at a table in a café in the terminal. From that, we found them in a hotel that they checked into. They were apparently booked on the train that was hit, but missed it and went to a hotel where we found them. The next morning, we were able to get their breakfast tray from their room."

Ralls, shocked at the speed, asked, "How did you get the French police and government to turn over the recordings of the train terminal so fast?"

"We didn't," Winger said. "We hacked into their system, as usual. It avoids all the delay and red tape."

"Well done," Ralls said. "Anything further?"

"Baron Von Limbach is well known for selling international arms and military equipment," Winger said. "But he was never known to be married until now. We do not have any background on the woman, yet. We can't find any."

"Where are they now?" Ralls asked.

"They boarded a 747 first class to Taiwan. He has an office there as well as in Berlin," Winger said.

"Nice work. But please see if you can find out anything more about the woman."

# CHAPTER 13

Mei Ling and the rest of the staff always stood when Baron entered the office. The office was expecting General Hisa Rong-Jee—family name first, and pronounced "tsee-ah." Two of the male employees had come from the Taiwan military. A good deal of Baron's business was with the Taiwan military and they enhanced the contacts and communication. Since the military always stood when an officer entered the room, the rest stood as well and it became a tradition at his office, which Baron did not mind in the slightest. When he came in, everyone stood. And since many of the people that came to the office were in the military, it was an excellent policy.

Mei Ling came into Baron's office with a steaming pot of Oolong tea. The slender Mei Ling, wearing her cheongsam, slithered around Baron's chair and served him the exotic tea from his own plantation. The aroma was delightful, and he had not been able to enjoy anything like it while in Europe. Even better than the aroma, the taste was extraordinary.

"First, it is General Hisa regarding the weapon for the military," she began. "Then, after lunch, the two Americans." She had not met the baroness yet. "How's the baroness?"

"She's busy on the Internet upstairs. She's obsessed right now with studying about serial murderers and rapists. I won't have her down for the meeting with Hisa, as it will be in Mandarin. However, I'll invite her to the meeting in English with the Americans."

His apartment was the on the floor just above his office, with each occupying half of a floor of the building in the expensive part of Taipei. To have a nice house with grounds in Taiwan required at least an hour and a half drive from the city center. So the only way to go was in a high rise.

"I've told Madam Baroness to let me know if she wants to go out or needs anything," he added. "I want to send her with Driver Chen to the National Palace Museum. Tonight we will dine out, so make reservations for two for us at my usual place."

In Taiwan, Baron did not bring Lachhiman to drive, as he stayed in Europe with the Rolls Royce. And Baron needed no body guard as entry into the island of Taipei was very restricted, allowing little leeway for bad elements to enter, combined with the fact that Baron enjoyed protection from the highest ranks in the Taiwan Army.

As Taipei was practically a synonym for a traffic jam, Baron hired a man named Chen, who was on full time when Baron was in residence, and in the traditional manner, Chen was called "Driver Chen." He had his own small SUV, as anything bigger could not get about in Taipei.

In a short while, Mei Ling announced General Hisa, the high-ranking officer in charge of procurement for the Army of Taiwan. Baron conducted the meeting in Mandarin, in which he was fluent, as General Hisa could hardly tie two words together in English. With Mei Ling serving tea, the meeting began.

"Baron, as you know, I'm here regarding the competitors for the trials coming up soon for the proposed new turret to be put on our M113 vehicles," General Hisa said. "I'd like to hear how you evaluate the French version of the competitors for the contract that you represent."

He referred to a contract soon to be awarded to modify

the older M113 armored personnel carriers, of which the Taiwan army had over a thousand, by adding a state-of-the-art, French-made, twenty-five millimeter gun turret on one hundred of them. The purpose of the vehicle was to hustle troops and supplies to any location that the Mainland Chinese Army might invade to fend them off until the Americans might arrive with allies to save the country. In reality, however, the likelihood of the Western World making war on China over Taiwan was next to nil. This started with President Carter, who knew so little about Asia. But, Baron thought, if it was not for the abandonment of Taiwan by the US, he would not be able to sell things like the turret. Each of the three companies had representatives coming to Taiwan for the trials, which involved sending over actual turrets by ship, with a crew to mount one temporarily to a M113, and then conducting actual field trials in southern Taiwan. Baron was the exclusive representative for the French competitor.

"As you know from the data that we have, the company I represent has the best scores in the various competitions elsewhere," Baron said. "In extensive testing, the French version has fewer malfunctions. We have the trials coming up here for the finalists."

Hisa pretended he knew how the thing worked. "Go on. Please refresh me on the specifications, so I don't get the guns mixed up in my thinking."

"This weapon has ideal specifications for defense of the island. Its twenty five millimeter cannon shoots in three or five round bursts, of either one hundred fifty or four hundred fifty rounds per minute, and the length of bursts can be programmed. The thermal imaging sight can find and hit ground troops landing here from China or target running engines in enemy vehicles all by itself. The stabilization mount means it can fire while moving at full speed. There are several types of rounds. The simple one uses regular 25 mm ammo. The next is the High Explosive Incendiary. Another interesting one is the Armor Piercing Fin Stabilized

Discarding Sabot, which has a tungsten inner projectile that comes out of an outer shell housing after it leaves the barrel and can penetrate Chinese tanks with ease. The tungsten projectile has a hardness of four hundred Brinell and can penetrate eighty millimeters of homogenous armor at one thousand meters."

Hisa, pretending he was well versed on the weapon, which in reality was over his head in complication, said, "Yes, I recall. But, don't the newest Chinese tanks have much thicker armor? If China lands its newest tanks, will these be effective against them?"

"Some of the newest ones have a meter of armor, but not the older ones, and even those that do have the thickest armor do not have it everywhere. Most of an expected landing from China would be the older ones, which make up the majority of their inventory. This weapon will stop most all of them. But, General, this conversion makes the personnel carriers into an Infantry Fight Vehicle, not a tank. The guns on tanks are much larger. If we put a tank gun on top of the M113 it would blow it over upside down when it was fired. This projectile will destroy any similar vehicle as the M113, any enemy field artillery, any trucks pulling artillery, stop troops on foot, wipe out older tanks, and stop even the newest tanks with the special projectile ammo. The projectile of this gun is more effective than what the competitors have. It would be very effective at repelling a mass landing of Chinese troops and equipment on our shores, and wreak havoc with their soldiers, while providing safe transportation in and out of the battlefield for ours."

"But, isn't this weapon more expensive than the other two?"

"Only slightly, including the targeting system, at four hundred eighty thousand United States Dollars each, including installation on the M113."

"So, Baron, tell me more about why I should be influenced to buy your weapon?"

This was the cue Baron had been waiting for. "With the

Americans, who are in the competition, they always state the price in the end user papers to get permission from the US State Department to sell such weapons outside of America. That end user permit has been known to take over six months, even to friends such as Taiwan and Israel and, in troubled areas, indefinitely. That, and the existence of the Taiwan law that makes it illegal for anyone to accept a commission on military sales to the government, makes it difficult for us to do business. The commission is usually paid by some foreign subsidiary of the company under some ruse, and the risk of leaks is high. However, the French will sell to both sides of the same war and will sign any document presented them, however false. Regarding commissions—the government, itself, does this for the business, not only the manufacturer. They will pay me my commission and, from that, you will receive your fragrant oil."

"How much is your commission?" the general asked.

If they water-boarded Baron to within an inch of death, he would not reveal the truthful answer to that question. "Very small, due to the fact that my version is more expensive and, therefore, I had to agree to cut it substantially to do business. It is only three per cent on all initial purchases, and only one per cent on parts, supplies, and ammunition, and then only for five years."

The general assumed he was lying, as no Chinese ever told the truth in such matters, and he assumed it was probably closer to seven per cent. The truth was that it was seventeen and one-half per cent on the initial order, and three and one-half per cent indefinitely on all future sales and parts as well as ammo.

"But you know I have my own expenses," Hisa said. "I cannot possibly go through with the contract with your version, unless I receive four per cent myself.

"My dear friend, Baron said, "we have had done much successful business together, and you know that I always provide handsomely. But this is a contract for conversion of one hundred vehicles for a price of forty eight million dollars plus spare parts and ammo. I obviously cannot pay out more than I receive. I have a considerable investment in the deal and many costs yet to pay."

"The lowest I can possibly go is three," Hisa said.

"As we go back such a long way and have had such good relations, I tell you what I'll do. I will stretch my goodwill with the French gun maker to the limit and make another trip to Paris to meet with its highest officials one last time. I'll ask them for an additional two percent, which would make it five per cent total commission. If they will, which is questionable, then you and I will split the commission at two and a half percent each. Considering my enormous expenses in putting this together, you would be making several times what I am on the deal."

This approach gave the general great face, the proposition elevating him to more money than Baron, and was effective. Before the general could respond, Baron added, "But, of course, the only way to get the French to pay out another two per cent would be to add it to the price, and the French do not care. That would mean we raise the initial order of forty eight million by two percent. Your fragrant oil will then be two and a half per cent of forty eight million, or one million two hundred thousand US Dollars."

Hisa acquiesced. "Agreed."

Of course, Baron knew full well that Chinese never quit bargaining and, unlike Westerners, Hisa would continue, or try to continue, to get more later. Baron had already cleared the higher price with the French, anticipating what the fragrant oil would cost. Once the contract was signed, Baron would send over a little gift to the general, probably a new Mercedes, which, in Taiwan with its high duties on cars, was very expensive. Presents were customary with the Chinese, and they especially liked Mercedes cars. In the meantime, Baron just raised the price of weapons for the country so he could have more money himself. He would also have to make some gifts to subordinate officers under the general.

"I can have the contract prepared today and delivered to you, so you can sign it just after the trials of the French weapon and the competitors," Baron said.

The general left the room, and Baron summoned May Ling, "Get me those reports on the wealth of that young, American heir who is coming in after lunch."

ℰↄℰↄ

The wooden door to Baron's Taipei office was thick and secure. Two tiny cameras, one above the door, another to the side, recorded who was visiting.

Shanta pushed the bell, as though afraid of what was inside. Mei Ling opened the door, smiled politely, and asked in English, "Mr. Saunders and Ms. Laxshimi?"

"Yes," Shanta answered for them.

"Please come in. My name is Mei Ling."

They passed a waiting room on the left and then went down a hallway with work stations to the right. Several stations had computers, scanners, faxes, and office machines, staffed with both sexes of Chinese, busily working away, with eight working there that day.

They were led into a meeting room with a sliding glass door that led to a balcony which overlooked the nearby buildings and part of the city from the next to top floor of the high building. In the center of the meeting room was a round rosewood table. Surrounding it were rosewood chairs with stuffed blue leather upholstery, set on heavy bases that allowed them to swivel and rock. On one wall was a LED screen for presentations.

Andrew and Shanta walked over to the balcony and looked outside at the rain that was pounding down heavily in the strong winds of the storm they had left outside. A mild typhoon was arriving, and the high winds between the tall buildings could be heard as a soft howling and pulsating.

Mei Ling stood by, dutifully waiting for orders for refreshments. "The baron is on an overseas call and should be with you shortly. While you wait, might you be interested in tea? The baron is known for having very fine Oolong tea."

Shanta looked at Andrew, smiling. "Oh, yes."

"Do you have any bourbon?" Andrew asked.

"Yes, we keep the major liquors here." Mei Ling disappeared and returned with the tea on a tray and a bottle of bourbon.

Andrew saw the bourbon and let loose. "I own that one!"

"How wonderful," Mei Ling said. She put the bottle in front of him on the table, along with a saucer of ice and a glass so that he could pour as he wished. He took the glass, put in a few ice cubes, and poured himself bourbon. He was not interested in waiting for anyone else to mess around with tea.

Mei Ling then turned to the tea. She first washed the tea leaves in the small pot with hot water and, while waiting, she warmed the small cups with hot water. She poured out the hot water in the cups and then poured out the tea with its rich, golden color. She passed it to Shanta.

Shanta took the cup and had her sip. Her expression changed to one of delight. "Oh my, this is wonderful!"

"The baron has his own tea plantation where this is grown," Mei Ling proudly announced as she refilled Shanta's cup. "See?" she asked, opening the lid of the pot, "the tea leaves have a purple color, even though the tea does not. Some say this is the best available."

"I like to think that it is the best."

The voice of a large set of lungs filled the room, their owner having overheard. They looked up to see Baron Von Limbach entering with his unforgettable presence. Just behind him was the red-haired, lovely Tak, in her same outfit, but now sporting makeup, since having learned how to apply it at the department store in Europe.

"Master Saunders." Baron addressed him as "Master" to provide him with a sort of title, done as a matter of great respect. He had learned of Saunders before the meeting, and knew that he was the heir to one of the larger fortunes. One of Saunders's holdings, that was easy to find, was the bourbon distillery, and Baron had Mei Ling get some flown in from the US.

"Yes," Andrew answered and shook his hand, enjoying the respect.

"And this must be the beautiful Mademoiselle Laxshimi whom the famous pleader Eschmann, Esquire, described to me."

"It is a pleasure to meet you, Baron, sir."

"This is my wife and business partner, Baroness Von Limbach," Baron said. "You may speak freely in front of her."

We are honored to meet you too, Baroness," Shanta said for the both of them as Andrew was not taking the lead in the introductions.

Shanta noticed Baron's outfit, a three-piece suit, made of gray wool with tiny specks of yellow-gold colored thread in the weave. His vest was gold in color. Across the vest was a gold pocket watch chain, with a rare, multi-colored jade fob.

Tak was wearing her alien outfit, which did not command the attention of Baron's, with his presence of elegance.

"Baron, I love your outfit," Shanta complimented, looking at him. Then she realized that she may have just insulted the baroness, but decided not to make it worse by saying anything further.

"Why, thank you," Baron said, devoid of modesty. "This one was made for me in Delhi. I especially like the vest, made of real Kashmir wool. That comes from the underside of the throat of the Kashmiri goat that is collected in tiny bits from many hundreds of goats by the local women and woven, in a painstaking process, into the softest wool on Earth. It takes many women hundreds of hours just to make something like this. Touch it if you like."

He opened his jacket farther, to allow Shanta to touch the vest.

She stepped forward, and touched his vest. "I've heard of this divine wool, but have never actually been able to touch it. It feels heavenly!"

"Rather nice on a cold, rainy day such as this," Baron said, having set the stage perfectly for a spectacular gift. He motioned to Mei Ling who, knowing her cue, picked up a box wrapped in gift wrap from a table against the wall and handed it to Shanta.

"A small token for such a beautiful lady."

Shanta opened the box excitedly, anticipating that it might be something made of that spectacular wool. Inside was a natural colored scarf of the legendary Kashmir wool. Her eyes widened in surprise, and she took it out to feel its softness, unlike any other fabric on Earth, and rubbed it on her face.

"For me?"

"Just for you."

"Oh my God!" she shrieked.

It was extravagantly big for the most luxurious material on earth, seven feet long and two feet wide. It was natural in color, a delicate brown.

She put it around her shoulders, continued to rub it on her cheeks, stood up, and turned around a few times, to enjoy and parade the most valuable present she had ever been given.

"Have a seat, please," Baron said, wanting to get down to business. "I see you have already tried the tea. Did you like it?"

"It is the best I've ever tasted," Shanta stated, still in awe of the scarf present, now enamored by the tea and the entire experience.

"Yes, the bourbon is great, too," Andrew agreed.

"I grow that tea myself," Baron boasted, "in the highlands, near Chang Rai, Thailand. Thank you, Mei Ling," he told her, which was her cue to leave. "I already know what you want as the most able pleader Eschmann told me. But I need to know just how committed you are. I have some questions." He turned to Andrew. "Can we speak freely, Master Saunders?" He was referring to the presence of Shanta.

Andrew caught on right away. "Yes, absolutely. Shanta and I are very much in this matter together."

"You wish to know if there is some way to put the Dalai Lama back in Tibet, correct?"

"Right," Andrew answered.

"Who else, other than Mr. Eschmann knows of what you want to do?"

Andrew and Shanta looked at each other and then at Baron. "Absolutely no one," Andrew said. "We're aware that this is extremely secret. We told only the minimal number of people that we were off to see Taiwan and then only to a place that we had not been to, on a holiday tour."

Baron looked at them, sizing up his new prospective employers as to whether or not they could be trusted. "Do you realize that entertaining such matters as something affecting an entire country will make you, if suspected, the target of an international manhunt? You can never tell a friend, relative, bartender, a priest in confession, or anyone as long as you live. Any breach of security whatsoever will make you a fugitive with no place on Earth to hide. There will be some out to find and kill anyone involved. Resources of entire governments will also be looking for anyone suspect."

Andrew and Shanta became concerned as they thought of the consequences of which Baron spoke. As it was not her money, Shanta, although willing to sacrifice, passed the decision to Andrew.

"Yes, we know," Andrew replied. "But atrocities continue in Tibet, and if anything can be done, we want to do it, and do it now—no matter what the cost or sacrifice. If not, there will soon be no more Tibet."

Baron's friendly face became all business. "The pressure from the rest of the world has not worked. The communist Chinese want to expand their territories and their race, which they imperialistically believe to be superior. Taiwan lives in constant fear that the United States and its allies will not intervene if China invades. Seven and a half million Chinese have been moved into Tibet to dilute the Tibetan culture. The only way that the Dalai Lama might be able to return to Tibet is if, suddenly, the Chinese no longer occupied it because of some catastrophe. Even if there were a catastrophe and the Dalai Lama returned, he would never be allowed by the Chinese to claim a new sovereign Tibet. You must not underestimate the number of communist Chinese soldiers and the formidable number of weapons in their arsenal."

Andrew considered what seemed to be an impossible task. Shanta could see his frustration and hesitation to speak, and said for them, "We understand that if anyone might know of a way to put the Dalai Lama back in Tibet, it would be you. Do you know how it might be done?"

Baron was gaining confidence in the two people and considered the request further. "If the Chinese, or a major part of them occupying Tibet, were to die or evacuate for safety reasons, the Dalai Lama might be allowed to back in, but only on a controlled basis. I know of a way that it might be done, but I have to confirm it."

"Are you referring to a nuclear bomb?" Shanta asked, impetuously. "What about the Tibetans?"

"Certainly not. The use of a nuclear weapon would make one the subject of an endless manhunt throughout the world, and there would be no safe quarter. Experts can tell exactly where the material from such a bomb came from. And, in any event, the use of a nuclear bomb would make Tibet uninhabitable. Out of the question."

"Then what?" Shanta said. "How do you propose to go about getting seven and a half million Chinese to move out of Tibet where they have been specially placed there by the Chinese government?"

Baron raised an eyebrow. "What if a large number of Chinese in Tibet were to die or flee? It might be arranged for the Dalai Lama to return in the wake of such a huge catastrophe, not permanently, but invited under special circumstances as a figurehead to provide spiritual aid for the dying Tibetan culture as a gesture to the world. It would give recognition to the rights of Tibetans, however small. I think this can be arranged. But then, you would have the souls of all those Chinese on your consciences. Do you think you could live with that?"

"Yes," Shanta responded emphatically. "The atrocities, that they are committing as we speak are so horrifying that they should all be put to death. It would serve them right."

"I agree," Andrew added.

Baron looked carefully at them. "But there is something else that I want you to consider. The Dalai Lama Himself would never agree to anything that would take the lives of anyone. What do you think of that?"

Andrew and Shanta looked at each other, but did not speak. They had not considered that. Baron, realizing they might like to talk, said, "Perhaps you would like to discuss this alone? If you'll permit me, I'll leave you to do that and go make a call." He looked at the clock on the wall. "I shall return in half an hour. But I do not wish to rush you. If you cannot decide now, you can go back to your hotel and we can meet again one final time tomorrow. If you have to take the topic back to the United States to consider it further, then you are not committed, and we will drop the subject and never mention it again."

He rose, took the hand of the baroness, and left the room, leaving Andrew and Shanta speechless. It was clear to them that he was not about to follow them through a soul-searching process as to whether or not they were committed—he was not going to waste time on such things. They had to decide.

Andrew poured another glass of bourbon for liquid courage, arose slowly with the drink in hand, and went to the window to look out at the pounding rain. Shanta came to his side and put her arms around him.

Andrew spoke outward toward the window. "He makes a point. How can we have anything to do with a plan that would kill Chinese in Tibet, even if they are communists, when the Dalai Lama would never approve?"

"When someone breaks into your home to rob, rape, and kill you, aren't you justified in doing violence to the person to stop it?" Shanta said. "And isn't that what is going on in Tibet? The Dalai Lama has called for immediate action. If none is taken now, Tibet and the Tibetan culture will be lost forever. The throne of the Reincarnate is lost to those horrible communists. If we do something soon, then He can return, His teachings can proliferate, and the Tibetan culture can be restored. I say we do whatever it takes to get Him back to where He belongs. Let's do it!"

Both of them watched and listened to the heavy Taipei rain beating against the window, wondering about what it would be like to take any part in anything on such a grand scale. Andrew turned around to look at her, placing him only inches from her face. She leaned forward and kissed him on the mouth in a long, slow kiss. That was the first time they had kissed.

When their lips parted, he said, "All right."

Shanta pulled him in again and kissed him in commitment. The tropical Taipei storm pounded against the window, and a decision had been made that would make a great change in the world, but they did not know yet how. Shanta went to make herself some more of the irresistible Oolong tea, but Andrew, less confident, turned and looked out the window as the mesmerizing rain pounded on it, wondering what he was getting himself into.

When the baron and baroness returned to the office, Andrew was looking out the window, sipping bourbon, and Shanta sitting down, sipping tea. Baron motioned for them to sit at his desk, and then he and the baroness sat behind it. "Have you had sufficient time, or would you like to go talk it over until tomorrow?"

Shanta answered for them. "We've decided to proceed."

Baron looked very intently at them both. He made a final decision that he would take the assignment, his most ambitious ever, and then stood up. He raised one hand with an extended finger on it up as high as his head and, raising his voice as well, said, "I, and only I, Baron Von Limbach, may be able to accomplish what you seek. If you accept my terms, in a short while, if I succeed, a very large number of the communist implants of Chinese in Tibet will die, and those that do not will flee to save their lives. This will leave the door open for the Dalai Lama to return. I do not promise what the Holy Man will do, as that is up to Him. But without Chinese communists in Tibet, He will never have such an opportunity again, and He will most likely take advantage of it—but, again, that part is up to Him. As to how to remove the Chinese, it is best that I do not tell you. Of course, you will come to find out. I'll tell you that it will not be by a nuclear bomb, or any bomb, and that the method will protect the Tibetans.

"There are a few contingencies which could prevent my success, but you must share in that risk. I require a non-refundable wire transfer of twenty five million dollars that will be paid into a bank in a country that does not disclose banking activities to other countries. I'll tell you where. This is necessary for the initial expenses of the effort. If everything goes well, and the contingencies are overcome, then in several weeks, or perhaps longer, I'll notify you where to wire transfer an additional sum of one hundred million dollars, which will have to be done within three days of when I notify you.

"This sum will be held by the bank in a form of escrow. It will be paid to a very discrete banker that I know, with instructions that, if within a month, the majority of

Chinese are dying or fleeing Tibet, and the Dalai Lama is invited or allowed to return, even if for a limited stay, the remaining money is to be paid over to me. If not, then the one hundred million will be returned to you and the effort will have failed. However, once again I must warn you, even if the Dalai Lama is invited to return, I cannot guarantee that he *will* return."

Andrew exhaled. "Phew! That is a lot of money!"

Baron looked at him. "Master Saunders, you are worth billions. The sum I ask is a bargain price for an entire country. The natural resources alone are worth billions, which of course replenish, and of course you are seeking to reinstate, or at least halt the extermination of, the Tibetan culture, which cannot be said to have any price of redemption."

Shanta looked at Andrew in awe, as she had no idea of the magnitude of his wealth—the number was staggering.

"A number of connections will be used up in this endeavor, as a number of those involved will have to flee and stay hidden," Baron told them. "And certainly this task may not be used as a reference for future business. If I undertake this task, it may be my last. I would ask for much more if I were younger, but the price I ask, after considerable expenses, will have to support me for my remaining years. My intention is to do this without leaving any way for anyone to determine that anyone is behind it.

"But there must be absolutely no one else informed of this at any time, and that includes the Dalai Lama as well. If it's suspected that anyone is behind it, and you jeopardize those involved by letting out information that could lead to a world-wide manhunt, those involved in the project will eliminate you as witnesses.

"You may count on this. You would do best not to discuss it even between yourselves, once things begin to happen, to avoid anyone overhearing. This means that you can never mention anything about it for the rest of your lives. If you were ever to confess your involvement as some sort of penance, you will be sought out and killed by those involved and, if they do not get to your first and a government arrests you, then you will be sent to China for a quick trial and execution. You must not underestimate my warnings. Are you certain that you are capable of holding your tongues forever?"

Andrew looked at Shanta, and she took his hand for support. She nodded at him. "We can."

Baron looked to Andrew for his commitment as well.

"Let's do it." Andrew said.

"Do you accept my terms?" Baron then asked.

"Mr. Eschmann said I can trust you," Andrew said. "I accept."

"I'll prepare written instructions for you before you leave as to where the money is to be wire transferred. Once the deposit of twenty five million is transferred, I'll begin. There need be no further communication between us until I'm ready. At that time I'll advise you where to send the balance. My timing is very important, and there can be no delays in the transfer of the one hundred million. It must be wired transferred within three days of my notification, so you must have it ready in advance. I'll provide you with a cellular phone for this purpose only before you leave. I'll call you on that phone when I'm ready. After that call, then destroy the phone and discard its remains where they cannot be found."

"Agreed," Andrew said. "I'll have the twenty five million transferred to you when I return."

When they left, Tak asked him, "I'm very interested to learn how you will kill Communist Chinese in Tibet. How do you intend to do it?"

"I know of a scientist in a place called Kazakhstan that has a unique ability. He can make a race-specific Ebola that will only kill one race and no others. I'll take you there when I hire him if the Americans send me the retainer I asked for."

"How many Chinese do you have to kill to accomplish what you want to do?" Tak asked.

"It has to be a large enough number to be considered an out-of-control epidemic. Probably several hundred thousand out of the seven-and-a-half million occupying Tibet will be enough."

"Is killing necessary to accomplish your goal?"

"The communists have no legal or moral right to occupy Tibet. It's not like they are innocents. They would expand into Taiwan in a heartbeat if they thought they could get away with it. Governments all over the world have tried, unsuccessfully, to get the Dalai Lama back into Tibet. My method, if I can pull it off, will work. But I do have to create the epidemic for it to work. By comparison, you say your captain might wipe out all humans on the planet if you were killed here. That's over seven billion, and that does not count all the neat dogs people have as pets. What do you say to that?"

"I see your point. Will it be interesting to go to Kazakhstan?"

"Oh yes. However, I have not been there myself."

He rang Mei Ling on the intercom.

She was already informed as to what to do. She walked in with another box, identical to the one given Shanta, and handed it to Baron.

He then handed it to Tak, and said with a big smile, "Did you think you would be left out?"

Tak opened it with childlike excitement, took out the exotic scarf, and wrapped it around her as Shanta had done, turning about.

"Marriage is expensive," Baron said. "And, if I keep this up, I'm going to have to buy you a bigger satchel for your return."

⌘

Just two days later, Mei Ling came into Baron's office. "I have confirmation of a wire transfer of twenty five million United States Dollars to your usual offshore account."

"Thank you, Mei Ling."

When she left, he checked the Internet to find the time in Kazakhstan, picked up his phone, and placed a call.

Dr. Volkova answered the call from someone who was speaking in Russian, asking for Dr. Dorogomilov.

She hurried for Dr. Dorogomilov. "Borislav, there is a phone call for you from Taiwan."

"Who can possibly be calling me from Taiwan?" Dorogomilov wondered.

"He says his name is Baron Von Limbach, and he speaks Russian."

"A baron?" Dr. Dorogomilov stopped what he was doing and went to take the unusual call. "This is Dr. Borislav Dorogomilov."

"Dr. Dorogomilov, I'm Baron Von Limbach. I have the advantage of knowing about you and your ability, but I doubt that you know of me. I'm interested in speaking to you about a project. It cannot be discussed by phone. If you are interested, I can be there in a few days."

"I could be very interested."

"Good. My staff will confirm the arrival date and time and call you on this number."

"The local airport is now unmanned, without a tower, and the runway is in disrepair," Dr. Dorogomilov advised. "A private jet cannot land here or the potholes will damage the landing gear. If you are planning to fly in, you can only do that in an Antonov AN-2. Are you familiar with that airplane?"

"Yes, I know it. I'll fly to Astana and charter one of those."

"How long will you be staying?"

"Two days, three days at most, depending on our talks. Can you reserve a place for me for two and, oh yes, and a place for the pilots of the Antonov?"

"The spring holiday is about to begin, but I can arrange it."

Baron ended the call and pressed a button on his phone.

Mei Ling appeared. "Yes, sir?"

"Call the baroness down from upstairs. She's on the Internet. Then I want you to make reservations for her and me to go to Astana, Kazakhstan, with no unnecessary stops, starting tomorrow. Then hire a private Antonov AN-2 airplane out of Astana to meet us at Astana to take us to Stepnogorsk, Kazakhstan. Make sure the Antonov will be there and ready for us. I want two pilots. Leave the return open. My host there will book us a room, as the spring fair is about to begin."

Tak appeared with a cheerful smile and sat down in front of his desk.

"How have the Internet searches been going for you?"

"I'm fascinated with the incredible amount of serious crime, especially those called serial murderers and serial rapists. I had no idea there was so much of that."

"Well, welcome to Earth. But, Tak, I think I may have something you may find very interesting. I have to go to yet another part of the world, where things are yet even different. It is called Kazakhstan. There I will see if I can find a way to do what the Americans want. We'll leave tomorrow, and you will get to experience a spring fair there called a Nauryz, which is very much different than what you have seen so far, and I think it will enrich your views on humans."

"Sounds wonderful."

# CHAPTER 14

octors Borislav Dorogomilov and Anastasiya Volkova," the Kazakhstani official announced to Christine Rhyes-Walters of the American Department of State at the hotel reception room. Present were two other governmental officials from Kazakhstan and two from the US, in addition to Rhyes-Walters. The doctors wanted the meeting to include Building 221, the ostensible purpose to show the testing of the fungi to kill poppies, but the real motive was to keep US money coming in. The tour of 221 included the frightening ten five-thousand gallon anthrax mixing vats, an impressive sight. Although there were interpreters, the doctors spoke in English to their sponsoring country's representatives. Rhyes-Walters wore a blue business suit, a blue skirt, and jacket, with a white shirt. She had gained weight since she bought the suit, and the skirt stretched out a bit at the seams. The jacket would not close due to the same extra fifteen pounds.

The inexperienced and overconfident Rhyes-Walters announced herself and her purpose as though the doctors had no idea why she was there.

As the group wandered about the lab, fascinated by the huge anthrax vats, Dr. Dorogomilov said quietly to Dr. Volkova, "The Idiots! They can't even stop the stealing of cars in the region, with the cars going mostly into Russia. How on earth does this idiotic, infantile woman think she is going to make any dent in the business of those who deal in drugs? Perhaps I should give the woman a little scare on the ability of the lab to start up again, in order to keep the money coming."

When they gathered, Dr. Dorogomilov did just that. "This is a complete, level four, bio-hazard lab. The lab and its equipment here can make the lab operate it as it did before. It is equipped with a pressure system and pressure suits to study and mass produce most any biological warfare agent. The suits we wore here during such studies were pressurized. In case there was a puncture, the air would tend to force any biological agent out, instead of in, to protect the person inside.

"As there are various instruments used in such studies that are sharp, cuts and punctures are not altogether rare. I headed the studies of bio-warfare right here and also led anthrax mass production. Many different types of biological weapons can be made here. But now, I'm working with nominal resources, developing fungi that attacks poppies, to be sprayed on poppies in the fields to curtail the opium trade and yet not harm the environment, people, or small animals."

Frightened by the idea of mass production of biological weapons, Rhyes-Walters changed the subject. "How is the progress with the fungi?"

"I could easily develop something to kill all the poppies in the world," he responded. "But my task is to develop an environmentally safe fungi that attacks poppies but yet is harmless to people, animals, and other crops, not merely another agent orange. I have made very good progress and can show you some of the effects right here."

He then led the ridiculous diplomat around the narrow lab aisles with Dr. Volkova to show her effects of his new fungi on poppy and on control plants and animals. There were live poppy specimens grown under special lamps for the tests and dead plants to show the results. There were also animal cages for rats and animals for testing by exposure, something that would horrify many Westerners. It was all staged.

Dr. Dorogomilov was, without question, a genius. And even though he was not a salesman, just having the opportunity to hear what he was doing was impressive. Rhyes-Walters was, indeed, impressed.

Following the lectured tour, they came back to the front of the building. Rhyes-Walters turned to Dr. Dorogomilov. "I'm favorably impressed. Have you any idea when you might have a final formula to recommend for production?"

She had gotten down to business. After all, that would be just about the only question put to her when she got back.

Even though Dr. Dorogomilov did not like such questions, he had to answer them to keep his funding and, having been under the Soviet Union's rule, he was very used to them.

And she could not go back and simply report that she had seen research and that funding should continue indefinitely. So she would have to bring something back.

On the other hand, Dr. Dorogomilov had already created the fungi that was environmentally safe and killed only poppies, which was safe for animals and humans, but he did not want to reveal that as it would cut off the funding money, whereupon he would lose the lab and his irreplaceable specimens of the exotic viruses that would then have to be destroyed. In addition, he resented the ignorance of these interrogations.

"Madame Diplomat," he said to her in English. "I'm a scientist, not a businessman. I have only one assistant scientist, Dr. Volkova, and practically no support staff to run controls and variables. If I had a dozen qualified assistants, I could expedite things greatly. But we have made progress and should soon have what you seek."

"I certainly think that you are working on a worthy cause, and keeping this lab doing something constructive is very beneficial," the diplomat replied. "I'll recommend that, pending a progress report to be reviewed by our own scientists, funding assistance be continued for the fungi."

When they all exited, Drs. Dorogomilov and Volkova stood together and watched, and then turned to wave goodbye as they left in a motorcade to Astana.

Dr. Dorogomilov put his hand on Dr. Volkova's backside and gave her a squeeze—sort of like the Russian kiss to the cheek, but this to another cheek. "God, it is good to get rid of those assholes. When does this Baron arrive?"

"The day after tomorrow," Dr. Volkova said.

❧❧❧

Tak and Baron disembarked from the commercial jet at Astana, Kazakhstan, and entered the modest terminal. Baron led Tak to a counter where the prearranged Antonov AN-2 flight to Stepnogorsk would be confirmed. The only person at the modest desk was a tall and robust woman with enormous breasts like watermelons. She greeted them and led them out on the tarmac.

On the tarmac stood an outrageous biplane, the Antonov AN-2. Over thirteen feet tall, it had a wingspan of sixty feet. It was a medium blue color and did not look like any other aircraft. Tak followed Baron and the large-breasted woman to the huge biplane and stared at it in apprehension. "What is this thing?"

"This was designed at the end of World War II, and flies at only one hundred twenty five miles an hour if there is no headwind," Baron explained. "We need a plane like this, as the landing strip in Stepnogorsk has not been kept up since the airport was closed a long time ago, and the extremely cold winters and hot summers have taken their toll on the runway. This is the only airplane that can land there. It'll be a much shorter trip in this plane—and more fun."

The pilots arrived, having finished studying the weather updates, and stood at attention to greet their most important guest.

Baron sized them up, realizing that there was no practical way to realistically assess their ability, and motioned for them to proceed. They loaded the bags and did a final check of the plane.

"We're ready to go now, sir," the captain said.

Baron and Tak climbed into the plane and took seats a couple of rows behind the two pilots. A tail-dragger, a plane with a tail wheel, the aircraft had its nose pointed up when at rest, and the two were leaning back in their seats. They would remain so until takeoff when the tail was raised up in flight.

The captain began the starter sequence, pumping the gas lever, turning on switches, and working the throttles a few times.

Then he pulled the starter flywheel lever and the flywheel began to spool up, whining as it did so. After 15 seconds, he engaged the flywheel. The massive 4-bladed prop began to spin and the huge radial engine belched, starting with a huge cloud of black smoke, followed by a roar—like that of a lion.

Tak feared that she might not live through the flight in the strange aircraft. But as the biplane taxied and then lifted into the air on its way through the Kazak Mountains, she was finally able to relax.

Over the noise of the engine, she called, "Baron, can you tell me about this aircraft?"

"Sure. It's powered by a Russian made copy of the American Wright Cyclone radial engine, provided to the Russians to copy at the end of World War II. The engine is reliable but goes through a huge amount of oil. It holds thirty two gallons of oil, but can still run on only six. It burns forty five gallons of fuel an hour when cruising. It can take off with as much as twelve thousand five hundred pounds and has special flaps and wing slats, which change the airfoil to add more lift to enable it to land on very short, rough, landing strips. It can land in a headwind with no discernible stall speed."

"Stall speed?" she said apprehensively.

"The speed at which a plane quits flying, due to low speed, so to speak. But don't worry. We won't fall out of the air. I promise"

"Why are we taking this strange aircraft?"

"The runway where we are going to land has been neglected since 1991 when the Soviet Union pulled out. I'm told that the runway has holes and is in bad repair. But don't worry. This special plane will land so slowly that there is no danger. It will be a piece of cake."

"A piece of cake," she repeated.

As the huge biplane worked its way through the mountains, the wind occasionally bouncing and tipping its wings, its Kazak-Russian pilots steadfastly kept it on course.

The airfield at Stepnogorsk finally appeared. The captain circled the field once, below which was a meter long strip of red cloth blowing downwind as a makeshift windsock put there by Dr. Dorogomilov. Off to the side of the runway were two cars, two men and a woman standing together. The pilot turned to base leg and set the plane up for a short field landing with full flaps down. When he slowed to forty miles per hour on the final approach, the leading edge slats on the wings extended by elastic bungees, providing a huge lift factor for slow landings by the increased airfoil. The slats would have to be reset from the ground after landing.

Landing into the headwind at the windy airport, the plane gently kissed the ground at the speed of a brisk walk.

Tak let out an audible sigh of relief.

After taxiing the plane to what used to be the terminal, the pilot shut down the monster radial engine. The silence was deafening.

Baron exited and Tak hurriedly followed. The waiting couple approached.

Baron presumed these were their hosts and said in his perfect, unaccented Russian, "Doctors Borislav Dorogomilov and Anastasiya Volkova, I presume?"

"Welcome to Stepnogorsk, Baron," Dr. Dorogomilov greeted in Russian. "We are indeed honored to have an aristocrat as our distinguished guest. How was the trip?"

"Not too bad, for such an old-fashioned aircraft." Then looking at Dr. Volkova so as not to ignore her, Baron said, "And you must be the talented Dr. Anastasiya Volkova. How do you do?"

"It's such an honor to meet an aristocrat," she said.

Baron, never outdone at introductions, said, "On the contrary. It's my honor to be in the company of such distinguished scientists." He turned to Tak and then back to them and, switching to English, said, "Please allow me to present my wife, Baroness Tak Von Limbach. Madam does not speak Russian."

Tak was beginning to fall into, and enjoy, the role. She nodded to acknowledge them as though a baroness in reality.

Realizing that English was the way to politely continue, Dr. Dorogomilov switched to English. "I speak English. The majority of the medicine and scientific journals other than in Russian are in English." He gestured over at the cars. "I've hired a separate car and driver here for the pilots, who will take them to accommodations as soon as they have secured the plane. They will stay at a different hotel than you and madam."

That, of course, meant cheaper, but Baron did not mind that the pilots would not be staying at his hotel, as this would minimize their knowledge of his activities.

Baron gave the pilots instructions. "Tie down the plane for tonight, but in the morning, go for fuel to the nearest spot to be sure we have enough for the return trip to Astana and return here. We will be leaving in two or three days."

Baron was shown to the front seat of one of the cars, Tak and Dr. Volkova to the rear, and with Dr. Dorogomilov, driving without a chauffeur so as not to be overheard, they headed for the hotel.

En route Baron said, "Doctor, I was very sorry to learn

of the passing of your lovely wife, Karina. I offer my most sincere condolences."

"Thank you," Dorogomilov said with a note of sadness. "I miss her greatly. But I see you are well informed and have the advantage of me. I know nothing of you, Baron, only that you must be a very important and powerful person."

"You flatter me," Baron said. He continued to show his knowledge by saying, "I hope that I've not come at an inopportune time as Nauryz starts tomorrow."

"How informed you are, Baron. I hope you and madam will be able to stay to enjoy the festival.

"We'll see," Baron said. "We may stay for a part of it."

To entice them to stay on, the doctor said, "Following the outdoor national games at the festival tomorrow, my deceased wife's family is having a special dinner. Would you be able to attend?"

"A Dastarkhan?" Baron asked.

"You know of Dastarkhan?" Dr. Dorogomilov was even more impressed. "You know this country as though you were local."

"It's my business to know of the people and places that I do business with."

"You will be the most honored guest at the dinner."

"But you pay me much too much tribute by making me the 'most honored guest.' I'm certainly not worthy of such honor." That was one thing Baron said that he certainly did not mean.

After he and Tak were settled in their rooms, Baron opened a bottle of red wine from his case—as the local wine was the equivalent of camel piss–and poured two glasses.

∞

Come morning, while sitting in the lobby, waiting for Dr. Dorogomilov, Tak said to Baron, "'Dorogomilov' is an interesting name. Does it have some particular background or significance?"

Baron chuckled. "Yes. It's Russian and means 'the cute one.' Russian names often have meanings like that."

Tak looked perplexed. "He does not seem to be cute."

Dr. Dorogomilov approached at that time. They both rose to greet him.

"Good morning, doctor," Baron said in Russian.

"Did you both sleep well?" the doctor asked.

"I did, but let me ask Madam Baroness." He switched to English, "Tak, the doctor is asking if you slept well."

Having practiced in her room, she said, "Da, spacibo."

Both the doctor and Baron laughed at her speaking Russian unexpectedly, and Tak joined in.

"Baron and Baroness," the doctor said, in English. "I'll now take you to my lab."

୧୨୧୨

The climate in eerie Building 221 was always gloomy, and the interior was musty and dank. The beauty of spring always found sites other than P.O. Box 2079, the only address the former anthrax mass production facility ever had.

Following a tour of 221, requested by Baron, Drs. Dorogomilov and Volkova, Baron, and Tak sat at a laboratory table as they sipped tea served in small glasses with silver base holders, Russian style.

Baron looked at Dr. Volkova and then at Dr. Dorogomilov, his signal that he was about to conduct business and a query as to whether Dr. Volkova should remain or leave.

Dr. Dorogomilov understood the silent inquiry. "Anastasiya has my complete confidence and will be working with me on every aspect."

"Madam Baroness is also my assistant in this project, and we can rely on her confidence," Baron said, regarding Tak.

Baron then announced why he was there. "Doctor, I'm aware of your achievements with Ebola of which you never told the Kremlin."

Dr. Dorogomilov arched an eyebrow as he waited to hear just how much Baron knew of his super-secret work.

"Doctor, I can put your ability to make race-specific Ebola to use."

Dr. Dorogomilov felt he had to probe the security leak of his secrets. "How do you know of this?"

"Please forgive me, Doctor, but it's best to keep such matters undisclosed. I make my living by being able to acquire such information. But rest assured that just because I'm aware of what you can do, it does not mean that it is known by many."

Dr. Dorogomilov certainly could keep secrets. He had worked for the Soviets on their most super-secret projects in bio-warfare. He wondered if perhaps the leak was from a former colleague he had worked with, which could only be one of about three, now off doing research elsewhere in Russia. Trying to guess as to which one of them might have sold such a tip made his mind very active. Baron dealt in arms and related high technology and ran in such circles. He might have learned of Dr. Dorogomilov years earlier, before the collapse of the Soviet Union, from his formidable resources and contacts. No doubt it had to be one of his ex-colleagues, and then only fragmented information that he could do it, that could not have been confirmed—perhaps only strongly suspected. But yet, here was Baron, presumably with money, claiming to know—and he did know. How?

"Am I correct?" Baron asked. "Do you have Ebola that can be made race specific?"

"I'll be back in a few minutes with your answer." The doctor got up and went to a different room, returning after ten minutes with a sealed glass jar a foot high. Inside was a second jar, isolated from the side by pieces of foam, as an additional safety measure against breaking, in case the jar was dropped. Inside was a black mass of several pounds.

"Baron, what you see here is the most deadly virus ever. It's stronger than the famous Ebola Zaire." He set it down carefully on the table and guarded it with his hands rather than passing it to Baron, to avoid it being dropped. "I'm the only source of this in the world. This is my own variant of Ebola Zaire, and not only much more virulent, but I, and only I, can make this race specific. And the RNA has been altered so that it will remain race specific after it finds its target race and replicates."

Tak and Baron moved in to have a closer look, but Dr. Dorogomilov stopped their progress. "Forgive me for not letting you handle it, but you will appreciate that if you were to drop it, we would all die."

"So my information is correct," Baron said. "Doctor, would you be interested in applying your skills?"

Dr. Dorogomilov sat, trying his best to hide his enthusiasm at finally being presented with the accolade that he was so clearly entitled to. "What do you have in mind?"

"I present you with an opportunity to realize your genius. I need a race-specific Ebola. If you do this, you can retire and live the rest of your life in luxury."

Dr. Dorogomilov, his respiratory system on medical alert, but well hidden, asked, "What do you consider luxury?"

"Five million United States Dollars."

Still trying to act cool, as though he was disinterested, he said, matter-of-factly, "You have my attention. What race?"

"Chinese. I want you to create a race-specific Ebola that will infect only the Han Chinese race. I need enough of it to spread about Tibet in a short time so that it kills a significant number of the seven and a half million Chinese living in Tibet, placed there by the Communist Chinese Government, enough to create an epidemic and a scare. The Chinese that do not contract it will flee the country back to China in fear. This has nothing to do with any hatred for

Chinese, but only to pave the way for the return of the Dalai Llama."

Dr. Dorogomilov's unusual eyes opened wide. When working for the Soviets, all he'd gotten was his modest pay but he had many privileges, and he had become very bitter since that was all gone, as was his car and income. This would be the retirement to which he was entitled. His mind began to drift to far away islands he had only seen in pictures.

Baron suspected that the doctor might be puzzled as to how to handle so much money and not be suspected of something, such as drug involvement, should he begin to spread such wealth around. "Doctor, I'm also aware that you would be suspected and caught if you were to receive such a sum here in Kazakhstan. I'm aware that the tax collectors here in Kazakhstan collaborate illegally with banks on how much money companies have, sharing arrangements between the two, based on corruption. The money will be put in an account for you elsewhere. I can also assist with travel visas for you, if necessary, to travel from Russia or Kazakhstan to some places that are not restricted."

Dr. Dorogomilov looked at Dr. Volkova, who wore a sullen expression, as she was being left behind, and then said to Baron, "Would you get Anastasiya a travel visa and passport also?" he asked, forgetting himself and referring to her by her first name.

"Of course," Baron said and gave her a smile to let her know she was to be included.

Hearing that she was not to be excluded from her lover's new wealth and future, Dr. Volkova lost a little self-control. She reached over and squeezed Dr. Dorogomilov's leg.

"Now, can you do it?" Baron then asked.

The doubt cast by the question changed the expression on Dr. Dorogomilov's already bizarre-looking face to one of slight contempt at the lack of respect for his genius.

He gathered himself, trying not to show offense, realizing that customers for his miracles were not exactly in line outside the door. "Can I do it? Can I do it? I'm the only one ever to have created a specific monoclonal antibody and a method of linking it to the Ebola virus. I'm the only one in the world with a working inventory of Ebola Zaire, as well as variants, the most virulent of which I have made myself. The closest achievement elsewhere is in the primitive accomplishment of using monoclonal antibodies with CD 20, in patients with non-Hodgkins lymphoma—an injection of that locates and kills the cancer. That is the one that Jackie Kennedy died of. Apart from that, no one else has ever done anything even close to what I have done. And I've done it working with the most deadly of substances on the planet. You'd be surprised how difficult it is to work with something that you can only get near in a pressure suit and in a bio-hazard-level-four-containment facility. Any mistake, however small, is fatal. I can create an Ebola that is race specific and will only kill a given race.

"But," he continued, "I've accomplished an exponentially greater feat. I've been able to modify the RNA of the Ebola, so that it will remain linked to the antibody upon reproduction. This means that the Ebola will continue to remain race specific when it kills its host and reproduces. Thereby, it will only kill the target race and continue to do so. This is my achievement!"

He looked at Baron to see his reaction and, seeing none, he decided to boast and up the ante of his miracles. "I've gone still further. I've even found unique antigens in the human brain that are associated with extremes in thinking patterns and have produced antibodies that can be linked to Ebola to go after such antigens. I did this with prisoners from Russia just before the breakup. I've discovered that there are two distinct types of brains, those who engage in extreme religious thinking, and those who do not. Those who engage in such extreme beliefs have an older type of brain, especially in the limbic system. It's as though evolution is not the same for all, or at least not yet. I have even found parts of the frontal lobes that are active in religious people when praying to God. Religious people have frontal lobe activity when praying to God that is similar to that of talking to people, which means that they envision God as a person. The initial process is Single Photon Emission Computerized Tomography."

And then he dropped a bombshell to clinch the business from Baron. "In other words, Baron, I can create an Ebola that only attacks fanatically religious people."

Baron let his emotion show, which was rare, and said excitedly, "You're joking!"

In a very serious response, the doctor announced, "I do not joke about my work."

Thinking that he might, in the future, find a client who would pay a fortune beyond belief to eradicate Muslim terrorists, Baron asked, "Is that something you have ready to go or can make easily?"

"No, not ready to go. There is one problem with directing it toward the brain, and that is the blood brain barrier. Not everything in the blood gets through to the brain. But I believe I could do that with a change in the RNA. I have already changed the RNA of the Ebola. But religious fanaticism is not what you want to address. The race-specific Ebola you seek would be made to attack organs such as the lungs. That's easy for me.

"For making a race-specific Ebola, I have the Ebola here, and I would only have to make more of it, which I can do. For a given race, I need subjects of that race. You see, the subjects that I have tested are, of course, all dead. Ebola eats its host. I need only make an antibody from a Chinese subject that I can link to the Ebola."

Baron got back to the business at hand and focused on what he needed. "But you have not created a Chinaman-specific Ebola, or have you?"

"Correct."

"Do you know for a fact that you can do it with the Chinese?"

"No question about it. I've worked with a few races, including Mongolians, and have had access to data from others. There are unique proteins in every distinct race. After all, the races are quite different, aren't they?"

The statement was so obviously true that it called for no answer. After a pause, Baron asked, "Explain to me, only a layman, how can it kill only one race and be limited to only that race? Won't this virus spread to others and create a worldwide pandemic?"

"No. I can guarantee that it will not."

"Well, my good Doctor, while I believe you have great credibility, your assurance that it will not end up in a deadly pandemic, out of control, is not exactly the sort of guarantee that I can depend on."

"Well, Baron, this is not the sort of thing that I can apply to a world bank for a guarantee that a race-specific Ebola that I will create will only kill one specific race. Perhaps I'm unable to convince you?"

"I'm not giving up, Doctor. But I want to be convinced that this virus will not become some sort of worldwide virus, killing everyone and not just the Chinese."

"Perhaps the best that I can do to convince you is to explain the basics as to how it is done. Otherwise, I'm unable to give you what you seek."

"Please do."

Dr. Dorogomilov assumed that Baron and his wife would be able to understand, and so he began. "I find a unique protein in one of the organs that does not exist in any other race. From that I make an antibody that will react to that antigen. I then link that antibody to an Ebola particle. Once linked, the particle will not spike, or enter, any other cell in the body that does not contain this unique antigen. Circulating about in a body, if it finds the unique antigen, the antibody is attracted to it, and very strongly. The linked Ebola then spikes the antigen, enters it, and replicates, much the same as ordinary Ebola. It would then become ordinary Ebola and kill anything else, but for the fact that I have been able to alter the RNA of the Ebola so that it continues to be linked upon reproduction. This is my accomplishment."

"I must be able to distribute it," Baron informed him. "My targets are not in a lab. If you can make this for me, what is the best method of distributing the Ebola? Will stomach acid, for example, destroy it?"

"It's true that stomach acid can destroy the linked particle, but I've conducted many actual experiments and found that the subject nearly always becomes infected even if it is subjected to stomach acid. If you put it into a water supply to go into the stomach, it will work, but it would take a considerable amount to create an epidemic. A better way to spread it is via airborne particles which are breathed in and spread into the body via the lungs, very much like a viral pneumonia that spreads into the blood steam and reaches every organ. No matter what the target organ is, it will find it via the bloodstream. So the answer is no."

"How do you go about creating it?" Baron asked.

Having to take a risk and reveal his secrets in order to make something of his genius after so many years and, only having one customer, the doctor went ahead and explained. "I must first have subjects of the target race to obtain tissues from so I can find their unique protein. There are usually a number of unique cells, and I locate one that I believe to be the best candidate for linking."

"What if you find more than one? How do you choose?"

"There are many factors to consider. They range from the physical size of the protein chain, so the resulting linked antibody with Ebola will not be too large to enter the target cell. If you wish to hear more, I'll continue."

"Can this be done with other substances, such as anthrax?" Baron asked.

"Absolutely. I have successfully linked anthrax to monoclonal antibodies. Anthrax, unlike Ebola, lives on very well outside a host. Spores, not anthrax, were found in Egyptian tombs, living thousands of years. Ebola, if you get enough of it around before it is discovered and contained, will infect a large population very fast. It's conceivable that the authorities might not know the Ebola was man made, whereas with anthrax they would know at once."

"Is your Ebola just as deadly as that found at the Ebola River, the Ebola Zaire?" Baron asked.

Dr. Dorogomilov raised his head proudly. "Even more so. Ebola, as I see you already know, was named after the river in Africa where it was first detected. The Soviets used to rush in a team whenever there was an outbreak, ostensibly to render aid, but the real reason was to get samples and bring them to me here at this lab. Unbeknownst to them, or, to anyone, I still have them here, kept alive with animal tissue. The only one I did not keep was the Reston virus found in the Philippine monkey, as that does not kill humans. The problem has to do with the length of the glycoprotein. I've retained the 1976 Ebola from the Yambuku Mission Hospital in Zaire. That was ninety percent fatal. I especially like that one. There are differences in the various viruses, and I use the most deadly. Some, like the Sudan, have only fifty per cent mortality. I've done considerable work on the genes in the Ebola molecule, learning the differences between the structural proteins, the membrane-associated proteins, and the replicating proteins. I've found a way to create a mutation over the years that is even more deadly than Ebola Zaire, with nearly one hundred per cent mortality."

"How long before death once a person is infected?" Baron asked.

"Two to four weeks."

"What about races partially mixed?" Baron asked.

"There will no doubt be some percentage of mixed races in the population you seek to infect, and they may not have the specific protein antigen as exists in the specimens of the Chinese I would use. I've no way of knowing if mixed races will have the same unique protein without testing. If they don't have the same unique protein, they will not be affected."

Tak decided to ask a question. "You say that your variant developed over the years is nearly one hundred per cent effective. But if you would link that to a cell from a Chinaman, is the resultant linked Ebola particle any less potent?"

"Baroness, that's a very informed question. Well, without actually testing the resultant linked virus on subjects, I cannot confirm its virulence, but I do have my earlier work in other races. However, since the new, linked Ebola will not penetrate cells unless it finds a cell or cells that its linked-monoclonal-antibody is attracted to, it could reduce slightly the number of subjects that will be infected with it. On the other hand, because it is so specific, when it does find the unique protein it seeks, it is even more potent at penetrating the membrane and infecting. Rather delightful, don't you think?"

Tak seemed content with the answer. Baron then asked, "What are the initial symptoms when a person contracts it?"

"With non-specific Ebola, the incubation period is usually from as soon as two days to as long as twenty one days, but usually from four to sixteen days. Fever may be detectible after two days. Severe frontal and temporal headaches occur. Generalized aches and pains follow. Watery diarrhea, abdominal pain, nausea, vomiting, dry sore throat, and lack of appetite occur. By day seven, maculopapular rash, that is, raised spots, and thrombocytopenia and hemorrhagic manifestations, especially in the gastrointestinal tract and lungs, with bleeding from all orifices and mucous membranes. By day twelve the skin starts to peel away from the rashes, and there is bleeding. Lesions are caused in almost every organ with necrosis. Although an organ may give way and fluid losses into tissues would be considerable, the effects are so severe that the actual cause of death is normally shock. The pain involved is enormous."

"Is there a worse way to die?" Baron asked.

Dr. Dorogomilov responded with absolutely pure scientific impartiality. "Not that I'm aware of."

"What about the race-specific Ebola?" Baron asked.

"It depends on where the unique antigen protein is found. If found in more than one organ, it will infect each. If in only one, it will only infect the one. For example, if the tissue is kidney, it will only infect the kidneys. Of course, if the kidney, being a very bloody organ, is being consumed by Ebola, and since it regulates many things, the entire body will be affected as the kidney is destroyed by the Ebola. The urine output stops, generalized edema occurs, along with blood pressure fluctuations and other problems, causing certain death. If in the lungs, then you have rupturing of alveoli and capillaries, coughing up blood, frothing of the mouth and nasal passages, difficulty in breathing, and the cause of death is likely to be drowning in one's own blood. Eventually it will consume the entire lungs, even after the person dies. There are other organs to consider if you would care to know."

Baron was content with what he had heard and changed the subject. "What about the life of your variant before it is taken in by the Chinese? How can it be kept alive to distribute it to a whole country before it dies?"

"That, of course, depends on how much of it is made and how many people you can use to disseminate it. Ebola is an interesting virus—it kills its host. People wonder how it exists for the usual three to five years before it pops up again in some African country and kills everyone in the village before it is contained. I have my own theory on that. I think it goes dormant. But what you need to be able to do is to keep it alive until you can get it there and distribute it. The best way to preserve it is to keep it very cold. The colder the better. Ice will work, but if you want to maximize the preservation of the entire stock, then liquid-nitrogen canisters. That can bring it down to about minus two hundred Celsius initially, and keep it very cold for a long time. Exposed to room temperatures, without any host tissue, it has lasted several days in numerous tests, and I've witnessed it lasting more than two weeks.

"But why go into the zone you seek to contaminate

with partially dead Ebola? In order to keep the stock all fresh, go with nitrogen-cooled canisters. Those are your best bet, and you will have one hundred per cent living Ebola, ready to spread about when you get there.

"If you don't spread it about quickly, you will have the government restricting everyone's activities and then it could possibly be contained. Once inside a subject, it then has a host and does not die off as long as the host is alive, or as long as it has tissue to feed on."

"What do you think would be the best method of distribution to an entire country?" Baron asked.

"Getting as many of the target race to get it into their lungs or mouths in as short a time as possible. When taken into the lungs, it enters the bloodstream and infects at once. So people breathing on others works the best. Taking it by food will work, especially if it is breathed into the lungs when tasting or inhaling the odor of the food so it goes into the lungs. Methods of getting it into the mouth result from the person getting it on his hands, which often end up in the mouth or passing it in food which enters the mouth. Sharing food, sex, using the same utensils, all this, in addition to close breathing on others will work. Placed on door knobs, currency, cigarettes, or other objects that are soon thereafter touched will result in infecting most who touch it. You can put a drop of it in fluid form on items at a vendor's food stand.

"Anyone who touches or eats the food that has it will become infected, and then spread it to many. All in all, people are the best vehicles to spread it. The ideal method would be to infect people at crowds, markets, gatherings, and travelers, and to do so at as many places as possible in a few days. The first person infected that enters a hospital will probably infect most everyone in the hospital, as they won't know what they are dealing with."

"Does it take a lot of the virus to infect someone?" Baron asked.

"Not at all. You realize that Ebola is a microscopic-sized item. It's about eight-hundred-five nanometers in length, and eighty nanometers wide. A nanometer is one-billionth of a meter. A single Ebola entering the body can infect and kill, and, unlike a flu virus, being in good health will not prevent it from taking hold and killing. Just ounces could theoretically infect the whole country, if you were able to spread it widely and rapidly. I can make it in a fluid medium and, bringing it in with liquid-nitrogen canisters disguised as mineral water or liquor bottles, for example, should work."

Tak realized that Baron was still learning about it and decided to ask her own questions. "I'm interested to hear more of the details of how the race-specific Ebola is made."

"Certainly. Actually, the techniques are very simple, but of course I know what to look for, having done it before. The hard part is the fact that it needs to be done in a level four bio-warfare high containment center like this, which would take several billion dollars today to make new.

"I first get tissues from the target race, which in your case would be the Han Chinese. I'll look at the stomach, lungs, and liver, but other organs work as well. I look for unique antigen protein of the target race. Some are much better than others for passing along the infection rapidly, and the lungs are the fastest for an application such as this because, if infected in the lungs, the infected person will cough up an aerosol of contaminated fluid which will infect others very well.

"To find the unique cells, I sonify the cells—that is to subject them to sonic waves, which makes up a homogene-ous paste of them. Then I begin looking for something unique about the cells. In this case, we have to find antigens that are not found in Tibetans. While I've done this with a few Chinese, but no Tibetans, I predict that I'll find just what I need. The Tibetans must not have the same antigen.

"After I sonify the cells, the protein is then mixed with an eluent solution, and put in a high pressure column. This displaces the cells according to weight. Then a tiny fraction of each is taken from the bottom of the column in a fraction collector tube—the most would be, say, five hundred to a thousand, but I can usually do it with a hundred as I've done it so often. Then the optical density of each sample is tested against a standard of two-hundred-seventy. Light is passed through each tube and recorded optically."

Dr. Dorogomilov stopped to prepare a freehand graph on paper. He drew an X and Y axis, and a hypothetical horizontal line across it with several vertical sections, one of which was very high.

"These elevations I have drawn are similar to what I'll find eventually in the sample antigens. Now, of course, I'm simplifying things for you, but the result is the locating of the unique peaks of cells, until I select one that is not found in the control, that is, the Tibetans."

"I understand," Tak said.

"Good. Now, once this process is done, the unique protein is concentrated," the doctor continued. "It's then put into a dialysis tubing that will retain the proteins but will allow the salts and electrolytes to pass. Then the solution goes into a beaker with ammonium bicarbonate and is freeze dried, just like foods at the market. That is called lyophilization. The result is a powder of a race-specific antigen, in this case Chinese."

Baron smiled. "A very special freeze-dried substance, indeed!"

"Yes, very special," the doctor answered. "This special powder is then dissolved with saline and injected into the inner canthus of the eye of a mouse. Detecting this substance in the mouse's eye, the mouse's spleen begins producing antibodies. The cells can then be identified from the spleen of the mouse that interact with the original antigen, the hybridomas yielding the monoclonal antibody. The identification has to be done by reading the original antigen peak, another process similar to the first one."

"How do you reproduce the antibodies?" Tak asked.

"Now come the rabbits," he responded. "The peritoneal

cavity of the rabbit is an excellent incubator for monoclonal antibody production. So I inject it there and let it grow, and the abdomens of the rabbits will be swollen with it. With a peritoneal tap, I remove the antibodies and put them in put them in the ultracentrifuge. The antibodies go to the top and the cells to the bottom with the help of ammonium sulfate. This is now concentrated, but not pure.

"You also need Ebola in sufficient quantity, depending on the size of the place you wish to infect. This is done with the monkeys. I infect the monkeys with Ebola in whose bodies it grows rapidly, even continuing after they die by living on the dead tissue. This means turning part of the lab into a deadly zoo. The monkeys will grow the Ebola and infect others in the cage. I then take the tissues much in the same manner as the non-infectious procedure, segregate the Ebola from it, and cleanse them. Extreme precautions are needed, so as not to allow a single Ebola particle loose or to come in contact with one of us, which makes this delicate work. One mistake and we all die.

"Then, I'll have the Ebola in quantity as well as the unique antibody of the target race. The two are then linked together chemically and reproduced in incubators. If anything goes wrong and Dr. Volkova and I become infected, you will not get your Ebola.

Tak looked at Baron, as though to communicate that she had no further questions and was satisfied that the doctor had a credible presentation.

Baron summed it up. "You have created a magnificent biological weapon. The beauty is that a small crew, disguised as tourists, for example, can take in Ebola into a country, spread it about, and not get infected themselves. They would never be suspected since there would be no trail back to anyone, as they would be long gone with so many other tourists. There is no other weapon like it. Terrorists would love to get their hands on this. This is so unlike an atomic weapon, for example, as the type of radiation can be easily traced back to the reactor where it was made and all involved would surely be caught. What do you need to undertake the project?"

"Money for some new equipment and for supplies. I'll need five expendable Chinese and two Tibetans, but they must not be related by blood. I'll take tissue from the subjects without killing them, and then use them later for testing on how well the Ebola works, which will kill them. There are jail cells here in the building that we used to put criminals in that were sent to me for experimentation. I'll need several very good security guards to help me with the Chinese, as they will object to being cut on for body parts. I'll also need to hire some help, but that is available here. However, I need money to pay them."

"What equipment do you need? Baron asked. "I thought that you would have most everything here in this billion dollar lab."

"There are vast resources here such as the electron microscope. But the primary asset is the level four containment of the place. That's the huge expense. There is simply no way to create a large quantity of Ebola without such a place. As for equipment, there have been advances in the equipment that, if I had it, would make the work go more quickly and more efficiently. I'd like to have a new ultra-centrifuge. That is one that slings the samples to one hundred thousand times normal gravity. The one left here only goes to forty thousand gravities. That is very helpful in isolating different parts of the tissue based on their density.

"Then I'd like to have one of the latest laser densitometers. I have a column chromatography and a gamma ray counter. I'd like a new cell fluorescent sorter—a fluorescent material can be added to the proteins, and actually lights up in the device so the proteins can actually be seen, and is very helpful in observing the linked virus to the antibody in the linking process."

The doctor became a little excited, like a kid in a candy store, adding whatever he could think of to his shopping list of goodies. "I've got a C02 water-jacketed humidifier which provides an atmosphere in which cells will grow very well. But a new spectrophotometer would be helpful. And, of course, I'll need supplies and lots of mice, rabbits, and monkeys. I already have cages here for them, but I might need to convert some rooms to large cages when I go into production. Oh, yes, and I would like to have two of the latest and fastest computers available. I'll put Russian Windows on one, and English on another, as I need both, and the two versions sometimes conflict. And, of course, the expendable subjects.

"I should buy a few pressure suits, as mine are old. I can possibly get by without getting the best of everything, but if I have what I want, and if you can afford everything, I can almost assure you that it will go very quickly. With the right equipment, I can probably isolate what I want in a matter of days.

"Then I'll need operating money for wages, but the wages are very low here. I would use as few people as possible, and limit their knowledge. I would tell them that I'm working on the fungi for the project of eradicating the opium poppy for the Americans, which the Americans are presently funding."

The doctor seemed to have completed his shopping list.

"How much will all that cost?" Baron asked.

The doctor looked up and calculated in his head. "I'd say about two hundred fifty thousand dollars, not counting the cost of help and local expenses. Three hundred thousand US Dollars altogether will be sufficient. As for the animals, the cost is not high, but they have to be flown in so they don't die in transit. There are places that grow mice and rabbits for labs, and those are easy to get. However, the monkeys are more of a problem. They can be bought in the Philippines, India, and Africa, and have to be flown in special cages. Not all the airlines like handling monkeys in cages, as you can appreciate."

Baron was relieved that it would only take so little for the equipment. "Here's my proposal. I'll pay for all the equipment from a special account, which will not go through the corrupt Kazakhstan government or banks. For your expenses locally, I will give you one hundred thousand US Dollars now in cash. As the equipment will come from Europe or the US, the payments made will go unnoticed and the arrival of equipment can be explained as from the US money for your fungi research. I will send some men here with the subjects, to assist with the handling of them and to keep an eye on the progress.

"I'll get you the Chinese and Tibetan subjects at my expense, within two to three weeks. They will be delivered here through Russia via Vladivostok on the TransSiberian Express.

"The deposit will be in the account in a few days. I want everything set up at once. I want you to obtain the nitrogen canisters. I'll get labels made to disguise them as Russian mineral water. They can be large sizes, perhaps a liter and a half on the outside. You will notify me when you are ready to 'bottle' your samples, and I'll have several men here to collect them. I'll have a crew ready to go on a tourist trip to Tibet and they'll take the bottles.

"When the product is shown to work in Tibet, the sum of five million additional US dollars will be deposited into the same account. I'll get started on travel visas for you and Dr. Volkova now, so I'll need copies of your birth certificates and Kazakhstan passports to take with me." He thought this would also make it easier for him to find them in case they bolted with his money. In which case, they would soon thereafter die at the hands of the Russian mafia.

"Agreed," Dr. Dorogomilov said.

"Of course this agreement cannot be put in writing," Baron said. "And we will rely on a gentleman's agreement where a firm handshake is our contract." He held out his hand to shake that of the doctor, and they sealed the deal.

Baron opened his brief case with his travel and other documents in it and took out one hundred thousand US Dollars in one hundred dollar bills.

"Do not show this about so as not to bring attention to yourself. You can rely on me, and I expect to rely on you. You are to notify me as to your progress, and I wish to be advised of any problem. Do not forget that I have friends nearby in Russia who can act on my command, and I will also have four or five here as guards with the subjects."

That was stated to let the doctor know not to take off with the deposit, in which case he would be hunted down and murdered.

The doctor, holding the stack of money, smiled for the first time since they had been there. "I'll make exactly what you want."

"Doctor, I recognize your genius. You will not have to work again after this. Oh, you may also keep or dispense with the equipment that you buy. However, you are not to take any risks by the selling of equipment that could lead to us."

"Why, thank you!" Dr. Dorogomilov, pleased that his genius would finally be appreciated, shook Baron's hand vigorously. "I leave it to you to name the new virus." This was bestowing an honor on Baron, to let him name it, even though there could never be any publication of it.

Baron thought for a moment. "Tibet Restored."

# CHAPTER 15

The transaction completed, Baron and Tak stayed on the following day to attend the celebration of the annual Nauryz event that coincided by chance with their journey. It was held at a playing field near Stepnogorsk. Kariat, the nephew of the doctor's deceased wife Karina, was their host.

The first event was the Kokpar. One of the several hundred horsemen, each wearing a black cape and black turbine, carrying a lance and shield, galloped toward the dead goat on the ground that was dropped by another. He then ran his lance through it, letting out a yell as he galloped off, carrying it toward the other side of the huge playing field. Several horsemen on the other side came at him head on, holding out their shields to ram him. There was a loud crashing of their shields, and he fell off his horse. There was scrambling around in circles by the attackers as well as the defenders who rushed in to lance the dead goat, and the man who fell off his mount was trampled. When the group moved out of that area, and the dust cleared slightly, it could be seen that the man on the ground was not moving and, without so much as stopping the game, an older man, formerly a competitor, accompanied by two young men, still too young to compete, ran in to pick up his body and take his horse off. The man was dead.

The horsemen, dressed in their traditional garments

adorned with turbans, ignored the incident and frantically continued the chase for goat's carcass, as though nothing had happened at all.

"What does the name of the game, *Kokpar*, mean?" Tak asked Kairat.

"It means 'fighting for a goat's carcass,'" he answered. "It comes from a Kazakh custom of sacrificing a goat to get rid of evil."

"Do you believe it rids of evil?"

"Many do, but I'm not sure."

After Kokpar, the large number of horses cleared the huge field. Then two mounted men came onto the field. "This is called 'Audaryspak,' which means wrestling on horseback," Kairat explained.

The two strong men fought each other while on horseback until finally one knocked the other off his horse. The crowd erupted in cheer for the victor.

Following that short event was a game where a young man put a handkerchief out on the ground in the field, not far from the bleachers, with an old silver coin in it. A horseman came at it galloping at full speed and leaned over all the way to the ground, off the side of his horse, to try to pick it up. If he missed, he was out of the game.

"This was shown to Alexander the Great," Kairat told her. "It is called *Kumis Alu*, which means *pick up the coin.* Alexander was very impressed with this skill performed on horseback."

Following that game, assistants set up for another. Appearing on the field were two teenagers on horseback, but one was a girl. This was the first female in the events. The horses had a woven blanket under the saddle and white lower leg wrappings, which looked very dressy. Both the girl and the boy wore traditional garb with head gear consisting of a white band two inches thick with a colored, round top of material with weaving. The girl wore a vest with a colorful woven pattern on the front. She also had a fearsome looking black whip in her hand.

"Is that female part of the game?" Tak asked.

"Oh yes!" Kairat said eagerly. "This game I have done myself. It is called 'Kyzkuu,' which means 'overtake the girl.' The boy and the girl start from the same spot, but the girl starts first. The boy then goes as fast as he can to try to overtake her. She can try to stop him by lashing him with her whip. If he can catch up to her, he will kiss her on her horse signifying a victory for him. If, by the time they reach the end of the course, he has failed to overtake her, she then turns around, follows him back before the crowd, and whips him all the way back as she does, signifying a victory for her and great loss of face for him."

"And you say you have done it?" she asked.

He smiled proudly, his chest puffing up. "Oh yes, even last year. But I always won easily, and this year the girls who are competing all know me and refused to compete against me. They don't want to be disgraced again."

Their conversation was interrupted by the first two contestants. The girl took off first on her horse at a full run, followed by the boy just afterward in hot pursuit. The male contestant was faster than her and was soon about to overtake her on the right side as they crossed in front of the shouting crowd.

He caught up to her and kissed her while riding. He led her back to the crowd and was declared the winner by an official, also in traditional garb. The crowd hooted and cheered, delighted at the male victory.

The second pair got ready to compete and Tak's interest mounted in the game. They galloped out and the chase was on! The boy worked his way toward the girl, gaining slowly as the crowd cheered them on. He overtook her and got his kiss. The crowd cheered wildly for the male victor once again.

A third pair competed and the results were similar to the first two.

Tak was now bored with the results of what did not appear to be a real contest. "They really are not very well matched. The males are much better at this than the females. I think I could do better."

Kairat looked surprised at her comment and fanaticized that he might win a kiss from the beautiful, foreign woman in front of his friends. "Why don't you and I compete?"

She wondered if she should dare to follow up on her assessment. "Oh, I don't have a horse, and I don't have the clothing. But thank you for asking."

The idea of defeating her and getting a kiss in public from the gorgeous, red-haired Westerner with his friends looking on was beyond irresistible to Kairat. "I can borrow a horse as well as the outfit for you. You are supposed to wear the traditional costume in the game. Why don't we?"

The opportunity of experiencing first hand this Earth sport was all too tempting. She looked to Baron for an answer to see if her Earth guide and husband would veto the idea.

"As you wish," he said.

She gave in to temptation. "I'll try it!"

Kairat led her to the area behind the bleachers and to a yurta, an Arabic tent used, in this case, for changing clothes. He called inside to someone in Kazakh, and a young woman came out. Kairat spoke to her and the arrangements were made.

"She will lend you clothes for the event," he said to Tak. "I'll go change and come back."

Kairat returned in a traditional outfit, wide-legged red pants, brown boots, a brown shirt, and a brown leather jacket. He wore one of the hats that the other contestants had, a dome-looking affair with a white band of cloth about the bottom and the top in a red cloth with weaving.

Tak exited in a traditional, bright yellow outfit of loose pants held up by a woven multi-colored sash, the legs of which were tucked in high-topped riding boots. She wore a black sweater, a matching yellow vest with weaving in blue and red on the front, and a black and yellow hat similar in shape to his.

"You look Kazakh," he told her, intending the statement to be a compliment.

"Good. I'm ready."

At the staging area, Kairat was recognized by the horse handlers, from his previous competitions, as a very good horseman. Kairat spoke to the handler, who smiled and agreed to what he wanted, a horse for the less-than-competitive-female that he would compete against.

The handler got a fast, healthy horse for Kairat, and then selected a smaller horse for Tak as though she needed an economy version as a female.

"No, not that one," Tak dictated to him. She looked around at the horses and saw a frisky black stallion that was standing alone on the far side. She pointed. "That one."

The handler understood from the pointing but doubted that she could handle the big fellow. He spoke to Kairat in Kazakh, who interpreted, "He says that the big one you pointed to is not safe for you."

"I want the black one."

Kairat assumed that this upstart, infidel female would fall right off such a beast and then decided to approve it for her, notwithstanding the fact that he was supposed to return her unharmed that day.

The handler reluctantly went to the black one and tried to get hold of its leather bridle. The horse reared up to stomp on him, and he jumped back just barely out of the way. He then went around from the side, came up, grabbed the bridle, and put his arms around the neck. The big horse pulled its head up and raised the handler two feet off the ground, but the handler would not let go. After several yanks up into the air, the frisky horse finally stopped and let the handler control him. The man then put on the traditional blanket and saddle.

Kairat and Tak walked their horses to the staging area and got in line behind a pair of contestants. Kairat mounted his horse.

The handler held the stirrup for Tak. She put a foot in it

but, in the anticipation and excitement, she forgot her additional strength in this lower gravity and jumped up on the horse in a single movement from the ground. Kairat was not sure if he saw her correctly and rubbed his eyes to take another look but, when he did, Tak was already sitting on her horse, smiling.

The assistant handed Tak a whip. Seven feet in length, light, and thin at the end, it was intimidating.

They moved up in line until it was their turn. The crowd was cheering at the victor of the round before them, the boy having again won as usual, and being kissed by the inferior female contestant.

Tak's mount, although not quiet, seemed to her to be worth the experience as weighed against the risk. After all, she told herself, she was here to experience the natives and their ways.

Her mount moved as though he knew that he was about to be on stage in the competition. His breaths were loud and he made more loud noises with his lips as he waited restlessly in the staging area. His bridle was held tightly by a large man who started the competition in the age-old manner of simply letting go of the horse. Another held the bridle of Kairat's mount and would let it go shortly after Tak was away. The men looked at Tak and Kairat and saw that they were ready. Tak leaned forward, in a ready-to-go position, and held the reins tightly in her left hand, the whip in her right hand on the side where Kairat would be riding.

Kairat was somewhat calmer about the competition, assuming he would have no difficulty in beating the completely inexperienced Tak, and was already anticipating the public kiss from the foreigner, which would give him great face.

The man let go of her horse, and off she went! The horse went into a full run on its own. Tak was startled, but leaned over and did her best.

Then Kairat came up just behind her. Tak's high-spirited horse put nearly two lengths on Kairat's mount, as he followed in hot pursuit. He closed the gap, but not enough to catch her before the finish line.

She was then entitled to follow him back to the crowd—whipping him all the way. As they rode back, she whipped him strongly with her whip, Kairat crying out in pain with each stroke.

Kairat tried to ignore the pain and dug his heels into his horse's belly, but she was still there with her whip, continuing the strokes. They came to the area in front of the crowd, and she continued the whipping.

The crowd cheered, but much more subdued than the last couple, not wanting to see an inferior female win. They mumbled among themselves about how it could happen, as the female almost never won.

Kairat gathered up his composure as best he could in front of the crowd, stood, and began to walk, back toward the tents, vanquished, totally humiliated in front of people he knew well. Tak and Kairat walked back, not together, each to their respective changing yurta.

Kairat began to boil. He had never lost any such event, and now, in front of all of friends, he was reduced to nothing, disgraced, and by an infidel and inferior woman. He concluded it would do justice for Allah to kill that infidel bitch, who did not have the decency to cover her harlot head with a Hijab.

He followed her back, unseen, to her yurta, and looked about outside. No one was watching. As part of his traditional garb, he sported a traditional hunting knife in his belt, an ornate knife with a Damascus blade and wooden handle with jeweled trim, encased in a jeweled sheath. He took out the weapon and opened her yurta, murder in his mind.

Tak had just removed her borrowed clothes and was standing, naked, her back to the yurta opening. She heard him coming and turned to face him. Looking at the knife and his violent expression, she knew what was about to happen.

As Kairat stared at the lower part of her naked body, he

knew it was not what it should be or anything he had ever seen and witnessing it unearthed a feeling of inadequacy deep inside him, making him lose the impetus of his intended violent assault. He regained his composure and determination and went for her, the knife in his right hand, intending to kill her.

Tak saw the knife coming at her and managed to grab his wrist with her left hand, and then with her right, to keep from being stabbed. She leaped at his torso with her naked legs and got hold of him around his throat with her agile toes—seven on each foot, which were like fingers—and choked him. Kariat dropped the knife.

Just then Baron came to the yurta, in time to see the attack. He grabbed Kairat by the back of his hair and yanked him away so hard he fell backward.

Tak made ready her wrist laser weapon, but Kairat was done in from the fight. He raced out of the yurta, leaving the knife behind on the floor.

Baron picked it up and handed it to Tak. "A souvenir for you. I guess Kairat did not like losing."

❧❧❧

The Dastarkhan dinner was arranged at the home of the relatives of Dr. Dorogomilov's deceased Kazakh wife Karina. Having been given notice that there were two special guests were visiting, supplemented by a gift of one thousand US Dollars expense money from Baron, the family had morphed the meal into not just a modest Dastarkhan, but a memorable one.

The living room had been converted to a dining hall with a number of make-shift tables and mismatched chairs. Baron was seated at the end, with the baroness to his side around the edge of table. Kairat was nowhere to be found.

The ceremony for the most honored guest was a performance for Baron, who was seldom matched in style. Naturally, he assumed he would be designated the most honored guest, and so he had prepared ahead by learning what to do when so designated.

Lamb was brought out on two large plates, the first with the meat. The second, called a koy-bas, was the sheep's head cooked intact, presented to Baron with great honor. He stood to distribute the meat from the head and other parts of the sheep that were on the plate, being very careful not to offend.

He asked who was who in the group, in Russian. "Who are the young men?"

Several young men held up their hand, although it was obvious.

"You take these ears to make you more attentive." He then cut off the ears from the head and cut them up to distribute among them.

"Now, the girls," Baron said, carving out the palate from inside the head of the sheep and passing it to them. "This will make you more diligent and hard working. I have hipbones here for the elder men, as honored guests," he said and served them ceremoniously to the senior men. "Who are the daughters-in-law? They get the breast." He passed the pieces to them. "Who are the married women?" He passed the neck bones to them and one to Tak. "The boys?" They got the kidneys and heart to grow into a man more rapidly. "Who are the sons-in-law?" Once identified, they got the breastbone. "Now, are there any pregnant women?" Baron looked about until one identified herself. "You get this vertebra. Now here are the brains, but not for children. It will make them weak-willed." Baron put servings of brains on plates, with that warning, as some of the women passed them to others sitting beside the children. "Here's an elbow and an ulnar bone. Anyone can have this, except an unmarried woman or young girl, as it will make her left on the shelf with no husband." Baron passed the elbow toward someone who wanted it.

When Baron completed his performance, all done as though he was born Kazakh, he sat down. The rest did not touch their food until Baron, the most honored guest, began to eat.

"Only a true Kazakh would know such things," Dr. Dorogomilov complemented.

"Common knowledge," Baron said in an understatement.

The head of the sheep on the table was facing Tak, and it was more than a little distracting. Completely horrified, she tried a bit of a few things to be polite. She looked at Baron, who chuckled at her shock, enjoying the effect it was having on her.

When no one was listening, she said to him, "Am I actually asked to consider letting these people go into space?"

# CHAPTER 16

*D*alai is Mongolian for *ocean* and *Lama* is Tibetan for *spiritual leader* and hence the translation *Ocean of Wisdom*," Shanta read to Andrew as they sat in the square living room of the boxy houseboat on Lake Cumberland. He listened, while assembling a radio-controlled model airplane on the dining room table and sipping a bourbon.

The Saunders family had always had a houseboat on the Kentucky Cumberland Lake. The vessel did not look like a boat at all, but more like a house trailer on hidden floats—hardly a seaworthy vessel. But it was not used in the same manner as ocean boats, as it had a relatively small engine. If the boat was in the middle of the lake, it was too deep to anchor so it would just sit as there, as there were no significant currents to make it drift appreciably. The typical day out on the lake would be to just cruise off somewhere and then turn the motor off. They could then soak up the atmosphere as the houseboat sat in the calm of the lake, which, especially in the mornings and evenings, was as flat as glass. One could fish, but Andrew did not care for fishing.

A small runabout motorboat, tied to the back of the houseboat, provided transportation if they wanted to go ashore to one of the few restaurants on the lake. It could also be used to go look about the lake, but there was not much to see, apart from a waterfall over a rock that one could take a runabout under, just missing the water.

"Have you always built models?" Shanta asked Andrew as he worked intently on the model.

"Yes. I stopped for some years, but now I like to do it again."

"What is that model you are building?"

"This is a Cessna 182, converted from wheels to floats so I can fly it off the lake," he said proudly as he held the fuselage up for her to see. "It is powered by a .90 cubic-inch, four-stroke engine. Here are the wings," he said, holding them up. They measured over five feet in length. "They go on and off for easy storage. I crashed the last one. This is a replacement." Andrew adjusted the neutral point of the control servos and then asked, "Where does the Dalai Lama actually live?"

"It's called *McLeod Ganj* and is just above Dharamsalah, India, just outside of Tibet in India. But He's coming again soon. I have His schedule here for His next United States tour which is in two months. Listen to the names of the sessions: Overcoming Negative Emotions, The Practice of Six Perfections, Compassion and Universal Responsibility, and Pathways to Peace."

"Are we going?" Andrew asked her.

Shanta got very excited at the prospect. "Can we?"

"Definitely. And now, this beauty is ready to test fly."

He fueled up the model from a can with a pump and started the motor outside the door with an electric starter motor. Shanta stood by his side, just to the rear, and watched intently, joining in the excitement.

He set it on the water and checked the controls. All seemed to be working, and so he set the model out from the boat, into the wind, and pushed the throttle control all the way forward. It gained speed and, eventually, was skimming along the water on its floats. He pulled back on the rudder, and it became airborne.

It went up and down, as Andrew was having trouble

controlling it. He got it stabilized, finally, and then flew it around the houseboat in circles with gentle left turns. After four circles, he became so nervous his lips were quivering, and he cut the throttle down to a quarter. It descended slowly toward the lake, out and away from the houseboat. Just inches short of the water, he pulled the stick back. It did a slow stall and splashed into the lake, bending the landing struts.

"A perfect landing!" he declared, overlooking the damaged landing struts.

"You're wonderful!" Shanta complimented. "Such talent!"

Andrew grinned from ear to ear like the Cheshire Cat.

⌘

Ralls answered the phone in his Washington D.C. office.

"Mike Winger, CIA, here."

"Any news?" Ralls asked.

"I have the results from the utensils taken from the Paris hotel. As the results were not credible, I had everything re-done."

"Why all the fuss? What's wrong?" Ralls asked.

"There were two distinct sets of fingerprints. One set is normal, and we believe that set to be the baron's, although he has none on file anywhere that we can access. The other set is presumably that of his wife, the baroness. We have no record on her, other than she has a recently recorded marriage certificate with him in Berlin, and her first name is Tak. And that set is not normal."

"Maybe she is some beauty that he picked up somewhere, like in Russia or a satellite country?" Ralls said. "Quite a few western men find a wife that way, and in some cases through a service that provides wives."

"Could be, but we don't have normal access to such records," Winger said. "Let me finish and tell you what we found before you interrupt with your ideas."

"Okay, sorry."

"She has seven fingers, that is, a thumb and six fingers. And she does not have any fingerprints. Her skin is textured, as though designed to assist with delicate work, such as picking up fine instruments. But it would not be enough to distinguish one person from another."

"Interesting," Ralls said. "Well, still, maybe she was born with that unusual characteristic with the seven digits."

"Please stop interrupting. You haven't heard the rest."

"Sorry."

"We got the DNA back and had it tested and re-tested. She's not human."

# CHAPTER 17

Baron and Tak were relaxing in their suite in the hotel in St. Petersburg, Russia, when Nikolay Bogomazov announced his arrival in the hotel from the lobby.

"Nikolay! Come up."

In the room, Baron said to Nikolay, in Russian, "I'd like you to meet my wife, Baroness Tak Von Limbach. She's my companion and with me on this task. She has my confidence and we may speak freely. However, she does not speak Russian. Yet."

"I had not heard of your marriage, Baron. Congratulations! And to you, madam!"

Nikolay was no stranger to hiring beautiful women from Russia, Romania, and the Ukraine, as times were hard there and a beautiful young woman had a much better chance for a better life outside the East, unless she was lucky enough to meet one of the new super-wealthy Russians, most of whom where the sons of former communist leaders who had acquired businesses and monopolies through corruption when the USSR broke up.

He had to ask again to be sure Baron had not gone senile or soft over a beautiful woman who would later blackmail him, even if she was his wife. "Are you absolutely certain we can discuss the matter freely at this time?" he asked, in Russian.

"Yes," Baron answered in Russian. "You may speak

freely in front of the baroness. She is along with me on this mission. So let's continue in English."

Baron explained the task, which involved spreading, the Ebola in Tibet, once it was made. He then came to the part about the needed subjects. "Nikolay, in order to make the Ebola, I need five Chinese—of both sexes—and two Tibetans, one male and one female. None of them must be related, except by marriage. I want healthy, young subjects, in their twenties. They must be brought to Stepnogorsk, Kazakhstan, and will not be returning. I need them there as soon as possible, but I think that by rail from Vladivostok will do."

"I think I can get the Chinese we need brought in from China to Taiwan," Nikolay said. "I should be able to get them from the mainland, and no one will report their absence."

"How'll you do that?" Baron asked,

"It's simple. We don't have to kidnap them in China—they will come to us. People from the mainland often sneak over to Taiwan to make a better life. I'll have someone on the mainland arrange to announce jobs and hiding places in Taiwan for five people, ready for them when they arrive. They will even pay someone to arrange their trip. They will not have anyone on the mainland expecting to hear from them for some time, as they will think they are sneaking in to Taiwan and must be incognito until established and secure. They'll voluntarily consent to being hidden when they first arrive. Then I'll get them onto a ship heading for Vladivostok as you have requested."

"Ingenious!" Baron praised. "You just invite them to Taiwan, and they come running. I love it."

"Thank you, thank you. Now, as for the Tibetans, I think that I can get some in Tibet who have been jailed there by bribing a Chinese official. They'll have been jailed for dissent. I hope to be able to get them to Hong Kong, where I can bring the ship. Then I'll have all of them on the same ship to Vladivostok."

"Once in Vladivostok, arrange for a Russian military officer to take them to Omsk, Russia, which is just above the border of Stepnogorsk, Kazakhstan," Baron said. "They can go by the TransSiberian Express from Vladivostok, as the train goes there. Arrange for an escort with a Russian officer and two guards to drop them off at the border. Then I need you and four big guards to come down and handle the Orientals in Kazakhstan for as long as two months. I want big ones, and they must be totally trustworthy and able to keep quiet when they return. If any of them start getting drunk and boasting of what he or she did, I want them silenced at once.

"When the Ebola is ready, it will be put into nitrogen-cooled canisters. There will be seventy of them. Then I want you to take them to your prearranged twenty Russians in St. Petersburg who will leave on a Tibetan tour for two weeks. Once in Tibet, you all can spread the virus. You will need twenty trustworthy people, and they all must appear to be tourists, wanting to take a sort of economy tour to Tibet— probably younger people, who appear to be students. But they all must be totally trustworthy, and they must realize that they cannot go on a spending spree with their money. If they become a risk, they will be killed. Let them know that."

"I'll get on it at once. I should have something for you by the day after tomorrow. Can you stay in town?"

"Yes, I will show the baroness the Hermitage tomorrow, and we can meet the day after."

❧❧❧

At their next meeting, Nikolay had results already and reported to Baron and the baroness. "While traveling, I decided on how to bring in the subjects. It'll be on the TransSiberian Express. There are often prisoners on that route. I'll do it with actual prisoner transportation papers."

Baron caught on fast. "Don't tell me you—did you?"

"Yes. I got an actual officer of the Kontora, the FSB. He will transport them with actual prisoner transportation papers. It's the real thing! How do you like that?"

"Nikolay, there is no end to your resourcefulness," Baron enthused.

"Or you to your money, Baron. This will be expensive." Then he chuckled at his own little joke.

"Go on, tell me the rest," Baron said, not finding the joke about spending his money quite so funny.

"I was able to find a relatively high-ranking member willing to take the risk—Colonel Vladislav Tupkalo. He is not informed as to what we are doing, but only that we have some Orientals in Vladivostok that we want to get to Kazakhstan via Omsk with no questions asked. He'll prepare actual orders for the military to transport the prisoners from Vladivostok to Omsk by rail and then by military truck to the border above Stepnogorsk. He'll fly to Vladivostok with two soldiers from Moscow and pick up the Orientals. The soldiers will be specially selected to accompany him from Moscow, as they are part of a unit that does covert operations for the FSB, and they will not be suspicious. Although it is not anticipated that anyone along the route will speak Mandarin or Tibetan, the soldiers will have orders not to allow anyone to talk to the prisoners, which is typical of such prisoner details. I'll also get him to bring along a package of weapons that we might need at the lab for security."

"Will the prisoners draw attention on the TransSiberian Express?" Baron asked.

"A little, but it's the best way. I'll meet them with my men at the border of Kazakhstan and take them to the lab in Stepnogorsk. Tupkalo and the soldiers, of course, have to stay at the border and return. They'll never have a clue as to what we're doing with them. I'll go into Kazakhstan and make sure that the border guard is informed in advance to let us pass for a bribe, and I'll have the men, who I'm hiring to stay with the Orientals at the lab, join us at the border and escort the test subjects to the lab. I'll have a total of four guards. I'll pick big, tough ones, as I want to be sure they can overwhelm the Orientals if they should try to escape or give us a hard time."

"How much do we have to pay the FSB Colonel Tupkalo?"

"Fifty thousand US. The soldiers will just be on assignment, earning their regular wages so as not to make them suspicious. I know it's a lot, but he risks his career if caught. And it makes the transportation of the prisoners official. They will be traveling with genuine military soldiers and actual orders."

"Excellent," Baron agreed. "What about the guards?"

"I've not contacted them yet, but that's easy. I have used them before. You should see the size of these monsters. They can easily handle the Orientals. I'll offer them money for all time away from home, plus expenses and food. They eat a lot of food, by the way," he said, chuckling.

"Just make sure they are not the kind that will get drunk later and start talking about what they did.'

"Don't worry, Baron. For what I'm going to pay, I'll get the best. I know of some already. And as they are used to working for gangsters, they know that if they talk, they will be killed very quickly. What is the plan to distribute the Ebola in Tibet?"

"The virus will be in a liquid, kept alive in nitrogen-cooled containers. The plan at this time is to take in seventy, one-and-a-half liter canisters, disguised as Russian mineral water. Twenty people should be sufficient, plus yourself, so each can take in three bottles, plus a few extra. I want you to arrange a tour group of twenty, plus yourself, to go to Tibet. They must be carefully selected and will be well paid. They must be the kind that can receive a small amount of money, initially, and receive the rest later. They must not get drunk and talk once they are paid. There can be no problems. You make sure they know that if they talk to anyone, they're dead—and so will their families be or anyone who they know who can give evidence. None must have any knowledge of me. Some of the group should be women, as it should appear to be a group of people learning about Tibet."

"How do we spread it around in Tibet once we're in?" Nikolay asked.

"Organize it as one of those budget tours from Russia to Tibet," Baron said. "They will have bottled water bottles as most are afraid of the local water, and the bottles will not be suspect. There is no control over travel in Tibet once you are inside, so you can splinter the larger group into several smaller ones to go off and hit the major cities where the Chinese have been put by the Chinese government. The smaller groups can each have something different about the country that they want to see, in case they are asked, to justify the splintering of the tour group into the smaller groups. The Chinese that have been brought in by China are almost entirely in the few cities and, therefore, concentrated, which will make the job easy.

"They can be found at strategic places like city markets, public buildings, and military bases. There are several military bases of pure Chinese personnel. And all that needs to be done is to go to the entrance of these and infect someone going in. Shaking someone's hand with Ebola on yours, passing a soldier a piece of contaminated paper Yuan for permission take his photo in his uniform when he is on the way into the base should work very well. The open food markets in the crowded bazaars should be perfect. Sprinkling it on the food on display will reach large numbers of people. Also, passing out contaminated cigarettes should work very well. Just put a drop on the filter end and give it to someone."

Nikloay, normally fearless, swallowed hard. "Is this potion really going to be safe for the person who is spreading it around? Ebola is the most deadly virus there is, isn't it?"

"It'll be perfectly safe," Baron assured him. "It'll not infect anyone other than a Chinaman."

"Is a two week tour going to be enough to spread the Ebola?" Nikolay asked

"Yes. The longer you stay, the more the risk of someone linking the group to the outbreak. Lots of people take a two week vacation from work, which usually has an additional weekend added to it that gets used up in the travel. You can split up into, say, three groups and should be able to hit the major places where the Chinese are. If you infect a soldier entering his compound, he will then infect many exponentially. You will want to infect as many as you can. The beauty of this project is that the Chinese people themselves will spread the virus. Any questions?"

"Not for now. I'll be off to arrange transportation for the Chinese and Tibetans to Vladivostok. And I'll get to work putting together a tour group."

℘℘℘

In Baron's Taipei office, he prepared to meet one of his local resources, Mr. Lee. As he spoke English, the meeting would be in that language, so Tak was invited.

Mei Ling brought Mr. Lee into Baron's office."

"So nice to see you, Mr. Lee," Baron said. "This is my wife and partner, Baroness Von Limbach. Please be seated."

Lee sat politely, but only on the edge of the chair, and did not relax as he had the one time previously when he'd had a private audience with the wealthy and powerful baron.

Within moments of his sitting down, Mei Ling came in with tea. "Please have some tea," Baron offered, as Mei Ling poured it before obtaining an answer. She then poured for Tak and Baron.

Mei Ling had been told in advance what tea to make. "This one is chrysanthemum flower pedal flavored Oolong. It has a very delicate aroma."

Lee picked up the cup that Mei Ling poured for him,

while Mei Ling stood back, waiting to see if the tea would be satisfactory.

"Very fragrant," Lee said. "It's very generous of you to serve me such excellent tea."

Baron nodded to Mei Ling, who then left the room and closed the door. Looking at Lee, he asked, "Have you made the arrangements?"

"Yes, sir. I've got you five healthy Han Chinese, both sexes, unrelated by blood, between eighteen and thirty, from Mainland China. They are ready to come here to Taiwan. They believe they will be given false identity cards, a place to stay, and jobs. As you requested, they all believe they cannot contact relatives for several months so as to minimize any detection. I've arranged for them to pay a boatman, who makes illegal runs across the Taiwan Strait regularly, the sum of one hundred dollars each to be delivered to the Taiwan coast. That is less than the actual cost, but your instructions were to find five straight away and that it would be financed in part by you. They did not have enough money for the full fare."

"Is that with Madman Cheng?" Baron inquired. That boatman that had a reputation for extraordinarily fast trips across the Taiwan Strait in a very unusual boat. Baron had used him before.

"Yes. It's set for three days from now. But the military has caught more and more of those who came across this year. I cannot guarantee that they will not be detected and caught. Those new Robinson helicopters with those special cameras can detect a man's head swimming in the ocean." Lee exaggerated slightly, but he wished to inform his employer that there might be a problem and Lee did not want to be held responsible.

"Yes, I know about them. Those are FLIRs, Forward Looking Infrared, thermal imaging cameras. I sold the helicopters and the FLIRs to the Taiwan military."

"Excuse me, Baron," Lee said. "I had not realized that you would, of course, know about such devices. Can you make arrangements to make the military look the other way?"

"Of course. I just need to know the estimated time and at which spot Madman Cheng will be landing. I'll make sure that the military is not looking."

"I'll get the details from Madman Cheng and call you," Lee said.

"My man from Russia is coming into Taipei tomorrow and will be with you on the shore to meet them when they arrive. You will escort them in a lorry to a Russian ship that we have chartered at the shipyard. The Russian will know what ship to go to. You will tell them that they must hide out on the ship in its hold for several days until everything is arranged. Stay with them long enough to be sure that they have everything they need before you leave. When the ship is ready to go, the Russians will take over. Understood?"

"Yes, sir."

"All right, and now we must discuss money." Although the amount was insignificant to Baron, especially since the ship and fuel that was taking them to Russia would cost two hundred fifty thousand dollars, he had to sit with Lee for a while, negotiating over the amount that would be charged, as was the Chinese tradition.

Lee asked for what Baron called an insultingly high amount and offered half that. More tea was poured and the negotiations continued. But if it had not been done in this manner, Lee would have suspected that there was something bigger going on, as he had not been informed about where the five Chinese were headed or why they were wanted.

Finally, after fifteen minutes of *nego-nego*—the name, taken from English, used in Taiwan as the term for negotiations—Baron, acting reluctant, agreed to pay the sum of two thousand five hundred dollars for the fee of Madman Cheng and another two thousand to Lee, but only upon the safe arrival of the five Chinese to the hold of the Russian ship— less the five hundred dollars, of course, that the five Chinese were going to pay Lee as the fee to be taken to Taiwan.

As Lee was shown out by Mei Ling, Tak said to Baron, "It was very exciting to watch you negotiate."

"Here it is a process," he said. "If I did not do it, he would have been suspicious and would have begun making inquiries to see how he had been cheated."

⌘

Under the bright moon in high Tibet, a prison guard opened first one and then another cell door in a Chinese military prison, located inside a Chinese military base. The base was not prestigious as compared to those in Mainland China. It was just set up to have troops ready for crowd control, rioting, insurrection, and any other problems that the Tibetans caused, which were mostly on the anniversaries of various Tibetan events, which had all been banned by the Chinese government.

The jailer had been given orders from his commander, which in turn came from a general in the Chinese Army in Beijing. The orders stated that Tibetan prisoners Neema Lhamo and Jamyang Gyamtso, being held pending an unspecified trial date for anti-government activities, were to be taken to a Hong Kong prison and then to be deported from China. General Lee Dai Kwok signed the orders. Unbeknownst to anyone at the jail, he had been provided with fragrant oil by Baron for the turnover of the two Tibetans.

Neema Lhamo and Jamyang Gyamtso saw each other for the first time in months. Jamyang had been beaten a number of times during interrogation, more so at the beginning of his incarceration. Neema had regularly been used sexually by several of the jailers.

They looked at one another but were afraid to speak, for fear of a beating for talking. Led to a desk, they were put into prisoner-escort chains around the waist, with handcuffs on either side of their waist chains, and a detachable chain in-between them so as to tie them together.

"You have been ordered deported from the country for your subversive activities," the soldier at the desk told them. "You are being taken to Hong Kong to be deported."

They looked at each other in shock and disbelief. Deported? Where would they go? What country would have them? Were they being sent to the Dalai Lama in exile in India?

The transport guards came in from a truck waiting outside and motioned for them to come. They had no idea where they might go or what would become of them.

☙❧

"Nikolay! It's so nice to have you here in Taipei." Baron got up from his chair to greet the resourceful man, which he did not normally do for subordinates. But since Nikaloy had come such a distance, Baron stood.

Nikolay came in and sat in front of Baron's desk. Tak was present, so they conducted the meeting in English for her benefit.

"It's always good to see you, Baron, and you, Baroness. Thank you for having the driver meet me at the airport." He had arrived the day before, and Baron had sent Driver Chen to fetch him from the Taiwan airport.

"You look well and rested," Baron said. "How is the hotel?"

"Splendid. And so were the girls!"

"Ah, I'm glad you were pleased," Baron said. He knew Nikolay's propensity for young girls, and so he'd had Madam Su, who had the very best prostitutes in Taipei, send over two of her newest additions. Su had assured him that she had two new girls who had only just begun in the profession, were just eighteen, and could please. Apparently, she was right, as usual.

"And so, when are the Chinese coming?" Nikolay asked.

"Tonight, after midnight. Is the ship ready?"

"Yes, I have set up living quarters in the hold. How many again?"

"There will be five Chinese, a mix of males and females."

"They are prisoners, right? It should not matter if they have to stay together."

"Yes, this is a one-way journey, but they must arrive healthy. You make sure that they are kept warm and have plenty of food. I don't want them to arrive all beat up and injured either."

"Done."

"Good. Now, I have two more prisoners for you to take. I told you that I would be sending over two Tibetans, if you recall?"

"Yes. Where do I get them?"

"In Hong Kong. They were imprisoned in Tibet by the Chinese for dissident political activities. I bribed a high official in the military and he arranged for their release and expulsion from the country. I'm told that they are young, probably in their early twenties. You had better put them in different quarters than the Chinese. I don't know if they will get along with the Chinese after what the Chinese have done to them."

"All right. Is there anything special I should know? The food will be coming from the ship's Russian cook. Do they have a special diet?"

"They'll do fine. But I don't want these political dissidents to try to martyr themselves by discovering they are going to die and assuming that they must die beforehand to promote their belief in the Dalai Lama or their homeland. Don't forget what I'm paying you for, which is their safe delivery in Stepnogorsk. Make sure that these Tibetans, who have already shown that they will risk jail rather than give up their beliefs, don't go on a hunger strike or start acting crazy. You might tell them that they have been brought out because they're on a mission to further the causes of Tibet, which is true, and then deal with them as a ship security matter on the ship as opposed to letting them get the idea that they are prisoners. You work it out. As for the Chinese, they will eventually figure out that they are leaving Taiwan, so you better keep an eye on them. They won't try anything like a hunger strike, but the less they know the better."

"Understood."

"Next I want you to start arranging the tour group to go to Tibet. I'll advise you when the material is ready, hopefully within a few weeks after you make your delivery of people to Stepnogorsk, according to Dr. Dorogomilov."

⁓⁓⁓

Upon returning from Europe, Ralls met with Hauser in his office. Ralls had sent his report in advance in case the director wanted to review before the meeting. As it turned out, he did.

Hauser started off with, "What is this about not being human?"

"I know, I know," Ralls said. "Winger had it checked three times at the lab, and then I sent samples to another lab. Same conclusion in all cases."

"If she is not animal, then she must be vegetable or mineral," Hauser said, still disbelieving,

Ralls smiled at the joke. "Well, perhaps a freak of nature?" He began summarizing what he had. "The mystery woman in the hypersonic craft may or may not have been the one that Baron Von Limbach drove from the salt mine in Poland to the hotel. He stayed at the Forum Hotel with a red-headed woman and took her to dinner in downtown Krakow. They left in his car to go to Germany, with me a few days behind. There was one strange thing along the way on the road they took, which was a hole in the highway, ten feet deep, with none of the dirt or debris that was removed from the hole anywhere to be seen. When I got there, highway repairmen were filling in the hole. But I could find nothing connecting the baron or the woman to it.

"The two went on to Germany. I could not find them, initially. They may have stayed with friends, or if at a hotel, possibly one of those small places, like on the Romantic Road, but I could not confirm that. He may have paid cash for the room and there was no computer record of it. The two were definitely in Berlin next, where their marriage was recorded. It looks as if this baron must have fallen in love with whoever he was traveling with, as it was not a church wedding, but a civil ceremony. I have been unable to find out anything about her background, which is, in itself, very odd.

"One theory is that she came from someplace in Russia with a very poor economic background. The baron might have found her through some dating or marriage service and had her sent down to Krakow. This is very easy for a Russian woman to do as the airfare is cheap, although paid for by the potential mate. But the main thing is, that young women can go freely to Poland, whereas trying to get a visa to the US, for example, is very hard. After Berlin, their next stop was Paris. They took a commercial airline to Paris from Berlin.

"Our CIA connection got me the information that Baron and Baroness Von Limbach booked tickets on the French Train a Grande Vitesse, but they weren't passengers aboard this same train when it was de-railed by terrorists south of Paris in protest for the law not allowing women to cover their faces in public. The CIA hacked into the French surveillance cameras at the train station after the sabotage and found the two sitting at a café table. There is a picture of them in the file, but it is low quality as it was taken by a surveillance camera some distance away. It seems clear that they intended to take that train but missed it. From there, the CIA found them in a hotel in Paris. Winger at the CIA sent one of their operatives into the Paris hotel for DNA and fingerprints, which she was successful in getting."

The director found the picture in the file. It was of the baron and baroness in the Paris train station, but it was not very good, as Ralls had said. Their faces were grainy and the number of fingers could not be ascertained.

"So what about the seven fingers and the fingerprints?" he asked.

"Extra fingers isn't so rare as you might think," Ralls said. "Or so I am told by a doctor friend of mine. Having six is fairly common, and more than five is called ploydactyly. If a baby has an extra digit at birth, and it is deformed at all, they usually cut it off. As for the bizarre skin pattern on the fingertips, it's a dead end. She has no record anywhere that we can find, including Interpol, and we can find no background information on her at all.

"As for the strange rocket craft, we were utterly unable to find any trace of it, who built it, or even who *might* have built it. We cannot find any motive for the trek the pilot took across the US. The only law the pilot broke was a misdemeanor of not filing a flight plan for any pilot going over eighteen thousand feet in US airspace. Can you imagine trying to extradite her? We go to a federal judge and say that we have a single sighting of a red-headed female from a nearby pilot through his canopy, but no rocket was found, and we have no other evidence, other than DNA and fingerprints that were probably taken illegally under French law. 'But judge, we would like you to issue an extradition order for the misdemeanor of flying too high without a flight plan.'"

"That would be rich," Hauser said. "We would be the laughing stock."

"What do you think about whether or not she was the hypersonic pilot?" Ralls asked. "I have a gut feeling that it could be her, but I do not have any hard evidence. I have tried to run down all possibilities, but I've found no sign of any involvement by anyone else. I'm reminded of a Sherlock Holmes quote from the *Sign of Four*, 'Eliminate all other factors, and the one which remains must be the truth.'"

"I cannot let a potential threat to the US, by someone

having a manned craft that can go that fast, just lie," Hauser said. "Even if they, or whoever made it, did not have sophisticated guidance systems, a suicide bomber could Kamikaze one of our cities with a dirty nuclear bomb and we could not stop it. I deal with actual or potential terrorist threats all the time and, to me, this has the potential. Keep on it."

# CHAPTER 18

The hands of Madman Cheng's knock-off waterproof wristwatch were all pointing up as midnight arrived. He was waiting in a dark cove on Mainland China for his passengers. The commotion of people coming down the trail could be heard, and he hid, in case it was not the people he expected. As they approached, he could see there were six people, and then he recognized the man who worked for him. Madman stepped out of his hiding place in the bushes and turned on a flashlight to lead them to him.

He greeted his helper and then the five passengers. The average age appeared to be early twenties, and none were married. They were all ambitious, trying to get to Taiwan for a better life.

Madman looked at his hand-written list of passengers and asked who was who.

"I'm Mee Noh Yew," the youngest of the ladies said.

"Do you have the one hundred dollars?"

She handed Madman a crumpled one hundred dollar bill from her pocket.

Madman looked at the next person, a male. "What's your name?"

"I'm Tai Won Ong."

"Good," Madman said to the young man. Tai gave his stack of Yuan to Madman, who looked at it disdainfully. "It's supposed to be in dollars."

"I could not get any in the time I had," Tai said. "I had to get some of this at the last moment from friends, and I had no time to get to a money changer."

Madman was unhappy about it, but it was too late. He took the Yuan and put it in his pocket. He turned to the next, a lady with short cropped hair.

"I'm Ma Tuyit To," she said. She then gave her money to Madman and he checked off her name.

The next was an older man of thirty. "I'm So Su Mee."

It was slightly unusual to see a Chinese man of thirty without a family, and these people were not supposed to have any family to leave behind in China.

"Where's your family?" Madman asked him.

"My wife and son were killed in an accident, and I have nothing left. So I'm going to start a new life."

There was no way to verify his story, but it really did not matter. Madman was going to take him anyway. He took the man's money and checked off his name.

He turned to the last, a man of twenty two years.

The man held out his money. "I'm Sum Ting Wong."

Madman completed the list. Everyone was accounted for and had paid. Madman would get the balance on the shore in Taiwan. It was not unusual for that to happen, as the Chinese had so little that they often did not have enough to pay the full fare. Relatives or contacts in Taiwan would pay the balance on those occasions. In this case, it would be Deng Lee, working for the baron.

"All right," Madman announced. "Now, we're going to cross the Taiwan Strait. It is very important that you do exactly as I say. If you do not, you will be knocked out of my boat and you will drown in the sea. To avoid being caught, we have to race across the sea."

The five passengers stared at the strange craft in fear and amazement. It was made of white, round, PVC drainage pipes, glued and tied together. There were two keels in the catamaran fashion, each fifteen feet long, made up of pipes a foot and a half in diameter. The front of the keels had tips made of cones that had the points turned up to cut through the waves. In between the large pipes was a flat platform of PVC pipes, each four inches in diameter, sitting out of the water the height of the catamaran's hulls. The rear had a makeshift bracket holding an enormous, American V-6 outboard motor with two hundred and fifty horsepower. The huge engine looked very out of place fastened onto a boat that was made up of so few dollars in PVC pipe. The motor had come from a Chinese ring in Southern California that stole cars and put them in shipping containers bound for China. Madman had gotten the engine for one-fourth the price.

The entire purpose of the materials used in the boat was to minimize any heat signature, as the Taiwan military FLIR cameras on their helicopters and planes could easily pick out the heat signature of a human body or a motor against the cold sea. The PVC pipe gave no signature at all. The major heat came from the motor, over which he had installed a cold water bladder that sucked up water from the sea and drained it out quickly, cooling the outer surface of the motor case and creating a cold buffer of water and neoprene in between the hot motor and the radar.

There was an overall benefit to the makeshift boat, which was that it cost almost nothing, except for the motor. If the boat ever flipped over and sank in high waves, got shot up by the government, or was seized—all of which had happened to him previously—he would not lose a major investment.

The passengers would give off a heat signature themselves and, to reduce that, Madman had acquired several blankets that were made for forest fire fighters to cover themselves in case of a flashover while they were fighting a fire. The blankets were made from a fabric developed with a coating that resembled aluminum foil on one side and was designed to keep out most all heat. With the reflective coating of foil turned to the inside toward the body, the blankets kept the passengers' heat signature contained and invisible to the expensive thermal imaging cameras and radar the Taiwan government had bought to monitor the Taiwan Strait.

All in all, Madman had a craft that gave off hardly any heat signature, was below the larger waves, and went across the ninety miles of the Taiwan Strait so quickly that it was nearly impossible to detect. But on important occasions such as this, Baron had also bribed someone in the military to make sure that no one signaled any alert during the designated time period.

"Now, each of you is to lie down on the floor of the boat and hold on with one of the short ropes," Madman told the group. "You are to lie down on the pipes and keep your faces down to avoid giving off a heat signature that can be detected by special equipment the military have. Do you understand?"

There being no questions, the Chinese, each with a knapsack of their most precious belongings—most of which were simply clothes—lay down on the plastic pipes and hung onto the ropes.

The passengers would soon learn that Madman Cheng had not earned his name by a fluke. He had been so named because he went so insanely fast across the Taiwan Strait that he was nearly impossible to catch.

Once the passengers were in place and huddled up close together, Madman put two of his heat-shield blankets around them and fastened them with a nylon rope, as if trying to bundle them. He put on a suit, consisting of a pair of overalls and a make-shift pullover top with a hood whose cord pulled tightly around the outside of his face, which he had made for himself of the same material with the foil to the inside.

"Everyone ready?" he asked.

The frightened Chinese grabbed on tightly to the little ropes as Madman pushed the strange craft away from the shore. The craft drifted out twenty feet and was race ready.

"Everyone hold on," he said loudly.

He started the monstrous outboard motor. As it sprang to life, Madman put a wide leather belt with two metal rings on it, one on each side, around his waist. Two nylon ropes were attached to the deck, each with a ring connector on it, which he fastened, one to each side of his belt. This would hold him to the boat. Otherwise, at the speeds he would be traveling when bouncing off waves, he would be thrown off. He also put on goggles, black plastic with clear lenses, and looked like a crazed WW I fighter pilot.

"Here we go!"

Madman engaged the propeller and pushed the throttle. The boat leaped, its front end pointing up, then slowly laying down into skimming position as its speed increased. Sixty, seventy, eighty, and then ninety miles per hour, the unusual craft bounced off the waves, pounding its passengers violently.

Madman was at his best. The horrified Chinese, scared nearly to death, managed to hang on for their lives, the salt water spraying them from time to time. On larger waves they were bounced into the air, each holding on to his rope for dear life. Madman stood to the aft, his ropes holding him to the hull, the spray of the sea soaking him as he maintained control of his stealthy craft, traveling at an unimaginable pace across the Taiwan Strait.

The wild ride came to an end, and Madman eased off the throttle as he approached his secret spot on the Island of Taiwan, formerly known as Formosa, where Deng Lee and Nikolay Bogomazov waited for them. As Madman approached the shore he shut down the massive outboard and coasted the final twenty yards. A big sigh of relief could be heard from the passengers and they started to chatter to each other, not having been able to talk during the ordeal.

"Be quiet!" Madman barked in Mandarin.

"Come this way, and no talking," Lee said, beckoning to them.

They scurried ashore like rats off a ship, grateful to be safe from the death-defying experience at sea with Madman

Cheng. Nikolay stood by, taking charge, but he could not communicate as he did not speak Mandarin. Lee and Madman huddled together regarding payment. Lee gave him the agreed amount, the difference of what the baron was paying and what the passengers had paid. Then, turning so that that Nikolay and the passengers could not see, Madman slipped a bag containing a kilo of heroine out of his coat, and passed it to Lee.

Lee looked inside and weighed it in his hand as best he could to see if it was a full kilo. "Is this pure and uncut? If you have cut this, you will owe me money. I'm paying for pure heroin."

"It is one hundred per cent pure." Of course, Madman lied, but the cut was only ten percent. If Lee had not ground him down so much in advance on the price, Madman would not have had to cut it. They had set up arrangements in advance on the Internet. The baron didn't know about the transaction, but such side deals were common. Their business complete, they parted and Madman left for another daredevil passage across the Taiwan Strait.

Lee addressed the group in Mandarin. "Mr. Bogomazov will be hiding you for several days on a ship in the harbor. I'll accompany you there for now, but then I'll go and he will be looking after you. You will stay there until all the arrangements are made for your papers, a job, and a place to live. You must not cause any problems for him. Understood?"

They all nodded. Then Lee and Nikolay led them to a minivan that was waiting on the road.

⁊ↄ⁊ↄ

The cargo hold was a plain, steel, dark room. There was no shortage of space on the freighter *Sokol* that had been exclusively chartered for the trip, so Nikolay had the crew set up good-sized compartments for the prisoners. The compartments were twenty feet square and just as tall, making it impossible for the prisoner to climb out. A minimal Russian crew had been hired and were only told of the destination. They were of a type, experienced in moving contraband, that knew not to ask questions about the nature of the cargo.

The walls were metal, plain, and without windows. Each of the compartments had an access door on one side, by which the prisoners' provisions could be brought, always with an armed escort. One was set up for the Chinese. Another was made ready for the Tibetans. Nikolay had been told to make them comfortable, so he had lowered a portable, construction-site toilet; mattresses; and a table and chairs into each of the compartments. He had also provided a mahjong set for the Chinese. A drop cord with electricity for light bulbs ran down the wall. The large hatch cover was to be kept open for them when weather permitted, but it had started to pour rain the day the Chinese came and the hatch had to be closed. Much to Nikolay's satisfaction, the group made no protest when the ship departed Taiwan, as they all presumed that the ship was simply being moved to another harbor on the island.

The ship was piloted into the bustling Hong Kong harbor. The human cargo was moved into two secret spots, created for smuggling, in the structure near the bottom of the hull. The cargo hold that had been set up for them was cleaned out, in case an inspector should want to examine the ship.

While the crew made the ship ready for its next journey, the captain, Nikolay, and two Russian members of the crew went ashore to collect the two Tibetans. They presented their documents—signed by General Lee Dai Kwok of the Chinese Army, stating that the two Tibetans were officially exiled from the People's Republic of China and were to be released to their ship for exile out of China—to an official in a building next to the wharf. General Lee Dai Kwok had been paid handsomely by the baron.

Nikolay showed the official the documents that ordered

the release of Neema Lhamo and Jamyang Gyamtso. The Chinese official read the document, picked up a phone, made a call, and talked for several minutes. He then looked over the counter at the captain and Nikolay and told them, in Mandarin, "The two people you are here for are in a jail. They will be brought here in two hours."

In the usual fashion of Russians who sailed, the captain, Nikolay, and the two Russian sailors utilized the time to find a bar that had vodka, while the captain filled out the necessary papers for the ship while in harbor.

Feeling better with vodka, Nikolay and the other Russians later returned for the prisoners but found that they were not there yet. Less irritated than they might have been, thanks to the vodka, they went outside to wait, sitting on a barrier and smoking. Half an hour later, a military truck, with a canvas top over the truck bed, pulled up and stopped in front of the office. Two soldiers with Chinese AK-47 rifles got out of the back. The two Tibetans got down, handcuffed together.

Nikolay noticed that, with their darker skin, the Tibetans were quite different looking than the Chinese.

Nikolay and the captain of the ship went inside, and the captain was given documents to sign that he was taking the prisoners out of the country. The soldiers who delivered them insisted on taking back their handcuffs and they retrieved them. Nikolay saw that the Tibetans had some slight facial bruises. Apparently, they'd had some differences of opinion with their jailers or transporters over something.

Although Nikolay had no handcuffs with him, he and the Russian crewmen presented a sufficient deterrent that Tibetans did not to try to bolt. They knew that they were being exiled from China, but that was all.

The Russians led them to the ship and ushered them into the hold adjacent to the one set up for the Chinese. At first, Jamyang Gyamtso resisted, but two crew members changed his mind by lifting him off the ground by his arms. The young lady, Neema Lhamo, followed without resisting.

The human cargo secured, Nikolay told the captain to set the good ship *Sokol* sailing to Vladivostok, Russia. Once outside the magnificent Hong Kong harbor, Nikolay and the crew went into the cells, setting them up for the comfort and safety of the prisoners, in accordance with instructions from the baron.

Gyamtso and Lhamo looked about as Nikolay and the crew brought in a table and two chairs, a portable toilet, and two mattresses, which were laid on the floor. Nikolay did not know if the Tibetans played mahjong, so he had bought them a new jigsaw puzzle, a jungle scene with tigers that would take many hours to complete.

The Chinese prisoners were brought from their hiding place in the secret panels in the lower hull and taken back to their compartments, followed by the crew bringing back the things for their comfort.

The group of seven was then en route from Hong Kong to Vladivostok, where they would be officially turned over to Colonel Vladislav Tupkalo of the Federalnaya sluzhba bezopasnosti Rrossiiskoi Federacii, who, with a group of Russian soldiers armed with assault rifles, would be officially transporting them, with written orders, as prisoners across Eastern Russia on the TransSiberian Express.

⌘⌘⌘

"Just call for me, sir, and I'll bring the car back to this spot," Roger told Andrew as he and Shanta got out of the limo in front of the VIP entrance to Churchill Downs. Andrew wore his usual blue jeans, but he'd put on a regular shirt and worn a tan sports coat, as the event called for that in the area where they would be seated. Shanta wore a green sari, the only sari at the event.

As they walked in, Andrew said, "My father used to have horses, and he brought me here." It was as if Andrew was coming to the race as a matter of recalling good memories of his youth and his father.

"Do you have horses now?" Shanta asked.

"No. But there are some at the stables on one of Dad's properties. I let the neighbor girls use them when Dad died. They don't have money for their own. Actually, I guess they are mine, come to think of it."

"Don't you like horses?" Shanta asked.

"Not really. I was thrown off a huge horse when I was little and never rode much after that. My dad liked them very much, however. He never had race horses, just riding ones. But he liked to come here, and he met lots of friends here. I preferred to ride a trail motorbike."

There was much excitement in the air with one hundred thirty thousand spectators. On the fourth floor of the clubhouse seating Andrew's company owned two boxes, one for the executives and a private one for his father, which was now his. They were in the best location, in what was called Millionaires Row in Skye Terrace. On Derby Day, there was a buffet nearby, but Andrew did not want to go there as he would, no doubt, have had to socialize with executives of the company. He ordered a bourbon, and Shanta her usual tea.

As they waited for the race to begin, Shanta said, "I hope we hear from the baron soon."

"Do you think we should call him for a progress report?" Andrew asked.

Shanta shook her head. "He said that there was to be no communications between us. We dare not."

They looked out at the race track, as the first race was about to begin.

"Do you bet on the horses?" Shanta asked.

"I just like to watch."

The truth was that she would have loved to place a bet, but since it was his money she dared not ask.

The first race took off. The excitement of the crowd felt like a tangible thing as the horses charged around the field and, finally, there was a winner.

After the first race, the crowd quieted down. Shanta

turned to him and took his hand. "Darling, I haven't much, but there is something I have that I have decided that I want you to have."

Andrew studied her curiously. "What?"

"My virginity."

# CHAPTER 19

Traveling on the TransSiberian Express, even though they were in chains, was, nevertheless, an interesting journey for the prisoners, who had never before traveled anywhere, except for the two Tibetans, who had been taken to Hong Kong on their way out of Tibet. They sat by windows enjoying the scenery. The blood-red colored railway cars, although designed for higher speeds, rumbled along at only sixty to eighty kilometers per hour, because of the condition of the rails, which was always bad, due to the severe weather conditions. The train went through several mountains with long tunnels, one of which took over ten minutes. They passed many little villages along the way that were made up of different races but, due to the unification tradition of the Soviets, they did not wear unusual clothing. Route Number One on the Express was from Moscow to Vladivostok, while Number Two was from Vladivostok to Moscow. The trip went by Lake Baikal, the largest freshwater lake in the world, so vast it took hours just to pass it.

Finally, on the fourth day, the train arrived at the town of Omsk. There was no trouble, as people in Russia were so respectful of authority, even after the breakup of the Soviet Union, that no one dared question prisoners under guard. Since the prisoners could not speak Russian, they could not communicate anything to others on the train, and it was easy to move them from Vladivostok to the remotest part of the country without incident. Obviously, the prisoners were in some sort of trouble, or so it seemed to the others on the train, and they did not wish to join them. The Russian soldiers selected by Tupkalo were in combat gear, armed, and had a formidable demeanor.

Omsk, in south central Russia just above the Kazakhstan border, was as close as they could get by train to Stepnogorsk. The prisoners were surprised to see a familiar face, that of Nikolay Bogomazov, who was waiting there to meet them.

Nikolay had arranged for a military truck and driver to meet his group at the railway station. It was a large, olive-drab truck, with a canvas covered truck bed with two benches, one on either side. The soldiers accompanied the prisoners into the truck, which would go as far south as the border. Four of the Chinese were put on one side, and one of the Chinese and the two Tibetans were put on the other. All the prisoners were chains. There was a protest from one of the Chinese, but a gun butt in the stomach from Tupkalo quickly ended that.

The ride to the border was on a very windy, narrow, dirt road. Snow could be seen on the ground off to the side of the road as they went through the mountains, but it had melted off the road. The road had giant potholes, occasional farm animals, and antique-looking tractors—going only slightly faster than walking speed—all of which made progress toward the border slow. Dust rolled up the back of the truck all the time and covered the prisoners, as well as the soldiers, who had to sit at the rear gate to prevent any of the prisons jumping out—although that would have been next to impossible with their chains locking them all together. Nikolay and Tupkalo rode in the front seat with the driver as they bounced along.

Under an overcast sky, they arrived upon the Kazakhstan border. The Russian soldiers ushered the prisoners out and stood by for the exchange in guards. Their journey had ended, and they would return to catch the next train back.

Four men, who Nikolay had hired, could be seen standing across the border in Kazakhstan. They were, however, some of the toughest available in Russia. The four were from Ural, the mountain chain in Western Siberia, where one had to be tough just to survive. The shortest was six feet, two inches and their weight ranged from two hundred sixty pounds to three hundred twenty. They were Zuhk, Opanasenko, Yageltchuk, and Timoshenko.

The sky darkened to charcoal gray, even though it was midday, and soon a spring snow began, rapidly increasing in intensity. Nikolay and Tupkalo walked up to the Russian border guard shack and went inside. The border guard was sitting in a chair behind a small desk. He did not initially rise, as there had been hardly any activity in the area, let alone from anyone important.

"I'm Colonel Vladislav Tupkalo of the Federal'naya sluzhba bezopasnosti Rossiyskoy Federatsii," Tupkalo said smartly. He took out his identity billfold, which displayed not only his current FSB card, but also, on the other side, his former KGB, or Komitet Gosudarstuennoi Bezopasnosti, card, which he liked to keep as a sort of badge of past honor.

The border guard immediately acted as if he'd gotten a shot of adrenaline, stood up, and came to attention, barking off, "Yes, sir!"

"I'm delivering seven prisoners to Kazakhstan," Tupkalo said. "I do not want to register the transaction." By that he meant that he wanted no record of their names, as would normally be taken down with persons crossing a border.

Russian soldiers were used to such things, and so the border guard did not question the high-ranking officer. "Yes, sir!"

Tupkalo went outside and ordered the soldiers to march the prisoners across the border and transfer them to the four huge guards waiting for them. The border guard raised the wooden gate, and the Russian soldiers ushered the prisoners across. The Chinese had their knapsacks returned to them to make them feel a little better. The colonel also delivered a package, wrapped in brown paper and containing six pistols, two automatic rifles, many extra clips, and lots of heavy ammo, to be delivered to the lab for security pursuant to Nikolay's request.

Once the prisoners were across, they were ushered into the back of a similar truck to resume their journey into Kazakhstan. Nikolay and Tupkalo went to one side of the truck, where they could not be seen, and Nikolay gave Tupkalo the fifty thousand US Dollars. In return, Tupkalo gave him the keys for the chains, allowing Nikolay to keep the prisoners chained.

Tupkalo counted the money with wide eyes, having never had such a sum at one time. He was rich!

On the Kazakhstan side was another guard shack, but it was tiny and the man inside did not even come out. He had already been promised a bribe by Nikolay for overlooking the crossing of the prisoners and, although actually not a lot of money, the bribe was the equivalent of two month's salary. Nikolay did not give him any more than necessary so as not to make him suspicious and, with so little activity in Stepnogorsk for years, he was quite glad to accept the amount offered.

All of the prisoners got into the truck peacefully, except for the Tibetan male, Jamyang Gyamtso, who refused to get in. He had a chain around his waist that was connected to the next prisoner in the truck and, since there was no slack in the chain, the man in the truck ahead of him was about to be pulled out.

Anatoly Zuhk came over him and thumped Gyamtso on the top of his head with his knuckles, making a noise like a drum. That quieted the man down, and he then got into the truck. He appeared dizzy after the tap on the head.

The snow and cold wind increased. Opanasenko passed out blankets to the prisoners to cover themselves, so they would not fall sick, as the truck headed into the narrow, mountainous, desolate trail to the south, heading for the place known only as Post Office Box 2076, where, known only to a select few, the deadliest organisms to humans existing on the planet were still alive.

℘℘℘

At Building 221, the sky was dark in the middle of the afternoon, but this was not unusual for the area. Spring snow fell, and a cold and unfriendly wind pierced the prisoners' clothes like that of an Arctic winter. Inside, near the lab in the back, jail cells remained from the days of the Soviet Union, built for prisoners brought in to be subjects for exposure to horrific bio-warfare agents. The main use of those condemned prisoners was for anthrax testing, as that was what was made in huge quantities at the facility in its heyday. But the anthrax had become so highly developed that there came a time when there was little need to continue testing, except to confirm that new batches were just as lethal as the previous ones. So there had been ample subjects for Dr. Dorogomilov to use for his own pet projects with Ebola. The jail cells had not been needed since the Soviet Union breakup, and so they were just used as storage rooms. He'd cleared them out for the current project and told the maintenance man, who stoked up the furnace in the mornings, that he needed those cells heated, along with another part he would use for the multitude of monkeys and rabbits that were to be brought in to be exposed—he said— to the fungi under development for killing opium poppies to make sure that the experimental chemical was safe for animals.

The high-containment operation recovery rooms were still there, equipped with left-over medical equipment. The high-containment area was insulated from the main building by a series of three chambers with air-tight doors to prevent whatever was being used on the subjects from escaping. The outer doors led into an additional, large containment hall, also with a fourth air containment door, where pressure suits were hung up in one of the chambers. They would have to be pressure checked regularly for leaks, and patch kits were on-site for repairs. The middle chamber to each room was built like a big shower with a hose that supplied chemicals to wash off the containment suits. The doors were all oval-shaped submarine doors, which was where they came from when the building was built. The airtight doors could all be locked from the outside to prevent the subjects or contaminated persons from escaping.

Mice, rabbits, and monkeys arrived in quantities, transforming the place into a smelly zoo. The monkeys shrieked and jumped all about when anyone entered.

Drs. Dorogomilov and Volkova hired six local women and three men, who were out of work, to help out. They were extended family of Dr. Dorogomilov's deceased wife, except for two who were close enough to be trusted. They did not, of course, have any idea of what they were really doing, only that they were working on the special fungi testing to kill opium poppies, and that details of the work were to be kept secret, in hopes that the process might be patented if successful.

All the helpers would go home in the evenings, as though it was an ordinary job. A special bus was hired to fetch them from several pick up points, designed to reduce the inevitable chatting and questions with other passengers that they might meet on the public bus. The help were not allowed in the back area where the prisoners were to be kept and, to reduce any interest in going to Dr. Dorogomilov's lab, the helpers were told that they could not enter the back without special showers and clothes just before going in, as they would bring contaminates in to the specially clean laboratory research areas.

The truck with Nikolay and the human cargo arrived. Hearing that, Dr. Dorogomilov rushed to the front of the building, much like Dr. Mengele at Auschwitz learning that more twins had arrived for experimentation.

Nikolay made the prisoners get out and stand in front of the huge building. Dr. Dorogomilov walked around them once and studied his new subjects. The prisoners stood quietly in awe and fear, wondering what was in store for them. They were led inside and past the section where cages had been set up with mice, others with rabbits, and larger ones with monkeys. Seeing the humans, some of the monkeys shrieked and others jumped from the sides of the cage bars, scaring the prisoners.

When they reached the rooms for the prisoners, Nikolay and his guards unchained and separated them. Tai, Sum, and So were motioned to undress and shown into a shower. Their clothes were gathered and taken away, they thought for cleaning, but in actuality to be disposed of as unsanitary. After the Chinese men showered, they were each provided a two-piece, gray, cotton outfit that would be their attire at the lab, one that could be washed like hospital scrubs. Shown to the cells, one of the men, Tai, resisted being locked up and was holding his head after Yageltchuk persuaded him to change his mind.

It was then time for Mee and Ma to shower. The two women modestly resisted undressing in front of the guards, and the guards began to chuckle. One of them moved in to force Mee out of her clothes, but Nikolay realized that they still had a good chance for cooperation and motioned him back.

"I'll get the women to shower. You go on," Nikolay said to the guards.

The guards left reluctantly with the three men, disappointed that they were missing the free show with the naked women. Nikolay led Mee and Ma to the shower door and allowed them their modesty by leaving the room. There was no other exit or trouble they could get into, and so he opted for obtaining their cooperation as long as it would last. When he heard the showers shut off, he waited a minute and went in. Ma and Mee had already put on their gray cotton outfits, to avoid being seen naked, and had bundled their clothes. He then led them to their cells, after which he told one of his men to make them tea, as he had been instructed by the doctors that they could not have solid food that night as there would be medical tests on them in the morning.

The Tibetans, Jamyang Gyamtso and Neema Lhamo, were next. Nikolay determined that they were getting along well together and decided to have them shower and dress together. They seemed to feel more comfortable together, speaking their native tongue to one another, and were given a cell to share. Tomorrow was going to be a special, and unfortunate, day for the prisoners, as experimentation was to begin on their tissues.

❧❧❧

Nikolay and three guards came to the Chinese subjects' cells at six o'clock in the morning to find them sound asleep. Sum was found praying in his room.

They led Sum to Dr. Dorogomilov's outer lab area and to a separate room with a guard placed outside.

Dr. Volkova appeared in a white lab coat and began Sum's medical examination. She took his vitals and drew blood for analysis. She was most interested in the blood analysis and took it to an analyzer in another room right away.

She returned several minutes later, bringing in a disposable cup of a clear liquid which she gave to him.

"What are you giving him, Doctor?" Nikolay, asked, speaking in Russian, as he knew the Chinaman did not understand.

"Klophelin," she answered. "It'll knock him out, and then we won't have to fight him to get him under the mask." She motioned for Sum to drink, and he complied.

"I know of that," Nikolay said. "Russian hookers sometimes put this in a man's drink to knock him out so they can steal his money."

Sum suddenly felt tired, lay back on the table, and closed his eyes. He was out in no time.

"Take off his clothes," Dr. Volkova told Nikolay.

He slipped off Sum's gray scrubs, and Dr. Volkova then looked him over as he lay naked on the table. She reached for a set of electric shears with an extension cord on the counter nearby and shaved the hair off his head, the hair falling to the ground. She then lifted his sex organ with one hand and methodically shaved around it as well.

Once finished, she said to Nikolay, "Bring in the gurney."

He went outside and returned with a gurney and one of his men. They easily put Sum, half their size, onto it and wheeled him behind Dr. Volkova toward Master Surgeon Dorogomilov's operating room and lifted the naked Sum onto the operating table.

"Please go tidy up the hair, so as not to frighten the next one, and then make another one ready," Dr. Volkova told Nikolay.

The operating room was large and filled with all the equipment one would find in a regular operating theater. The operating table was in the center, under lights. Behind it was an anesthesiologist's cart set up with the usual tanks and breathing equipment, ready to go.

Dr. Volkova opened a jar of sterile wipes and began to wipe Sum with them in the area over the liver, the stomach, the scalp, and then his chest. They were going to do all the areas at one time. Any later complaints about the lack of bedside manner would not be a factor.

The door opened and the Dorogomilov entered. Dr. Volkova pulled over a table of instruments selected for the procedures. "This one has been praying in his cell every day," she told him.

Dr. Dorogomilov first went for a sample of liver tissue, which he took in the form of a needle biopsy. He ran a huge, size sixteen needle with a trochar, a plug inside the needle blocking the opening, right through his abdomen into his liver. Once inside his liver, the trochar was removed and Dr. Dorogomilov put a huge syringe on the needle, applied vacuum, and rammed the needle on into the liver, whereupon he sucked out liver material into the syringe, and then set the syringe in a stainless-steel pan with the tissue samples.

"What next?" Dr. Volkova asked.

"Lungs."

Dr. Volkova wiped Sum's chest once again so Dr. Dorogomilov could make a cut over the lung to one side. He then cut through the intercostal muscle and spread the ribs. Taking forceps to pinch a piece of lung for his specimen, he then stapled the lung tissue together leaving the specimen in-between the staples so that when he cut it out, the lung would be already pre-sealed. He then cut the piece of lung in between the staples, and had his specimen.

After stitching up the open chest, he started on the stomach. He shoved a fiberoptic endoscope down Sum's throat and sniped off a piece of stomach tissue.

"I'm going to take some brain samples as well," Dr. Dorogomilov told Dr. Volkova.

"What? You have never made a workable race-specific Ebola from brain tissues. The blood brain barrier does not permit it."

"Hush. This modified virus is more virulent, and I predict it will get past the blood brain barrier. In any event, do not mention it to the guards or to the baron. Sum has been praying since he got here. He may have the difference in the brain that I believe exists between deeply religious people and those who are not. Now that I am back in operation, with resources, I have the chance to test my theory that I can make an Ebola that will only attack fanatically religious people. It is only my knowledge that is bringing me the five million from the baron, and I want to learn what I can now that I have the chance. I will compare parts of Sum's brain to others as Sum is deeply religious. Imagine what that knowledge could be worth one day."

Dr. Dorogomilov drew a circle on Sum's shaved head with a red pen over the parietal area and drilled a pilot hole in the red spot with a drill. With a craniotome saw he cut a hole. The bone fragments sprayed about like sawdust from a woodworker. With a scalpel, he cut the dura, allowing clear, cerebrospinal fluid to seep out. There it was, brain tissue for the taking. Pausing a moment to look at the bounty, he then put a probe deep into the brain, to an area that he had learned of, and then took out what he wanted. He then put in a bipolar cautery electric probe and cauterized the wound to prevent hemorrhaging, as bleeding in the brain was quite often fatal, although the removal of part of his limbic system in the brain would probably keep him from regaining consciousness.

The doctor closed the dura mater, stitched it, but did not bother to put anything back in the hole in the cranium, as there was no need, given the situation.

When he was through with Sum, he looked up at Dr. Volkova and nodded, indicating that the procedure was completed.

He took off his bloody gloves, and tossed them into the wastebasket to go have a tea and then scrub for the next subject. Dr. Volkova methodically put the tissue samples in containers and labeled each one with its place of origin, as well as with Sum's name, and placed them into a refrigerator.

Dr. Volkova covered Sum with a sheet up to his head, went to the door, and called for Nikolay. He came in, with Zuhk pushing the gurney, transferred Sum to it, and wheeled him out to a recovery room. Timoshenko and Yageltchuk were standing by.

Not wasting time, Dr. Dorogomilov utilized the rest of the day completing the tissue sampling from all of the remaining four Chinese, Tai, Mee, So, and Ma. They were brought in one at a time, two hours apart, for the same treatment.

No one put up any resistance except Tai who, when he

saw some cut hair on the floor around the table where he was told to sit, decided to try bolting. Rather than voluntarily drinking his Klophelin drug from the cup, he had to be held, with each of four huge guards on one of his limbs, as, shrieking and kicking, he had a gauze filled with chloroform held over his mouth and nose until he became limp.

Within an hour or two following their operations, they came to and were then wheeled to their cells and placed onto their beds by the guards so they could sleep off the final effects of the gas and procedures.

Later that day, they were given strong pain killers, as they awoken in horrible pain and were suffering.

By the end of that long day, Dr. Dorogomilov had the initial tissue samples he needed. He looked at the tissues in their containers through the glass refrigerator door, wondering just what specifics he could expect to isolate.

The following day, the two doctors performed the operations with the Tibetans, the control group.

Everything had gone well. Beginning the next morning, Dr. Dorogomilov would start early.

⌘⌘⌘

Drs. Dorogomilov and Volkova sat admiring the new equipment that had arrived. Dr. Volkova turned to Dr. Dorogomilov and asked, "Which do you want to start with?"

"I read a study just last night on the Internet that the Han Chinese have a high incidence of liver disease, so we can go there if we don't find it in the lungs, which I would prefer."

Dr. Volkova went to the refrigerator and brought lung tissue from one of the subjects. Dr. Dorogomilov first put it into his new sonicator and blasted the sample with sonic waves until it was broken up and blended into a homogeneous brew. He then put the cells into his new density gradient ultracentrifuge, which swung them in a circle at an amazing one hundred thousand times normal gravity. The result was that the dense cells were slung to the bottom of the containers, resulting in cell separation by density into relevant fractions.

Next the doctor added an eluent, to dissolve any contaminants, and put the cells into a high-pressure liquefying chromatography machine which separated the mixture into vertical columns. One cc at a time was removed from the end of the each column and put into a tube, over and over again, until a hundred cc's had been taken, each with a different density. The cells were then subjected to a densitometer with a light scanner. Once the light scanner turned on the cells, peaks and valleys appeared on the monitor, along a horizontal axis, displaying the differences of the protein components.

He had gone through two thirds of the hundred cc's with the light scanner, when he noticed that one had a huge vertical peak, clearly distinguishing it as a unique protein.

"Here's one!" he exclaimed. "Have a look." He moved aside to let her in closer to the monitor. "Now, Anastasiya, I want you to repeat this with the other lung tissues from each of the Chinese to see if they all have it. As we know that the unique cell is in the lungs, you can shortcut the process by starting with the lung samples from the other subjects and taking the sample from about two-thirds of the way down, or at least very close to it, so you only have to test a few tubes on either side to find and confirm. If you get confirmation with the other four, you can go ahead and concentrate it by mixing it with ammonium carbonate in a dialysis tubing. Then we will see if the Tibetans have it. While you do that, I will get started on tissue from another organ. I'm hoping that if I can't find it the lungs, I will be able to find it in the liver, so I will try that next."

He went to the refrigerator for liver tissue to start the process on that while she went to work repeating the experiment on the remaining lung tissues.

As he had done back in the lab's heyday under the Soviet Union when he was hot on a project, Dr. Dorogomilov had set up small living quarters in the building, so as not to waste time going back and forth to the city, and worked constantly when not asleep.

Since his wife died, he had no family, other than hers, and no social life. Dr. Volkova was working on changing that.

She stayed in with him, but only on alternate nights, as she had to make sure that provisions were being provided to the prisoners as well as to the animals.

Dr. Volkova went to his quarters at midnight. "Can I help you relax, darling?"

He nodded and began to take off his clothes.

She began to talk about non-scientific things as she undressed. "All I can think of is going to some tropical island, darling. I've always wanted to see a beach of sand. I want to go to one of those places where they have tropical fruits. I've never had a coconut."

"Stop daydreaming until we finish this project," he replied.

She watched him lay down on the bed. Then she moved in to do what he liked and that would help put him to sleep.

೮⊃೮⊃

Tai Won Ong was awakened by Nikolay at six in the morning four days after the operations. He was taken by gurney to a special room which had been set up for him in the high containment area, adjacent to the lab in the back of the building. The room had a toilet, a table, a chair, and a bed. The unusual feature was that, to get to it, one had to go through three sets of high containment doors much like the oval doors in submarines.

Off to one side of the door into the room was a small latch over a shelf where food could be passed to him in the room without anyone opening the door.

At just before seven, the small food access door opened. In came a bowl of steaming rice. On top of the rice were fried strips of the local produce, in addition to egg and meat, which had been prepared by the doctor's deceased wife's aunt that morning. The food contained a special additive, however, provided by the doctor, who was serving it while wearing a pressure suit. That special additive was a sprinkling of the doctor's deadly virus, newly linked to the antibody created to seek the unique protein located in the lungs of any member of the Han Chinese race.

Tai became very excited at the delicious smell and appearance of the meal. The doctor helped him take it to the table and Tai eagerly dug in, using the chopsticks provided.

Outside the cell, the doctor watched Tai through the double window, until Tai had eaten a good portion of the special breakfast.

In a short while, Nikolay brought one of the Tibetans, Jamyang Gyamtso, to an adjacent room set up similarly to Tai's. Jamyang was fed the very same dish, which he was pleased to receive after eating bland foods ever since the tests.

Sum was unable to eat, being still unconscious after having had a part of his brain removed, and so he was fed intravenously.

෪

On the third morning after the special breakfast—after suiting, up but before working with the infected monkeys—Drs. Dorogomilov and Volkova stopped by the cells to look in on Tai and Jamyang.

The first cell they came to was Jamyang's. He was moving about restlessly, pacing one way and then the other, frustrated about being confined.

The doctors walked over to the observation window of the next cell and looked in on Tai, who was, in complete contrast to Jamyang, lying on his bed, perfectly still.

"Tomorrow, after we suit up, let's go in and get Tai's temperature and take a blood sample before we start work with the monkeys," Dr. Dorogomilov said to Dr. Volkova. "It looks like we have done it."

"You have done it, dear."

❧❧❧

On the fourth day after Tai had been given the virus, Drs. Dorogomilov and Volkova made their rounds, suited up in the pressure suits for safety.

Looking in on Jamyang the next day, they saw that he was as healthy as ever. It was so obvious that he was feeling no effects from the virus that they did not even bother going in. Moving on to Tai's cell, they unlocked the door and went in. Tai lay on his mattress, moaning. Dr. Volkova drew blood from his arm and took his temperature, which was elevated to one-hundred-and-one degrees. He had horrible stomach pains and was nauseous.

By the seventh day, Tai was unconscious. Blood, the color of coffee grounds, bubbled out of his mouth, creating a dark froth. He looked ghastly and had to struggle mightily just to get a breath.

"Note the coffee grounds color of the blood coming from his mouth," Dr. Dorogomilov said to Dr. Volkova. "That is older blood from the stomach, so he is definitely bleeding in the stomach now. Later on, there will be bright red blood coming both from his mouth and rectum. This is very good. Now, do you see the frothing at the mouth?"

"Yes."

"The frothing shows that the lungs are infected as well. The virus is in the bloodstream and lungs. Lungs usually infect much more quickly, as there is no stomach acid to destroy the particles, no liner like the stomach has, and no food to mix with. The lungs are fast and simple. I really like it when we can use the lungs.

"Let's go ahead and bring in the Tibetan Jamyang as

well as another Chinese and put them in with Tai so they can breathe his air," he continued. "That will tell us if it is working as planned and if the linked Ebola will pass to the Chinese subject through aerosol means. Since we should be in the pressure suits, they might get scared and put up a fight when they see us, so it might be best to knock them out first. You go get the Klophelin, and I will have Nikolay see that they drink it. Once they are out, I'll have them put onto gurneys wheeled into Tai's room."

Nickoly was located and, with Zuhk, brought a soda spiked with Klopheli. They gave one to the female Ma and one to Jamyang. As it appeared to be a treat, both drank the sodas without being forced to and, in a very short time, both were unconscious. They put them on gurneys, and Dr. Dorogomilov, still in his pressure suit, wheeled them both into Tai's room.

Two days later, Ma was ill and lying down on her bed. Jamyang was still energetic and pacing about. Looking through the window at Tai, the doctors saw that he was writhing on his bed, with red blood dripping out of his mouth and mixing with the froth.

Dr. Dorogomilov turned to Dr. Volkova. "That's it! We have it! Now all we need to do is to confirm the extent of the infection. I'll have to get tissue samples from Tai. I'd prefer to wait until he dies and do it as an autopsy, as that way we can also record the time it takes for the Ebola to kill. From the looks of Tai, that should not be too long."

༄༅

Five days later, Tai expired. He was moved to the operating room so an autopsy could be performed. Lying naked on the operating table, Tai was a ghastly sight. The doctors donned their pressure suits in preparation for performing his autopsy.

First Dr. Dorogomilov made a huge cut over Tai's abdomen, exposing the stomach—or what was left of it. It was surrounded by blood, some coagulated, some not. Dr. Dorogomilov sucked out the mess, as well as some red blood that filled the abdominal cavity, with a vacuum tube. He then took a sample of the tissue and put it into a solution of formalin to prepare it for microscopic examination. "Note how the lining of the stomach has sloughed off," he said as he cut into the stomach. "Good! Let's have a look at the lungs."

With an electric saw, he cut open Tai's sternum, exposing the lungs. Then he cut into the lungs with a scalpel, revealing an ugly mess of bloody tissue.

"Perfect! Both the lungs and the stomach are infected. Let's get samples and check them. If the next subject reacts in the same way, I think it will be time to contact the baron."

☙❧

As they sipped their Russian tea in the morning, Dr. Dorogomilov turned to Dr. Volkova and Nikolay and began to plan the day. "It's time to begin making the finished product in sufficient quantity for the baron's project. We need a large amount of lung tissue for the finished product and we are running short. Bogomazov, please go fetch me a Chinese and bring him to the operating room. There we will go ahead and remove both his lungs for the tissue we need."

"Any particular one?" Nikolay asked. "Male or female?"

Dr. Dorogomilov shrugged nonchalantly. "You pick."

Nickolay and Zuhk left to go get Yageltchuk and Opanasenko and then to go fetch one of the remaining three Chinese who were not infected.

"We're right on schedule," Dr. Dorogomilov said to Dr. Volkova. "All the monkeys we have brought in are now in the same cage in the containment area and they should be all infected. This will put a strain on us, as we will need to work long hours to collect the Ebola virus from them. They will all fall sick over a fairly short period time, unless we want to wait and work on them after they die. Once we start collecting, we will flash freeze each day's production in liquid nitrogen."

In the monkeys' area, instead of the usual, wild screeching and jumping about the monkeys had done before when someone entered the room, they were lethargic and listless, clearly infected.

"We'll start the large scale production of Ebola after we get the lungs and process them for antibodies for our assistants, who can work in the front," Dr. Dorogomilov said, referring to the non-containment area. "Also," he reminded himself aloud, "we need to set up the incubators for the mass production of the antibodies after they come out of the rabbits, as we'll need them in a day or so. It's time to start removing the antibodies from the peritoneums of the rabbits. We'll use five per cent carbon dioxide, mixed with purified air in the humidified incubators, as that will be the best environment for producing more cells." He sighed. "It is going to be a lot of work, Anastasiya, especially because we will have to do it in pressure suits. Are you ready for some long work days?"

She smiled at him. "Sure. I'll start staying up here at night."

They arrived at the operating room, where Nikolay, Timoshenko, Zuhk, and Opanasenko each held onto one of So's limbs. So lay on the operating table and, in spite of the weakness caused by the disease, was still struggling and doing his best to escape. Dr. Volkova wheeled her anesthesiologist cart up to the head of the operating table. She lifted the mask from its hook and put it over So's face. She turned on the gas and held the mask firmly over his nose and mouth, forcing him to breathe through the mask. In just thirty seconds, he was quiet.

She started an IV and dripped anesthesia into him until he was in deep sedation. The four big Russians relaxed their hold, slowly at first, and then altogether, before stepping back, as the four of them took up too much space around the table.

With a pair scissors Dr. Volkova cut off So's top and tossed it into the wastebasket. Dr. Dorogomilov, who had been in the scrub room during the preparation, came in, ready to operate. So would not live through this one as he would have no lungs when they were done.

♥つ♥つ

Ma, in the bed next to Tai, was two days behind him, and was actually in more pain as she had remained conscious longer. She was bleeding out of all of her orifices.

"Do you think we should give her morphine for her last days?" Dr. Volkova asked.

"I'd rather not, in order to get a more accurate estimate of how long it takes them to die. Often the death is from shock itself, and the morphine may extend that time by reducing the shock."

"But she is suffering so."

Dr. Dorogomilov ignored what to him was idle chatter as they went back to the monkeys. The animals were now very quiet as many had died and been dissected for the Ebola tissue that continued to live on their cells for a time. The remaining monkeys were all very sick. The production was nearly half done by this time and progressing well. From the start of the day to around one or two in the afternoon, the doctors would extract the live Ebola cells from the monkeys, both alive and dead.

"Oh!" Dr. Volkova said. "I forgot to tell you. The liquid-nitrogen cooled canisters arrived yesterday."

"Good." Dr. Dorogomilov reached into the cage for one of the recently deceased monkeys to begin the day's work. The incubators were all going. Everything was in good order and progressing more rapidly than predicted. "We might as well infect one of the two remaining Chinese later today or tomorrow," he said. "And we can then compare the Ebola's progress with another subject. Even though they have been consistent, another subject will add more reliability to the timetable." He shrugged. "We have no need for the Chinese now and they have to be eliminated. There is no other use for the remaining two, unless we run short of lung tissue, but I doubt that we will. We have more left over. I'll tell Bogomazov to fetch me one of them later."

દ૭

Dr. Dorogomilov sealed up the lid on the last nitrogen-cooled bottle. "There it is, Anastasiya. That makes seventy," he said as the two doctors left and sterilized their pressure suits.

Tai and Ma had died of Ebola, and So from removal of his lungs. The remaining two Chinese, Mee and Sum, were now infected and being observed as the virus overwhelmed them. Both the Tibetans were still perfectly healthy, but unfortunately for them, they were witnesses.

The incinerator at the back of Building 221 bellowed out a blast of flame when Dr. Dorogomilov opened the door. Drs. Dorogomilov and Volkova were in pressure suits and had wheeled up a table with a tray on top filled with a horrific mass of black, disgusting-looking organic material.

Dr. Dorogomilov stepped back from cart and studied it. A substantial amount of tissue was on it, easily fifteen pounds. He dumped the mass into the fire.

દ૭

Andrew lay in bed, awake, in his suite at the New Orleans Windsor Court. Next to him, asleep, was his ultimate prize, Shanta. On her left hand was a diamond that looked too big to be real, but real it was. It had belonged to his mother. His father had gotten it for her as her second ring, long after they were married, when he became rich.

Andrew and Shanta had been married that afternoon,

with Eschmann as a witness. Eschmann had arranged a quick annulment of Shanta's first marriage, as it had never been consummated. He'd had to simply guess as to the particulars, as Shanta did not have any of the paperwork from Singapore.

Andrew did not want to get married in Kentucky, as it would have become a media event for the local papers. Instead, he'd contacted Eschmann who had arranged a private ceremony in New Orleans. They had a wonderful evening, and Andrew finally had sex with her, but only after, not before, he took her hand in marriage. It was his biggest day.

The cell phone, which was solely for the call from the baron, which Andrew had been carrying with him day and night, was sitting in its charging stand on the table. Andrew got up and grabbed the phone.

"Hello?"

"Master Saunders? Baron here."

"Yes! Good evening!" Then Andrew remembered the time difference. "Is it evening?"

"Actually it's morning here in Taipei. How have you been?"

"I married Shanta today!"

"My congratulations. She is one of the most charming women alive, to be certain. You are such a lucky man."

Andrew knew why the man was calling. "Is it time?"

"Yes," Baron said. "Everything is ready. Transfer the money to the same account, and I'll verify that it came. Keep this phone until you hear from me further to confirm the payment. Then dispose of in a way that no one can possibly find it."

"Will tomorrow be soon enough for the wire transfer?" Andrew wasn't sure if he could do it at night, and he wanted to get back to his bride who was now stirring.

"That'll be fine," Baron said. "My best wishes to your new bride, Mrs. Shanta Saunders."

"Thank you, Baron."

When the called ended, Baron turned to Tak. "Andrew Sanders and Shanta Laxshimi just got married."

"Love is in the air," Tak said.

৩৩৩৩

"What are we going to do with that ridiculous American diplomat Christine Rhyes-Walters from the State Department, who thinks fungi is going to end the drug traffic?" Doctor Dorogomilov asked.

"We have to see her," Dr. Volkova said. "And we must not let on that anything unusual had been going on here. There will be Kazakh officials as well."

"Should we tell her now that I have already created it?" Dr. Dorogomilov said.

"I don't think so," Dr. Volkova said. "They will tell the press, and there might be journalists and others wanting to come here and interview you. She will want you to go lecture others in the United States and elsewhere on how to make it. And if you don't go, it will arouse suspicion. It is best to say you are making great progress. Perhaps after you get your money, you could forward your work on it to some scientist in the West to verify that it works. Let him make the announcement and donate the formula to the world. We don't want anyone coming around here."

# CHAPTER 20

Nikolay began his talk for the twenty people in his now-crowded St. Petersburg office. Extra chairs were found so sixteen of them could sit, whereas the monster-sized Yageltchuk, Opanasenko, Timoshenko, and Zuhk stood behind Nikolay's desk, as they would be the leaders of splinter groups who would spread out in the Tibetan cities. The sixteen additional people consisted of eight men and eight women, all carefully selected.

"Tibet consists of six million Tibetans and seven and a half million Chinese. Nearly all of those seven and a half million Chinese have moved there after the 1949 Chinese invasion, and ninety per cent have moved there since 1990. That includes thousands of soldiers that China brought in to maintain control. The military bases there, however, are non-hardened, that is, they are not built up with concrete, as they would have been had the Chinese government expected to defend a war. Rather the bases were built just to house troops should there be any problems with demonstrations or control of the Tibetans. Practically all of the people who have moved into Tibet of late are Han Chinese, which is what we call the Chinese race. They were and are still encouraged to go there by China to dilute the Tibetan population and culture. Racially, in Tibet, nearly all are either Tibetans or Han Chinese. There are extremely small minorities of a few other races who do not matter.

"We will be spreading Ebola virus around. The Chinese who have moved into Tibet have all moved into the few major cities and work in commerce, mostly in stores selling to tourists, owing hotels, owning or working in restaurants, and things of that nature. In the downtown areas, the Mandarin language is spoken, as nearly all the government officials are Chinese, appointed, of course, by China, with Beijing actually ruling the country. In the rural areas, Tibetan is the spoken language. The vast majority of Tibet is not populated, consisting of huge mountain ranges on the south and, on the north, the arid plateau six thousand meters above sea level. Travel in the winter is next to impossible, but as we go in the summer, one might see Tibetan herdsmen drive pack animals, yak, or sheep far distances. The newcomer Chinese have not had any interest in joining the hard life of the nomadic Tibetans or the rural farmers who farm barley or raise yaks or sheep.

"So infecting Chinese is made easy by the Chinese themselves, as they are concentrated and also live and mix with other Chinese exclusively. This is a perfect country for this task. Even though the country is large in size, only a tiny portion has any concentration of people, and those are the areas where the Chinese have moved to and where the military's soldiers are based. We can infect nearly all of the areas where the Chinese are in just two weeks and rely on them to spread it to others."

Nikolay held up a bottle, a perfect replica of Essentuki, a well-known Russian mineral water, named after a town that had a spa. "These are special liquid-nitrogen-cooled canisters. The outer layer is insulated with a high-tech material, and there is an inner wall forming a chamber filled with liquid nitrogen. The contents are very cold Ebola in a fluid medium.

"I'll give each of you three of these canisters to put in your check-in baggage. I'm supplying a piece of bubble wrap to wrap each one, which will not be suspicious as the bottle is supposed to be glass. These containers are metal made to look like glass. You will be given two bags, one carry on and one small check-in size. Make sure you leave enough space in your check-in bag for three of these and for a smaller, flexible bottle. The nitrogen keeps the contents at close to two hundred degrees below zero Celsius. The Ebola inside is a clear fluid, one that will not freeze up like water, and is preserved by the frozen temperature. It will live for some time at room temperature once it is out, possibly as much as several days, but we want to preserve it as much as possible. We will only take out each day as much as we need for that day.

"Regarding customs, should anyone at customs in Tibet, for any reason, ask why you have the water, you tell him that you were informed by the tour organizer that the water in Tibet is not safe to drink, and the tour host provided the mineral water for your own health and safety. The Chinese customs officers in Tibet will never have seen Essentuki and will have no reason to suspect you.

"I'm also providing you with one of these traveling water bottles." He held up a half liter water bottle. It had an insulating, thin, foam- rubber sheath around it with a sports logo on it. Each had a shoulder strap that allowed the bottle to be slung under the shoulder.

"The top unscrews and, in the hotels in Tibet each day before you leave, the bottle will be filled with the estimated amount that you will need for that day. The top has a squirting type of lid." He held one up, demonstrating. "These are made to allow you to squirt water into your mouth like a cyclist. By squeezing it, it can shoot the liquid six to eight feet."

He squirted water from it to demonstrate. "But don't waste it, as you only need just a drop, not a cupful for each person you infect. I'm putting in your bag a small funnel, so you won't spill this exotic stuff in the hotel rooms. Put several teaspoons into the sport bottle and fill the rest with water. Then you can refill when it is empty.

"Naturally you don't want to be seen standing back and

squirting the bottle on things. You will have to be as subtle as you can. For example, at an open air market, you can start handling foodstuffs with some of the virus on your hands. While cooking the vegetables may kill the Ebola, the vegetables will be first handled by someone and, if that person is Chinese, they will most likely catch it. Therefore, it should not be necessary, although it is better, to put it on things that will not be heated such as fruits and nuts. When paying, give a note with some of the virus on it. In public buildings, you can squirt a little on your own hand and then just rub the doorknob, door push plate, or any railing that looks like it is used often.

"Now, I'm giving each of you a cheap digital camera so as to look like tourists, and you can use them as an excuse to get in close and pretend to take photos. Also you will have six cartons of luxury western cigarettes. Two cartons are the most you are supposed to bring in, but I have checked and there are no reports of anyone being hassled over excess cigarettes or liquor. We are especially keen on targeting soldiers, as they will be in contact with more soldiers as they return to their base at night and this will render the military helpless very soon.

"We also want to hit the police. An excellent way to infect someone is to offer him a cigarette. Either squirt the filters or put a drop of the fluid on your finger and pull out a cigarette with that finger. Then pass it to the Chinaman. If he takes it and puts it in his mouth, he will be infected. If the person doesn't smoke, offer him money for him to stand beside you while another one of you takes a picture of you together. Smear Ebola on the note or coin you offer him. The money will pass the virus to his fingers and should end up infecting him.

"Now, you are all selected because of your ability to blend in and not be suspected, which does not include knowledge on how to travel lightly. So I'm going to tell you how. I'm passing out these bags." He reached down and picked up two lightweight bags. One was the correct size for carry-on bags for planes, and it had the name of a tour agency written on it.

"These are all you will take. It's the hot season there, and you will not need warm clothes. I've purchased a bunch of wash-and-wear clothes from which you can choose what you want. You should only take the slacks you wear and one extra pair. You should only take the shirt you wear and two extra. Three undergarments in total. One sweater or sweatshirt. Only the one pair of shoes that you will wear. Make sure they are your favorite sort of walking shoes and, preferably, ones that are broken in so you won't get blisters. Some of you may want hiking shoes with thick, soft soles, some tennis shoes. That's up to you.

"The clothes that I'll be passing out are all drip-dry and can be washed in the hotel room at night and hung up. They will dry before morning. As I said, take a jacket, sweater, or sweatshirt, but wear the one you take. You don't have to take the clothes that I'm passing out, but if you take your own, I want everything to fit in the check-in bag because, once we land, you will transfer the bottles from the check-in bag to the carry-on. You also need to leave room for six cartons of cigarettes, three liter and a half bottles, and the squirt bottle.

"This is not a fashion trip. I don't give a shit what you look like. You are not going over there to find a fucking spouse. The Tibetans do things like eat Cordycepts fungus for their health, a fungus that kills the brains of insects and most likely theirs as well. So forget about falling in love. Anyway, if you veer off your duty, you will have to answer to me, and you will not like that. You won't fall in love with me.

"If you can't get everything in the carry-on, then re-organize and cut back until you can. You must be mobile to do this job, and not laden down with heavy or extra bags."

There were several groans in the room at not being allowed to take all their favorite things.

One of the younger men asked a question that he had

already been told the answer to. "Are you absolutely sure that this will not infect us?"

He apparently needed reassurance, and Nikolay had expected the question. "The best answer to that is that I'm going with you and will be right there the whole time. I've personally witnessed the effects of the Ebola on the Chinese, as opposed to others, and am convinced enough to join you and be part of the operation. It will not affect any of you. And this is not something that you might get a bit of, like a cold. This will either do you in or not affect you at all. And it won't. So shut up and stop asking the same question."

He scanned the group to see if there were any more questions. "Very well, then. You will be picked up between seven and eight tomorrow. We're flying to Lhasa, Tibet. I don't want anyone to forget his or her passport. I'll have your tickets and visas tomorrow, and some spending money for the trip.

"Now, I remind you that you were selected because you were considered reliable, and I want to emphasize that, no matter what, no one is to hint or tell anyone that they will be coming into money right away or do or say anything that will arouse suspicion and lead to questions. You are not to spend any great deal of your money immediately upon return so as to make your friends connect the trip to your new money. If we hear of any breach of confidence, no matter how slight, you will be visited by one or more of us here and you will be killed at once."

ͽͼͽ

The meaning of the word Lhasa was "goat dirt," Nikolay read in a paperback book on Tibet as he practiced what he was to do on his way in from Russia. The name, it said, for the city that was three-thousand-six-hundred feet above sea level, meant that the city was built on dirt carried by goats. The highest mountains in the world were in Tibet, and the average elevation of the entire country was four-thousand-nine-hundred meters, or sixteen-thousand feet, the highest country on the planet.

The tour group got off the plane at the Gonga Airport in Lhasa, Tibet, and entered the terminal. The group all had the same travel carry-on bag, with the name and logo of a travel agency on it, and all were wearing the wash-and-wear clothes that had been provided. They all looked mostly the same, except for the four giants, Yageltchuk, Opanasenko, Timoshenko, and Zuhk, for whom Nikolay had purchased special clothes, as they were all 5X or 6X size.

No one hassled them at customs. They got their check-in bags, small as they were, and assembled.

Nikolay decided to start in the airport. He took his luggage into the bathroom, beckoning for one of his male operatives to follow, so as to show him how not to waste the super substance.

Once the two of them were alone in the bathroom, Nikolay took out the sports bottle. He produced the tiny funnel, the size used to fill a pocket flask with whiskey, from his pocket. He opened the Essentuki bottle carefully, as it was the first time he had opened one. The contents, extraordinarily cold, gave off a slow moving, white-colored fog, due to the temperature difference. The fog exiting the special bottle gave off no discernible odor and rose above the opening, then slowly sank around the bottle, as though it was heavy.

He poured a teaspoon of the special contents into the flexible sports bottle. He closed up the supply bottle and then topped off the sports bottle with water. He then opened a packet of cigarettes, pulled the ones in the front row out slightly, and squeezed a drop of fluid onto the tips of the filters. Pushing them back in the pack, he was ready.

Outside in the terminal, the group had assembled, waiting. Nikolay got their attention and led them toward the exit. As they approached the doors, they could see the Tibetan tour guide, who had been hired through a travel agency, holding up a small blackboard with the name *Bogomazov* written in chalk, just outside.

Nikolay acknowledged him, and he approached. The Tibetan guide smiled, and greeted Nikolay in horrible Russian. Nikolay had insisted on Tibetan tour guides—so as not to be provided with a Chinese who would become infected with the Ebola—and also one who spoke Russian. But it seemed that Russian may not be the lingua franca for the tour, if this man was to be their guide. At any rate, it was better than a Chinese under the circumstances.

Just in the parking area were two large tour vans, each big enough for half the group, with Tibetan drivers, all as ordered by Nikolay. The group assembled outside the building, having their first look at Tibet.

At the exit, just outside the door, stood two Chinese soldiers in uniform acting as airport guards, both looking very bored due to the lack of any action at the airport. Nikolay's group was watching, trying hard not to be noticed, what their leader was going to show them.

Nikolay turned to the soldiers, taking out his cigarettes as though to step away from the group to smoke. Acting as if he just noticed the soldiers' presence, he pulled two cigarettes halfway out and offered them to the soldiers.

The soldiers both smiled widely, each taking a cigarette from the pack.

Smoking was allowed by the soldiers on duty, when outside the terminal building, and both put them in their mouths. One produced matches, lit his, and then the other's. They thanked Nikolay for the gift. He turned around and joined the group, which were watching and learning from their leader as to how it could be done.

Nikolay smiled and said, in Russian, "One and two."

# CHAPTER 21

One of the green Rolls Royce's from the Hotel Peninsula's fleet picked up Baron and Tak at the Hong Kong Airport. In the car, Baron's cell rang. It was a local call from Hor Chew Guat.

"Hello, Baron. I called your office and heard you were coming. Mei Ling gave the flight number to me. I take it you have landed?"

"Yes, I'm en route to the Hotel Peninsula."

"It is such an honor to welcome the famous baron," Hor said. "You must let me take you to dinner! I'll not accept no for an answer."

"I have a special guest. I was married recently, and I must bring her if I am to come."

"Bring her along. A larger group is better for a Chinese dinner. And I was hoping to bring my wife. She will be delighted to meet her."

"I accept your gracious invitation."

The arrangements were then made for one of the most exclusive restaurants in Hong Kong.

Baron concluded the call and turned to Tak. "I want to show you Hong Kong. An old friend found out I was coming and insisted we join him. I have accepted a dinner invitation. This is Hong Kong, but not what the average tourist will experience for dinner. This fellow will order exotic foods that you might find somewhat strange. Here in Hong

Kong, it is a custom to impress your guests with the most rare and expensive dishes. Would you like to experience that?"

"I'm not sure, Baron, after that savage experience in Kazakhstan."

Baron laughed. "Tak, you are here to experience what the natives do, which includes cuisine. Now, to occupy the afternoon, after we check in and freshen up, and to let you experience the people of the city, I'll take you shopping."

Later, Baron led her out onto the bustling streets, with Lachhiman, who had been summoned after he delivered the Rolls Royce to Berlin, walking behind as a bodyguard. They stopped at a window, taken in by a small statue on display, carved from rosewood from Mainland China. Tak could not help but stare.

"Can I look at that?" She went in, picked it up, admiringly, turned it about, and then set it back down.

She looked at the proprietor, who understood English. "What is it?"

"It's a Chinese general," the proprietor said.

When she put it back down and looked around further, the proprietor made a face and cursed her in Cantonese in a low, but quite voice for touching his goods but not buying. "*Diu ni lo mo!*"

Baron, who understood the slander perfectly, turned around abruptly, and snapped back, "*Gan ni niang de tzo de bi!*"

Lachhiman, standing by, caught the tone of the insults and stepped forward, ready for action. But this sort of situation was not the kind that got resolved by fighting, only with words, and Baron was the master at that game.

Unaware of the threat posed by the Gurkha, but hearing the baron, the Chinaman was speechless. Not so much because of what the baron had said, but because his curse had been so easily understood by the white-skinned devil, and that the *qui*, or devil, had returned a curse even more effectively and in Mandarin.

Outside, Tak, who had detected the tension and heard Baron's sharp retort, could hardly wait to ask, "What was all that?"

"If you window shop here in Hong Kong, and you go in and touch the goods but do not buy, you will be very likely be cursed by the owner. As I'm white, he did not suspect that I speak Cantonese, so he said his curse out loud. These Cantonese are the rudest."

"Would you mind translating?"

"Very well. The man said to you in Cantonese, 'Fuck your *mother*!' I said back to him, in Mandarin, 'Fuck your mother's smelly pussy!' The curses you witnessed are typical and common. But I spoke to him in Mandarin, rather than in Cantonese, which had the further effect of degrading him as Mandarins are higher class."

She was startled by what she had heard. "It's interesting that the communications are addressed to or about one's mother, whom the person obviously does not know. It suggests a genetic claim to superiority. I learned of this in Auschwitz. Is it the same?"

"You are a most observant guest. More than any other alien I have entertained."

⊱⊰

Dinner with Hor Chew Guat was on the second floor of an exclusive restaurant that did not have a street frontage or a big sign to lure in tourists. Hor, when he entertained someone of the baron's status, intended to impress with exotic and extremely expensive dishes. In his late fifties, Hor and his wife, Xiu Mei, were at the restaurant before the arrival of their honored guests.

Tak, with her Western-sized breasts, red hair, and beautiful face, was the subject of envy of the Chinese who saw her as they walked in.

Baron was in his element, as usual, receiving great face as they entered, with looks of admiration for him with his escort of the best looking woman, especially with a "round-eyed" knockout.

They found Hor, and greetings and introductions were exchanged. Xiu Mei wore a yellow cheong sam with an ostentatious diamond necklace, a matching diamond bracelet, and a ring with an enormous diamond surrounded by many smaller ones.

After the introductions, in keeping with his reputation, Hor signaled the waiter and it was then obvious that he had pre-arranged the menu ahead of time with the chef for an exotic meal, as there was no ordering at the table. A waiter came with a big plate and set it in the center of the table.

To Tak's amazement, the first dish was covered with black scorpions, each fully intact and arranged around the plate with its head pointed in and its tail curved up and forward, as though to strike. Rice was also brought, which Hor and his wife put on their plates to eat with the scorpions.

"Ah, fried scorpion," Baron said. He took one and ate it as Tak looked on in utter amazement.

"Must I eat these insects, or draw attention by not doing so?" she quietly asked Baron, who was seated next to her.

He just looked at her and smiled.

She took one and put it on her plate to try it.

"Don't eat the tail, as it has poison in it," Baron said.

Her eyes wide in shock, Tak stared at him, but he said nothing more. She studied the one on her plate, trying to make sure which was the tail. By watching the others, she determined where the tail was and took a bite of the other part. Disgusting.

The next plate was filled with light-brown objects the size of kidney beans, and each had a small black spot. Fifteen hundred or so filled the plate.

Tak looked to Baron, as she was now used to doing, for an explanation. Baron waited for their host to present the dish.

Hor spoke in English for Tak's benefit. "These are

miniature clams. Each was shelled and cleaned by hand. It's done by women along the coast on the mainland. They are called *hin*."

"This is nice," Tak said, a relief after the scorpion.

The waiter then brought out a tureen of soup and opened the silver lid.

Tak's eyes opened wide. Inside was a huge animal hoof.

"This is camel's hoof soup," Hor said. He then, with gusto, put some broth in Tak's dish and then the others.

Tak was bewildered. "Do we eat that thing?'

"No, just the broth," Baron whispered.

After the others, she sipped a tiny bit of the broth. It was not as bad as it looked.

Then came two plates of cooked vegetables, both of which Tak tried and found to be quite delicious. But then came another "spécialité" dish. The waiter put down a plate with a huge, black paw on it, surrounded by vegetables. Tak turned to Baron in despair after looking at what was clearly a hand cut off of some animal resembling a human, except that it was larger, black, and had claws.

"This is bear paw," Baron told Tak quietly. "A bear is a large animal with fur that lives in the northern territories."

Hor gestured to the dish, for which he would pay quite dearly. "Yes, these are poached in North America and smuggled over."

Tak stared at Baron in disbelief that he expected her to sample something that resembled a hand of a human and was so like cannibalism.

He leaned over to her and said quietly, "It's illegal to kill bears for food, so it is considered very rare to have the dish."

To fit in and be polite, she took a small bit of the re-volting-looking dish when it was passed to her. The taste, she found, was somewhat disguised in the vegetables sur-rounding it and not altogether bad.

Then the final dish came, a huge, hand-made clay pot

on a silver tray. The clay pot was completely enclosed, including the top, and a foot and a half high, narrowing to a point near the top. The waiter broke the clay top free from the bottom, by hitting it with a large knife several times, and then lifted off the top in one piece, revealing the contents.

Oh no! To her amazement, inside was an entire, roasted, small animal, upright, with its arms and legs wrapped around a natural stick, poking up from the bottom of the pot, as though to be in its natural environment. It had tiny finger-like digits and big, sympathetic eyes that were cooked in the open position.

Hor proudly pronounced. "Clay pot surprise! Roasted lemur!"

Xiu Mei's eyes opened wide. She grinned widely in excitement and began to clap her hands in great delight at the marvelous treat.

Tak fought to keep from throwing up. Just ahead of her was the dead, furry creature with its big eyes open as though looking at her, its hands and feet with fingers holding onto the stick, and steam coming off of it from being roasted.

Baron laughed aloud.

She then realized that he was once again amusing himself at her expense. She sighed, wondering, how she could avoid having to try a piece of the poor little creature. When she got the opportunity, and their hosts were not listening, she said softly to Baron, "Is there nothing about this planet that is not barbaric?"

He smiled. "Only you."

# CHAPTER 22

Lhasa was easy. The government capital, the largest city, and the center for trade and commerce, it contained the most concentrated population of Han Chinese in Tibet. Two large military bases kept soldiers to squelch demonstrations which the Tibetans liked to have on their religious holidays. Nikolay and the tour group split up into two groups, each going to one base. The photo sessions with the passing of coins and cigarettes worked easily on soldiers who were on their way in to the military bases. The two groups then went to different shopping areas, where food was being sold, and transferred the virus from their wet hands to the food, passed wet money to pay for goods, and gave away cigarettes to many Chinese shop owners.

A few of the bolder Russians offered some Chinese a drink from their portable water container and were able to get them to actually squirt the Ebola right into their mouths. Several mail carriers were seen and stopped for pictures, lured by a free cigarette, the idea being that a mail carrier might infect hundreds on his route for several days before he became too sick to work, not to mention infecting other mail carriers back at the post office where he would return at the end of the day. Those postal carriers would, in turn, infect hundreds more on their routes. Police were also thought to be good targets, but tended to be a little more reluctant to be photographed. They all readily accepted the free cigarettes, however as they couldn't resist an expensive Western cigarette.

The tour bus driver took them as part of the tour to Potala Palace, a thirteen story building with a thousand rooms, and the Jokhnag, the most important Buddhist temple. Both of the sites had a great many Chinese-owned shops, were wonderful places to infect. The Drepung Monastery, built in 1416, named for a pile of rice, was another major tourist attraction, and similarly surrounded by many Chinese merchants, excellent for infecting large numbers with Ebola.

After three days in Lhasa, by pre-arrangement, the group split into two, with nine driving by private tour bus to the second largest city, Xigatze (Shigatse). Two-hundred-twenty-five kilometers west of Lhasa, Xigatze was also an important trade and commercial center and, as such, was chock full of Chinese just ready to be infected. A large military base and a downtown concentrated with Chinese businesses made it a cinch to ensure massive infection. Their group was scheduled to spend four days there, as it was nearly as large as Lhasa, and the group had been cut in size to less than half. There were government buildings, markets, military, police, and many merchants that were easy to infect in very little time, even though only there were only nine operatives in the group. The tour bus driver then took them to the Tashilhunpo Monastery, around which there was a huge number of Chinese shops owners, merchants, and customers, all easily infected.

In Xigatze, one of the Russian women, Marina, decided to get bold. She went up to a Chinese on the street and started talking to him in Russian. When he could not understand, Marina, a light-haired, good-looking Russian woman with big breasts, started flirting with him and pretended to show him how to pronounce her name by touching his lips as though to teach him how to hold them. In doing so, she put Ebola right on his lips. That she was a woman and an attractive, light-haired foreigner made the gesture non-threatening and fun for the unknowing man. He was done in, for sure.

Another Russian woman, Tatyana, picked up on it and the two of them started trying to outdo each other on how bold they could be, something that worked very effectively and, at the same time, added a little sport to the task. Tatyana went so far to outdo her friend that she put some of the fluid on her lips and kissed a soldier for a picture that Marina pretended to take.

Another one of the group, Sevastiyanov, was at a market where chilled beer was sold. Outside the market were two soldiers, standing on the street. He purchased a bottle of the beer inside the store and opened the top. He then squirted in a few drops of the Ebola and took it outside. He went up to the soldiers and smiled at them, showing his camera. They agreed to allow the photograph, which Sevastiyanov took. He then held up the beer, offering it to them as a gift. One of them took it and the two turned and went off to drink it out of sight of the crowded street. Sevastiyanov watched as they went alongside a building and drank from it, sharing the bottle. Perfect, Sevastiyanov thought. They would go back to their base and multiply the effect.

Their group then took the tour bus south to Sakya, then east to Gyantse. Gyantse, the City of Heroes, so-called for its resistance to British invaders in 1903, was known for carpet production.

It was the Tibetans who made the carpets. But it was the Chinese merchants who had set up many shops to sell those carpets and other Tibetan goods to the tourists. The shopping areas attracted many Chinese. This large concentration of Chinese was excellent area for Yageltchuk and Opanasenko's group of to infect the Chinese in large numbers.

Their group then headed back to Lhasa, stopping along the way to infect Chinese merchants and customers at several roadside stops.

⋐⋑⋐⋑

Nikolay, Timoshenko, and Zuhk took the other group of twelve, by plane, east to Chamdo, the only other city with a major airport. After two days there, that group split into two groups of six, with Nikolay leading one to the north by tour minibus to Jukundo, then southeast to Derge, then east to Kandze, and farther east to Sungpar, stopping at each for a full day. The group then returned to Chamdo.

Timoshendo and Zuhk took their group, by hired bus, southeast to Dartsedo, then west to Litang, then Batang, and back to Chamdo where they were reunited with Nikolay and his group.

Along the way, the groups stopped wherever there were Chinese travelers and Chinese-owned rest areas where they could infect others. At the airport of Chamdo, they did their best to infect as many personnel and military guards as they could, becoming much bolder at it as the end of the trip drew near.

The group arrived in Lhasa in the evening, and everyone had most of the next day to see more of the city before their return flight the next evening.

The only report that anyone heard about any illness, while the group was still in the country, was the night before they left. In their hotel rooms, watching a newscast from a European television station, they heard reports stating that a large-scale epidemic had affected many in the Tibetan region of China, but no details were said to be known.

At the Gonga airport, Nikolay looked around for a newspaper either in Russian or in English but could not find one. Once on the plane, however, there were Russian newspapers, and he was able to read a report that some unknown disease was wide spread throughout the Tibetan region of China, infecting thousands, and that a few deaths had occurred. It said that the government was doing what it could to find out what it was.

Nikolay turned to one of his group sitting next to him, and handed him the paper. "Perfect!"

# CHAPTER 23

In Taipei, Baron had a scheduled meeting with military personnel in a test area for a demonstration of a weapons system he was selling. He wanted Tak to join in, keeping with his promise to include her as he was her Earth guide.

"Tomorrow morning, I'll take you to military trials in the south, as I'll be supervising a demonstration of military equipment that the Taiwan government will buy from me."

"I'll be interested to see that and learn about the nature of the weapons you are selling," she assured him.

The next day, the hot, summer sun baked Baron and Tak as they stood in a narrow field owned by the government, in the south of Taiwan, surrounded by private pineapple orchards, including some in between them and the target area. Demonstrations by several contestants had been set up with the contestants vying to win the lucrative government contract.

Tak wore her regular outfit, but Baron wore an outfit of brand new camouflage fatigues, combat boots, and a camouflage hat, as though he was at the front of a real war. He wore a gun belt, with a stainless-steel Sig .45 pistol and two extra clips

The outfit and gun were just for show, to make it look like he was one of the military. The outfit was so new it looked a bit conspicuous—like a dressed up soldier.

Baron's suppliers, with their various experts, were there, demonstrating the gun turret they wished to have mounted on a number of Taiwanese M113 personnel carriers for the Taiwan army. Those owned by Taiwan had no weapons, and were used as armor-plated personnel and equipment carriers, the idea being to move soldiers, supplies, and small weapons and ammo safely to the site where the Mainland Chinese might one day land to take over Taiwan, which China had often promised to do.

One of the guns had been affixed to the turret on a M113 for the demonstration. The other participants in the trials had already demonstrated their equipment over the past three days.

There were a number of observers. General Hisa was there and was in charge. There were a half dozen junior officers, another dozen enlisted men, two Taiwan officials, and several persons from the French gun manufacturer, as well as from the subcontractors who made the gun mount and targeting system. They were putting on the demonstration and would be expected to fix any problems that might arise.

A target had been set up down range by the army so that a designated Taiwanese officer could shoot the weapon. The man at the trigger was one of General Hisa's junior officers, a nephew of Hisa's. Unfortunately, he was not versed in the intricacies of the new gun, which had a complicated, computerized system to account for the speed and movement of the vehicle that it was mounted to, as well as the heat of the barrel, wind, range, type and weight of the ammo, and a few other factors. This data was all fed into the controlling the computer which would, or at least was supposed to, allow the operators of the M113, with the turret attached, to shoot and hit a target while the M113 was charging forward into harm's way.

But General Hisa had decided it did not matter much what the results were as the bribe was so large that he was going to buy the baron's system, whether it surpassed the others or not. Therefore, he decided to have his young nephew gain face by having the distinction of firing the first round of the test rather than the European expert who had come to Taiwan just for that purpose and who understood the weapon perfectly.

When everything appeared to be ready, he gave the command to his nephew, "*Fire!*" as though in a real war.

His nephew, Captain Fei, was not an accomplished marksman with such a device, nor, in reality, with any gun at all or, for that matter, accomplished at anything and had no idea how to program the necessary details needed to hit the target. Instead, he just looked down the barrel and gave it his best guess, notwithstanding the million dollar system behind it, which he had no clue how to use, and activated the trigger.

*KA BOOM*! It struck with its explosive round well short of the target, landing in the pineapple field that was in between the gun and the target. A blast of dirt shot into the air, followed by an ominous trail of black smoke.

The foreign crew took the lad's incompetence in stride and prepared for another shot. Down range the smoke was growing rapidly.

"General, it would be a good idea to get the fire brigade down there," Baron said to Hisa. "I think we have set fire to that farmer's pineapple field.

Not wanting to embarrass himself by calling the fire brigade if he did not need it, Hisa commanded, "Get fire extinguishers down there at once!"

The enlisted military personnel ran toward the smoke with the small fire extinguishers from their vehicles that were entirely inadequate to put out the rapidly growing fire in the middle of the pineapple field, the owner of which looked on in desperation and bewilderment.

Soon flames could be seen rising up high through the bellowing smoke, and it was clear to all that a substantial fire was in the making. Soon enormous flames rose out of the smoke, blasting up to the sky. Baron realized that it was time to do something more effective or there would be a huge fire and possibly bad news in the press about the incident, all of which would draw unneeded attention to the contract with General Hisa that was already agreed would be awarded. Baron sprang to his feet, taking over leadership of the situation, as it appeared that General Hisa was not going to do it, or at least not fast enough. The flames were now eighty feet high, very wide, growing fast, and the winds were spreading the fire rapidly.

"General, get the fire brigade!" he yelled to General Hisa.

General Hisa stopped watching the fire, came to his senses, and gave a command to contact the fire brigade. The subordinate hurried toward a jeep to go to the nearest communication hut to make the call.

The fire was now out of control. "Tak," Baron yelled at her in the midst of the commotion, "you run off with that man going for the fire brigade! It may be unsafe for you here soon!"

She complied, jumping into the jeep with the soldier, leaving to go to the communications hut some distance away.

They arrived at the communications hut, got out, and went inside where a soldier sat behind a communications desk. The soldier who had been driving said excitedly, "Hurry, call the fire brigade!" He then explained where the fire was.

In Taiwan, however, the fire brigade was set up under the jurisdiction of the air force, for no particular reason, or at least for no reason that made any sense. In ten minutes, but what seemed like an eternity, an air force colonel drove up in a military vehicle.

"I'm the colonel in charge of the fire brigade," he proudly announced in Mandarin.

The two enlisted soldiers saluted and then began excited telling of the emergency. Tak stood just behind them.

"The air force had no notification of this operation or a

contingent would have been deployed," the colonel said. "And it is a Sunday, so mobilizing men will be difficult. I do not think that the air force can be of any help."

The driver pled for assistance, describing how the fire was spreading. But, the colonel did not seem to care.

After the conversation seemed to come to a stalemate, Tak stepped forward and said, in English, "What would it take to get you to send the fire brigade to extinguish the fire?"

The officer spoke English. "The fire brigade is really not interested in this army fire that resulted from an operation of which the air force had no prior notice."

Tak motioned the colonel to the side, turning her back to the others so they could not see or hear what she was saying. "How about some fragrant oil?"

The colonel's frown changed to a smile.

"I'll give you ten thousand United States dollars if you'll call out the fire brigade and put out the fire," Tak said. "I'll give you half now and half upon completion." She took the money from her bag, counted out five thousand, and gave it to him.

The colonel took the money then turned to the other soldiers. "Given the fact that this is an emergency, the air force will be most willing to come to the assistance of the Army."

He went to the communications console, picked up the mic and headset, and called in orders for all available men to come and put out the fire.

Soon all of the available men of the fire brigade, and all other available enlisted men on duty, headed for the fire. Tak and the driver returned to the original burning field, which, by that time, was toast. The surrounding fields were now catching fire.

Two fire trucks arrived, speeding dangerously. The driver of the first did not see a ninety degree turn ahead in the dirt road, until it was too late, and slammed on his brakes. The fire truck following too closely behind drove right into the rear of the truck, pushing it off the road into pineapple field.

Men began to arrive and in, what was clearly a completely unorganized, chaotic effort, tried to put out the fire. More fire trucks came, and more men. They scrambled about and, with some luck, by working all afternoon and into the evening, the fire was contained, but not until several hundred acres of field were toasted into ash.

Tak and Baron looked on, soot falling all around them, as the fire subsided, stopped mostly by the surrounding roads that created fire breaks, rather than from the unorganized fire brigade. Baron's new camouflage fatigues were covered in soot, and he was shaking his head at the debacle.

He saw Tak looking at him and smiled. "To enhance your English vocabulary, there is an expression in English for what you just witnessed, a chaotic event, which is said to be a 'Chinese Fire Drill.'"

☙❧

The following Saturday evening, in order to celebrate his soon to come wealth, under the guise of an award ceremony to award the winner of the trials, which, oddly enough, was the same company for which the baron was the sole representative, General Hisa had already planned a magnificent, twelve-course Chinese banquet.

The engineers, programmers, and other staff from the French company making the gun and the subcontractors who were at the trial were invited. Also invited were the officers that attended the trials, a few of the general's high-level friends in the military, and a few government people involved with budget approvals. And everyone brought their wives. No one from the air force and their corrupt fire brigade were invited. Eighty were in attendance. Naturally, Hisa had the army pay for it.

Tak sat next to Baron, who in turn sat next to General Hisa, in the most honored seat next to the podium.

General Hisa was nearing retirement, which would now be expedited with his new wealth, diminishing his respect for regulations. To show his appreciation for what the baron was providing, he had decided earlier that day to reciprocate. After the dinner was completed, he stood and asked for the attention of those present.

In Mandarin he announced, "As an award for the bravery of all that courageously participated in the emergency yesterday, I'm decorating everyone involved." Loud applause rang throughout the hall.

"However for Baron Von Limbach, as well as his distinguished wife, the baroness, for taking the initiative to get the fire brigade to the scene, and instrumental in extinguishing the fire, they are to receive what they deserve. I present them with the *First In Combat* medal."

The presentation of the First-In-Combat came as a surprise to the audience, who were in awe of the majesty of the award. All broke into deafening applause. In recent times, no Taiwanese soldier had ever gotten the First-In-Combat medal, as Taiwan soldiers had no battles. But the Taiwanese soldiers were very much into recognizing titles, degrees, and the like, and so everyone in the Taiwan Army knew of it, and would thereafter snap to attention for the baron whenever he came, giving him even more face, as a true hero.

He was now the equivalent of a prestigious officer as the medal included all of the privileges of officers to enter officer clubs and the like. Once awarded, this medal became the most distinguished part of the Taiwan uniform and, in the Taiwanese Army tradition, anyone in the Taiwan Army would thereafter consider the baron to be a true hero. And, after all, anyone that paid as much bribe money as the baron did was a true hero to the general. The baron had suggested earlier that the general include Tak in the award and he complied.

The general motioned for the baron and the baroness to stand and come next to him at the podium. They were presented with a plaque, a medal, and sew-on cloth badges. These were intended for a military shirt or jacket, but could be worn on any jacket.

Baron and Tak graciously accepted the award, and the audience broke into deafening applause. When they returned to their seats, and the audience stopped staring, Tak turned to Baron, still in shock.

When the applause subsided, she said quietly to Baron, "What have I done to receive such an honor, or any honor?

Baron was smiling widely, almost in laughter, enjoying the situation immensely. It occurred to her that she was beginning to get to know him well and to appreciate, not only what he could do but also his unforgettable sense of humor.

She was now decorated with the most prestigious award available from the Taiwan Army, and all she had done to earn it was to observe a bungled weapons trial, resulting in the burning of pineapple fields caused by the incompetence of the general's dolt of a nephew. And she provided the assistance of offering a bribe of fragrant oil to someone in the fire brigade that was supposed to help anyway, all to orchestrate an actual, as opposed to a metaphorical, "Chinese Fire Drill."

⁊℧⁊

Baron and Tak sat in a small boat, its driver maneuvering through the exotic Bangkok floating market. Flowers, fruits, and artifacts were sold from boats as they passed. Lachhiman sat behind them, just ahead of the boatman. Their boat was one of the typical Thai boats, with the long, extension propeller shaft running nearly horizontally out the back, as far as the boat was long.

"The Thai people are quite different from the Chinese," Tak observed. "Do you speak their language as well?"

"Yes, I do."

"You speak many languages, don't you, Baron?"

"Yes. Do you?"

"Yes, but none that you would recognize. Oh, except English, of course."

It was a hot Bangkok day, but that was not unusual. Baron wore a wide-brimmed panama hat, light shirt, and slacks. Tak wore her usual outfit as she did not have anything else appropriate, but her usual outfit kept her air-conditioned comfortably.

"You really must let me buy you a sort of local outfit," he said at one point. "It won't be air conditioned, however. I think a batik top and perhaps some shorts? What do you say to that?"

"I'll give it a try," she joked. "But I will have to go back home with more than one satchel."

Tak looked on, fascinated at the various things for sale in the boats, and also in the shops at the water's edge. Children bathed in the dirty water, and women washed their clothes in it as well as their pots and pans.

That evening, with Tak dressed in a very colorful batik top and white, loose pants, they went to a famous Thai seafood restaurant/market where the fish was selected open style, like a market. Some, quite large, fresh from the day's catch, were laid out on ice. They took a grocery shopping cart from the entrance of the restaurant and entered a line along a long, ice-packed counter filled with fresh seafood, some still alive. Baron selected a very colorful fish, caught that day; crabs, still alive and moving; squid; prawns; sea snails; cockles; and oysters. He then picked from a section that was not seafood—kangkong, or Chinese watercress, and vegetable greens.

After purchasing the food much like at a supermarket, it was then taken to their table by an attendant. The chef came out from the back to greet them and to discuss how they wanted everything prepared. To the surprise of the chef, Baron spoke to him in Thai, and they entered into detailed discussions on just exactly how everything was to be prepared, and with exactly what sauces. Baron was in no mood to leave it up to the chef and spent a great deal of time making sure that they agreed on each dish. Then a certain kind of rice, noodles for the oysters, and various other additives were agreed upon.

As he and Tak enjoyed the spicy Thai seafood, Baron thought he might push for more information. "Have you decided on your recommendation to the Federation about this planet?"

Switching to professionalism, she said, "Before I make any decision, I'll return, evaluate all I've witnessed, and study what my computer has taken in. After careful consideration, I'll then make a recommendation to the Federation, and it'll make its own choice. Baron, I have to be honest with you. For some planets, it is not entirely a question of just joining or not joining. In some cases, a planet may be considered a threat and the Federation might do something about that."

"I expect they will follow your recommendation. Are they all human like?"

"Oh no! Not at all! But no more questions."

☙☙☙

At the hotel in Bangkok, Baron turned on the television to a world news program in English. As Tak and he watched, a female reporter gave the news story.

"…in the Tibetan region of what is now part of China, there is a widespread outbreak of Ebola, the deadly disease that was formerly confined to the African continent. The Chinese government reports that Ebola has been confirmed as an outbreak in the cities of Lhasa, the capital and most populated city, and in Xigatze, the second largest city, located two-hundred-and-twenty-five miles west of Lhasa. The number of cases is presently unknown, but it is believed to be in the thousands and spreading as an uncontrolled epidemic. Ebola is said to be the most deadly virus known and nearly always fatal. The Chinese government has suspended all travel to and from the region.

"Anyone who has plans to visit Tibet should be made aware that the Chinese government is not allowing any travel to Tibet, and any travelers already in Tibet cannot leave and are being held in quarantine. The Chinese military has been mobilized to cover the borders, and roads leading in and out of Lhasa and Xigatze, and are setting up camps to quarantine anyone leaving those cities. Unconfirmed reports state that there are also outbreaks in Tibetan cities of Chamdo and Gyantse.

"The World Health Organization, made up of one hundred-ninety-one member nations, said in Geneva today that this may be a medical catastrophe of the largest magnitude ever known since the plague in Europe. The origin of the outbreak is unknown, but a government official in Beijing said that the source may have been a traveler from Africa who was infected and visited Tibet. A spokesperson for the World Health Organization stated that Ebola has no known cure, and medical personnel must wear special suits with special equipment to treat patients. But there is no such equipment available on the scale needed. We'll bring you updates as we learn them..."

"The race-specific Ebola of Dr. Dorogomilov's is working very well," Tak said. "How do you plan to get the Dalai Lama back into Tibet to fulfill your deal?"

"With the epidemic spreading into a major catastrophe, it should be possible to get Him invited back with well-placed fragrant oil," he answered. "But it is not yet time."

♥♥♥

The US President conducted an emergency meeting of select staff and a few others, including the head of the CIA and of the FBI. It also included Raymond Hauser, the vice president, the secretary of state, the national security advisor, and a dozen others. Ralls was not high enough up the ladder to be invited.

The president asked the national security advisor to

open the meeting as the president thought maybe he had more to offer. The subject was the epidemic in Tibet.

He began. "There is clearly a huge epidemic of Ebola in Tibet, Mr. President. Due to the incubation period, we do not have an accurate count of infected people yet, but the World Health Organization has told me that it may be over a hundred thousand. But there is no doubt that it is spreading rapidly and exponentially. It has been identified as similar to Ebola Zaire, the most deadly kind. But what is most interesting is that, so far, only Han Chinese have become infected. There is no record yet of any Tibetan or other race becoming infected."

"Isn't it just a matter of time before others get it?" the president asked him. "Possibly the Chinese are more susceptible?"

"Could very well be," the NSA director said. But it's hard to imagine that a hundred thousand of one race can get a virus without a single case of any other race. In any case, we should take steps to locate and quarantine any travelers that have arrived from Tibet in the past several weeks. There is a case reported of a Chinese couple who are students in Canada who visited Tibet and returned, bringing the Ebola back with them. Anyone that they came in contact with is being quarantined, and they are chasing down the passengers on the jet at this time. We have put our best doctors on it, and we'll see what they can find out."

"Does anyone have any notion as to where it came from?" the president asked.

Stella Buchanan, the secretary of state, said, "I think it came from a traveler from Africa. I think we should quarantine African visitors as well."

"But there has been no outbreak in Africa reported yet," the NSA director pointed out.

After everyone who wanted to talk had their chance, the president turned to Hauser. "Raymond, you have not said anything yet. What have you to say?"

"Since only Chinese people are getting this virus, we

should be asking, why only in Tibet?" Hauser said. "Why not mainland China with a billion? Why not Taiwan? Why not the many countries where there are large populations of Chinese such as Singapore, Malaysia, and other countries of Asia? The Tibetans are desperate to get the Chinese out of Tibet, and someone, somehow, might be using Ebola as a biological weapon to free Tibet of Communist Chinese."

Stella Buchanan rudely repeated her message. "I don't believe that the Tibetans could do that. I still think we should pursue a visitor from Africa."

Hauser was obviously displeased with her lack of foresight. "What if it is a biological weapon? It could be directed one day toward black people, Jews, Arabs, or another race, even Caucasians. I would like to put some effort into finding out how, where, and when this virus could have been made, in case it is a biological weapon."

No one disagreed with him as he was not asking them to preclude any other areas of inquiry. The president began to delegate duties to the staff members as to what they might do to find out more about the epidemic.

# CHAPTER 24

The tea plantation manager brought Baron's big Mercedes sedan to the Chiang Rai airport in Northern Thailand to greet them. Lachhiman, who was along on the flight, took over the driving and drove them outside of town up in the hills to Baron's house on his plantation.

The house was not a mansion, but still very grand with its ten-thousand square feet. The road in was done in fine gravel, very densely packed, rather than concrete, much like an old European estate's driveway. There was an additional home, just down from the crest of the hill for servants. The two-story house with rounded sections was on the highest point of the plantation. The roof had blue tiles, much like some of the older castles in France, but there were occasional small points that stood up slightly from spots of the roof, in the Thai tradition. The house was clearly a mixture of design. There was a round observation tower with a panoramic view of the entire plantation, as well as the surrounding area. Off to the right was a building for drying and storing teas, as well as for the keeping the harvesting equipment. Around back of that was a long garage for holding several vehicles. The help for planting and harvesting in season came in daily from nearby villages to work. The planation consisted of many acres, with tea plants of the most exotic and unique Oolong teas in the world.

Baron did not keep a large staff there, only enough to

maintain the house and to take care of him when he came in, as he rarely had a house guest there. As they pulled in through the gate, the head chef, two housekeeper girls, two grounds keepers, and a handyman lined up in front of the house in respect for the owner. The staff for harvesting the tea were currently out in the fields, working with the plants.

Baron introduced the staff to the baroness, and they went inside. "Do you like my house?"

Tak looked about the grand entrance hall, with a curved staircase winding up to the balcony surrounding the hall below.

"The floor of the hall is blue lapis granite imported from Brazil," he explained. "Note the gold streaks in it. The staircase is of local teak wood."

Coming down the full length of the staircase, in the center of the steps, was a brass and ivory hand rail, attached to each step by brass stair rods. Black, wrought-iron circles and patterns of an art-deco design made up the bottom of the railing.

"It's beautiful!" Tak exclaimed.

"I'm glad you approve. But, considering your mission, you might be more interested in the turned-up points on the roof outside. Those are popular with the Thai people to ward off evil, and most all Thai structures have them. Some homes have miniature houses on the grounds to house spirits of the dead family members, and daily offerings of fruit are brought to them."

"That explains what I saw on the way in from the airport. I saw several of them, about the size of a bird house."

He nodded. "We'll dine here tonight. You may be surprised at just how great my chef is. This will be Northern Thai food, which is different from what you had in Bangkok. Tomorrow we can go into the nearby areas on a tour and look about, until the day you leave, which will be a sad one for me."

He smiled at her and led her to the master bedroom, something to behold. The outside wall was rounded. The floor was done in multi-toned granite, with light blues, creams, and rust colors, all in swirls. A huge window, in sections, covered most of the outside wall, overlooking a significant part of the plantation and the countryside beyond. In front of the huge window was a granite table, six inches thick, with baroque edges, broken off and irregular, at barstool height, with a chair on either side.

He led her into the bathroom, a modern rendition of a Roman bath. There was a pedestal lavatory, toilet, and bidet, all carved out of solid granite. There was a granite shower and Jacuzzi of a multi-colored beige granite. The ceiling had three skylights, two in the main area, and one making up the top of the shower, which was tilted so as to drain off the water. Made of clear glass to illuminate by natural light, the skylights opened by electronic motors.

Tak looked about in awe. "This is magnificent, Baron."

The staff had filled the Jacuzzi for them. Baron turned on the pumps and heater. "Let's freshen up. I have arranged for some local clothes for you. They are in the closet."

ひとひ

In the early evening, they sat watching the sunset to the west from the crow's nest tower atop the house. The view covered three hundred sixty degrees, but at this hour one could not help put look past the plantation to the fire in the sky from the setting sun behind the high clouds, coloring them from pink to crimson red. From the wardrobe closet Tak had selected a sarong with brocade and a matching, slim-fitting top. Baron wore loose-fitting, white pants and a hand-printed, Malaysian batik shirt. Tak wore no shoes over her seven-toed feet.

"How do I look?" she said. She turned around like a model.

"Extraordinarily sexy and beautiful, like most seven-toed aliens."

The young female assistant to the chef stood by to

serve Baron's finest Oolong tea, while the chef continued in the kitchen on what would be a delightful Thai meal. The tea was served in demitasse tea cups from Germany, a century old, very thin, and with gold leaf flowers set in royal blue china. Caviar and tidbits on crackers were served with the tea, along with an assortment of slices of local fruits.

"And so, you must tell me, my lovely wife and baroness, how do you find my tea?" He was enjoying, to the nth degree, being the only human to ever marry an alien.

"Exquisite. What do you have in mind for today's culinary extravaganza?"

Baron laughed. "It seems you need no help from anyone with the language. We'll start with Khao Soi noodle soup, and after that I'm not sure."

Dinner was prepared in the most elaborate style that the chef could accomplish, enhanced by the fact that he had been called well in advance and told to put on the finest meal that was in his ability, and to bring in whatever his imagination might come up with without any regard whatsoever to the cost or effort.

Tak came down the stairs for dinner, dressed in another outfit from her wardrobe closest. It was a green sarong with intricate brocade and a lighter green tight-fitting top that left her stomach bare. Baron was waiting for her at the bottom of the stairs to see her beauty and how she handled the local costume.

Tak saw Baron at the bottom of the lapis granite staircase, and realized that she was on stage. She came down the steps with a sway, exhibiting sexy moves, something she had seen in the movies she watched to learn English.

"Breathtaking!" Baron announced.

Tak had learned that silence could be an effective communication and tried it. In old world fashion, Baron held out his arm so as not to let an unattended woman enter the dining hall. Of course, no one was looking besides a peeking staff member who would later gossip it to all the others, but that was not the point. Tak took his outstretched arm and he led her from the bottom step to the drawing room before dinner.

Baron led her to the bar, where he poured chilled champagne with the additives of a shot of bourbon, a dash of Hungarian bitters, and a slice of an Asian pear before dinner was to be served.

⌀⌀⌀

The following morning, Baron led Tak to the garage. The manager had polished and made ready for them one of Baron's favorite things. Tak saw it shinning with chrome and polished paint. "What's that?"

"I call it fun," he said. "But more correctly, it is an American V-Twin Motorcycle. We will use that to go about the north here, whenever the weather is nice."

Tak walked around it. "I saw these on the roads, but none as pretty as this. I bet this will be fun.'

"That is what I called, it. Fun!"

# CHAPTER 25

The video in the briefing room depicted a newsman for a British news service. "…this is a report from Tibet, where there is an epidemic of what has been confirmed to be a hemorrhagic viral fever. It's believed to be a virus similar to Ebola Zaire, the most deadly on the planet, named after its outbreak at the Ebola River in Africa. I'm reporting from Lhasa, which is in a state of chaos. The government in Beijing has sent in all of the available bio-warfare suits and breathing masks for soldiers to use, but there are not enough to go around. There are also reports that many of the Chinese-made bio-warfare suits are defective, causing some soldiers to catch the virus."

The film panned to the background behind the young newsman to focus on a street in Lhasa with two soldiers in the special suits with AK-47 Chinese-made rifles in hand.

"The sight of soldiers," the newsman continued, "instills fear and even panic. Here is a scene from downtown Lhasa."

The film then switched to a scene depicting Chinese running about in panic.

"The Chinese government put more of the same suits into immediate production, but it's too little, too late. Worse, much of the military is infected, and thousands more are becoming infected daily. But oddly, only Chinese are getting sick. It is uncertain if the bio-warfare suits are working or not, as so many of those using the suits are becoming infected. One government official was allowed to leave Lhasa at the early stages of the epidemic to go to Beijing, and he later was diagnosed with it in Beijing. He infected several persons on the government plane as well as three hospital staff in Beijing, all of whom, along with anyone he came in contact with, are either dead or in quarantine.

"The task of the military, as they tell us, is to try to keep order, to segregate parts of the cities from others, to prevent looting and riots, and to set up bases on the outskirts of town for citizens to come to if they do not have Ebola.

"Anyone not obeying a soldier is shot on the spot."

The camera switched to a scene depicting a Chinese person lying face down, clearly dead, with blood stained bullet holes on the back of his jacket. The scene then switched to a large fire, with soldiers in bio-warfare suits throwing bodies onto it.

"Large fires have been built to put the bodies in, as the virus lives quite well on dead tissue for some time, and the bodies are a further source of spreading the epidemic."

The picture switched to soldiers in bio-warfare suits forcing a couple at gunpoint to enter a tenement.

"People are ordered to stay in their homes. Every medical facility is trying to operate at several times full capacity, and we have reports that many of the staff people at the hospitals are infected. The cities of Xigatse, Sakya, Gyantse, Jukundo, Derge, Kandze, Sungpar, Chamdo, Dartsedo, Litang, and Batang all have the same epidemic. The cities of Choni and Labrang to the north, and Amdo and Nagchu to the west report occurrences as well, but not as widespread, indicating that the epidemic did not start there, but may have traveled there with people traveling to those cities from the major cities that are in such a horrible state…"

Colonel Doctor Chamberlin of the US Army Medical Corps turned off the video and addressed the group of five volunteers and a dozen others in the room, who would be in contact with the volunteers or who were otherwise participating in the event. The lecture was at the US Army Medical Research Institute of Infectious Diseases, or USAMRIID, in Frederick, Maryland, the main location of four where research on US bio-warfare was conducted. The facility was well equipped with the various air locks, pressure suits, and equipment needed to work on volatile things like Ebola.

"That news film was taken by a British news service with a news person already in Tibet," the Colonel said. "Since he was already there on another assignment, he was able to provide that report via satellite. He is not infected as you can see. We are going over to collect samples and to determine whatever we can about this epidemic. We have been granted permission from Beijing to proceed.

"Each of you is very brave to volunteer, as the possibility of infection if anything goes wrong is extremely high. You are all trained in bio-warfare and Ebola, and you have been selected because of your medical background. We are not allowing any Chinese volunteers.

"Let me give you a quick refresher in Ebola. It has never been considered as a likely tool for bio-warfare, as it is simply too damned dangerous. It always kills, whereas things that make a person swell up, get red-eyed and temporarily lose vision, get sick, go to sleep, or become temporarily incapacitated have been considered more valuable as bio-warfare agents. When an anthrax victim dies, his body can be disposed of without much risk as anthrax is not carried from one person to the next. This is not the case with Ebola. An infected person, and even a dead body, has many pounds of tissues for Ebola to feed on, and it will live, using the remaining tissues, even after the victim dies.

"Viruses associated with most hemorrhagic fevers are zoonotic, which means that these viruses naturally reside in an animal reservoir host or arthropod vector. They are totally dependent on their hosts for replication and overall survival. Animals can be carriers, as well as humans. It is well known that monkeys carry it. We must assume that quite a number of animals can feed off the remains, and spread it—rodents, possibly vultures, and who knows? Maybe even insects.

"Ebola can enter the body by the mouth, by being breathed in, by sexual contact, by ingestion of water or food, by getting it on a hand or utensil which later ends up in the mouth, and, of course, through an open wound. Close contact with an infected person will transmit it by breath, much like catching the flu.

"Regarding early detection, there is simply no way to tell that a person on the street has just contracted it. You might think that taking a person's temperature would reveal he just caught it, as it is a hemorrhagic fever, but that is not the case. There is no rise in the person's temperature until the body starts to react to the infection, by which time, he will be close to very seriously ill and most likely unable to get about very well. After two days, a person might get a cough. Only after a few more days, will he usually show a fever. Soon there will be bleeding from the urinary track, nose, mouth, or anus, all of which are clear signs, but these usually do not show up in the first two days. As to the contagiousness of it with a newly infected person, Ebola is highly contagious shortly after a person has first become contaminated with it, and this means that people who look healthy and have no idea that they have it are spreading it like wildfire. For several days after a person is infected, he will be unknowingly infecting many others, and they will infect many others, exponentially.

"We have detection systems for many biological warfare agents, like the Biological Integrated Detection System, or BIDS. However, none of these will detect Ebola. So, we simply have to assume that it is everywhere where you will be going.

"We are to treat this as the most dangerous, level-four hazardous substance known. We must exercise the most extreme precaution in decontaminating. We are going over in a Boeing C-17, and the plane will let us and the equipment off and then take off right away, leaving without being touched or fueled by anyone at the airport. It'll be flown to one of our bases and immediately sprayed upon landing in case it picked up any of the virus.

"As for equipment, we'll be in a Block II Nuclear, Biological, Chemical Reconnaissance System, or NBCRS, when we roll off the plane. If any of you have not been in one, it is the eight-wheeled reconnaissance vehicle made just for this sort of mission. We will be in our Self Contained Toxic Environment Protective Outfits, or STEPOs, before we open the hatch of the NBCRS. If it is too hot in the suits, you will also have the new Advanced, Lightweight Microclimate Cooling System, or ALMCS, to attach to the suit, which will keep the temperature inside your suits comfortable. If any of you have not yet used them, your metabolic heat is transferred to the fluid in the ALMCS. Communications among us when in the suits will be by the PRC-127 headsets.

"We will be living in one of those inflated tents, an M20 Simplified Collective Protective Equipment, or SCPE. We will also take a spare in case it fails or gets ruined. We will inflate it inside a building like a big bladder. We'll have a motor blower for inflation, portable toilet, and cots inside for sleeping. We'll use M291 decontamination wipes. The batteries of the suits are good for four hours, and then they need re-charging or replacement, so we better plan on getting back each time we go out with enough reserve to make it in case of problems. When we get back to the tent, we will first spray ourselves with a decontaminate. Once back inside, you can use the toilet, rest, eat, and then go back out for another four hours. We'll stay there only three days, and then the plane will return for us. The Chinese government is providing us with soldiers who will guard our tent and will also defend us as we go out to observe. They will have their own bio-warfare suits.

"We'll make observations, get samples, and get out. The samples will land with us in Guam and then be packaged to come right back here. Hopefully, we'll learn more about the virus and come up with recommendations. England may also send over a medical team, and possibly other countries. However, it is not feasible that members of other countries to go together with us as they are not trained on our equipment nor we on theirs, and time is of the essence as people are dying by the thousands.

"I frankly don't have high hopes that we can do very much, as we already have good information that it is Ebola or a variant for which there is no cure. As for recommendations on how to keep it from spreading, I suspect it will be hard to do much, considering the standard of living there, which is so low, with people sharing utensils, sharing food, and living in close quarters with one another. And, there is chaos. But we are commanded by our president to try, and it will be an interesting, but dangerous, challenge.

"We have reports that the Tibetans have not been contaminated, and their monks attribute their lack of infection to their holy status. We suspect the Tibetans have something that resists the infection. But frankly, we have many reports of crazy things there, some conflicting, and we really don't know what to believe. And, of course, the Chinese are superstitious and inclined to add their own interpretation on things—so much so, that we have reports that sound crazy.

"Now, for coming back, we will be sent to quarantine upon return to Guam, to make sure that we don't have it. Chances are that if any one of us gets it, the whole group might, as we will be together when not suited up, eating, and sleeping, just the same as the Chinese.

"Any questions?"

Lisa Chapman, one of the volunteers, asked, "Is there any information on how it got so widespread so quickly?"

"Nope," the colonel answered. "That is one of the highest priority issues that we have to address. But that may be best addressed when we return and evaluate what we learn there. Perhaps we can glean information to better theorize just how it happened. Right now, the only plausible explanation is that some traveler or travelers got it in Africa and then went to Tibet and brought it there. There are many students that travel in the poor areas of Africa and Tibet, and it could have been brought in by a student or a group of students. But as yet there is no evidence, or at least none that the Chinese government has given us, that any such person or persons have been found or traced.

"But the fact that it did spread so quickly to so many is of great concern, something that presents a new way of thinking to people like us in the US. We simply are not prepared to deal with anything so large in scope. It is of the magnitude of the largest epidemic ever and so overwhelming that it presents an entirely new challenge. The White House wants full reports as soon as we can provide information."

ⱭⱭⱭ

The huge C-17 airplane made a most impressive drop off at the airport at Lhasa. Planned for just such a bio-warfare scene, the plane performed its designated task by coming in and touching down on the runway. It did not stop, but instead, kept rolling at a slow speed so as to minimize contamination from any bio-warfare agent that might be present. The rear cargo door was opened and out rolled the olive-colored NBCRS. With four wheels close together on either side, it rolled easily off the plane, even with its attached trailer full of equipment. As soon as the vehicle cleared the ramp, the pilot of the C-17 hit the throttles and closed the cargo doors as the C-17 picked up speed and took off, away from the biological hazardous area. The NBCRS then motored over to the area near the terminal where soldiers were waiting in their Chinese bio-warfare suits.

One of the soldiers came over from where he was standing near his jeep to meet the group. Colonel Chamberlin got out to greet him.

The soldier spoke English, but he had to speak inside

his mask, making it hard to hear him. "I'm Captain Zeng. Greetings on behalf of the People's Republic of China."

Chamberlin spoke up loudly, so as to be heard. His team had on short-range headsets under their hoods for communication amongst themselves, but that did not work with the Chinese in their suits.

"Thank you," he practically shouted inside his hood. "I'm Colonel Doctor Chamberlin in charge. We are a group of six. We would like to be led to the area that you have selected for us so that we may begin our observations."

"Very good. Please to follow me." The captain went to his jeep, one of three, with soldiers there to protect the guests.

The NBCRS, pulling a trailer, could not go as fast as a jeep, but the soldiers went slow enough to allow it to keep up. After an hour, they arrived at the designated location. They stopped inside the city of Lhasa, in a large lot with a one-story, small building set back from the street. It was a government building, used for warehousing, that had been cleared out for the insertion of the M20 tent.

Chamberlin's group of six got out of the NBCRS and looked about. The team then unloaded the trailer and carried the M20 inside the building to unfold it. It was a package three-by-four-feet in dimension when folded and included a second pack with the door and air pump. They set up the inflation blower, and it began to fill the room like a giant bladder, lining the sides, as the positive pressure filled it. Once inflated with the air lock door in place, the group began setting up their things inside the room, making ready for their mission. By the time they had everything in place, and safe, it had been nearly four hours since they came off the plane and time to take off the suits to change the batteries, use the toilet, take a break, and get a snack and some water before suiting up again to go out and observe. The suits with their re-breathers weighed thirty-eight pounds each, which made working in them a chore, and the rest break was welcome.

එෘඥෘ

"Let's get some tissue samples and blood from this man here," Colonel Chamberlin said to his team, utilizing the PRC-127 headset communicator inside his STEPO. The team looked like men in space suits with the breathing packs, except that the hoods and face shields were not small like space suit helmets. The hoods were roomy and the face shields quite tall, making visibility much better for working.

The team gathered around a body on the street in Lhasa. The body was still warm, having expired only minutes earlier. Blood was coming out of his nose and mouth, and he had red blisters on his face and hands with bloody, open sores. A red patch in his crotch indicated bleeding from the anus as well.

Sitting or lying down against the buildings on either side were several other people, not moving, either dead or dying, who had apparently collapsed there, unable to go farther. Six Chinese soldiers in their bio-warfare suits and breathing masks stood by, guarding the team, their AK-47 rifles in hand.

Two of the team members bent down and opened their special container for samples. One of the team, Lanier, cut away the man's shirt, revealing open sores on his chest that were dripping with blood. Lanier cut tissue from the open sores and took blood via a syringe.

A military truck came down the street with a stake-bed rear section completely filled with dead bodies. It did not stop for the bodies on the street, as there was no room for more. The activity of the men in the special suits attracted a Chinese man nearby, who was obviously infected with Ebola as he had open, bleeding rashes on his face. He came up to the group, yelling something, with his arm out in front of him. The soldiers yelled at him, but could hardly be heard in their suits. The soldiers all pointed their guns at him, in a warning not to continue to approach. The man looked like he was too sick to know what he was doing—but knowing or not, he continued to approach at a rapid pace. At about fifteen feet away, all of soldiers opened fire with bursts of bullets, pumping dozens of rounds into him. He fell, right in front of the group, very dead, which was probably a relief over having to die slowly of Ebola.

Chamberlin looked on and then went back to work as there was nothing he could do. The soldiers had to guard them, and that was what they were doing.

"Okay, got this one," Lanier said, putting away the syringe and tissue samples in the container.

"Let's get some more from two or three other victims and then head back," the colonel said. "We're supposed to observe what we can and make any recommendations on how to assist in containing it, but I don't see much that can be done."

He looked up the street at the shops and buildings, formerly filled with Chinese merchants, now completely abandoned. Looking at the clock on the outside of his sleeve, he sighed. "We've been out two hours. It's about an hour's walk back to the M20, so we should start heading back in about a half hour. That'll leave us with a thirty-minute safety margin on these four-hour packs."

They went down the street and found a dead woman lying in the street with blood around her mouth.

"This will do for a specimen," the colonel said. "Let's go get more."

☙❧

"It's time to go," Chamberlin said to his group on the third day, as he was one of the first awake inside the M20.

The others awakened and made ready for the welcome trip home with their samples. When they arrived back at the airport in the NBCRS, ninety-odd Chinese were gathered restlessly behind the fence separating the tarmac from the terminal. Most were from the airport or had found out that there was a plane coming. They had hopes of leaving on any plane that might come. Chamberlin's group stayed in the NBCRS just outside the terminal building waiting for the C-17 to come, so as not to cause the group of desperate Chinese to follow it or start a riot.

"This could get ugly," Chamberlin said to his group inside the NBCRS.

On schedule, the big C-17 could be seen coming in for a landing. The Chinese all looked and pointed, chattering among themselves. The soldier who had accompanied Chamberlin stood by and watched as the NBCRS drove toward the gate so it could get out onto the tarmac near the landing strip where the C-17 was touching down. Several other soldiers stood by the gate. The C-17 touched down, slowed to a stop, then turned around quickly, and taxied back to where it had landed, ready to take off into the prevailing winds. It came to rest on the runway, not taking the chance of coming up to the terminal where the unruly crowd looked on.

The cargo door lowered. The Chinese soldiers opened the gate to let the NBCRS vehicle, with the six specialists inside, pass through. Chamberlin drove the vehicle toward the C-17 out on the runway and started up ramp of the cargo door. Two US soldiers in STEPO suits stood ready inside the plane and secured the vehicle with nylon straps to the airplane deck. They began spraying the vehicle with decontamination fluid.

Seeing a perceived escape out of the country, the Chinese behind the fence went into a frenzy, trampled down the fence at a spot near the terminal, and rushed toward the plane. The pilot could see the group coming and pushed the throttles forward to spool up the engines. He radioed to the back for status on the loading. When he got an affirmative answer, he released the brakes and started the plane rolling.

"Close the cargo door," he commanded his co-pilot.

Chamberlin got out of the NBCRS once it was secured to the plane, the rest of his group following. As the door began to close, he could see the Chinese running as fast as they could, nearing the plane. It appeared that several of them would make it to the cargo door as the big C-17 was still moving slower than they were running. This he could not allow.

The Chinese soldiers that escorted Chamberlin's group were giving chase to the group, yelling at them to halt, but to no avail. They opened fire, hitting them in the back, dropping them as they ran.

Eleven of the faster ones made it to the cargo door, trying desperately to get into the plane, in hopes of saving their lives. The two soldiers inside the plane went for their weapons, M4A1 rifles with extended magazines in case of just such a situation. Both readied a round in the chamber and aimed.

A few dropped away, but seven got to ramp, which was closing slowly, and grabbed on, trying desperately to climb in. They had their hands on the door, and their heads were visible just above the edge. One was pulling himself up into the inside of the plane.

The C-17 began to rotate its nose up preparing to lift off. This had the effect of lowering the rear of the cargo door toward the ground, making it easier for the men to get in. Five were now pulling themselves up and in.

The two soldiers opened fire on them, riddling them with holes, blowing them back and out the door. Those hanging on were shot in the head. The doors finally closed, and the big C-17 lifted off.

One of the two soldiers lowered his smoking rifle and looked at the other. "That'll teach 'em!"

⍟⍟⍟

Colonel Doctor Chamberlin, his medical team, and the four-man crew of the plane came down the ramp of the C-17 at Guam, at the far end of the runway where the quarantine had been set up. The C-17 was parked at an out-of-the-way spot, where it could remain until decontaminated by chemicals, waiting for the added safety of the passage of time, all before it would be put back into service. The remote possibility of a rodent or other animal getting on board was considered, and chemicals were sprayed around the plane and then inside, just to be sure.

The team left their suits in the plane, and wore ordinary clothes. Outside were two Nuclear Biological Chemical (NBC) men, in STEPOs. They had a pressure sprayer set up on a truck, with which they sprayed the outside lower parts of the plane, especially the door areas. They would then go in—after the team was led to their quarantine quarters—collect the samples, decontaminate the outside of the containers, decontaminate the inside of the plane, and collect the team's suits and other things to put into a large fire that they had set up for the disposal.

One of the men in a STEPO came up to the colonel and spoke to him with the radio gear. "I'm Captain Dudley, sir. Your quarantine building is just there." He pointed to a building about eighty yards away. "Please follow me. I'll lead you there, come back for the samples, and take care of supervising the decontamination procedures."

Dudley led the team and flight crew to the quarantine building. Temporary facilities were set up, including a shower, toilet, ping pong table, two big screens TVs with satellite antennae, a stack of the latest magazines, Internet-ready computers, and phones, all to try to make this very important crew comfortable—if infected—in case it turned out to be their "last supper."

"I think everything is pretty obvious," Dudley said, as he went inside the room with them following, looking about at all the goodies set up for them.

Colonel Chamberlin went to the food service area, where there was a place for meal preparation and a table with two long benches for the group to sit at. There were two refrigerators full of many things—too many, as Dudley had set up everything he thought they might possibly want, in case they were going to end up infected. A filing cabinet had been moved in and converted to a pantry of dry foods ranging from pancake mix to peanuts to chips. Locally grown tropical fruits filled a large bowl on the coffee table. A makeshift bar was stocked with the usual liquors and cases of beer were on the floor nearby. They would no doubt either gain weight—or die after suffering the tortures of the damned if infected.

"Boy! This is first class," Chamberlin exclaimed, his eyes wide.

"You can call your families, or just dial *0* and you will get our command post," Dudley informed them. "I will be there most of the day, but if I should go out for a time, there will be someone at the phone at all times, around the clock, twenty-four/seven, if you need anything, or, if you detect any sign of infection. I have arranged a special medical and nursing team of four, with suits and equipment, should it be needed, and more who are standing by and can be brought over at once from the mainland.

"Do not leave the building. After ten-to-fourteen-days, evaluation, a decision will be made as to whether or not your team can be let go, or if additional time in quarantine is needed."

"I understand perfectly," Chamberlin said.

Dudley left, and closed the door.

Chamberlin opened a box of medicines that he had pre-arranged. One of the small containers in the box had a few special pills. He recognized them at once. They were cyanide capsules that, if broken in front of the nose or in the mouth, would kill instantly. They came from the CIA, as they were not the sort of thing you could find at a CVS or Walgreen's pharmacy. Some in his group, and certainly he, would rather end life quickly than take the slow death of Ebola, should they get it.

Two guards were posted outside, taking positions that were believed to be a safe distance away from the building, which was two hundred feet. They were under orders not to let anyone in, or out. They would be replaced in shifts and further confined to special quarters, where only they and their replacements would be living, away from anything and anyone—similar to the confinement of the team they were guarding, only not as extreme, for the entire period of the team's confinement.

In the meantime, the samples in special containers, collected by Dudley and his helper, were wiped with decontaminates on the outside, then taken for additional decontamination. The samples were then hurried into a plane waiting to carry them to USAMRIID. It was there that the best analysis in the US could be undertaken.

☙❧

The president's staff and other important people were summoned for an update. To expedite an updated report, a special link was set up from USMARIID, with the scientists there, and a camera was positioned against a wall to transmit the image of the scientist or doctor in front of it. A big screen was already in place in the president's situation room and had been hooked up for the report.

"Our volunteers are still in Guam, right?" the president asked Christy Elniff, the lead doctor in Maryland.

"Yes, still in quarantine," she responded. "But we received the tissue and blood samples by a special jet shortly after they landed in Guam." Elniff then switched the image to an electron microscope enlargement of a long-tailed figure. "This is an actual filovirus from the tissues of a victim in Tibet. Note the interesting shape. It has the long tail of known filoviruses, but the head is much larger and much more complex. It is certainly different from any of the Ebola or related viruses that have, to date, come from Africa."

She switched the screen to an existing picture taken from an Ebola Zaire textbook, which clearly showed the difference. "This is a picture of an Ebola Zaire filovirus." Then she switched it back to the current enlargement. "You can see the difference. The morphology is different from any known Ebola. It's not just the usual nucleocapsid and surrounding helical capsid. It appears to be much more complicated. It is as though it has mutated either into something different or perhaps combined with something that is not usually combined with Ebola. One theory here is that it may have become linked to an antibody that must find an antigen that only exists in Chinese. This would explain why it only attacks Chinese. But this does not explain why, after it infects a Chinese, that it remains race specific. We think that it has to be in its RNA.

"Since we know it causes bleeding, it must still have the glycoprotein sticking out from the surface that destroys the endothelial cells that line blood vessels, causing them to leak.

"There are several travelers that left Tibet before the quarantine. A Chinese couple from Vancouver, Canada, returned to Vancouver from Tibet and infected their Chinese family in Vancouver and, as far as we know, no one else. Another Chinese traveler from London brought the virus back from Tibet to London, infecting his Chinese family in London. The reason it affects the Chinese and not the Tibetans must lie in the makeup. This is only our preliminary studies, as you requested immediate information. We will learn more in time, to be sure.

"I'm sure that we can learn a great deal about it, but I don't know what good it will do the dying Chinese. We have no cure for the virus, no matter whom it infects. We hope that it will mutate out and become less virulent in time."

The president thanked her. "Contact my office with any new developments."

# CHAPTER 26

In St. Petersburg, Nikolay received a call from Grigoriy Mishkin, one of the crew who went to Tibet. The call was in Russian.

"There's trouble. I went out with Yaroslav Ivchenko last night. He invited me to a nightclub. He has not been working and has been drinking very heavily since his new-found wealth. Although already drunk when we got there, he proceeded to drink quite a lot of vodka. He invited two women, young ones, to entertain us. After a while, he began boasting how it was he that had spread the Ebola all over Tibet and that he was responsible for the epidemic."

"Who was listening?" Nikolay asked.

"Only the girls, about age twenty. I don't know how seriously they took him as he was drunk, but the point is that he was talking and is a security risk."

"Thanks," Nikolay said. "I will do something about it at once. Tell no one else."

☙ℰ❧

Two days later, at ten in the morning, Nikolay knocked on the door of Yaroslav's apartment. Yaroslav was still asleep and very hung over. Stumbling about with a huge headache, he got up and let Nikolay in.

Nikolay brought a small bag with breakfast rolls and

tea leaves in a small carton. He went to the stove and put on a kettle for hot water. Then he went to the small kitchen table and sat. "Sit down here and have a roll and the tea. We must talk."

"Why are you here?" Yaroslav asked.

"You have been talking about what you did in Tibet," Nikolay told him. "I came here to warn you that it has to stop at once!"

Yaroslav groaned, so hung over that he could not say much. Finally, he said, "I don't recall anything like that."

"You did it, the night before last, in front of Grigoriy Mishkin and two girls you picked up."

Yaroslav stopped denying it, as his memory began to return. "I don't know how I screwed up like that."

"I do," Nikolay said. "You got drunk on your ass, and you started boasting. Aren't you working?"

"No, I lost my job, and I have still not found a new one yet.'

Nikolay translated that to mean that Yaroslav went on a binge with the money he made from the job in Tibet and was not about to work until that was all gone.

The kettle began to whistle. Nikolay got up and found a cup, not cleaned, and rinsed it. He put the tea from his bag in the cup and poured in boiling water. He brought it over to Yaroslav.

"No thanks," Yaroslav said.

"*Drink* this!" Nikolay commanded, as though it was needed to sober Yaroslav up to talk.

Yaroslav went along and sipped the tea.

"Take a bit of the roll also," Nikolay told him. He complied. "I'm here to warn you that you are a security risk," Nikolay continued. "Do you recall that I told you when I hired you that no such leaks could be tolerated? This is your absolute last warning. Do you understand?"

"I'm sorry, Nicolay. It won't happen again. I've been drinking way too much."

"Finish the tea and get sober. I don't want to have to come back again."

Yaroslav drank the rest of the tea as ordered.

"I'll leave you now," Nikolay said, "but you must get your act together. Do you understand?"

"Yes, I do. It won't happen again."

Nikolay left. Yaroslav returned to bed to nurse his hangover.

Given the amount of Polonium 210 in the tea, about 1000 times the lethal dose, Yaroslav would probably not leave the apartment alive. If he was taken away in an ambulance and anyone took X-rays at the hospital, those would not show anything, as the Polonium 210 did not give off gamma rays. Unless specialized doctors looked for it, no one would ever know what ate out his insides. It was produced in a Soviet reactor, which made a small amount of it each year, about eighty-five grams. It did not burn the epidermis, It only began to work once inside the stomach and then very effectively.

Nikolay had kept some he had obtained from a payoff to a corrupt government official at the reactor where it was made. As no one would conduct any autopsy, the death would just be written up by the medical examiner as the deadly effects of advanced alcoholism.

# CHAPTER 27

Baron and Tak returned from a motorcycle sightseeing trip to the Golden Triangle in the north of Thailand.

Inside their home, they went to the flat screen and tuned on the satellite news. There was a news report, estimating the infection of Chinese in Tibet at over one hundred fifty thousand. Travel to and from Tibet was forbidden, and there was rioting and chaos there. The report confirmed that only Chinese were subject to this strain of the Ebola virus.

It was time. Baron looked up a number in his cell phone and called one of the most powerful generals in Mainland China, General Chew Won Hor. He was in and, hearing who was calling, quickly took the call, notwithstanding the emergency going on in Tibet and the needed efforts to keep the epidemic out of Mainland China.

"General, Baron Von Limbach here," Baron said, in Mandarin. "How are you?"

"I'm fine, but the epidemic is a catastrophe. How are you, Baron?"

"Good, thank you. The epidemic is why I'm calling. I have it from my sources that the Tibetans are not being infected. Is that so?"

"That is the same information that I have."

"I have a source that would like the Dalai Lama to be invited back to Tibet to give spiritual comfort to the Tibetans in this catastrophe. Since Tibetans are immune from the Ebola, He could travel there. Do you think you might arrange it for me?"

"Baron, so many of the devil-infested countries of the world have been putting pressure on China to allow the Dalai Lama to return. Why do you think that it would be allowed now?"

"I have two reasons. First, it would show the world that your country is compassionate to the devastation that is going on there in allowing a spiritual leader to return and give comfort."

"But Tibetans are not becoming infected! He would not be providing comfort to the Chinese."

"I have yet a second, more compelling reason. I'll also pay you one million US dollars cash, as soon as the Dalai Lama sets foot back in Tibet."

There was a pause. Of all the international efforts to put the Dalai Lama back in Tibet, all of which had been rebuked, no one had ever offered anyone in such a position of power in China a bribe, as the countries of the west did not do that. They offered aid, trading benefits, and the like. But this would put Chew Won Hor into luxury beyond his dreams.

"With this catastrophe, I can arrange it," Chew said. "But I would have to share some of that, and there would not be much left for me."

The Chinese always bargained, and Baron was prepared. "I'll tell you what. If you succeed in obtaining the invitation within two weeks, I'll make it one million five hundred thousand dollars. But the Dalia Lama has to be given the right to travel in Tibet freely, without restriction, and allowed to stay, although with restrictions. I cannot guarantee that He will come, but I rather think so, as soon as He is convinced that He and the rest of the Tibetans are safe."

"Done," Chew said. "I'll make the arrangements. With all the chaos in Tibet now, I don't think it will be too hard to arrange to let Him in. Some of the party members might want it at this time, thinking He will come down with Ebola if He comes in, as there are many here that refuse to believe the Tibetans are immune. They would like to see Him die from it."

"Good," Baron said. In actuality, he had been prepared to go much higher in money to please his customer, Master Saunders.

"Baron, I'll call you with the confirmation within a day or two if I can arrange it. Will I find you on this number?"

"Yes. I'll wait for your call, as I wish to finish this business before moving on to another."

"Consider it done," Chew said, deciding not to wait.

Baron looked at Tak. "Governments have spent billions on all sorts of committees, organizations, conferences, salaried idiots, and expenses, all trying to get China to allow the Dalai Lama to return and give the Tibetan culture recognition. I, on the other hand, with a little virus, a call to the right place, and a paltry one-million-five-hundred-thousand, did it single handedly. Actually, I might not enjoy retiring as much as I thought, as this is business is really all too rewarding."

☙☙

If one looked for a singular aspect of the Dalai Lama's accomplishments in His later years, one had to consider the importance of the contacts He made. He spent most of His time going from one head of state to another, being received publically as a great exiled leader as though receiving Him attributed to them great social awareness of the oppressed. He was awarded many prizes, including the Nobel Peace Prize. He could call on heads of state, and that is just what He did when, by the most unusual turn of events, He received a formal invitation from China to return to Tibet to provide spiritual support for all those in the turmoil of the epidemic. He was offered an expiring visa approved for a single entry. The actual invitation was signed by a General Chew Won Hor, instead of a political leader, but He assumed that the military invitation was because of the turmoil from the epidemic and the need for martial law. To inquire into His own safety, He first called on the offices of the Prime Minister of India, in which country He and His Tibet-In-Exile government had been granted sanctuary. So as not to offend India by ignoring protocol, He contacted the Indian government first. Although He knew India was not in any way able to deal with Ebola, as it could hardly handle its own impoverished with their illnesses.

He was told, as He knew in advance He would be, that in spite of the excellent medicine in India, its doctors had no clue as to how to deal with Ebola, nor did the country have the resources. He then called the Prime Minister of England, the White House, and the Prime Minister of Australia, to ask about the safety of possible travel to Tibet. The consensus was that, while all the reports available stated that there were no reports of Tibetans becoming infected, that He should not go as there was no way to ensure that every Tibetan was not subject to infection and, further, that things were in such a state of chaos that the risks of riot or uncontrollable lack of safety conditions made it unsafe to go.

But evaluating all this, and hearing that no Tibetan had become infected, He found this to be a spiritual calling, no doubt the most significant in His life since His exile and perhaps the last significant act He would ever do for His Tibet. He gave an announcement that the catastrophe in Tibet that was killing the Chinese was most unfortunate, but that if the Chinese would allow Him to enter Tibet and provide spiritual comfort, it would be a magnanimous gesture by the Chinese government. Had He said anything else, His visa would never have been issued.

Once He decided to go, a military plane from India was provided with volunteer pilots. A bonus of one year's salary offered to the two Indian pilots willing to take the risk helped locate the needed crew. It was unknown if Indians were susceptible to the virus, but it was thought that the drop off of the passengers at the airport could be done in such a way at the end of the runway that exposure would be very minimal. The plane would fly in only long enough to drop off the Dalai Lama and His minimal contingent. It would then leave the airport immediately without having any service or fuel so as to minimize contamination. The plane and crew would be quarantined at a military base upon return to India.

The followers of the Dalai Lama wanted to make His return into as big of an event as possible. While no new visas were issued to newsmen to enter Tibet, the local Tibetans were able to assemble video gear from local media stations and cameramen to get the event of His return on video. Tibetans in exile were also provided with video gear and arrangements were quickly made, with the help of the West, for satellite hookup to record the historic event live.

A few days later, the Indian military cargo plane came in for a landing at the Lhasa airport. The plane came to a halt near the end of one of the runways, and the cargo door opened. The Dalai Lama was the first to exit. In His orange robes, He knelt down and kissed the ground. Following were His contingent, including some of His most loyal and life-long followers, and a half dozen Tibetans that had been trained to use camera equipment provided them by several news services.

Unaffected by the epidemic, an enormous crowd of Tibetans, estimated at two hundred fifty thousand, came to the airport at Lhasa, or as close as they could get, lining the road to greet the holy man.

The crowd overwhelmed the airport and the roads in. The hundred Chinese police and military monitoring the event, dressed in the limited bio-warfare suits and masks available, were so helpless and useless that they gave up very early in the morning and went back to their base of operations.

Satellite transmission was set up by the Tibetans following Him in so the interested world could witness the historic event.

In the family room of the Saunders home, Shanta and Andrew were closely watching the media event by satellite.

At a stand erected for His initial speech in the holy country, the Dalai Lama seated Himself in the traditional Buddhist fashion and made ready the microphone to give a prayer in Tibetan to the huge crowd. The satellite photographers were bringing His image and speech around the world to news stations everywhere. His initial prayer in Tibetan was followed by the ritualistic chanting. Then, so as to communicate with His many supporters since His exile in 1959, He spoke in English.

"For my many followers and supporters around the world that do not speak Tibetan, I wish to say a prayer in English. This one, which I gave in 1960, at the Swarg Ashram at Dharamsala, Kangra District, Himachal State, India, came to me following my exile. It is 'Words of Truth,' and honors the three jewels, Buddha, the Teachings, and the Spiritual Community. I think it is appropriate for this event." He began his prayer: "O Buddhas, Bodhisattvas, and disciples of the past, present, and future…"

On the other side of the globe, in front of their screen, Shanta said to Andrew, "We accomplished this!" She went to Andrew and held him tightly. And overcome with their achievement, they both began to cry.

<div style="text-align:center">~~~</div>

Mike Winger from the CIA came to Ralls's office to give him an update on the mystery woman.

"I still can't find out any background on the woman," Winger said. "It's as though she never existed. She married Baron Von Limbach recently in Berlin, but he is so connected that his file is sealed like our president's so no background information is accessible. She has no cell phones in her name that we can find. The only thing we know about her is that she only began to show up in places when she started traveling with Baron Von Limbach.

"I've been able to find out that the two of them, as husband and wife, booked a flight to Astana, Kazakhstan. She has a German passport. From there, they hired a plane that is common there, but not allowed to be imported here, called an Antonov AN 2. It's a huge biplane that has been used all over Russia and the former USSR satellites to ferry officers around. It holds about ten with the pilots. It can land anywhere, much like a Super Cub in Alaska. It flies very slowly, at about one hundred twenty five miles an hour, and it can land at a very rough field. It turns out that the two of them chartered one to Stepnogorsk as that has an abandoned airstrip which is full of potholes from years of weather and no maintenance since the Soviets left. I could only get information out of Astana, and that was that the plane returned on the fourth day.

"There was a very special spring fair in Stepnogorsk at the time, called Nauryz. It is some really crazy event with all sorts of medieval horse games going on. So it's possible that the baron, being very rich, took his new bride to the Nauryz fair that almost no one in the West has ever seen or will ever see as part of a very special honeymoon present."

Ralls became impatient. "Why are you telling me all this about a honeymoon?"

"I just thought you might like to know that, in addition to the Nauryz spring fair, there is something else of interest there."

"What?"

"A level-four bio-warfare lab put there by the USSR."

∽∾∽∾

Christine Rhyes-Walters entered Ralls's office.

"I want to thank you for coming to Homeland Security," Ralls said as he stood to greet her. "It's nice of you to take your time for us."

"No problem. You caught me just before I have to go to a conference in Europe. I'm leaving tomorrow."

"I won't keep you long," Ralls said.

"I understand from your call that you want to know about what I observed at the former USSR anthrax production lab in Stepnogorsk, Kazakhstan?"

"Yes, just that," Ralls confirmed. "I'm looking for any lead that may arise regarding the outbreak of Ebola in Tibet. Since that place was a former mass production lab of anthrax, and a level-four bio-warfare lab, of which there are only a few, and they cost billions to put in, I wanted your first-hand impressions as to whether or not there was any sort of bio-warfare activity going on there. This outbreak in Tibet has us very worried to say the least."

She got interested and asked a delicate question that involved security matters. "Do you have information that the Ebola epidemic in Tibet is manmade as some sort of bio-warfare attack?"

"No, no, we do not have any such information. We are just tracking down any possibility that it was not a natural outbreak. It might have been just an outbreak, perhaps initiated by someone bringing over the virus from Africa where these Ebola viruses originate. But it seems strange how a virus would originate in Africa that only infects the Chinese race since there only about a million on the entire continent of Africa, compared to about 1.5 billion worldwide."

"This is not a suspected terrorist attack, is it?" she asked.

"Not that we know of. There is no evidence that some group is attacking Chinese. But our interest is in if it is possible to make an Ebola that attacks only one race. It would be an incredible weapon. For example, what would a Muslim group do with a Saudi financed Ebola that only attacks Jews? One sect of Muslims against another like the Sunnis and the Shiites warring in Iraq? Possibly an Ebola that attack Caucasians and not Arabs? What about an attack on Blacks?"

"I see what you mean. Pretty scary!"

"Please help us out. However, I must inform you that this comes under your agreement with the government as to confidential information."

She answered his plea for help. "I was there with a small delegation. We were shown the building where the anthrax was made years before. There were other buildings, now closed down, that we did not go into, but those were not part of the lab itself in the back of the main anthrax production building, which is where we did go. The place is anything other than bustling. It's dreary, cold, unheated, windows broken, and in decay. If not for the fact that the buildings are modern in shape, you might think it was an abandoned castle where Dracula lived.

"Other than maintenance, there were only two people working there, a Dr. Borislav Dorogomilov and his assistant, Dr. Anastasiya Volkova. They are aged and former USSR scientists. We have been providing them with funds to work on creating a fungus that will kill opium poppies but is not harmful to the environment, people, or animals. I saw nothing that was in any way suspicious, or that might lead me to believe the lab was used for anything else.

"And I'm happy to let you know that, just recently, our investment and my recommendations to continue the funding were realized as worthy, since Dr. Dorogomilov did create such a fungus and sent us all the details. In fact, he donated the method to the world and did not ask for any patent or compensation for it, although he was obligated to give the method to the US as part of the compensation he has been receiving. So it was not like he was giving up that much.

"When he sent the details to us, we asked him to come here to be given a recognition ceremony. I might have been able to raise some sort of monetary award, but he has not yet come or indicated that he will. Perhaps he's not the sort who wants the limelight of public notoriety or recognition."

"So then, you saw no indication that the lab, which I

understand is huge, could be making any bio-warfare agents?"

"None whatsoever. We only saw one other person working there, an elderly man who maintained the small part of the place that Drs. Dorogomilov and Volkova used. I think he only gets the heat going in that horribly cold place and does janitorial work as far as I could tell. I would imagine that it would take a large staff of people and a very busy place to create any bio-warfare agents."

"I'm interested in why he has not come here. Was he aware that there might be a bonus here for him? How much of a bonus were you planning to give him?"

"Nothing was promised in terms of money. He was paid for work on the fungus. For a bonus, I was hoping to get something together if he accepted the invitation. But there are a number of doctors who would like to have him give presentations to them, as doctors have to have a bunch of hours of continuing education every year, and attending approved seminars counts toward their quota. His would be an approved seminar.

"So he would be in demand to go around and give speeches. He would also probably be paid about fifteen hundred per speech, plus expenses. And, as he would go to various places, he would be asked to attend teas and dinners funded by doctors, who characteristically take good care of themselves.

"I wrote him by Internet about coming over, but I have not heard from him. I don't know if he is even still at the lab. Since the fungi project is now finished, maybe he left. I can't imagine why anyone would want to live or stay on there. It was the dreariest place I have ever been to."

"Well, my many thanks. Based on your observations, it does not look like the lab is being used for bio-warfare. But nevertheless, please keep in mind that all this is confidential."

Hauser and Ralls met in Hauser's office. Hauser started out, as he sometimes did, with light-hearted joking as a way of salutation to begin the meeting. "What have you got on the hypersonic, female, redheaded pilot who does not have human DNA? Is she an alien invading us? Maybe she is connected with the epidemic in Tibet, having brought outer space Ebola to Tibet to reduce the population since aliens don't like Chinese?"

"Hah!" Ralls answered. "That's a good one. The way you put it, she is the ultimate terrorist. An Ebola-toting alien!"

The salutation and joking over, they got down to business.

Ralls told what he knew. "The only candidate that I have been able to find for the pilot of the hypersonic space craft is this one redhead whose trail I picked up in Poland where the hypersonic craft landed. There's been no sign of the craft since that day. There have been no ransom demands as you know. There are no clues as to who built it, or even who might be able to build it. There is no trace of the craft taking off or orbiting before it entered the atmosphere above White Sands. No one who is involved in aerospace has any notion of how anything can go seventeen thousand miles an hour in the atmosphere without burning up. Aerospace engineers whom I have spoken to do not know of any material that could make up the skin of such a craft that would not burn up in the atmosphere at the speed she achieved.

"As for the redhead, her given name is Tak, which, oddly enough, means *yes* in Polish. She has no background, almost like someone invented her. Her marriage to Baron Von Limbach was recorded in Berlin, but the forms with the background information in Germany are sealed, much like here for the president and high officials, as the baron is very influential and in the arms business. They might say, for example, where she was born and parents' names, but we can't get them.

"We can find no history or records on her anywhere. We know of no language that she speaks other than English. We can't even find out what country she came from. She has no driver's license. She attended no schools that we know of. And—speaking of flying at hypersonic speeds— she does not have a pilot's license.

"She has been traveling with Baron Von Limbach, and it appears that he may have found her in Poland at a salt mine tourist attraction then took her to Krakow and later into Germany, where they married. Keep in mind that Poland is where the hypersonic craft landed.

"She is now a baroness as they married in Berlin. He then took her to Taiwan and later to Stepnogorsk, Kazakhstan to a special spring fair there with medieval horse events that few Westerners ever see. There is an almost closed-down level-four bio-warfare lab there, a tiny part of which has been kept open with US money to fund two doctors who created an environmentally safe fungus to kill opium poppies. That lab was visited by a representative of ours from the state department, shortly before the baron and his wife went there.

"In case there was any possibility that the lab might have been used to make the Ebola, I interviewed the representative, and she saw no signs at all that there might be any bio-warfare activity. The two Russian doctors there recently developed the fungus, sent the details to us, and have now apparently left. So it looks like the baron and his new wife the baroness were there just for the spring fair on their honeymoon.

"But there are curious facts. She has seven fingers and all well-formed. She has no fingerprints. And the strangest part is that she does not have human DNA."

"So is she a freak of nature?" Hauser asked. "Or do you mean to imply that she is actually an alien?"

Ralls was not sure if his boss was seriously asking if she was an alien. But he did not appear to be joking. "It would be most interesting to pick her up for questioning.

But we can't just do that and take her to Guantanamo for waterboarding as though she was a captured combatant. The only crime she is even suspected of is the misdemeanor of not filing a flight plan to enter US airspace at over eighteen thousand feet above sea level, which is called class-A airspace and requires a flight plan. The baron with his arms business stays clear of the US, as he is wise enough to know that we might charge him with some violation of US law and pick him up one day like Adnan Khoshoggi. And since his wife the baroness travels with him, we don't expect either of them to ever come to the US.

"We have nothing to connect her to the epidemic whatsoever. She has not been to Tibet, as far as we know, nor to Africa, to our knowledge, where Ebola always originates. We can't extradite them without legitimate charges pending here. The baron has an office in Taiwan and is very well connected with the Taiwan Army. He and his wife would be protected by the army itself if we tried to arrest them. The baron does have, however, a tea plantation and a house in the north of Thailand. We could go in there and pick her up. But he also has connections there, and we certainly would have to release them after a short interrogation. I would like to take her to one of our ships for questioning."

"How could she be picked up in Thailand?" Hauser asked.

"I think we might just go in with one or two helicopters and pick her up without getting anyone's permission," Ralls said. "Maybe use the Navy SEALs."

"Like we did with Bin Laden?" Hauser asked.

"Yes. We did not notify the Pakistani Government as it was a given that someone in the government there would have alerted Bin Laden if we had announced we were coming. Whether Bin Laden would have been informed because of his rich Saudi family, or his supporters in the immensely corrupt Pakistani Government who would have been paid money for revealing we were coming, or because of some Muslim loyalty thing, he would not have been there if we had notified the government that we were coming when we did. That is certain.

"But there is no Muslim connection with the baron, the baroness, and Thailand. Bribery is a possibility, but not as bad as with the Pakis. I still recommend we do not tell anyone if we want to pick her up."

"To do that, we have to get the president's okay," Hauser said. "He would run it by his staff. It's a pretty big deal going into someone else's country with the military. Imagine if some other country came in to the US in their military helicopters, arrested someone, and took him out? It would be an act of war!"

"I've been on this woman day and night for some time," Ralls said. "I've been working with the CIA, checking and rechecking, all to prove that she is the mystery pilot in the hypersonic craft as it presents a genuine security threat. But to answer your earlier question, I honestly think that she might be an alien, as far-fetched as that sounds. I think we should go pick her up and take her somewhere for questioning."

"Oh, sure, how could that be a problem?" Hauser snapped. "I'll just ask for an audience with the president and tell him we are on the trail of an extraterrestrial, who is also a German baroness, and we want to go into Thailand in armed military choppers with Navy SEALs to her home without notifying the Thai government so we can cart her away in handcuffs from her influential husband, a baron, to one of our warships for interrogation, as she is suspected of having entered US airspace without a flight plan, which is a misdemeanor. That'll work for sure."

"Not so good, huh?" Ralls said.

☙❧

The final arrangements were made but with a compromise. The Thai government was notified and agreed to a plan including the Thai Army. Ralls decided to pick up both the baron and the baroness for questioning, instead of just her. The Thai military, not the US Navy SEALs, would go to the tea plantation with one of its helicopters, taking Ralls, to collect them for interrogation at a Thai military base. The interrogation would be conducted by US representatives, which would include Ralls, with a Thai representative monitoring. They would then be returned to the tea plantation after questioning, unless there was further reason to detain them.

# CHAPTER 28

Baron and Tak returned from another motorcycle tour, this time to the Mekong River, where they had taken a tiny boat across the half-mile width of the Mekong to Laos. Once in Laos, they had walked up the steep bank of the river to see Ban Houei Sai, a quaint Laotian village. The roads were dirt, the huts teak, and the living primitive, but the people were warm and wonderful to visitors. The archaic living conditions were something completely new for Tak. She and Baron returned the same day, and just in time, as rain was about to fall.

After they showered together to refresh from the dust and heat of the day, they retired to the tower, overlooking the plantation. From the tower of the hilltop tea estate, they could absorb the ambiance of the many acres of lush, deep green tea trees.

The rains, combined with the harvest of fresh tea leaves, provided a unique and lovely fragrance.

As they sat in the tower overlooking the plantation in the late afternoon, a torrential downpour fell and then subsided to a steady rain.

Over the sound of the rain, she brought up the subject that they both knew to be inevitable. "Baron, I have completed my study. The starship will soon be nearby and I must go."

A hollow feeling overcame him at the reality of losing

his lover. "Is there any chance I might talk you into staying here on Earth with me?"

"Baron, now that I've seen a great deal of Earth and your lifestyle, especially after the contrast of visiting the village of Ban Houei Sai in Laos, I realize that traveling with you is hardly a typical example of life on Earth. But I have loved it and you as well."

Baron knew there had to be a "but," and there was.

"But there is an unimaginable amount of worlds yet for me to see as a Federation anthropologist. I simply cannot end my career here on this one planet, even though it has you."

She looked at him, took a sip of her drink to fortify herself for making a suggestion that she feared might, if accepted, compromise her impartiality on the starship as an independent anthropologist. "Why don't you accompany me? I believe I could get permission to make you part of a team of the two of us. As I would be sent to places with beings that are much like us, and that use oxygen and water, you would fit right in. You have unique language skills, and could easily learn languages of other beings in the places that I would take you."

Baron was quiet. He looked at her, then out to the plantation, taking in the lovely rain, wondering if he could give up the luxuries he had created, his influence, wealth, powerful contacts, properties, languages, collections…

As he did not jump at the chance, she added enticements. "There would be benefits for you if you come. You will not need to worry about being wealthy, as where you will be going, you will not need money. You will not need to worry about medicine, and your life will be greatly extended. I know you like weapons, and I'll get you some that you will *really* like. I understand that Earthlings consider there to be seven wonders of your world, and I assume that you've seen them. You would be amazed to learn of the wonders of the universe."

Contemplating her offer, he asked, "When is your starship coming?"

"In about four days, and I'll know exactly when they contact me. But I must warn you, if you do come, you cannot plan on returning. I wouldn't be allowed to take you on a sightseeing tour of space, only to have to bring you all the way back if you got homesick." She paused. "Would you be able to come with all of your business here?"

"I have made provisions for Mei Ling that are in my safe in Taipei if something should happen to me. I could send her an email to set things in motion."

She leaned over and kissed him, her tone changing, "I want you to come. After all, we are married."

He did not answer, as he was unable to accept her invitation to leave everything that he had worked for behind. He considered his mastering of many Earth languages, the many connections he had made, and his possessions. He was very comfortable here on Earth.

He avoided giving her an answer. "Now that I have been able to get the Dalai Lama back into Tibet, and my mission is accomplished, there is something I would like you to do if you can. With your advanced medicine, when you return, could you make a formula for an antidote for the race-specific Ebola? Maybe even for all forms of Ebola? It would have to be able to be made with substances and equipment available here on Earth. You could transmit the formula to the World Health Organization without saying who it is from. It would put an end to the suffering in Tibet."

Tak seemed a bit surprised at the request and looked at him for a few moments as she considered the interference with Earth activities.

She made her decision. "A piece of cake!" and kissed him passionately.

He then decided it might be time to get some information since she was going to be leaving. "Now that you are leaving, can you tell me what all that fancy wrist computer of yours can do? I've seen it act as a weapon and translator. What else?"

"Sure. It's a sort of intergalactic laptop. It has knowledge of the parts of the universe that we have visited, which is relatively small on an intergalactic scale, and it can recall those images. Watch."

She gave it a command to show a planet that she knew of. It sprang to life and projected a three dimensional holograph just above it of the solar system of that place, three feet in size in each direction. A projection of the planets circling their sun appeared, also showing their moons. The view moved in to a planet, a blue one, covered partially with water much like Earth. Some of the cities showed up by their lights on the dark, nighttime side.

"Here is one in your Milky Way, similar to yours. There are inhabitants, but they are not like you or me. There are so many of inhabited planets logged in our computers that you could spend your lifetime studying." She shut down the image.

Baron decided to add a bit of humor. "Does it have a battery that needs recharging?"

"Of sorts. It uses something similar to what you call atomic power, but without radiation. I think if used continuously every day, it might grow weak in two hundred years."

Wishfully thinking, he said, "I could easily spend the rest of my entire life doing nothing else but watching that."

❧❦❧

The night before Tak was to leave, Baron had still not declined her offer to join her, but she had taken his silence as a "no." He obviously could not bring himself to relinquish all that he had accumulated on Earth.

It was still raining when they finished a Northern Thai meal made by the in-house chef, a meal featuring his version of Khoi Soi, a dish of egg noodles in a creamy, spicy, coconut broth.

This, their last evening, when they retired after dinner for a drink at the bar, he brought to her a briefcase covered in brown ostrich. "A small token for my favorite alien," he announced, presenting it.

She took it, but hesitated to open it, the sadness of the gift representing the acknowledgment of her departure the next day.

She finally, and ever so slowly, opened it, revealing its sparkling contents. The inside top of the case was a map of Earth, with tiny precious jewels stuck in holes in the map in different countries. The bottom was filled with jewelry, enormous versions of the small stones stuck in the world map. Its bottom glistened like a treasure chest from a pirate movie.

"This is my private collection of the best gems from various parts of the planet. I enjoy collecting gems, and they increase in value. I want to give them to you as a going away present. Note that the inside of the top of the case is a map of the planet to show you where on the planet each gem inside came from. See here?" He pointed to the Island of Tahiti. "See the small, dark pearl? That is where the best pearls come from, and where this came from."

He picked up a huge, nearly iridescent, dark green pearl on a gold chain from the lower part of the case.

Tak took it, turning it about. She then looked at the map and figured out what the gift was all about.

"It's fantastic!" she nearly shrieked.

She turned her attention to one of the jewelry items in the bottom, a white dragon pendant of two inches, made all from one piece of exquisitely carved jade, with rubies for eyes. "What's this?"

"Nephrite Jade, from Yunnan, China. See if you can find it on the map. The color in Chinese is called 'mutton fat.'" He chuckled. "The Chinese are not known for romantic names."

Tak found it, pointing. "China!"

She then lifted three matching objects with deep green,

oval stones, mounted in platinum, partially surrounded by tiny diamonds.

"A ring and earrings in Burma Imperial Jade," he told her. "It's the most valuable jade."

"Wow!" She put on the ring on one of her seven fingers and held out her hand in front of her, turning it from side to side, admiring it.

Baron then pointed to the earrings in her hand. "These go on your ears."

She fastened them to her ears and went to the nearest mirror. She then returned and looked at the country called Myanmar where she found both a green stone as well as a red one. "There are two from this same country. One is red. There must be two gems from this country."

She found a huge single ruby in a ring and held it up.

"This is an authentic, pigeon-blood Burmese ruby," he said. "That is the name for the very best. I got it as a gift from the Sultan of Brunei, although it came from Burma, which is now Myanmar, very close to us. Try it on."

Tak put it on, changing fingers on her hands until she found one that it fit.

"Why would a person give you such a beautiful thing?"

"I did him a favor."

She looked at the map and pointed back to Myanmar, which had both the green jade and the ruby in it. "Myanmar!"

She next lifted an opal necklace with a single stone, wide and thin, an inch and a half in diameter, in a natural shape, edged in gold.

Colors radiated from it, as though it was backlit by light through a prism. "What's this beautiful thing? It appears to be giving off light. Does it?"

"No, no light. It's an opal, but a very special one with what they call 'fire.'"

"It's beautiful!" She held it in different directions to see the colors. She then found a small opal in a county in the southern hemisphere. "Australia!"

"Right!"

She then took out a bracelet of huge emeralds wrapping all around, set in twenty four karat gold.

"Oh my!"

"They're called emeralds."

Tak found a small green emerald on the map. "Columbia!"

The next piece she held up was a diamond necklace, covered with so many diamonds as to be a task to count. A line of large stones were set end to end around the length, and there was a huge pendant diamond surrounded by many smaller ones. Tak held it up to catch the afternoon sunlight, which struck it and refracted the light through the stones, creating a display of light and colors on the walls.

"This is like the necklace of Xiu Mei at the dinner in Hong Kong."

"That's right."

She found a small embedded diamond in a country on the map. "South Africa! Absolutely beautiful!"

Tak next lifted up two, huge, blue sapphire earrings. "Earrings?"

"Yes. They're Laotian. There is a pendant in here to match," he added, finding the pendant. The monster stone was two dozen times the size of the earrings, and mounted in platinum with diamonds surrounding it.

Tak set out to find the small blue stone on the map. "Here it is! Laos. We were just there!"

Next, from the bottom, she lifted a light blue, star sapphire on a neck chain. The stone was an inch in diameter, and the upper part of the setting had diamonds surrounding it. She held it up and gazed at it. The light made a crisp, white crisscross across the front of it—the star.

"It's a star sapphire, from India," he said.

Tak found India on the map. "Gorgeous!"

The next stone she lifted was a pendant of yellow amber.

"This is amber, from the Baltic Sea," he told her.

"These are available where I met you. This is not rare as the others, but still interesting. You will see, if you look closely, that the piece has an insect frozen in it, from prehistoric times."

"I see it, I see it. How neat!" Then she went to the map, now a very interesting game, until she found a piece of small amber. "Poland." She held her finger on the country, and Baron looked at where she was pointing. "It will be very special to me," she said, "as that is where we met."

She stopped looking, even though there were a few more. "Oh my, Baron, I suspect that these are worth a fortune." Tak got up and came to him, kissing him. "I shall cherish these always." Then she took out her pocket watch from her pocket that he purchased for her in Rothenburg ob der Tauber. "But this will still be my favorite as I will always remember where and when you bought it for me.

⁊

The following morning was overcast, and light rain was falling. It was time. Tak gathered her things, which now were much more than the contents of the satchel she had landed with, and put them just inside the front door.

The wrist computer lit up and spoke in her language. She looked at Baron. "The shuttle is near. But there's a problem. There's an Earth warship coming from the south. I believe it's called a helicopter."

The helicopter came in under the rain clouds, arriving from the back side of the hill. It swung around the house and landed in the front yard, back far enough to clear the rotor blades. It was a US made Sikorsky gunship in the service of the Thai Army with Thai Army soldiers, consisting of a pilot, a gunner inside behind a .50 caliber machine gun, and another soldier with an M-16 assault rifle. It also had a non-Thai passenger, Richard Ralls.

It shut down its engines and Ralls exited, accompanied by the Thai soldier with the M-16. Ralls had a .45 pistol on his side. The soldier and Ralls walked toward the house, the soldier two paces behind, looking about, ready with his M-16. Tak and Baron had heard the noise of the helicopter and watched from a window.

At the front door, Ralls announced loudly, "I'm Deputy Richard Ralls, US Homeland Security. We are here for Baron and Baroness Von Limbach. The two of you are ordered to come to a Thai Army Base for questioning."

Baron and Tak heard the order well. They stood just inside the door, looking at each other, wondering what to do.

Just then the shuttle from the starship descended through the clouds to the front of the house, across from the helicopter. It made no noise. It was a gunship, sent in precaution to remove starship personnel from planets that were not peaceful, in case of trouble. It was black, seventy feet long, fifteen feet high, with two, fearsome laser weapons pointing out the front, a laser on each side, another in the back, and a weapon in a turret on the top capable of destroying an Earth warship of any size.

It was a menacing sight to Ralls and the Thai soldiers, with its configuration that gave it almost an ominous expression, as if it were alive.

It descended near to the ground and landing gear extended. Just before setting down, it rotated to face the helicopter, weapons pointed at it.

Ralls looked on in fear and amazement, backing away from the door. The soldier beside Ralls got scared, retreated back to the security of the helicopter, and kneeled down to one knee, pointing his M-16 at the alien gunship.

The gunner in the helicopter, seeing the menacing gunship, got ready behind his .50 caliber machine gun. He chambered a round and aimed it at the gunship.

Baron and Tak opened the door and stood in the doorway. "We'll not be joining you today, Deputy Ralls," Baron said. "If you want to leave here unharmed, get back in your helicopter and go."

Not willing to stand down, Ralls took the .45 pistol out

of his holster and pointed it at the two of them. "You are ordered to accompany me to the Thai Army Base. You will now get into the helicopter."

The gunship was manned with starship personnel, but they did not initiate the first shot. The front lasers of the shuttle moved a few degrees to aim more precisely at the helicopter and the soldiers. When the Thai solder behind the .50 caliber machine gun in the helicopter saw the weapons of the gunship moving, and Ralls take out his .45, he panicked and opened fire on the gunship, letting go a burst of bullets. The bullets did not penetrate the armor of the gunship, bouncing off, and so he kept firing. The kneeling soldier joined in the fracas and began shooting his M-16 at the gunship.

The gunship responded with a loud laser blast from both front lasers, one at the helicopter, disintegrating it completely with its pilot and gunner, the other at the kneeling soldier next to it.

The helicopter, the noisy machine guns, and the three soldiers, disappeared as though evaporated. The silence became deafening. Ralls stared in disbelief. Stunned, he did not move, but continued to hold his .45 on the couple.

Standing in the doorway, Tak held up her arm with her wrist computer and its laser. She touched the lapis jewel on the top, targeted the .45 in Ralls's hand, and commanded the computer to fire. Its penetrating bright blue beam hit the .45, disintegrating it and, unfortunately for Ralls, some of his fingers. He cried out in pain and dropped to his knees, holding his wounded hand with his other.

Baron and Tak stepped backward into the house where Ralls could not hear them. Looking into Tak's eyes, Baron said, "This means a change of business for me. Now that the US Homeland Security wants me, the CIA will be hunting me as well. My business as I have been conducting it is over. I will take you up on your offer and come with you."

"What about all of your affairs?" Tak said.

"Mei Ling knows that if anything happens to me, she is

to open a safe at my office where there are instructions for what she is to do. I had planned that one day I might have to flee, but it would have been to a tropical island where I could hide out. I never dreamed it would be into space. It's ironic for me. I never thought that my life would be undone by a woman."

"I'm not exactly a woman," Tak corrected.

Baron chuckled and quickly packed a small satchel of his own with a couple of changes of clothes and other essential items he didn't feel he could do without. Then they gathered up Tak's bags that were just inside the door, including her new jewelry case, and headed toward the gunship. They walked by Ralls, still kneeling on the ground in pain.

Ralls gathered himself enough to say as they passed by, "I knew you were an alien! This proves it! But no one will believe me now as there are no witnesses left to back up my story." The woman and the baron did not respond but continued to the gunship. The door to the space shuttle opened, and they stepped inside. Ralls remained where he was, afraid to move, and stared at her. "I've been following you a long time," he cried. "Who are you? Please, at least tell me who you are."

Just inside the door, secure in the protection of the gunship, Tak listened to the plea of the government man with his injured hand, kneeling on the ground in the light rain. She looked at her Baron. He nodded his silent assent.

She then presented herself. "Tak, United Federation of Planets; Field Anthropologist; First Officer; Baroness Von Limbach; Honorary Officer, Republic of China, Decorated First In Combat."

The gunship door closed and the ship ascended at an unearthly rate straight up, disappearing into the clouds.

End

# About the Author

Brent Ayscough or Ace, as he is known to friends, retired from the practice of law and lives in a house overlooking the sea in Southern California. He has always loved machines, from airplanes to motorcycles, structural design, and other interests. He has enjoyed the acquaintance of diverse and interesting people and is widely traveled. Bits and pieces of characters he has known, places he has been, seasoned with the spice of his imagination, help him create unusual stories and characters. Extensive collaboration with experts and sources, hopefully, make his stories credible and interesting.